The Ogress and the Orphans

Kelly Barnhill

Piccadilly
PRESS

First published in Great Britain in 2022 by
PICCADILLY PRESS
4th Floor, Victoria House, Bloomsbury Square
London WC1B 4DA
Owned by Bonnier Books
Sveavägen 56, Stockholm, Sweden
www.piccadillypress.co.uk

Published by arrangement with Algonquin Young Readers,
an imprint of Algonquin Books of Chapel Hill,
a division of Workman Publishing Co., Inc., New York

A CIP catalogue record for this book is available from the British Library.

ISBN: 978-1-80078-302-7
Also available as an ebook and in audio

Printed and

Picc

The Ogress and the Orphans

Also by Kelly Barnhill

The Girl Who Drank the Moon
WINNER OF THE NEWBERY MEDAL

The Witch's Boy

To Rose,
who is the reason the Ogress bakes,

∾

and to Charlie,
who first discovered the Dragon—

∾

this book is lovingly dedicated.

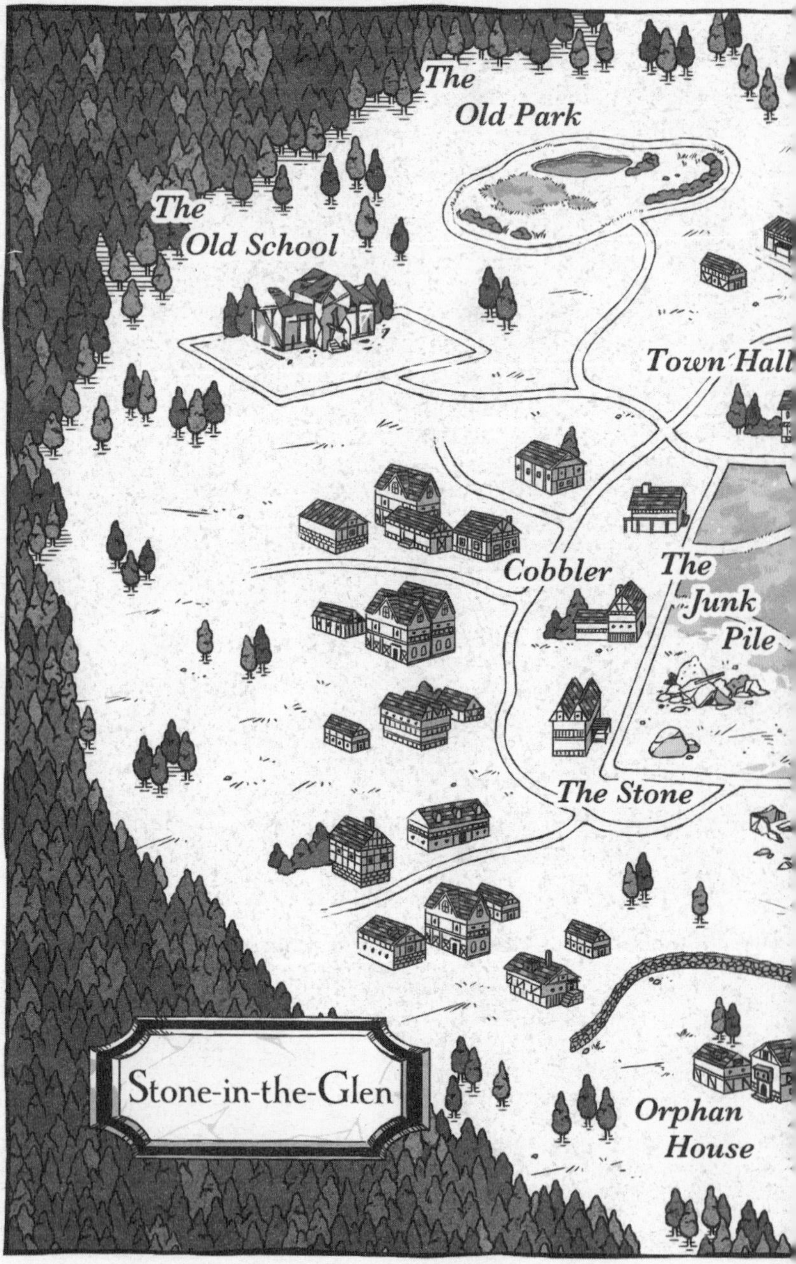

The
Old Park

The
Old School

Town Hall

Cobbler

The
Junk
Pile

The Stone

Stone-in-the-Glen

Orphan
House

The Mayor's House

The Ogress's Farm

Toy Shop

Dais

Butcher

Town Square

Apothecary

Old Library

Ignorance is the cause of fear.
—SENECA

No act of kindness, no matter how small,
is ever wasted.
—AESOP

Pay Attention.

Listen.

This is a story about an ogress.

She is not who you might think she is.

(But really, is anyone?)

The Ogress lived in a crooked house at the far edge of town. She enjoyed baking and gardening and counting the stars. Like all ogres, the Ogress was quite tall—even sizable adults would have to crane their necks and squint a bit to say hello. She had feet the size of tortoises, hands the size of heron's wings, and a broad, broad brow that cracked and creased when she concentrated. Her skin was like granite, and her eyes looked like brand-new pennies. Her hair sprouted and waved from her head like prairie grass—stiff and yellow and green, sometimes spangled with daisies or dandelions or creeping ivy. Like all ogres, she spoke little and thought much. She was careful and considerate. Her heavy feet trod lightly on the ground.

This is also a story about a family of orphans. There were fifteen orphans living in the Orphan House at the time our story begins, several years after the Ogress first arrived in town. There were too many children for one house, but they made do. Their names were Anthea, Bartleby, Cassandra (who preferred Cass), Dierdre, Elijah, Fortunate, Gratitude, Hiram, Iggy, Justina, Kye, Lily, Maude, and the babies, Nanette and Orpheus. They were good children, these orphans: studious and hardworking and kind. And they loved one another dearly, ever so much more than they loved themselves.

The Ogress, too, was hardworking and kind and generous. She also loved others more than she loved herself.

This can be a problem, of course. Sometimes.

But it can also be a solution. Let me show you how.

The Dragon

This is also a story about a dragon. I do not like to talk about him much. I don't even like to think about him.

I should clarify: It is not my intention to speak ill of dragons generally. It is a terrible practice to prejudge anyone, be they ogres or orphans or dragons or nosy neighbors or assistant principals or people with unusual manners. It is important, always, to treat everyone with compassion and respect. This is well known.

As for dragons in particular, they are as diverse in their dispositions as any other creature. I, myself, have encountered dragons of every personality type—shy, gregarious, lazy, fastidious, self-centered, bighearted, enthusiastic, and brave.

But *this* dragon, I'm sorry to say, was none of those things. This dragon was greedy, perfidious, and indifferent. He felt no remorse, and he had not been redeemed. He delighted in discord and sowed acrimony wherever he went. These are all large words, and I apologize for them. But my feelings about this dragon are *large*.

Listen.

I would like nothing more than to tell you that every person—human, dragon, or any other kind of creature—is fundamentally *good*. But I can't tell you that, because it is not in my nature to lie. Everyone starts fundamentally good, in my experience, and nearly everyone stays mostly good for the most part. But *some* . . . well. They choose to do bad things. No one knows why. And then a small number of *those* choose to *stay bad*. I wish it weren't true. But it's best you know this now, at the beginning of this book. Every story has a villain, after all. And every villain has a story.

The Town

This is also a story about a place, called Stone-in-the-Glen, which used to be a lovely town.

Everyone said so.

Stone-in-the-Glen had been famous for its trees. Shade trees in parks, blossoming trees in the walkways. Fruit trees lining the neighborhood streets, with limbs that bent under the weight of an abundant harvest each season. Anyone—any neighbor or friend or visitor from far, far away—could reach up when the time was right and simply help themselves. People filled their baskets with apricots and persimmons, cherries and plums, apples and pears, depending on the time of year. They perfected recipes for tarts and pies and jams. They cooked fruit into candies, which they kept next to their front doors to give out to neighborhood children as they passed by.

The streets in Stone-in-the-Glen were a thing to behold in those days. People walked slowly under blossoming, or green, or fruiting boughs, taking their time as they enjoyed the dappled shade. Each night, street sweepers and scrubbers washed the cobblestones clean. The lamps, made from blown glass and polished lovingly by hand, glittered at night, like stars. The street signs hadn't yet gone missing, nor had the public art, back when it was a lovely town.

In those days, townspeople lounged in the promenades and the public square, discussing literature or politics or philosophy or art. All roads in town then led to the Library, which had wide windows, tall shelves, and deep cushions on the sofas, and which welcomed everyone. There were hand-bound books and modern books and ancient scrolls, and even texts carved into stones. The librarians bustled this way and that, sorting, preserving, shelving, and shushing. Even their shushes were lovely.

Neighbors worked together to make soup for the sick and cookies for classrooms. They swarmed like worker bees when a tree fell on a fence or when a roof needed mending or when somebody's mother had broken a leg. Neighbors cared for one another once upon a time. Back when it was a lovely town.

But then, one terrible night, the Library burned.

Different people remember terrible events differently. There were many stories explaining what happened that night in Stone-in-the-Glen, and nearly all of them disagreed. Some insisted that it was a miscreant who set the fire, claiming that they had heard footsteps echoing with sinister purpose, moving toward the venerable building and then scampering away once the flames erupted. Others swore they had heard the wings of a dragon flying overhead. Dragons were more common in those days than they are now, after all. And who loves fire more than a dragon? Others shook their heads and said that the fire had been inevitable—the place was a tinderbox. Old wood and old paper and the occasional candle that someone left unattended. *A disaster waiting to happen*, they said gravely.

(If anyone had asked me—and no one did—I could have told them that they were all correct. There was indeed a candle left burning. And then, I heard the malevolent footsteps, approaching in the dark. Within moments, a dragon unfurled itself into the fullness of its size and power at the back of the Library, the bright gleam of its scales shattering the night. I watched as it slithered up the side and coiled its long neck around the western turret. It grinned as it unhooked its jaws. I would have told anyone if they had asked me. But no one asked.)

While there was little consensus among the townsfolk about the fire's cause, everyone was in perfect agreement regarding what happened next—how the bells rang in the middle of the night and everyone, from the oldest to the youngest, raced from their beds, pulling coats over their nightclothes and sliding bare feet into galoshes. They ran through the darkened streets, carrying buckets, following the billowing smoke and that awful firelight. The fire, they say, rose in great towers over the Library, so bright it hurt their eyes just to look at it.

Heat poured from the building in great waves, crackling people's eyelashes and shriveling the leaves in nearby trees. Books flew out the melting windows like panicked birds, their wings bright and phosphorescent. They were beautiful for a moment, the town remembers, the way a heart is beautiful in the moment before it breaks.

The people of Stone-in-the-Glen arranged themselves into a line, desperately passing buckets, throwing water onto the flames. It was a useless exercise. The fire was too big. The wood beams were too dry. And paper has no choice but to burn.

For years after, the burned library remained in place, a tangle of ash and old metal and fallen, charred stone, situated between the Orphan House and the Center Square. No one had the heart to clear the debris away. No one could bear to touch a single stone. When people walked by, they held their breath.

The children in the Orphan House grew up next door to the remains of the Library. They could smell the smoke and ash. At night, the ghosts of old books haunted their dreams.

After the Library burned, the town's school, too, burned down. A tragic coincidence, everyone agreed. They held on to one another and grieved. Soon after, several other buildings burned as well—homes, shops, beloved spaces—in a rash of fires that spanned a little more than a year. After the fires, the fruit trees, and then the blossoming trees, and then the shade trees began to die off. A blight, people said. Perhaps caused by the smoke. Or that terrible heat. Or terrible luck. The people in town watched in sorrow as tree after tree came down.

And with the trees died the shade. The light in Stone-in-the-Glen became a constant, searing whiteness, and difficult to bear. People squinted to look at one another, their faces creased into permanently angry expressions.

Without the trees, there was no root system to soak up the water when it rained, and Stone-in-the-Glen began to experience damaging floods, one after another, which finally caused an enormous sinkhole to open up right next to the beautiful park where the children in town used to play, nearly swallowing it whole. It was too dangerous to play there anymore.

Indeed, it began to feel too dangerous to play anywhere in Stone-in-the-Glen. There was no shade. There were no trees to climb. The whole town seemed to scowl. Neighbors glared at one another with creased brows and narrowed eyes.

People retreated into their homes. They stopped letting their children wander freely. They locked their doors and latched their shutters. Shut away and apart, they stopped thinking about their neighbors and stopped helping their neighbors. There was no more soup for the sick, no more sweets for children, no more cookies for classrooms (well, that goes without saying, as there were no more classrooms). Best, people thought, that we keep to ourselves.

And so they did. They peeked through their shutters at the empty streets, with a sadness in their hearts.

It used to be such a lovely town, people said.

But it isn't anymore.

The Mayor

The town of Stone-in-the-Glen had a mayor, and everyone loved him very much. How could they not? He cut a fine figure and had a blinding shock of blond hair and a smile so bright they had to shade their eyes. He glittered when he spoke. He was well mannered and seemed *so sensible*. When people went to him with their problems, well, they came away feeling so fine that they completely forgot what had vexed them in the first place. And isn't that, really, what a mayor is for?

People recalled the arrival of the Mayor, back when Stone-in-the-Glen was still a lovely town, like it was something out of a storybook. They remembered the click of his fine boots as he sauntered across the cobblestones, and the sweep of his great coat, and audacious twinkling of his eyes. Each time he spoke, he thrilled them to their bones. He set up a booth during Market Day with a sign that said WORLD-FAMOUS DRAGON HUNTER: INQUIRIES AND ADULATION ACCEPTED.

"Well," remarked the butcher (and the blacksmith and the tailor). "World-famous, you say? I am certainly convinced!"

"What a lucky town," exclaimed the cobbler (and the apothecary and the constable), "to host so noble a guest! What a lucky town indeed!"

They couldn't wrest their gaze from the world-famous dragon hunter. He dazzled their eyes. They shivered each time he spoke.

By sheer serendipity, several dragon sightings were reported in the weeks just following his arrival. And then they continued, month after month. What a lucky coincidence to have a world-famous dragon hunter in their very midst at the exact same time when an unknown number of dragons began lurking in the woods nearby! Each time they saw the dragon hunter emerge victorious from the woods, the dragon once again driven away and nowhere to be seen, the townspeople erupted in cheers. They elected him mayor. They reelected him year after year. A landslide, every time.

After a while, the dragon sightings dwindled, and then became haphazard, and eventually mostly ceased. No doubt the dragon hunter's reputation had frightened them off. And while the townspeople prided themselves on their mayor's beauty and charisma and bravery—and while they still loved to say to the town's visitors, "He defeated a dragon, you know; he defeated *so many dragons!*"—over time, his shine had begun to dull, just a bit. And perhaps that un-shining would have continued.

But then the Library burned.

And then the school.

And the other buildings.

But then the trees died, and the shade vanished, and the sinkhole took the park.

How they looked to their mayor *then*. How they needed him. The Mayor, they knew in their bones, would solve their problems. Their world had become, quite quickly, chaotic and dangerous and *mean*. Their mayor seemed to have all the answers. "I can fix it," he promised. "I, alone, can fix it." They pressed their hands to their hearts when they heard him speak, emotion swelling in their chests. Their eyes became wide, and their smiles became stiff, and their faces turned to their mayor in a state of adulation and static joy.

Indeed, one could say that the fire in the Library was the best thing—*the very best thing*—that had ever happened to the Mayor.

A lucky coincidence, even.

The Crooked House

Not long after the burning of the Library, the Ogress arrived in Stone-in-the-Glen. She found an abandoned farm at the far edge of town, and she decided to stay for a while. It was an out-of-the-way sort of place, but that suited her fine. It was several years after her arrival before anyone in town even noticed her living there. Ogres are reticent creatures, you see. And shy. They don't announce themselves.

On the evening she arrived, the Ogress dug a burrow in the ground, barely big enough to fit the whole of her in while the sun was out. She came out each night, with only the creek and the grass and the sky for company. She needed very little: some protection from the sun during the day and a comfortable place on the ground to lie back and watch the stars.

It took some time before she felt at home enough to want to stay for good. And it took a bit more time before she got it in her head to start building a house.

But I'm getting ahead of myself.

The Ogress had lived in many other places before coming to Stone-in-the-Glen. Ogres live so very long, after all. If an ogre passes away before hitting the age of one thousand, other ogres come to the funeral and say, "So young! So tragic! Struck down in the brightness of youth!"

She lived with her ogre parents when she was small—*no bigger than a boulder!* as the ogres like to say—until it was time for her to grow up and seek her fortune. The Ogress loved her parents and would have preferred to stay in her family home forever, but they explained that this was the way of things for ogrekind, and that it was time to get on with the business of growing up. And so the Ogress kissed her parents and held them tight and wept bitterly as she went into the world.

For a while, a cave made a nice home—but it was damp, and rather lonely, and she was curious about the wider world. And so she moved on. Later, she lived on a rocky crag in the middle of the ocean, where sometimes she swam with the whales. But it, too, was lonely. The ocean is wild and fierce and full of storms, and whales never stay in one place for long. It wasn't much fun always being the one to wave goodbye.

She tried her hand at being a swamp ogre for a little less than a century, but she didn't much like how it smelled. So she moved on again.

She lived for quite some time with two trolls and a ghost in an abandoned castle. It wasn't a particularly happy place, trolls being trolls. She would have left right away were it not for the castle's laboratory, which took up the entire eastern wing of the building, and which was a marvel of moving parts—intricate gears and numerous clocks, and racks of glass bottles with substances inside that changed colors depending on the time of day or the weather or the particular quality of the wind. There were shelves and shelves of books that she could not read (ogres, as a general rule, never learn how to read), but many had maps and pictures and diagrams and detailed plans that she could largely figure out.

It was in this laboratory that the Ogress learned how to draw, and build, and invent. It was here that she learned how to mix pigments and stretch a canvas and paint the world as she saw it. It was here that she learned to experiment with the fruits and nuts from the orchards outside and the honey from the hives in the hollows, and to bake marvelous confections. And it was here that she learned how to use a telescope, and follow a star map, and track a trajectory, and behold the wonders of the night sky.

While she liked the castle well enough, and loved the laboratory, the trolls were mean, and the ghost was a terrible conversationalist. Eventually, the Ogress grew lonely. On the day she left, the ghost tilted her head sadly but the two trolls merely belched and farted in her direction before walking away, scratching their bums as they did so. The Ogress shouldered her bag. "I'm just trying to find a place where I can truly belong," she said, more to herself than to anyone else. And with that, she took her leave, bringing a few items from the laboratory with her—a telescope, some books, and several sets of plans for different machines that she thought she might want to build some day. No one waved goodbye, and the Ogress knew she was making the right choice.

She lived for a few pleasant centuries in an ogre village, deep in the mountains. Such villages were a rarity in those days, as they often found themselves targeted by small-minded people with backward views about ogres. This one was far enough off the common routes and remote enough that it avoided such unpleasantness. It was a happy place, that village, both warm and welcoming, and there she made her living growing vegetables for the market and drawing pictures for the ogre children and teaching the other ogres about the mysteries of the stars. And there she might have remained but for a sad turn of events. One day, after the Ogress had been away on a long journey (ogres get restless, you see, and find the need to take a turn about the world every now and again), she returned to discover that in her absence the entire village had been burned to the ground and abandoned. Everything—*everything*—was gone.

The Ogress, after the shock of the destruction had finally worn off, knew that she had no easy way of discovering where her neighbors had gone. Since ogres don't learn to read and write, sending letters was never exactly an option. Ogres simply assume that they will see one another again eventually. Life is long, after all. And over time, the paths we take tend to intertwine and overlap.

She traveled extensively and tried to make herself useful as a laborer, or a builder, or a maker of ingenious contraptions. She found unused animal dens to sleep in during the day and did her best work by moonlight. Sometimes, she had to beg for her supper. Sometimes, she begged and then gave her supper to someone else. It felt good to be able to share and help others. It was its own sort of belonging. She discovered that she didn't need much, and she didn't want much, either—just a bit of shelter, and perhaps a hearth for baking and a pot for soup. Something for herself. Something to share. A way to belong. She learned to trade in kindness and discovered the tremendous value in small mercies and selfless giving. The more she gave, the more she seemed to have. It was the best sort of magic.

During her travels, the Ogress heard the stories of the terrible fire in Stone-in-the-Glen. She heard how the trees there were dying. She listened as people told tales of the town's sorrow and growing poverty. The Ogress held these stories deep in her heart. She knew about loss. And sorrow. She thought that she might have a bit in common with the people of Stone-in-the-Glen. Maybe, she thought, this was a place where she could belong. So she set out to find it.

When she arrived in the middle of the night, the town, over a year after the fires, still smelled of smoke and ash. And sorrow, too. No one was about, of course. People hunkered in their houses behind latched shutters and locked doors. No one saw her make her way through the sad streets. No one heard the quiet footsteps of her large, soft shoes.

(Well, I did, of course. But no one asked me.)

She walked until she came to the far end of town, where the roads began to twist and the thickets grew tangled. Where the heavy limbs of the sycamores creaked in the breeze. There she found a farm, fallow and abandoned, the remnants of the old house and barn heaped in a hollow. But the soil was good. And the grass was soft. She could stay a season or two, plant a garden, perhaps. Live off the land until it was time to move on. She lay back on the ground and watched the stars, and dug her burrow just before the sun came up.

After a week or two, she had sprouting plants and had found a clutch of tubers, which made a tasty snack when they were roasted. She found glass in the ruins and started polishing the pieces into lenses so she could build a new telescope. She didn't know how long she would stay. But the farm felt comfortable. And there was something about this town. It *needed* her. She could feel it. Perhaps, she thought, once she was able to overcome her shyness, she might introduce herself to the townspeople nearby. Her neighbors. What a beautiful word that was: *neighbors*. It thrilled her to her core.

The first friends she made were not townspeople. A massive flock of crows arrived one sunset to the winding road at the far end of town, because they had heard that an ogre—an actual ogre—had come to the area and seemed intent on staying. Crows, like the orphans, are curious creatures. The birds settled on the sycamore branches to see for themselves.

The Ogress stopped her work. She looked up at the crows.

The crows curled their talons into the wood, prepared to hold their ground. "Caw," the crows said, which in their language meant "You are a stranger. And we would like to know your business."

"Caw," they added. "We have never met an ogre before, but we have heard the stories and have learned that your kind are prone to wickedness. Have you heard of the undeniable power of crows? Have you heard about our rapacious talons and our razor-sharp beaks? Have you heard that we hold grudges and remember our enemies and sometimes use weaponry to defeat those who wrong us?"

The Ogress did not speak Crow. Instead, she smiled at the crows, and she bowed low. So low that the top of her head nearly touched the ground. The crows were impressed with her excellent manners. "Hello, my friends," the Ogress said. "And welcome. I don't have much to offer guests, I'm afraid, but I do have a bit of hardtack in my bags. And some dried corn. If I crumble them together, they will make a fine meal. There is no use in keeping it to myself. Everything tastes better when you share it."

The crows were deeply moved. In town, no one greeted them at all. In town, no one offered them a meal or referred to them as guests. In town, they were only called pests. Or varmints. The people in town had become grumpier than usual since the Library burned down. Even earlier, some of the older crows insisted—ever since that blasted shiny mayor showed up. Some people were so grumpy that they even threw rocks at the crows from time to time. Rocks! The very idea!

The Ogress crumbled the tack into the corn and scattered it on the ground. As the crows ate, she told them something about her life. She left quite a bit out. Her life was very long, after all.

The crows listened carefully as she spoke. They hopped from branch to branch. They hovered in great dark clouds overhead. They conferred to one another in murmurs.

They liked the Ogress very much. But they were worried about her, too.

"Caw," the crows said. "People have said that this is a good town. And maybe it was, once. And maybe there is still goodness somewhere. And loveliness somewhere. But there is an unkindness that grows every day. It spreads the way the blight spread through the trees. If a town can be so unkind as to throw rocks at crows, what else might they be capable of?

"Caw," they added. "We like you fine, but you might want to consider a different place to live."

Of course the Ogress couldn't understand a word of any of this. Instead, she smiled, her heart full and her spirit light. "What wonderful neighbors you are! What delightful friends! What a lucky ogre am I! Please, come any old day you like. I will share whatever I can. After all, the more you give, the more you have. It is the only true thing I know."

The crows stayed with her as the night grew darker, and gathered close as she lay back on the tall grass.

They all looked up to count the stars.

The Orphans Have Several Theories

Was it the fire that changed the town?

Was it unneighborliness?

Was it the loss of the school, or the sinkhole that swallowed the park, or the dead trees?

The library fire occurred many years before any of the orphans were born. They had no memory of Stone-in-the-Glen as it had been. They only knew the town as it was now: a drab, tightfisted, mean little place. The Orphan House was kept separate from the town by locked gates and tall stone walls, and the orphans were not allowed to wander by themselves. As a result, they had a lot of time on their hands to consider the problems of Stone-in-the-Glen.

How does a lovely town become an unlovely town?

And if it is unlovely now, could it have ever been lovely to begin with?

And furthermore, assuming it was lovely in the past, was it possible, really and truly, for it to ever become lovely again?

"It *was* lovely," Anthea, the eldest (and in her view, the wisest), said often and emphatically. She was a tall, serious girl, nearly fourteen. She had dark hair, which she kept in two neat braids, and dark eyes, under dark brows that were perpetually creased in a curious, keen expression. She had narrow hands, with long, clever fingers, which were often at work making something useful for someone else. A new pair of booties for one of the babies, for example. Or a more efficient type of spoon.

"Stone-in-the-Glen, once upon a time, was the loveliest town," she said. And because Anthea was the sort of child who believed in details, she had the pictures to prove it. She had in her possession a collection of woodcuts and watercolors, and tiny dioramas that could only be viewed through a pinhole in a small carved box, each showing different aspects of the town as it had been—orchards, gardens, girls in pretty dresses strolling down promenades, patrons busily searching the shelves in the long corridors of the Library.

"You see?" she offered. "Lovely." The pictures, she felt, settled the matter.

"But what *made* it lovely?" Bartleby, the second oldest, asked one afternoon, when the heat of the day pressed firmly on the whole town. Bartleby enjoyed philosophy, which is to say he enjoyed arguing. He had dark curls and mismatched eyes and an easy, ready smile. "Either we must assume that the source of its loveliness was removed somehow or we must assume that the stories of its loveliness are somehow overblown. If the former is true, it might be possible to return the town to its earlier loveliness. If the latter is true, then we must accept the town for what it is, warts and all." He paused for a moment, brushing his curls out of his eyes. "Not that there's anything wrong with warts," he said with a grin.

Bartleby stopped the matron of the Orphan House as she bustled by, attending to one of her endless tasks, to get her opinion.

Matron had no time for philosophy. There were many children in the Orphan House. Too many. And she had too much to do. She hoisted heaped laundry baskets in each arm and hurried down the stairs. Matron seemed impossibly old to the children, but she was surprisingly strong and spry, and always hurrying.

"You're too young to remember," Matron said breathlessly. "If you had seen, you would have known. It was lovely once. And safe. And kind." She glanced out the window, the deep lines in her face growing deeper, and her eyes becoming careworn and sad. "It's a shame, really," she sighed. "A terrible shame." Then she shook her head and hurried away.

But the orphans weren't done. There was an answer. They were *sure of it*. They had long listened to the muttering as people walked past the gate, blaming the Ogress in Stone-in-the-Glen, the very *fact of her living in town*, for causing the town's alteration from *lovely* to *not*. The orphans, for their part, dismissed that notion out of hand.

Anthea called it "too stupid to consider."

Bartleby declared it "philosophically untenable, and morally gross."

Cass, the third oldest, as usual said nothing, but she glared when anyone spoke that way.

The orphans' reasoning was obvious: The Ogress stayed in her crooked house at the far end of town all day long and, as far as anyone knew, never went anywhere except into the forest, and only in the evening. People would see her occasionally, always from far away ("She waved menacingly!" neighbors complained), but these sightings were few and far between. No one knew how she spent her time. So how on earth could the whole *town's* unlovelying have anything to do with the fact that it had an ogress for a neighbor?

Still, the question remained. If the town truly was lovely once upon a time, *where did the loveliness go?*

The two ten-year-olds, Fortunate and Gratitude, were of the opinion that Stone-in-the-Glen had never been lovely at all. They folded their arms across their chests and set their faces, prepared, as always, for disagreement. Despite the fact that they looked nothing alike—from their faces to their hair to the color of their eyes to the starkly different hues of their skin—both Fortunate and Gratitude insisted that they were identical twins. Which would have seemed ridiculous if it weren't for the fact that they were strangely difficult to differentiate. Fortunate was constantly being confused with Gratitude, and Gratitude was often mistaken for Fortunate. And then there was the way they finished each other's sentences and seemed to share each other's thoughts. It was widely believed among the family that Fortunate and Gratitude had identical souls. Everyone in the household simply referred to them as the twins.

"Look," said Fortunate.

"All of us wound up here," continued Gratitude.

"In a basket."

"Our kin either gone or dead."

"And no friends or neighbors willing to take us in."

"Do such things happen in lovely towns?" Gratitude wondered aloud. There was a long, pointed pause.

"No," Fortunate said flatly. "They do not."

And with that they left, hand in hand, in a huff.

Dierdre thought that the town had been doomed when the school burned down, as it had clearly made everyone stupid, while Elijah declared that it was the sinkhole that did it, since the very idea sounded *terrible*. Hiram, Iggy, Justina, and Kye didn't much care about whether the town was lovely or not, only that it was *absolutely unfair* that they weren't allowed to go out and play in it.

"At least we should be able to climb on the old smoky stones," Justina complained. "They're so fun and dirty!"

"It's too hot inside," Hiram announced. "Let's go outside and wrestle." Hiram could run faster on his one leg and crutches than most of the other children could on their two, and, as usual, he was gone in a flash. The rest of the younger children followed him out at a sprint and launched themselves into the garden, to roll on the grass or chase the chickens or play with the two milk goats. Elijah told stories to the twins as Dierdre drew elaborate scenes from his tale on the outside walls of the chicken coop with chalk. The cats stalked the flower beds for mice, and the babies napped indoors as Matron's husband, a very, very old man named Myron, gave the toddlers their baths.

It was a normal day in the Orphan House.

Anthea, Bartleby, and Cass all sat together on the front steps, watching over the younger children. And thinking. If it was true that the town had changed, perhaps the library fire was the primary cause.

This was Anthea's preferred theory. She was the sort of girl who believed in logic and progression, cause and effect. She enjoyed using the word *ergo* whenever possible. The fire, Anthea knew, had destroyed the Library's numerous fine books, but it also had damaged the trees nearby. Without a library, the town had no reference section and couldn't look up strategies on how to save the trees. The trees died, and then the floods came, which caused the sinkhole, which meant that it wasn't safe to play in the park. Fences appeared. Then walls. Then locks. No one wanted to be the only one helping, because no one wanted to be responsible for solutions that perhaps might fail.

"You see?" Anthea explained. She, Bartleby, and Cass leaned back on their elbows, legs stretched out across the porch steps. They pressed their shoulders together, enjoying, as always, one another's company.

"It's just logic," Anthea continued. "Because A is true, then B must be true. And B causes C. It's no one's fault that the town became unlovely. The fire did it."

"I question your assumptions," Bartleby said.

"I question your face," Anthea countered. "Also, I'm older," she added, as though this made any further argument unnecessary.

Bartleby was unconvinced. The younger children played in the grass as the sun sank low. They tilted their faces to the sky, enjoying the angle of the light. A cat climbed onto Bartleby's lap and curled into a ball. Bartleby stroked it absently. His eyes were two starkly different colors. One was hazel with flecks of green and gold, while the other was pale—like the color of skimmed milk spilled across the sky. The hazel eye was able to see tiny details at great distances, but the other eye was only able to see light and shadows. He often said this allowed him to practice seeing things in two separate ways, and to be of at least two minds on most subjects.

"I can see it both ways," he said to Anthea now.

Anthea was instantly annoyed. "This isn't a *both ways* situation, *Bartleby*," she said.

"Everything is a *both ways* situation," Bartleby countered. "All situations contain multitudes."

Cass snorted. She didn't argue. She never argued with Bartleby. Or Anthea. Or anyone, for that matter.

"See? Cass agrees with me," Anthea said under her breath. If Bartleby heard her say so, he didn't mention it.

Cassandra, Bartleby's sister, went by Cass most of the time. She kept her hair short and preferred trousers and boots instead of dresses and stockings, and she didn't say much, as a general rule. Bartleby spoke enough for the two of them. Cass was more of a doer than a talker. She was the one who always kept the walkway swept or the firewood stacked, or quietly placed a nice cup of mint tea in Matron's hands before anyone even thought to ask for any of it.

"You don't need to speak for Cass," Bartleby said. "*Cass speaks for Cass.*" Cass leaned her head on her brother's shoulder and pressed the heel of her boot to Anthea's narrow shoe. She closed her eyes and enjoyed for a moment the sensation of sun on her skin, and the company of Anthea and Bartleby, who were her two favorite people in the world. It didn't matter, Cass knew, who was right, or how many ways there were to think about a situation.

Because Anthea, if left to her own devices, could logic herself into a corner, while Cass's brother could think himself into a hole. Someone had to be there to pull them out. And that someone was usually Cass.

It didn't much matter in the end *whether* the town was originally lovely or not, or *how* that unloveliness first had begun. In the end, *the town didn't matter.*

All that mattered was the Orphan House. And that all the orphans in the house took care of one another. And that they took care of their matron, as well as Matron's husband, Myron. And that they always would. Because inside the Orphan House, it was all of them, together, and that was *something*, regardless of what happened on the other side of the gate. The town could be safe or not, or good or not, or lovely or not, and how it got that way didn't change the fact that the Orphan House was *good.* And the people in it, all of them, were *good.* And within those walls, each one of them was unshakably and unchangeably safe. And that was that.

We take care of one another, Cass thought. *We look out for one another. We belong to the Orphan House, and we belong to each other, and that will never change.*

And Cass was right. Until she wasn't.

The Stone

Listen.

There is an actual stone in Stone-in-the-Glen, which is situated at the center of what once was an actual glen. The glen, once upon a time, before the town was built, was thick with trees. Mostly oak and ash and sycamore. Ancient things, they were, and so numerous you couldn't see past the wide trunks and sprawling branches. That was a long time ago. Eventually, people came. And, being people, they saw the utility in those long, straight trunks, those broad limbs, and decided to use them to build homes, then furniture, then a school, then the broad beams of fine buildings, constructed sturdily so as to last through many generations. They cut down the trees and they built the town. They didn't ask the trees how they felt about it. This is not unusual, alas.

(The people who built the town didn't notice the Stone. And, as time progressed, people went on not noticing the Stone. The Stone insisted it didn't mind.

It mostly didn't mind.)

People say that the posts and beams and pillars made from those original trees have memories.

And not only that, but they say that each post, each beam, each pillar, each stick of furniture made from those original trees, will sometimes whisper their stories. Late at night. In the dark.

Or, at least, so I've heard. I, myself, am not in a position to be able to sneak into people's homes at night to listen, so I cannot verify whether or not any of this is true.

It's a pity, though. I remember those stories.

While ash trees tend to be, I'm afraid to say, rather silly creatures, and their stories are often too vacuous and meandering to matter much, there is no better storyteller on earth than an oak tree. Long ago, before the town was built, when the original trees still grew here, the glen of Stone-in-the-Glen rang with stories, and those stories had deep roots and wide, expansive arms—they stretched outward and upward toward the sky.

But that's all gone now. Each story fell with the blade of an axe. I still shudder at the memory of it.

The Stone remained. It wasn't going anywhere. Not that anyone noticed. Or mostly they didn't notice.

The Stone sat just off to the side of the Center Square. It was, and is, rough and asymmetrical and rather drab in color. It wasn't a stone that announced itself. It just blended in. It didn't seem at first glance to be so large a stone—perhaps the size of a comfortable chair—but in truth, it was much bigger than it seemed, as much of its bulk extended deep under the earth and extended in many directions. How deep? How wide? Well, no one could say.

No one but the Stone.

And stones don't talk.

Usually.

All anyone knew was that it could not be moved. Not for anything.

If you were to travel to Stone-in-the-Glen now, and if you were to find the Stone, and if you were to look very, very closely, you would see that the Stone has writing on its surface. Much of it was rubbed away years ago, by the wind and the rain and the touch of hands. And the writing that remains visible is in a language that no one has spoken for centuries.

Since no one noticed the Stone much, no one had noticed the writing . . . until that period of time after the Library burned. People were wandering about in a state of grief and trauma and disbelief. It was in this state that their eyes fell on the Stone. They told their neighbors to come and see. There was a symbol that some thought looked like a mountain. There was another that a few people remarked looked a little like a dragon. And another that looked like an oak tree felled by an axe.

And the more they looked, the more they saw.

"Well, I'll be," people said. "Doesn't that look just like a house?"

And it did. Everyone agreed.

"And look! It's a village right there."

And, yes, it did rather look like a village, if you squinted. But even more, when people placed their fingers over that symbol, it seemed to them that they could *feel* the village. Deep in their bones.

"And here!" They pointed to another symbol. "It's a fire."

And indeed, it was. The symbol itself was hot to the touch, and, for some reason, filled everyone with a crushing sense of loss.

"And look, there!" some people pointed out. "It's an ogre." So many mysteries contained in the symbols on this stone!

Word spread. People gathered. They sat by the Stone and tried to untangle its many paradoxes. Theories developed. And arguments about competing theories. A lively debate arose, along with spontaneous lectures, organized discussion groups, and even a sing-along for the children. Ideas were swapped. It wasn't the same as having their library back, but it still felt nice to be together.

Eventually, this sort of talk reached the ears of the Mayor. He emerged from the fine doors of his great mansion, bathed, as usual, in a golden light. He had beautifully coiffed hair and a dazzling smile. He glittered when he spoke. He defeated dragons, you know. After all those years, it still felt wonderful to say. He had been mayor for quite some time now. It was difficult for people to say how long. Whenever anyone tried, it made their eyes begin to cross and their head hurt. What was time anyway when one had so fine a mayor?

The Mayor frowned as he approached the crowd in the Center Square, where they discussed the meaning of the Stone. "Pray tell," he said with a smile. His teeth were so white it hurt to look at them. "Whatever is the meaning of all of this?"

The former librarians discussed the text on the Stone and their theories of its origin, while the unemployed linguists speculated on the roots and meanings of each symbol, and the teachers provided their thoughts on the scholastic applications of the Stone and how it might be utilized in a classroom setting once a school was rebuilt, and the artists proposed a community installation, and the builders suggested a gazebo around the Stone so that people could gather together to think and discuss and lounge in the shade.

The Mayor frowned. He reached out to touch the Stone. Nothing happened for a moment. Then his face grew livid. And then alarmed. He pulled his hand away, as though burned. If anyone had noticed his sudden change of expression, no one said so. It was more likely that no one noticed anything at all.

(I did, of course. But no one noticed my noticing. I am used to this sort of thing.)

"You see . . ." one librarian began, but she was quickly cut off.

"Enough!" the Mayor said with a click of his fine boots, his golden buckles flashing in the sun. The people in the Center Square had to shade their eyes. The Mayor adjusted the drape of his excellent coat and inclined his face toward his adoring subjects. He shook his head. "It pains me to see such disagreement in our beloved community." He pressed his hands to his heart and bowed in sorrow.

The townsfolk gasped. It grieved them deeply to see their beautiful mayor in pain. Had they unknowingly become disagreeable? Each person cast a hard look at their neighbors. Mouths twitched, brows furrowed, and soon every face bore a sour expression.

Without delay, the Mayor had his carpenters build a heavy wooden box to fit over the Stone, to keep it out of sight and out of mind. The polished grain and skillful joints withstood the wind and weather for a good long time. Thanks to the box, people didn't see the Stone anymore. As a result, they didn't really think about the Stone anymore. In time, they forgot about it altogether.

Eventually, though, wood rots. And joints fail. Eventually, the box became a pile of cast-off lumber—one more broken thing in a run-down town. Eventually, more trash and debris landed upon the pile in the Center Square. People tut-tutted about it and complained about the mess, but they didn't think about where it came from, or why it was there. They still didn't notice the Stone, which sat, drab and ordinary, in the shadow of the trash heap. Their eyes just slid past it, as though it weren't there.

Listen.

What happened, you might wonder, on that day when the Mayor placed his hand on the Stone? What happened when his expression changed? What, you might be wondering, did the Mayor notice? Well, who could say? The Mayor certainly didn't.

You could ask the Stone, of course. But I know what you're thinking: *Stones don't talk.*

And you're right. They don't.

Usually.

Tick, Tock

Like the matron of the Orphan House, her husband, Myron, was impossibly old. The children often tried to guess their ages, but neither Matron nor her Myron would ever say. (Fifty? One hundred? One hundred and fifty? Each number sounded like a lot, and therefore each was entirely plausible.) One thing was for sure: even though the children knew that Matron and Myron had been friends and sweethearts since they themselves were children (in this very Orphan House, no less), and even though Myron was a couple of years younger than she, it was Matron who was decidedly the more robust. Despite her age, she was all muscles and sinews and speed—sharp, agile, and in possession of boundless energy.

Myron was not. He had deep scars on his hands and arms and the back of his neck, as well as on one cheek—they were bubbly and angry and very, very red. Like burns. The children often asked about them, but Myron would never answer directly. The marks were too difficult to talk about, and they pained him, even now. Also, Myron became ill more often than anyone else in the house. He coughed a lot and wheezed terribly. His face sometimes grew pale, and his eyes looked as though they were seeing through murky water. And he was sleepy. More so with every passing month. The older children noticed this more than the younger children did. They did their best not to worry. They put a blanket on Myron's feet when he got cold and brought him a mug of mint tea to perk him up, and did whatever they could to tell themselves that this was fine. That he was fine. That everything was going to be just fine.

Still, there were nights when Anthea would lie awake staring at the ceiling, thinking about Myron. While his body was fragile, his mind remained as alert as ever—quick, curious, and keen. Anthea was a big believer in the power of the mind. Had not her own mind allowed her to learn languages and mathematics and logic, not to mention tinkering and carpentry and needlework? There was nothing, Anthea felt, that a well-tuned mind could not accomplish. She trusted Myron's mind to carry his body along for as long as necessary. The family needed him, after all.

These thoughts churned in Anthea's head as she walked with Myron down a potholed street in Stone-in-the-Glen— she held Myron's left hand while Elijah held his right. Myron gripped their hands very tightly, and his gaze darted this way and that. The sun was high and bright, with no shade to be found, so that every sagging doorway, every scattered bit of trash, and every boarded-up window on which someone had scrawled ugly words was shown in harsh relief.

Elijah told a story as they walked. Elijah was always telling stories. Anthea had stopped listening quite some time earlier.

Details flowed and tumbled from his mouth in an endless stream. There was, in Elijah's tale, a stone that knew more than it ought to have known, trees that spoke and dreamed and told stories, a dragon that was so mean that no one wanted to even mention him, and something about a bunch of ogres deep in the mountains. Elijah's story bent and weaved and twisted about. Anthea could *not* pay attention.

"Come, children," Myron said, picking up his pace.

"And *then*," Elijah continued, "you will *not believe* what the crows said next!"

Anthea rolled her eyes.

They passed through the Center Square. It wasn't Market Day, so by law no one was supposed to be selling anything in the square (there were signs reminding people of this, with the town's latest slogan, ORDER ABOVE ALL, printed at the bottom), but there were still occasional vendors calling out their wares on the sly to whoever might listen, but they were ready to roll up and scoot away if it looked like they were about to get in trouble.

"Clothing!" a woman called from a makeshift table. "Buy, sell, or trade! Cast-off, run-off, one-off, come-off. Rags, tags, and velvet gowns! We have it all!" She scanned the square again and again, making sure that no one was getting ready to report her.

"Nips, pips, and old drill bits!" a man bellowed from next to a pile of trash and debris that heaped off to the side. "Clockwork gears and springs and screws! Need bracing? Need tracing? Need wire? Need fire? Anything your heart desires!"

Anthea glanced over. All he had was a collection of odds and ends—likely just picked from the pile of trash right next to him, and he was trying to sell it as though a person couldn't have just picked through the junk on their own. Someone nearby threatened to call the constable.

"That man stole my idea," Anthea complained.

That pile of junk in the Center Square was incredibly useful. Anthea had been finding bits and pieces in there for her projects for as long as she could remember, but only when she was accompanying Matron or Myron on an errand, as she was not allowed to go to the Center Square on her own. It's where she had often scavenged a handful of perfectly straight nails. Or an assortment of screws. Or strong string. Or broken clocks, whose gears and springs could be repurposed into something else. Or knitting needles. Or cast-off yarn. There was always something new to be found. Anthea had a knack for finding value in abandoned things.

"People shouldn't steal other people's ideas," Anthea grumbled. She wrinkled her brow and gave the seller a hard look.

"An idea, my dear," Myron tutted, "can never be stolen, because it cannot be owned. Just as the sun cannot be owned and the air cannot be owned and the rain cannot be owned. A seed is planted in the ground and grows thanks to the gifts of sun and rain. Does the seed *own* the idea of growing? Does the sun *own* the idea of shining, or the rain *own* the idea of watering the earth? Of course not. Ideas are self-replicating. The notion that they can be limited or hoarded is nonsense."

Anthea scowled. Myron, like Bartleby, enjoyed philosophy, which only ever succeeded in making her cross. "I disagree," she said.

"But you *see*," said Elijah, who was *still* telling his story and not paying attention to what either Anthea or Myron were saying, "his face was actually a *disguise*! What the people in town did *not know* is that—"

"Here we are!" Myron interrupted. They had arrived at the butcher shop, and he bustled the children indoors. Anthea wrinkled her nose. She didn't like how the butcher shop smelled—of salt and smoke and fear and sorrow. She reached into her pocket and grabbed the sachet she had made from garden herbs, inhaling deeply.

A man stood at the counter, arguing with the butcher. Or at least the butcher was arguing. The man he was arguing with was standing placidly and nodding his head. He was very tall, with wide shoulders. He wore wool trousers with many loops and pockets, each one containing some kind of tool. Anthea was impressed. She admired tools. And clever places to keep them. The man spoke quietly, his voice firm.

The butcher had thin arms and a distended belly covered by a stained apron. He had dark circles under his eyes and a sallowness in his cheeks that made Anthea think that maybe he didn't spend very much time out of doors. As he raged, red splotches appeared on his face. The veins on his neck bulged. Anthea watched, holding her breath.

"A fine display of friendship this is!" the butcher said. Spit flew from his mouth. His lips twisted with scorn. "Very fine indeed! After all I've done! To be treated this way!"

"I'm not sure what you mean, Jonathan," the man with the tools said. He folded his hands and rested his chin on his knuckles. "I am not the one who altered our agreement, nor would I ever be, as doing so is neither friendly nor honorable. I am in need of leather to make shoes. You are in possession of a regular supply that would go to waste without a buyer, and the two of us negotiated what we both agreed was a fair price. We shook hands and wrote it down. It is *you*, my friend, not I, who is now going back on your word. I wonder why." He let his hands fall open, palms up, on the counter.

"Oh! Insult me now, will you?" The butcher threw his hands in the air. He added several rude words that made Anthea gasp. Elijah clapped his hands over his ears. The butcher turned his back on the man, and paced back and forth, throwing a towel on the floor and clattering the dishes. "Rascals and sharks! What has this town come to? When it used to be so lovely, once upon a time!"

The man with the tools continued to speak mildly, and the butcher continued to insult and explode. This went on for some time until, finally, Myron cleared his throat. "Pardon me?" he said, his voice like dry twigs. Anthea gave his hand a squeeze to help his courage. He was a timid man on a good day. The butcher's red, angry face was enough to knock poor Myron over. The man with the tools turned and caught Myron's eye, and both their faces lifted into bright smiles. "Oh!" Myron said. "It's you! Hello, Arthur."

"Why, Myron!" the man said, and he strode over. The two embraced, clapping each other on the back. "It's been some time. I've been meaning to pay you and dear Matron a visit, but these days it's hard enough just to keep a roof over our heads. I'm afraid time gets away from me."

Before Myron could reply, the butcher crossed his arms over his stained apron and harrumphed. "Oh!" the butcher said, gesturing toward the man and Myron. "Ganging up on me now, are you? Well, it figures! Please, old man! Tell me how you would like to swindle me as well!"

Myron carefully approached the counter and began speaking in a low voice—something about *accounts*. Anthea hung back with Elijah, their backs pressed against the door. Myron had told them earlier that he needed them to come and look charming, just in case, and Anthea now understood why. The butcher was not very nice. She put on what she hoped was her most charming face.

"What's wrong with your face right now?" Elijah whispered.

"*Hush,*" Anthea admonished.

"There's a story about this, you know," Elijah said. "You see, there was once this dragon who—"

"Ugh." Anthea sighed. "No one wants to *hear* it, Elijah."

The butcher raised his voice. "Liars and thieves!" he lamented. "That's all that's left in this town. Liars and thieves. And I see you are training them young, are you, Myron? Is that your gambit? The Mayor warned me that dirty deeds were afoot, and he was right! An orphan house dedicated to the production of the criminals of tomorrow, it seems. You should be ashamed!"

"Really!" Myron huffed. "I never!"

"*Jonathan,*" the other man said, trying to calm things down. "You aren't making any sense at all."

"How old is that one?" the butcher asked, pointing a finger at Anthea.

She flinched.

And then she remembered to be charming. She gave a mild smile and curtsied quickly, which was a thing that happened in books and seemed appropriate for the moment. "I'm thirteen, sir. I turn fourteen in the fall."

The butcher pressed his mouth into a savage twist. "Fourteen, eh? Well, well. Tick, tock. Clock's ticking, my girl. Soon you'll be out on your bum, just like that. A terribly nice birthday present, don't you think? But rules are rules. Or didn't they tell you?" He flashed her a nasty smile.

Anthea blinked. She had no idea what he was talking about. She looked at Myron, who glared at the butcher. "What?" she said. Her voice fell from her mouth like a pebble into a pond.

"That's . . . well, that's just," Myron sputtered. "It's ridiculous is what that is. I mean . . ."

"Jonathan, honestly," the man with the tools said. "What on earth is going on? Where is all of this coming from?"

"The Mayor was in here just this morning. Warning me about all sorts of wicked doings afoot. Schemes! Gambits! Fraud every which way. I've been on my guard! No one will trick me! Not even my so-called friends." He shifted his glare toward Anthea as a redness crept up from the skin of his neck and spread blotchily across his face. "And you, thief in the making! Surely you know that orphans are only allowed to stay at the Orphan House until they are fourteen. It's in the charter. You layabout kids are supposed to go out and seek your fortunes! Become apprentices! Become useful! It's the law, that is, you being useful! Not that you've ever been useful a day in your life. My taxes support you orphans, and for what?"

Myron threw his arms out like wings and herded the children to the door. "Outside," he said quickly. "Both of you." Then his eyes grew wide and his gaze darted this way and that. "But stay by the window. Where I can see you. It isn't safe to wander off."

As he shooed them out, he whispered, "Don't trouble yourselves, my darlings. He's talking nonsense. A madman!" He gave them both a squeeze and a kiss on the cheek and then returned to the shouting butcher.

Anthea stood with Elijah on the cobblestone street. The sun beat, hot and relentless, but Anthea wrapped her arms around her body and shivered with cold. Her eyes were so dry it felt as though they were made out of sand. *Fourteen*, she thought. *Is that true? Why did no one tell me?*

When Anthea was very little, there had been four older children who lived in the house. They had not arrived, as she and the others had, as babies, but rather had come as already-older children, due to some sort of family tragedy, and none of them had stayed there for very long. They were simply cared for by Matron and Myron until they started the next chapter in their lives.

That was how things were supposed to work at the Orphan House, once upon a time. Before the Library burned. Before the town changed. It was supposed to be loving and safe and *temporary*. It used to be that everyone worked together and did what was necessary to help their neighbors in need. But now, there wasn't a place for the orphans anymore, so the children arrived as babies, and then they just . . . stayed.

Anthea had assumed she would simply stay forever. Where else could she go? She looked up and down the street—at broken windows, boards covering doorways, missing cobblestones, the remains of various buildings that had succumbed to fire, like gaps in a mouth left by missing teeth.

Elijah, sensing her distress, curled his hand into hers. "There's a story, you know, about the old library," Elijah said. Anthea was too upset to tell him to hush. "About what happened on the day it burned. Did you know that the Library was magic? Or maybe just the books were."

Anthea closed her eyes. "Nothing is magic, Elijah," she said heavily. "You're old enough to know that by now."

"I think a lot of things are magic if you think about it right. And some things might not be magic exactly, but they're pretty close." Elijah always spoke quickly, as though there was not enough time in the day to release all the words and thoughts in his head. "Look at the Reading Room. I once found a book in there that released smoke from the library fire when I opened it. I mean it, Anthea! Real smoke! So maybe the Reading Room is magic because books really are magic. I read once that books bend both space and time, and the more books you have in one place, the more space and time will bend and twist and fold over itself. I'm not sure if that's true, but it *feels* true. Of course, I read that in a book, and maybe the book was just bragging."

Anthea closed her eyes and tilted her face to the sky, expelling a long breath from her nose. "Books don't brag, Elijah," she said, exasperation fraying the edges of her voice.

"Well, maybe they should," Elijah said. "Anyway, there's a story about a book in the Library that was disconnected from time, and that told history in four directions—forward, backward, inside, and outside. That's not magic, either, I suppose. But it's definitely close."

"That doesn't make any sense," Anthea said.

"It does if you think about it," Elijah said with a grin. He let go of her hand and wrapped his arms around her waist. Elijah was small for his age. His head didn't quite reach Anthea's shoulder, so he fit under the curl of her arm. He hugged her tight. "Don't worry about that man's nonsense, Anthea," Elijah said. "I already know how this story ends. The orphans save the day. I'm not exactly sure how, but I know that we do. All of us together. Trust me."

Anthea shook her head. Of all the children in the house, Elijah was by far the strangest. Still, his confidence was comforting. She hugged him back. Just then, Myron came stumbling out the door.

"And don't come back!" yelled the butcher.

"Don't worry, Myron," the man with the tools said. "I'll discuss this situation with the Mayor. He'll know what to do. He alone will solve this, just as he solves everything else!" The man's face became languid at the thought of the Mayor, his eyes unfocused.

Myron dropped his gaze to the ground and began to fidget. He almost looked embarrassed. Anthea frowned, looking at Myron, then the man, then back to Myron.

"Does he now?" Myron muttered, but he said it under his breath. The man with the tools didn't seem to notice. His eyes remained unfocused, and then he simply . . . wandered away, as though dreaming.

Myron gave Anthea and Elijah a forced smile. "Some people certainly do love the Mayor." He cleared his throat. "Well, off we go, then, my dears. Our beloved Matron is likely wondering where we are!"

Elijah frowned. "But weren't we going to buy meat?" He put his hands into his pockets. "You know. For supper?" Elijah's stomach growled, as if in response.

Myron clenched his jaw for a moment and sighed. "Not today, Elijah," he said. "It's a new policy at the butcher shop. Cash on the barrel. No more credit accounts. Do not trouble yourself, my love. This is fine. We are all going to be fine. We will delight ourselves with vegetable soup until we fill our jar with coins. And, oh, what a feast we shall have then! Come along!"

"Oh, good," Elijah muttered, making a face. "More vegetable soup. Breakfast, lunch, and dinner. Who could ever get tired of it?"

Myron took their hands and hurried away.

Anthea tripped on her own feet trying to keep up. Then, without meaning to, she stole a glance over her shoulder, back at the butcher shop. There, in the window, stood the butcher, glowering at their backs as they scurried down the street. His eyes locked on hers, and his mouth slid into a smirk. He raised one finger and tilted it back and forth, back and forth.

Tick, tock, he mouthed. *Tick, tock.*

Anthea turned forward and gulped. She had never really thought about time before this. What is time, really, when there is so much work to be done? In her mind, she calculated the weeks she had before weather changed and the leaves turned color and the night winds blew cold. And then her time would be up.

What the Ogress Saw in the Periscope

If you were to ask the Ogress how long it took her to finish building her crooked little house, she would likely be baffled by the question.

It isn't that time works differently for ogres—how could it? Time is time.

And yet.

We might think time is stable and consistent—seconds and minutes assembled like marks on a ruler—but that isn't true at all. Time stretches and bunches and wobbles about. It loops and twists, and sometimes lays itself flat and sometimes ties itself in knots. A stone buried in the earth experiences time differently than a comet hurtling through space.

Time, as they say, is relative. It's not magic, obviously, but it can feel that way. Ogres, for example, experience time differently than humans do. This has something to do with their long, long lives. You may have noticed something similar in your own family. A child might ask a parent how long she must wait for something, and the parent might say, "Five minutes." From the parent's point of view, five minutes is hardly any time at all. From the point of view of the waiting child, however, five minutes can feel long—unbearably long, or infinitely long, depending on what she is waiting for.

From the point of view of the nearby farmers, the Ogress took an astonishingly long time to build her house. Season after season, year after year. So long that some of them had forgotten that she had come in the first place, and had forgotten that they even had an ogress for a neighbor at all. They never saw her. She spent her days in that burrow she had dug, and only came out at night. She built her house by hand. Quietly. Calmly. And very, very slowly. Her neighbors barely noticed it. What they did notice was the crows, whose numbers had begun to increase. Instead of roosting all around town, the crows now massed on the Ogress's farm—a great, loud, chattering mob of black wings and sharp beaks. A growing menace in the sky.

This got the neighbors muttering. A group of crows was called a *murder*, neighbors were quick to remind one another. What sort of creature consorted with not just one murder of crows, but with many murders? More murders, in fact, than they could count?

The Ogress had no idea of her neighbors' mutterings, and focused her attention on the slow and careful construction of her house. She did not want to claim what was not hers. She gathered only the trees that had already fallen in the forest, carrying them on her back in the dark of night to let them dry and cure until they were ready to be split into lumber. She used only stones that she had dug up from her own ground or found in the stream. She used tools that she found abandoned in the forest, but only if they remained in place for a year and a day, to make sure that their original owners wouldn't be back to claim them.

The Ogress had memorized the entire forest. She knew every stump and stone, every berry patch and walnut grove, every mushroom bloom and salt deposit, and even the spot where she had last seen a partially broken but still usable cast-off hammer, either off on its own in a gully or in one of the many heaps of trash that dotted the forest.

Some people in Stone-in-the-Glen, I'm sorry to say, occasionally used the forest to dump their garbage. The forest was large, the thinking went, and what was the harm? Obviously, this is a terrible thing to do, but it was useful, in the end, for our ogress, who excelled in finding value in things that other people disregarded. Ogres, as a group, have a knack for finding what they need.

The Ogress knew that a dragon sometimes wandered the forest, which was an obvious concern. In her nighttime wanderings, she had found evidence of the creature, almost always coinciding with the new moon. She found the occasional shining scale or a discarded bejeweled claw. Other times, she found small trees casually uprooted and tossed aside, as well as wide swaths of undergrowth flattened by the lumbering bulk of a dragon as it sauntered through the green. And every once in a while, she encountered the remains of an animal eaten from the inside out, its eyes burned neatly away from the initial fright. These, too, were few and far between. She had never seen the dragon, as dragons prefer to go about their business during the day, and enjoy taking long naps while lounging in a sunbeam. They are rather like cats in this way.

Indeed, in all her long life, the Ogress had never once met a single dragon. Still, she knew that while they generally were reticent, wise creatures, it was possible for a dragon to go . . . *bad*. Just as it is possible for any creature to go bad. Like, for example, the dragon who had destroyed her village. She never quite forgave herself for being far, far away during her neighbors' time of need. And now, here was a dragon, right in Stone-in-the-Glen. She knew it was wrong to cast judgment without evidence, but still she stayed wary and alert, in case this dragon turned out to be the nefarious sort.

She asked the crows to keep an eye out for her, but the crows had no idea what she was talking about—she didn't know the word for *dragon* in crow, and her stilted, wandering explanations didn't help. The crows just shrugged and tried to steer the conversation on to more agreeable topics. Like dinner, or stargazing, or "astonishingly excellent crows."

The Ogress tended a hive of honeybees, only because she had invited them to stay and they had graciously agreed. She took the honey or the wax only when the queen consented. In return, the Ogress spread wildflower seeds so that her bee friends could have plenty to eat. By spreading her flower seeds far and wide, the Ogress grew a field of flowers that increased every year. The bees increased along with them. The more the Ogress gave, the more she had. This magic was everywhere.

Sometimes, the Ogress walked through Stone-in-the-Glen during the night's darkest hour. It was always quiet—a tight, fearful, closed-off sort of quiet. The crows didn't like it, which was why she usually went into Stone-in-the-Glen after the crows had gone to sleep.

The crows were exasperated at her obsession with the town. "Caw!" they shouted. "You shouldn't give that town a passing thought! We certainly don't!"

"Caw!" they added. "They used to care for one another there, but now they shut their doors and lock their windows and seethe!"

"Caw!" one crow muttered. "Their suspiciousness and unneighborliness make them dreadfully unattractive, if you ask me. Why think of them when you can be thinking of handsome crows, such as myself!" He strutted and preened for the Ogress to prove his argument.

The Ogress loved her friends and told them that they all had excellent points. But still, there was a sadness in Stone-in-the-Glen. And a loss. She could feel it even at the far edge of town. And the Ogress wanted to help.

Back at home, she cleaved boards from the dried trees and polished branches into table legs and chair frames, and used river stones to build a chimney twice as wide as she was and three times as tall. She melted sand into panes of glass and used the fluff from pussy willows to make her hand-sewn cushions deeply soft. The crows, in their wide-ranging travels, found ornaments for her windows and pretty papers to put on her walls. They found her forks and spoons and even a few perfectly good pie pans, which glinted in the moonlight as the crows presented them with a flourish of wings.

"Caw!" the Ogress exclaimed happily. She had been trying to learn the nuances of speaking in Crow, but she was not very good at it yet. She had meant to say "What lovely friends you all are, and I love my gifts very much!" but she accidentally placed a slightly incorrect emphasis on her caw, and instead said, "Your feathers have the delicate and enduring scent of manure in the sun! How stinky and wonderful!" Fortunately, the crows knew what she was trying to say—it was a mistake a little crow might make when first learning to speak. And they appreciated the Ogress's attempts to speak to them in their language.

Very slowly, with the crows' help, the Ogress's crooked house took shape. Finally, she was able to move out of her burrow and into her new home. The crows hoped that this would put an end to her fascination with Stone-in-the-Glen, and she could focus instead on her garden, and building a barn, and her study of the stars, and also the very important task of telling them what wonderful crows they were.

But they were mistaken.

As she dug and planted a large and productive garden, and as she built herself a fine barn in hopes of filling it with animals someday, and as she studied the stars each night, the Ogress could not stop thinking about the people in Stone-in-the-Glen. She had been living on her farm for a few years at this point. With every passing season, the town became a little bit shabbier, a little bit dirtier, a little bit more broken. The Library still hadn't been rebuilt. Nor had the school. Nor had the other buildings that had burned. They all remained as ashy ruins, utterly untouched. And other buildings were abandoned, even collapsed from inattention. Whole families boarded up the windows of their ancestral homes and left town, their possessions piled in carts or on the backs of donkeys or stuffed into rucksacks. Every year, the Ogress could feel more sadness radiating from people's locked doors.

What does it mean to be a good neighbor? The Ogress pondered this question. It was all she ever wanted to be. But first, she would need more information.

For that, she would need a very special tool.

During her time in that castle with the trolls and the ghost, she had developed a special fascination with telescopes. There was an almost limitless supply in the laboratory—some housed in polished wood, some in brass, and others in stretched leather, like a drum. Two were the size of tree trunks and were made of polished metal. They used a series of cranks and springs and gears and other intricately designed mechanisms to lift and extend the sliding sections of the housing, and a similar mechanism to open a section of the roof. She had taken some of them apart and put them back together again to better understand how they worked.

She paged through her many books until she found the diagrams and plans to build what she needed. The contraption was similar to a telescope, but it used internal mirrors and extra lenses to allow the viewer to see around a corner. Or up and over, through the roof of a house. You have probably heard of such a contraption. Often, people call it a periscope. The Ogress had no idea what it was called—she couldn't read the title at the top of the page. She usually referred to it as a Look-Arounder or a See-Paster. Or simply the Excellent Invention.

As she worked on her periscope, time wobbled and stretched, and sometimes even stood still. She designed gears and mechanisms that allowed her periscope to turn this way and that, to widen or narrow the focus. She wanted to be able to see all of Stone-in-the-Glen, every nook and cranny, and she didn't hurry. Time passed, even when she didn't notice it passing.

"Caw," the crows said as she polished the quartz that she had dug up on her farm and shaped it into lenses. "What on earth are you doing?"

They fussed at her as she sanded and whittled the wood. "Is this food? It doesn't seem to be food."

"Hmm," they added, as she measured the placement of the mirrors and made sections that could slide easily. "I hope this is for gazing at the stars. Oh, how we love the stars!"

The Ogress knew how the crows felt about Stone-in-the-Glen and the people who lived there, and so she didn't tell them exactly what the periscope was for. She searched her knowledge of the Crow language to give them something by way of explanation without encouraging an argument. She wanted to say, "This is my Look-Arounder," but she didn't have the proper Crow vocabulary. Instead, she said, "Caw," which she intended to mean "I am building a thing to help me see important things," but her pronunciation was garbled, and what the crows *heard* was "I see that which is the most important thing."

The crows puffed their feathers and beamed. It was true. They were *very* important.

"Well," the crows said. "Obviously."

In the cozy dimness of her crooked house, the Ogress peered through her periscope. She adjusted the lenses. And she saw her town in the daylight for the very first time. It was, truth be told, a dreary place. She could see how it had been lovely once upon a time. But now it was dingy, broken, and sad. This was even more obvious in the harshness of the light. The loveliness of Stone-in-the-Glen was only a memory now.

She saw a family begging in the street. She saw ash blowing in great clouds from the ruins of the Library. She saw boarded-up windows and sagging eaves and buckled doorways. Empty storefronts. The charred foundation of a house that had been burned. And another. She watched as a donkey, carrying far more than it should, tripped on a gap where a cobblestone had broken and collapsed on the ground.

Then the Ogress noticed a tiny house, far from the Center Square. The woman who lived there had three of the last producing fruit trees in town. Two plums and a pear. Over the course of several weeks, the Ogress watched her gather the low-hanging fruit, take what she needed, and set out the rest in small bags in front of her home next to a sign. The Ogress had no idea what it said. People walked by, saw the sign, and took a bag of fruit. Oh, the smiles on their faces! Every day, more plums and pears. Every day, more happy faces. Sometimes, the old woman encouraged people to climb into the trees and gather fruit. She was too old to do this herself. She handed them bags. She waved as they took the fruit away. They waved back.

One day as the Ogress watched, a child climbed the pear tree, holding a bag between his teeth. He climbed higher and higher, until he got himself stuck in the branches. The woman, as old and frail as she was, rolled up her sleeves and climbed up to help. The disentangled child climbed down and ran off, as though afraid of the tree. The woman, though, missed a step and fell to the ground. Hard. She hobbled inside and didn't come back out for days.

The Ogress kept watch, but no one checked on the old woman. No one paid her a visit. When the bags of fruit were gone, people walked by and didn't give the house a second glance. It was as though they had forgotten about the woman who lived there.

"She might be hungry," the Ogress thought after watching for more than a week. "Someone should do something." And, without thinking too much more about it, the Ogress went into the forest that very night. She gathered acorns and wild nuts and berries. She asked the bees' permission to take some honey. She peeled and boiled and dried the acorns, and then ground their meat into flour. She pinched together a pastry that she stuffed with honey and nuts and berries. Delicious. Then, when night was the darkest, she set the pastry on the doorstep of the woman's house.

The next morning, just before the sun came up, the Ogress paused and took stock of her garden. She noticed the thick bunches of beans, the heavy tomatoes, the astonishingly large squash. Her blueberries were fat to the point of bursting. Her raspberries were heavy on the vine. Her garden was producing so much—too much for just the Ogress alone. Even too much for herself and the flock of crows. And the forest was producing even more.

The following day, she made more treats in the quiet dark of her crooked little house. Some honey candies. A mushroom tart. A sweet-potato cake. A tureen of squash soup. And that night, she left gifts on three other doorsteps.

"Caw," the crows warned. "Be careful."

But she waved them off.

This is what it means to be a neighbor, she thought to herself, happiness glowing in her chest.

This is how I can belong, she thought in the center of her heart.

She came home and planted more ground-cherries. She planted cuttings from wild grapes and strawberry vines that she had gathered in the forest. They grew vigorously in the good soil of the Ogress's garden, and she sang to her plants under the stars to help them along. Ogres have always had a knack for gardening. Perhaps this is due to their long lives. Perhaps it is due to their little bit of magic. Perhaps it is simply evidence of their gentle demeanors—after all, the earth so loves those who love it back.

As her garden grew, the Ogress kept baking. Pies and breads and cakes and cookies. Muffins and turnovers and hand pies and rolls. She fired clay pots with tight-fitting lids and filled them with soup. She built boxes and filled them with vegetables. She built a handcart to help her make more deliveries. She delivered to as many people as she could, as many days as she could. She hoped it was enough. Surely, she told herself, what she did was helping a little bit.

Months passed.

Then seasons.

Then years, followed by years.

The bees hummed. The plants grew. The crows added to their numbers, with more crow babies born in the spring. The Ogress discovered more nut trees in the forest. More mushrooms. More everything. She increased her garden again. And yet again. The more she gave away, the more her abundance multiplied, which meant she could give even more. Every day, she watched the town through the periscope. Every day, she hoped things would improve. And yet, every day, she saw things that broke her heart.

A man who lost his wife. A woman whose children left town and didn't tell her where they were going. A small girl with a cough that didn't go away. Another family who had to beg to survive. She couldn't fix these problems. So instead she just kept baking. And delivering. And sharing.

Every day, she would grind flour, chop nuts, separate the honey from the comb.

And then she would bake and cook and prepare:

A tart for the woman who used to light the lamps.

Soup for the butcher, whose wife had passed away, and whose grief had twisted his face into an angry knot.

Cookies for the cobbler and his wife.

A box of cupcakes for the former teacher—who, the Ogress knew, missed her classroom and missed her students so much it was like a needle in her heart. The Ogress saw the teacher's sorrow through her periscope, saw how the woman still walked to the remains of the schoolhouse every day and pressed her hands to her face, to stop herself from crying.

Acorn bread for the former street sweepers.

Walnut pies for the day laborers. Most of them, the Ogress observed, had to go weeks between jobs, tightening their belts further and further during the lean times.

Rolls for the constable.

A jar of honey for the organ master, to sweeten his broken spirit.

Was it enough? She had no way of knowing. But she hoped.

"Caw," the crows warned her. "No good deed goes unpunished."

The Ogress cooled her pies and pretended that she hadn't heard.

She walked through her garden rows, her large, stony fingers drifting along the leaves. Each plant shivered a bit. She loved her garden, and her garden truly loved her back. Her greens and herbs and beans, ground-cherries and tomatoes and squash thrived. Her rows of corn grew taller than her house (the crows helped her pick them), and her cucumbers were the size of work boots. When the Ogress went into town in the darkest part of the night to deliver all she had made, the crows circled overhead, cawing at the Ogress, who cawed in return. She pulled savory tarts and cornucopias behind her in a cart. She balanced pies on her head and cakes on her shoulders.

The crows followed her through the town, moving in great, undulating clouds overhead and settling on trees or roofs or chimneys or the ground. The Ogress named each crow and knew them all by sight and by their particular calls. And she loved them all dearly.

With each gift, she left a small card she had painted on paper she had made herself. She mixed wood pulp with dried flower petals and strained it through sieves. She crushed leaves and berries or ground seeds to make her own ink, and drew a picture of a cricket or a butterfly or a curious snake. Sometimes, she drew a whale in a stormy ocean. Sometimes, she painted a sky full of crows. She never signed her cards. She didn't even know how.

One night on arriving at the Orphan House, the Ogress paused, as she often did, letting her hand rest on the iron gate. The crows settled on the wall surrounding the Orphan House.

They landed on the roof. A few fluttered into the garden, to see if anything had fallen to the ground. They didn't land on the ashy rubble nearby, where the Library used to stand. The Ogress never paused there, either.

Her box of vegetables was heavy and overstuffed. The peas were abundant this year. As were the melons. And the squash. The carrots and turnips were as heavy as bricks. Children probably ate quite a bit, the Ogress reasoned. Vegetables were nourishing, after all. She hoped it was helpful and could supplement what they surely already had. She hoped it was enough.

Her last stop was the Mayor's house. It was always her last stop of the evening.

The Mayor's house was a strange place. The crows didn't like it, though they couldn't say why. Something about it made them uncomfortable—a wrongness they couldn't shake. It smelled of smoke and ash and money. They scattered as soon as the Ogress got near—the one place they refused to follow. Every night, a contingent of cats stalked the perimeter of the yard, their tails aloft, their ears stiff and alert. The cats were not interested in the Ogress. They kept their eyes fixed on the house.

The Mayor was inside somewhere. A cold, golden light seeped through the gaps at the edges of the windows and the crack at the bottom of the door. There was always a light on in the Mayor's house. From time to time, an inclination to knock on the door and introduce herself welled up inside the Ogress. His light was on, after all. And he seemed so lonely. Even the light that leaked through the gaps felt lonely. When she saw him through the periscope, he always stood apart from everyone else. He was so bright it was hard to see him clearly, and sometimes he disappeared altogether. It's a terrible thing, to be all alone. The Ogress knew this better than anyone. She hoped the pie would ease his loneliness.

At the edge of the yard, the cats watched, their eyes shining in the dark. Their fur stood tall on their backs. They flicked their tails. They inclined their noses. "Meow," the cats said, their voices low and agitated.

But the Ogress did not speak Cat. She had no idea what they meant.

Mine

The former schoolteacher woke up in the morning and checked her front stoop.

Once again, there was a box.

Cupcakes this time.

Before that, it was a fresh loaf of homemade bread and a jar of honey.

Before that, it was a cheese tart.

She had no idea who kept giving her gifts. A former student, perhaps. There was a card, but, once again, it wasn't signed—just a carefully painted picture of a cat sleeping by a fireplace. The other day, it was a crow standing on an open palm. So strange. Who doesn't sign a card?

In any case, she felt it best not to mention the small bits of abundance on her doorstep. This had been going on for some time—only once in a while at first, but lately, she found a gift more often than not. Maybe it was magic, like those elves in that story. Or that strange fairy obsessed with teeth. But she didn't want to call attention to herself, not when most everyone in town was out of a job. Not when it was a bad crop year, again. The Mayor had said it best, after all: *The more they know you have, the more they will try and take from you.* Once upon a time, when it was a lovely town, she used to trust her neighbors. But not anymore.

The former teacher peered up and down the quiet street to see if anyone had noticed the gift on her doorstep. Satisfied that her secret was safe, she snatched the cupcakes and hid them away indoors.

Down the road, the woman who ran the apothecary shop thought it best not to mention the honey turnovers that had appeared on her doorstep.

Just as the woman who used to light the lamps didn't mention the freshly baked tart to anyone.

The cobbler didn't mention the cookies.

The constable didn't mention the rolls.

The organ master didn't mention the honey.

The matron of the Orphan House didn't mention the enormous box of vegetables—or the fact that it seemed to get more abundant with each delivery (which was useful, because the children kept growing). The box of vegetables was a godsend . . . but it wasn't always enough. Every year, it was more difficult to make ends meet. Matron tried to ignore the knot of anxiety that tangled in the pit of her stomach whenever she thought about the number of mouths there were to feed.

Because no one in Stone-in-the-Glen discussed their gifts with their neighbors, the questions of *who* and *why* had to be wrestled with on their own. They were grateful—of course they were. But they were suspicious, too. And there were no answers to be had.

∞

The Mayor opened his wide front door and stepped into the light. He stretched his spine, and spiraled his shoulders, and lifted his face fully into a sunbeam, enjoying the intense brightness that warmed him all the way to his bones. He looked down on the front steps and saw a pie. There was always a pie at his front door. This had been true since . . . well, he could hardly say. What was time anyway? This morning's pie had a pinched crust and eyelet openings. A silhouette of a bird flew across the diameter. It was a beautiful pie.

It was a perfect morning in Stone-in-the-Glen. Not a cloud in the sky. The air rang with the sounds of crushed metal and breaking glass and the staccato pulse of people yelling angrily at one another. The Mayor closed his eyes and drank it all in. He adjusted the drape of his coat, the shine of his shoes, the fit of his skin. He flashed a dazzling smile at no one in particular.

The cats at the edge of the yard hissed. They arched their backs. The Mayor paid no attention. He brought the pie to his nose and inhaled deeply.

"*Mine*," he said as he beheld the pie. He said it without curiosity or hesitation. He had no idea who had given him the pie, and it didn't occur to him to wonder. "*Mine, mine, mine.*" It was his favorite word in all the world. It was the best sort of magic.

He went inside and shut the door.

One More Note about the Library

The Library, before the fire, was the oldest building in town. Every street, once upon a time, led to the Library. Every overlook was positioned just so, to provide a perfect view of the Library's wide lawns and gardens, its intricate stained-glass windows depicting outlandish tales, its tall carved doors thrown open every morning, inviting the whole town inside.

The Library allowed the people of Stone-in-the-Glen to indulge their curiosities, awaken their sense of wonder, and come together as a community. Stone-in-the-Glen was famous for its trees and famous for its loveliness, but it was beloved for its library. When travelers visited the town, the first thing they were asked was, "Have you visited the Library yet?"

If the answer was no, then the people would grasp at their hearts and say, "Oh, but you must! Let us go this very minute!"

If the answer was yes, then the people would grasp at their hearts and say, "Oh, but only one time? That isn't nearly enough! Let us return at once!"

It was said that the Library housed the heart of the town. And the mind of the town. It had stately towers of carved stone, and wide windows, and books so numerous they seemed to bend both space and time. What a lucky town, people said, to have such a marvel in their midst! How lucky indeed.

So imagine, then, what the town must have felt like on the night of the fire. I was there. I heard each heart crack, one by one. I heard the guttural cries as they watched the building collapse into an ashy heap on the ground.

On that terrible night, before the panicked townsfolk arrived with their buckets, I saw the shine of a dragon emerging at the foot of the building. I saw the glint of malevolence in its eye. I saw its large, sinuous body unfurling itself from the back to the front, its tail unwinding like a rope around the neck of the Library and its agile legs crawling along the stone wall. It was as nimble as a spider, and as deadly, too. The jaws unhinged and opened wide, as the pit of its throat poured out flames—a harsh, bright whiteness that hurt the eye and assaulted the night.

I could do nothing to stop it. I listened as the beast hummed and preened and then giggled as the flames exploded. I watched him as he slunk away, disappearing into the night.

But I saw something else as well. There was one person who didn't stand in line with the buckets, but who instead ran in and out the side door, again and again, even as the flames surged throughout the interior of the building, to rescue as many books as he could. I watched him throw his arm across his mouth, in an attempt to block out the smoke. I watched him sprint out carrying boxes, bags, and stacks of books, even as flames licked at his heels, clung to his gloves, and crept up the collar of his shirt. I saw him return, even when it was far too dangerous to do so, even when the books in his arms were already burning beyond any hope of rescue. I watched him fall to his knees as he gasped for breath, his lungs damaged by smoke and heat. Indeed, I worried that they had been damaged beyond repair.

Books are funny things. The ideas and knowledge contained inside their pages have mass and velocity and gravity. They bend both space and time. They have minds of their own. There is a power in a book that surpasses even that of a dragon.

The man fell upon the heaps of books he had rescued, nearly insensible from exhaustion and injury. He fainted, briefly, from the strain of it. But he wasn't safe. And neither were the books. The dragon was nearby. I didn't know where. But I knew the dragon would return.

Hide them, I pleaded. *Oh, please hide them.*

Did he hear me? People usually didn't. I tried again. *These books aren't safe*, I said.

The man pulled himself to his hands and knees. His burns were deep and angry. He coughed until blood came out. I did my best to make myself heard.

The danger hasn't passed. The danger is here. He is still here. Hide the books. Please.

If I had eyes, I would have wept. If I had a mouth, I would have screamed.

The man looked up. He saw the flames tearing at the night. He sobbed as the first tower fell. So many books were lost that day. He looked at the books he had saved. A great heap of them. An astonishing number. He frowned, as though wondering if they had somehow multiplied when he wasn't looking.

(Listen. They had.

Books do that sort of thing. More often than you might think. It isn't magic, exactly. But it's close.)

He coughed again. "These books aren't safe," he said out loud.

He looked up. He pressed his hands to his heart. He could barely tear his eyes away from the Library as it collapsed.

"The danger is still here." He spoke to no one at all. "I should hide the books."

And so, as the rest of the town dumped bucket after bucket of water onto the unrelenting flames, Myron carried box after box of books into the Orphan House. He didn't tell anyone. He didn't know who he could trust. He shelved them in the Reading Room and never mentioned it again.

(The books, on the other hand, remembered. And they still do.)

Facts Matter, Anthea Said

Anthea had been in a foul mood all afternoon, and it was making everyone cross.

She shouted at Dierdre for leaving a full diaper on the hallway floor (Dierdre *tried* to explain that she was coming back for it), and she fussed at Bartleby for swaddling the babies *wrong* ("But I've always done it this way!" Bartleby complained), and she scolded Kye for wasting paper *and* pencils during their mathematics lessons ("Pencils are hard!" wept Kye), and she nearly kicked Elijah in the shins when he suggested that maybe, just maybe, she was a little bit *tetchy* today ("I rest my case," Elijah muttered to anyone who would listen). And when Myron asked her to please help him hang the washed laundry on the clothesline, she held her breath for a long moment, going a bit red in the cheeks. And then she burst into tears.

Myron regarded her with a stricken expression on his face, his hands curled around his cheeks. As always, when Myron got upset, his scars became quite red. "Why, my dear," he said desperately, "don't cry. Please don't cry. I can't bear it!" He called out to Fortunate and Gratitude, who were nearby, and asked them to make a nice cup of tea for their dearest and darlingest Anthea.

Both Fortunate and Gratitude paused in unison, and, as one, they dug their fists into their hips and frowned identically. (Their faces, as I mentioned, were nothing alike—and yet it was ever so difficult to tell them apart.)

"Why on *earth* would we get her *tea*," fumed Fortunate, whose nostrils were beginning to flare.

"When *she* has been so *mean*." Gratitude glowered. "And not just once. *All day*."

"On *purpose, probably*," Fortunate added with a frown.

In response, Anthea held perfectly still for a second or two and then crumpled to the ground, curling herself into a ball. All at once, she began to sob. The air around her bent with sorrow.

The twins gulped in unison. "Oh! Oh no!" Gratitude whispered. "Oh, *Anthea!*"

"I think . . ." said Fortunate, whose eyes suddenly became quite wide.

"That maybe we should make some tea," Gratitude finished.

And, arm in arm, they scurried away.

Myron helped Anthea to her feet, his arm across her shoulders, and guided her to the chair by the window, tutting and coughing as they went. "There, now," he said. "There, there, now." His scarred hands shook slightly, but that was nothing new. And the folded skin on his face was so delicate it looked like paper left too long in the sun.

Anthea's face produced tears and snot in great waves that poured onto her dress. Myron gave her a handkerchief, which she soaked through almost immediately. "Are you hungry?" he asked. "Being hungry can profoundly disrupt the mood. Perhaps you need something to eat."

"No," Anthea replied. "I'm not hungry." She blew her nose.

Myron looked disappointed. It was clear that he wanted to find something he could fix. "Well, then," he mused. "What could it be? Are you sick?"

"No."

"Tired?" He peered into her eyes as though the answer to her distress was lurking somewhere behind her pupils.

"I'm really not."

"Then why are you crying?" Myron's rheumy eyes became slicked with tears. Anthea knew how much it weighed on him when the children were upset.

"I'm fine, Myron. I really am." She wiped her face again and attempted to smile. "Honestly, I don't know what's wrong. Maybe nothing is wrong. Maybe I'm crying for no reason." This wasn't true, but it sounded good. One of the cats stalked in and leaped lightly onto Anthea's lap, curling up and purring with profound concentration and purpose.

Fortunate and Gratitude returned with the tea and then backed slowly out of the room, clearly afraid of another eruption of tears. They ran to the kitchen and began sweeping the floors and wiping the surfaces, just to give themselves something to do.

There was always something to do in the Orphan House. Too many things. The roof leaked, and the windowsills were rotting, and the wind sang through the gaps between the eaves and the walls. The floors sagged, and the ceilings wobbled, and several stairs were dangerously close to breaking. There was bread to be made (when there was flour) and porridge to be cooked (when there was grain), and every once in a while, the pile of vegetables left by a mysterious benefactor needed to be sorted and washed and peeled and chopped and combined into a soup that would keep everyone fed for at least a couple of days, or maybe even a week, depending.

"Myron?" Matron called from the cellar. "Could you please help me?"

Myron was about to call back, but Anthea put her hand on his wrist. "Go help," she said. "You don't have to worry about me. I'll hang the laundry, and then I'll gather the Littles for their lessons."

It used to be that children who lived at the Orphan House attended school just like any other child in town. The people of Stone-in-the-Glen, once upon a time, felt it was important that children in their time of need felt supported and connected and cared for by the whole of the community. But then the school burned down. Later, a teacher came by every day to conduct lessons so that the children might be educated and productive citizens when they grew up. But the money from the town coffers to pay for a teacher began to dwindle. She came three times a week. Then twice. Then once. And then the money disappeared altogether. Because Anthea had gotten the longest time with an actual teacher of anyone in the house, she was in charge of everyone's education, including her own. It was a great responsibility.

"I'll come and help with the lessons after I've helped our dear Matron," Myron said.

Anthea smiled. "Of course you will," she said, knowing that he likely wouldn't. He often promised to help her teach the lessons. And Myron was a good, if scattered, teacher. But there was always so much to do. And he was getting old. And everything exhausted him so. And sometimes he fell asleep on a chair without meaning to.

She kissed his cheek. "You see?" She stood and looked him squarely in the eye. "I'm much better now. I'll see you in the Reading Room later."

Neither of these sentences was true.

The space inside the wall surrounding the Orphan House wasn't particularly large. It contained a smallish lawn and a smallish garden, and behind that was a smallish raspberry patch (which produced smallish berries) next to a smallish row of other useful shrubs—blueberry and witch hazel, and two types of tea bushes, and a tangle of hawthorn. There was a chicken coop and a small house for the milk goats (the children had painted it a lurid color of pink several years ago, and now the paint was peeling, making it a mottled mess of pink and gray) and a shed that contained an assortment of tools—as well as a small, neat, and well-organized workbench, which Anthea had built herself, along with the shelves. She had placed hooks and cubbies and had cut holes in perfect circles on the eastern, southern, and western walls, fitting each one with the bottoms of broken bottles, which filled the space with mottled light. There was a chair that she had built, and a stack of hand-bound notebooks that she had sewn herself, each filled with her designs and drawings.

She felt guilty sometimes, having this space that was almost entirely her own. Not in theory, of course—in theory, anyone in the house could come and sit at the workbench and sew a baby carrier or build a puppet stage or invent a collapsible seat to let Myron rest his old bones from time to time, or precisely assemble and tune a hand-cranked music box to help the babies fall asleep. Anyone could sit and design a series of clever pulleys and levers to safely and efficiently lower the piles of bedsheets out the window of the dormitory to the laundry vats below to be boiled. But, really, it was only Anthea who did any of these things, so it was Anthea who had full possession of a space where she could close a door and sit inside four walls with only her thoughts for company. It was a delicious secret.

Anthea needed to sit at her workbench. She needed to *think*. But not quite yet. She stood at the clothesline and hung up the unraveling diapers and the overdarned socks and the much-mended shirts and the pants that had so many patches that even the patches had patches. They knew how to make do in the Orphan House. They had been making do all their lives.

As Anthea worked, her mind began replaying that moment in the butcher's shop. Myron hadn't mentioned it again. Elijah had steered clear of the subject. And Anthea was fairly certain that Myron hadn't brought it up with Matron, because Matron certainly would have enveloped her in hugs and soothing words by now and would have told her to stop worrying and being such a silly.

Did that mean that it wasn't worth worrying about?

Maybe.

And maybe not.

Anthea set the empty laundry basket on the back steps and, after quickly making sure that no one noticed, slipped into her shed. And then she let herself cry again, just for a minute. Just to get it out. She wiped her face and steadied herself, leaning against the bench for support.

Anthea was good at collecting things—unused tools from the cellar, and odds and ends from the attic, and her gleanings from the junk pile in the Center Square. She had stacks of fabric scraps from the remains of unsalvageable clothes. Buttons. Old nails. Gears and levers from ancient machines and broken clocks. Cast-off bits of wood that could be assembled into useful boxes or sanded into knitting needles or fashioned into toys. Everything was sorted and arranged. Every object had its place.

From a lower shelf, she retrieved an antique box with an ornate latch. It was a bit larger than a loaf of bread, had a dark, oily sheen to the wood. It had arrived in the same basket that contained baby Anthea, on that cold, winter morning long ago. The box once held the locket that she now wore, but it contained other things as well. A newspaper, for example. Someone had written, *This is the day you were born* at the top. There was a pair of spectacles and a magnifying glass, because someone, it seemed, had guessed that her eyes would go bad eventually. Also in the box: a small, carefully painted portrait of a young woman in an old-fashioned dress, sitting on a chair with her hands resting on a pile of books, and a slide rule on her lap. Her grandmother, Anthea supposed. She could see the resemblance when she looked in a mirror.

Anthea picked up the newspaper and looked at the date. She would be fourteen right after the leaves were done changing and the branches became bare. It was now late summer. Fall was coming fast. Certainly, there were other fourteen-year-olds in Stone-in-the-Glen who were working hard to support their families. Anthea had seen them on Market Day and on the occasional days when she was permitted to accompany Matron or Myron on an excursion. But she also knew that a great number of young people had left Stone-in-the-Glen to seek their fortunes in other towns and other lands, and they often didn't come back.

She added the finishing touches on a harness that would allow her to climb to the roof safely and fix the leaks. She sewed button eyes on a soft doll for Iggy, who had been having nightmares lately, and finished stitching the pages of a picture book that Elijah had written and that Dierdre had carefully illustrated. And she finally completed a pair of mittens that she had been knitting for Matron, whose hands were always so cold.

There was always something to do at the Orphan House. It was good to keep busy.

Anthea couldn't imagine Matron or Myron actually asking her to leave after her birthday. But the fact was that there wasn't enough for everyone at the Orphan House—even with the box of vegetables that was sometimes left at the doorstep. How often had she gone to bed with a grumbling belly? How often had Matron and Myron simply gone without? Even though the boxes of vegetables were larger now than they used to be, and came more often. As the boxes of vegetables had gotten bigger and more generous, the stores of flour and dried beans and oil in the larder had gotten smaller, because the town was providing less and less. It took a lot of food to keep fifteen children fed, after all. More every day. Because children grow.

Another fact.

And that fact mattered a lot.

It wasn't unkindness. It was just arithmetic.

Matron and Myron loved her. They might not *want* to ask her to leave, Anthea knew, but they might *have* to. Especially if it was a rule. Why had no one told her?

She put on the harness she had made and headed out to the rope she had set up outside to fix the roof.

"The more we are, the less we have," Anthea told herself. "But maybe if I *do* more, there will be *less* of the general less." She hadn't checked the math on that one. She hoped she was right.

On the roof, she hammered repurposed shingles over the weak spots, securing each one in place, keeping each bit fully attached to the Orphan House.

"What are you doing up there?" Bartleby called.

Anthea kept hammering.

"Just making sure nothing breaks off and falls away," she called back.

She hoped it would be enough.

Once Upon a Time, a Dragon

Listen.

I really don't want to talk about the Dragon. But, given the damage he caused to the Ogress before she even came to Stone-in-the-Glen, and everything that came after, it might be useful to explain a little about dragons, in a larger sense. Dragons in general, I mean.

Dragons, as we all know, are as unique as snowflakes, as unique as fingerprints, as unique as a particular baby's laugh to its particular mother. Some dragons are funny. Others are known for their prodigious kindness. Some dragons are shy. Some are studious. Some are generous. Other dragons have marvelous minds for analysis and problem-solving. Some are greedy. And, occasionally, some dragons are cruel.

Dragons, by and large, have glittering personalities: they are quick-witted, erudite, and persuasive. They are in possession of a small amount of magic, which assists them as they move about their days. Their magic allows them to fly, breathe fire, and camouflage their great bodies to blend in with their surroundings. It comes at a physical cost, of course—it gives them dreadful dyspeptic stomachaches, for starters, and it starts to whittle away at their health and vigor, and, over time, even their size—which is why they use it rarely.

Which brings us to the issue of the skins.

In ancient times, a dragon went hunting one day on the wide plains and caught himself a small antelope, which he intended to devour for his dinner. Using his sharp talons, and with great care to keep himself clean (dragons are quite fastidious), he removed the animal's skin with a sure cut. He roasted the meat over a campfire. (He did not produce his own fire for this, as it would have given him a stomachache and put him off his meal.) As he sat under the emerging stars, he found himself wondering what it must feel like to actually *be* an antelope. He marveled at the creature's speed and grace, and it made him curious. Curiosity is a powerful state of being—full of possibility. Curiosity doesn't sit still. It *moves*. It's awfully close to magic.

For a creature in possession of actual magic, curiosity has the potential to make all sorts of unexpected things begin to happen. That night, under the stars, the Dragon brushed his forepaw against the edge of the antelope's discarded skin. The magic in tandem with the curiosity did the rest. The Dragon looked down at the antelope's skin and saw, with some amusement, that it had begun to move about. Without thinking too much more about it, he picked up the antelope's skin, which was light and lively with the energy of magic and curiosity, and put it on.

And, just so, the Dragon *became* an antelope.

Can you imagine what that must have been like for that dragon? To be accustomed to so great and lumbering a body and to find oneself, all at once, small and light and gifted with marvelous speed? As an antelope, the Dragon raced across the plains, his hooves as light and delicate as fireflies. His antelope eyes glittered like stars. For a full year, he lived on the grasslands among the antelope herd. He ate as the antelope ate (and blessedly free of dyspepsia, which almost never afflicts antelopes) and spoke as the antelope spoke. He grazed on the hills with his antelope friends and wept whenever one of them was eaten by a predator.

And then one day, the Dragon-as-antelope was stalked by a lioness. Just before she pounced, the Dragon slipped out of his antelope skin and revealed himself, leaving his antelopeness on the ground. A dragon once again, he was smaller than he had been before, and weak, due to his long time inside the skin of the antelope, but the lioness didn't notice. She had expected an antelope and found a dragon instead. Terrified, she bounded away. Gazing at the retreating lioness, the Dragon recognized with some discomfort the hungry look he had seen in the predator's eyes as one that had once been in his own, and he felt ashamed. He remained rooted there for a long time, deep in thought.

He lounged in the sun for a handful of days to restore himself to the fullness of his size and power, noticing with interest that the day preceding the new moon, when both the sun and the faint outline of the moon hung in the sky, was the most potent of all and returned him fully to his normal strength, speed, and magic. He stretched and yawned and delighted in his dragon-ness. The other antelopes, once his friends, avoided him now, terrified of his teeth and claws. His heart broke at the pity of it.

He was, he realized, *more* now. He was a dragon who had learned what it was like to be an antelope. He had been an antelope who knew what it was to be a dragon. Each experience expanded the other. There was more *him* in himself now—his mind was enlarged, and his soul was enlarged as well.

Very carefully, he picked up the magic-imbued antelope skin and held it tenderly in his arms. It felt precious to him now, and the key to something important. "Others should experience this," he said to himself. "Other dragons need to know."

The Dragon took the antelope skin around the world, to all of dragonkind. One by one, the dragons put on the antelope's skin. One by one, they learned the delight in an antelope's speed and agility, as well as the joy of being a part of a herd. They learned to love the scent of grass in their damp nostrils and how to listen for danger. They learned what it meant to feel fear. They rejoiced with their antelope friends when a new calf was born, and they wept when one of their number was lost, offering comfort to the bereaved. Most dragons, as a result of this experience, became vegetarians. The antelope skin—the First Antelope—became a holy object to dragonkind. They wanted to understand *all* creatures in this way. All places. They wanted to understand the whole world.

Over time, skin-wearing became a sacred practice for dragons. By becoming other creatures, they could better understand how dragons were perceived by others, and through this understanding they could endeavor to make themselves nobler, kinder, more generous. It was through skin-wearing that dragons could seek enlightenment and openheartedness. Wearing skins became prayerful, holy, a state to be admired, and often dragons who had done so would preach what they learned to other dragons, who would sit and listen. Temples were built. Icons adorned treasure caves. And the dragons who had taken on numerous points of view were venerated as saints. This came at a physical cost, of course. It took magic to animate the skins, and magic to wear them. The dragons would emerge weakened and ill after their time in the skins—made worse the longer they did it. Still, dragonkind considered this discomfort a worthwhile fee for the benefit. The enlightened dragons spent their recovery time in a state of contemplation and gratitude.

One might say that the accidental encounter with the original antelope was, for dragonkind, a good thing. And this would be a largely true statement. But while it is true that *most* dragons became kinder, more generous, more good, and more empathetic thanks to their time in the skins of other creatures, there is something important that you must never forget:

Not all dragons are kind.

Not all dragons are generous.

Not all dragons are good.

And the years they spend in the skins growing in empathy—with their glittering dragon personalities and their erudite dragon ways just lurking inside—can sometimes cause problems of a different sort.

Even knowledge can be used for wicked purposes. Even understanding can be twisted by those who wish to twist it. Even empathy can be transformed into a weapon.

I wish it were not so.

The Philosophical Implications of a Box of Vegetables

Bartleby woke up before the sun did. This happened a lot. It was an excellent time to catch up on his reading.

He was, once again, under a pile of children, which made the process of getting out of bed difficult. He had fallen asleep next to Hiram, but sometime during the night, Iggy, Justina, and Kye had all piled in as well, curling into the available space and making new spaces that weren't there a moment ago. Sprawled atop the lot of them was two-year-old Maude, snoring loudly. Bartleby had to move carefully in order to extricate his limbs and wriggle himself away without disturbing anyone.

He slid into his sweater and slippers and tiptoed out of the room. Anthea, Dierdre, and Elijah cuddled together on one cot. Fortunate and Gratitude each slept with a baby tucked into the respective crooks of their arms. And Cass and Lily snored loudly in a corner. Even the walls seemed to be dreaming.

There is no better place, Bartleby thought in the fullness of his heart, *than the Orphan House in the almost-morning, and no better family in all the world.*

He tiptoed out of the dormitory and closed the door, making his way to the Reading Room. The cats, all awake (the cats were always awake in the morning), followed him through the corridor and down the stairs. They slid their sides and tails along Bartleby's legs, reminding him that they required adoration.

"Meow," demanded a black cat with tufts of white on his chest and paws.

"Meow," said another cat, the color of butter.

"Good kitties," Bartleby said, reaching down and stroking the cats. He sat on the floor. They immediately stalked away and ignored him, until he reached over and grabbed a book. Instantly, a fluffy gray cat sat on his lap, purring luxuriously, and an orange tabby insinuated herself under his elbow. Bartleby sighed and tried reading around the cat.

A white cat and two brindles came slinking from under the shelves and perched themselves on his knees. He closed his milky eye and saw the cats in sharp detail, from their mottled noses to their careful paws to the rhythmic rippling of their fur. He closed his hazel eye and saw them as permutations of light and shadow, moving in and out of view. Both ways of seeing, he knew, were correct. It was a great pleasure, he thought, being able to see in multitudes. Everything is details. Everything is light. Both at the same time. He carefully opened the book around the cats and began to read.

He sat that way, on the floor, under an increasing number of cats, until he was interrupted by the approaching slippered footsteps of a very old man. "My dear boy!" Myron said. "There seems to be a feline adhered to your head."

Bartleby would have nodded, but he was worried about the cat falling off. It was one of the littler ones—just a small puff of yellow fur. It purred into Bartleby's skull. Myron scooped the cat up with one hand, nuzzled it briefly, and set it down with a soft "Good kitty." The tiny cat settled herself on Myron's slipper and began to lick her paws.

Bartleby kept his eyes on the book, intent on finishing his paragraph. "That's Phyllis," he said. He knew that Myron could never keep the names of the cats straight. "She likes sitting on people's heads," he added, as though it were merely one of those little quirks.

"Ah," Myron said. "I see." He produced a small glass bottle full of goat's milk and a shallow dish. "Puss, puss," he called to the cats, setting the dish on the floor and filling it.

The cats abandoned Bartleby at once. "Meow," Phyllis said in a distinctly disdainful way. Bartleby had no way of knowing what it meant but was fairly certain it was something along the lines of "*You* could have *thought* to bring us *milk* if only you *loved* us enough!"

This was why he didn't want to learn to speak Cat.

Myron inclined his chin in the direction of the book. "Your companion this morning?"

"*The Altruria*," Bartleby said, still not looking up from his page.

The volume on his lap was an ancient copy of an even more ancient book. He had to be careful turning the pages. It was, according to the introduction, the last work that the philosopher Timaeus had ever written, and was largely disregarded by historians and scholars, as it was short, imaginative, and not satisfactorily conclusive. All throughout, the speakers interrupt one another, digress, threaten to leave the room, and never actually answer any specific questions directly. Instead, they slyly slide this way and that, forcing the readers to find the answer on their own. Bartleby thought it was the greatest book he had ever read.

"Ah!" Myron said, clapping his hands together. "Dear Timaeus!" He cleared his throat. "'It is our enemies from whom we learn enmity, and it is our friends from whom we learn friendship. The question, then, is not 'What shall we learn?' The question is 'What shall we choose to teach?'"

Myron, like Bartleby, also enjoyed philosophy. Unlike Bartleby, he enjoyed warm socks and a soft chair, and a long, long nap. Sometimes, even reading made Myron tired. He perked up his ears and peered down the hall. "Listen, my lad, it has been two days since our anonymous benefactor has been by with another box of vegetables, which makes me think that we might have something waiting today." Myron paused. An expression passed over his face that Bartleby couldn't quite decipher. "Would you mind helping me? The gate is a bit much for my old hands, I'm afraid, and I would rather let Matron sleep. She was so tired last night."

Bartleby looked at Myron's hands. The scars were quite red this morning, which meant that Myron was worried about something. And the tremor was decidedly worse. Bartleby repositioned the cat, closed the book, and stood to shake off his own prickly worry. "Of course I'll help," he said. He took Myron's hand in his, his thumb unconsciously running back and forth along the scars on the old man's skin.

The sky was pink and gold as they walked outside. Bartleby took in a deep breath, as though trying to fill his lungs with color. The two goats munched on the grass, and the chickens hunted for bugs, while a flight of chickadees murmured in the raspberry thickets. Myron turned the iron key in the gate and opened it slowly. The rusty hinges moaned. Myron peeked his head through the gap, looking furtively to the right and to the left. And then he looked down. Bartleby saw the old man deflate. When he turned back to the yard, Myron's face was the color of ash. The old man grimaced and then heaved a smile into his mouth that had no brightness in it, which made Bartleby feel worse, though he didn't entirely understand why.

"Well," Myron said. His cheeks shook a little bit. "No matter. Surely we'll be luckier tomorrow. It doesn't do to become overly reliant on . . ." His voice trailed off. He curled his hand around his mouth and tilted his gaze to the brightening sky. This did nothing for the prickly feeling in Bartleby's skin, which dug in so deeply he could feel it in his bones.

"Don't worry, Myron!" he said desperately. "Please don't worry. Look! No one's even up yet. I'll get baskets, and we can get what we can out of our garden. It's not as nice as what we get in the box, or as much, but it's still pretty good! And maybe the hens laid lots for us last night. And look at the goats! They're so ready to be milked they look like they might burst." He paused and made a face. "But, honestly, I'd rather you do that part, because it's kind of gross." He glanced at the goats and shrugged. "No offense." The goats did not respond.

They went to the shed and retrieved baskets and buckets. Bartleby ventured into the chicken coop and collected ten precious eggs while Myron relieved the goats of their milk. The garden was productive in its way—the tomatoes were small but flavorful, and there were a few good handfuls of broad beans ready to be picked, along with cucumbers and several colors of summer squash. Dark greens crowded the back edge of the raised bed. Altogether, there were two rather small baskets filled with different vegetables and another basket heaped with berries.

The milk was heavy, so Bartleby carried it into the kitchen, where he poured it into the large pot to be heated on the stove and made safe to drink. Myron followed behind. They set the harvest from the garden on the counter and took inventory. Bartleby frowned. What had seemed like a lot in the garden appeared pitiful now compared to what they received from the benefactor, who gave them tomatoes the size of Bartleby's face and beans the size of his forearms, all stuffed in a box so heavy it took two people to carry it.

Fifteen children needed an awful lot of food, after all. Bartleby curled his fingers around the back of his neck and held on for dear life.

Myron clapped his hand on the boy's shoulder and gave a squeeze. "No matter, son. We still have flour and oats and dried lentils in the larder. And a bit left from that precious tub of butter. We'll be fine."

But Bartleby had seen inside the flour bin and the oat bin and the lentil bin just yesterday: there was more air than anything else. He had to lean very far into the barrels in order to scoop something out. It was enough for now, but what about the days to come? How long could it last? He didn't mention these worries out loud.

Myron mixed oats and water and set it on the woodstove to cook into porridge. He handed Bartleby a knife to help cut the vegetables, which they would then make into a soup to feed the family for the rest of the day. They stood shoulder to shoulder, chopping carrots and onions, greens and herbs, red tomatoes and green tomatoes and squash, and a few wrinkly potatoes from the larder, keeping each vegetable separate in its own pile.

Over at the window, Matron had pinned cards to the wooden frame, each one carefully drawn or painted by the benefactor and tucked into the boxes of vegetables over the years. Bartleby walked to the window to get a better look. He ran his fingers over each small piece of art. One was a painting of the Orphan House itself. Another was a small goat in the arms of a child—the child looked quite a bit like Cass. Another was a tree with a setting sun behind it and a sky full of crows. Another was whales in the ocean. Another was a village nestled in the mountains. Not one was signed. But there were so many of them, because there had been so very many gifts to the Orphan House over the years. Necessary gifts, Bartleby knew. *Where would we be without them?* he found himself wondering. He didn't want to even think about the answer.

Bartleby unpinned one card—a picture of a tree. He examined it closely. Each crow in the sky seemed to have its own personality. The tree looked like it wanted to tell a story. Bartleby turned it around and around. Like on the others, there were no words. *What kind of person gives a bunch of strangers the gift of food—not once, but often, more than once a week—and doesn't even want to be thanked for it?*

This made Bartleby think about philosophy.

"Is kindness sometimes a trick?" he asked aloud. It was a question raised in *The Altruria*, and he couldn't stop thinking about it. "If someone is kind for selfish reasons or cowardly reasons, I mean. What do we call their actions then? If the reason for the kindness isn't kind, do we still call it kindness?" Bartleby shook his head. His thoughts swarmed and buzzed.

Myron folded his hands together and rested his chin on his knuckles. He closed his eyes and took a long breath through his nose. He didn't answer Bartleby right away. Instead, he said, "My dear boy, will you please stoke the fire?"

Bartleby wondered if Myron was avoiding his question. He opened the stove's side door with a rusty creak and started adding small pieces of wood.

Myron coughed. And then he coughed again, this time with such force that he had to sit down. He wiped his mouth with a handkerchief and quickly shoved it into his pocket. He looked up at Bartleby's stricken face and smiled, waving his worries away. "Consider this," Myron said. "Perhaps the only thing that matters is what *you* make of kindness. What matters is how you see these questions appear in your own life, how you think about them, and then how you choose to behave. Do you think it matters that people are kind?"

Bartleby was startled by the question. "Of course!" he said. "Just look at where we are! The Orphan House is the kindest place in the whole world." Even though Bartleby had not seen the whole world, he felt in his bones that this was true.

"Indeed. A kind place situated in the midst of a less-than-kind community. And perhaps that is why someone chooses to give to us. Or perhaps it is because we ourselves are kind. Or because the benefactor is kind. Or because we desperately need that kindness. Or because the benefactor has more than they need and feels obligated to share. Or because they simply *enjoy* sharing. Or perhaps it is some other reason that we can't even think of. But the *reason for the kindness* is never as important as *the fact of the kindness*. Someone was kind. We need that kindness. Therefore, we are grateful. It is the great lesson from *The Altruria*, one that I treasure. We can choose to be filled with suspicions, or we can choose to accept grace, and then continue to extend kindness to others. Which do you choose?"

Bartleby wasn't sure. He didn't know if Myron was right. It *did* feel important to know who was responsible for helping the Orphan House. It *did* feel important to know why they gave and gave and kept on giving. If for no other reason than to arrive at the truth.

Matron appeared in the doorway. Her shoulders sagged, and her face was gray. Bartleby wondered how much she had actually slept the night before. Her eyes scanned the kitchen, and landed on the smallish, thinnish, unabundant pile of vegetables on the counter. "No gifts today, I see," she said, her voice hoarse and ragged.

"But look at what we gathered from the garden!" Myron said brightly. "Look at the berries we shall have for our breakfast. And look at the milk. And the eggs! Ten of them! What a feast!"

In response, Bartleby's stomach grumbled. Ten eggs for seventeen people. He didn't even want to think about the arithmetic of it. Math, Bartleby decided, was mean. He cleared his throat and pretended to cough to distract attention.

Matron placed her hands on the edge of the counter and pressed down hard, closing her eyes in deep thought, her fingers tapping the air as though she were going through the numbers in her ledger. She squinched her face tightly for a moment and then relaxed. She knocked the wood for luck.

"This is all fine, of course." Her voice was bright and brittle. "Of course this is fine. I believe we still have more potatoes in the root cellar, after all. And, my word, look at all that milk! What good goats!" She kissed Bartleby on the top of his head and kissed Myron on his cheek, letting the back of her hand linger on his forehead, as though checking for a fever. "And don't forget Market Day is the day after tomorrow. We always sell quite a bit this time of year. Nothing to worry about. We will be fine. Of course we will be fine."

Despite Matron's words, the prickling sensation in Bartleby's skin returned. He folded his arms across his chest and curled his fingers around each elbow. He looked from Matron to Myron and back again. Both had tight smiles pinned to their faces. Both had deep grooves around their worried eyes.

"What else should I do?" Bartleby asked.

"Go wake the family up. The porridge is almost done," Matron said. "And, oh, what shall I do with these wonderful eggs? Hurry now!"

Bartleby scrambled up to the dormitory. He carefully stepped over the cats sleeping on the stairs and scooped up a yawning Phyllis, as she loved to wake up the toddlers, who in turn loved being woken up by Phyllis. He turned his conversation with

Matron and Myron over and over in his head, his thoughts clouded and confused.

Even as he woke up his sister, and Anthea and Dierdre and Elijah and the twins and the Littles and the toddlers and the babies, even as they all yawned and washed their faces and stumbled out of the dormitory into the day, Bartleby couldn't stop thinking about what Matron and Myron had said that morning.

And what they had *not*.

Some Sheep, a Lost Dog, and a Mysterious Something in the Woods

From the very start, the crows objected to the Ogress's practice of giving gifts to the people in town. They voiced their opposition as often as they could.

"Caw," they said. "Why on earth would you leave a plate of muffins for a man who has done nothing for you? Not a single thing!"

"Caw!" they added. "It used to be that our grandmothers and grandfathers would sit on the windowsills of the old library and listen to poetry, back when the town and its people were lovely. Nothing is lovely anymore, though. There is no more library. And no more poetry. Only mean-spirited men and women who throw rocks at crows. Rocks, I tell you!"

"Caw," they pouted when they realized that the Ogress was *not* listening to them. "Why must you give that mayor a pie? He is a strange one, and we do not like him. Our grandparents did not like him, either. He doesn't move right. And *also*, he has never given *you* a pie. Or us. There are no pies for us at all!"

"Caw," they said at last. "Well, fine. We will come with you. We cannot bear the thought of you being alone!"

They loved the Ogress so, so much. They did not like it when she went away, so the crows always flew with her as she delivered gifts to the people of Stone-in-the-Glen. The Ogress studied each person in town through the marvelous contraption that she had built. A few of the crows had been curious enough to follow her inside her house and watch as she peered into one end. They attempted to do the same, but they didn't understand it much. The Ogress explained that it helped her to observe the town, but why would a crow ever need such a thing? Crows see what they wish and need no assistance. It was one of the many excellent aspects of being a crow.

Inside the Ogress's house, she mixed paints and inks, fashioned paintbrushes, and painted portraits of every single person in town. She hung them from the ceiling and watched them spin in the breeze. She covered her walls with faces. Often, she pressed her fingers tenderly on the painted cheeks by way of greeting.

"My dear, dear neighbors," she said.

"Caw," the crows would sometimes reply. "Are they?" But they usually said this under their breath, and anyway, the Ogress still didn't always understand what they were saying. She was doing her best to learn Crow, but it would take a long time, and misunderstandings were bound to happen.

She also painted portraits of each of her crow friends, which the crows all agreed were far more handsome than the portraits of the townspeople. Why, they wondered, would she paint anything else?

Each night, the Ogress readied herself to head into Stone-in-the-Glen to deliver gifts, and each night, the crows complained. "Must you?" they cawed. "Can we not lie in the grass instead and count the stars?" But the Ogress insisted, and night after night, the crows followed.

After a while, they didn't mind so much. The Ogress, after all, was performing acts of kindness in a town that did not deserve it but still needed it all the same. They were proud of doing this work with her. It made them feel like very important crows indeed. At least they knew that while the Ogress loved the town, she certainly loved the crows best of all. Which was as it should have been.

One day, the crows and the Ogress were deep in the woods, gathering mushrooms. Crows don't care for mushrooms (they cause them terrible stomachaches) but are adept at finding them, due to the strong, earthy smell.

They called out when they found a colony of shy morels.

Or a large bloom of chicken-of-the-woods.

Or a fruiting of beautiful red mushrooms whose caps all looked like flower petals opening delicately in the dark.

And then, without warning, they saw a troop of muscular creatures coming through the gloom on cloven feet. The beasts' eyes glinted menacingly in the moonlight. Their matted wool was as thick and broad as armor, with sticks and vines and even growing plants bursting out of the tangles, making them look like walking weapons. They bounded over rock and root and fallen log. They were agile and wild and *terrifying*.

"*Baaaaaa*," the creatures bellowed.

"*Caw!*" the crows screamed, fluttering madly and circling back toward the Ogress. "*Monsters!* Run for your life!"

They weren't monsters, though. They were sheep. "*Baaaaaa*," the creatures bellowed again.

The Ogress clapped her hands and waved. "Oh!" she said happily. "Well, hello!"

There were ten all together: four ewes, one ram, and five lambs. The lambs were the most interested in the Ogress. They approached her with their nostrils flared. They regarded her with their large, damp eyes. Their wool was in such a sorry state that the skin underneath had lesions that festered and wept, and their feet were wretchedly sore. The Ogress had some dried corn in her satchel. She reached in and grabbed a handful.

"*Caw!*" the crows complained. "*That was ours!*"

But the Ogress shook her head. "That's not how it works," she said. The sheep ate the corn. They sniffed the Ogress's hands. They closed their eyes as she stroked their faces. "Quick," she said to the crows. "See those trees there? See how they are thick with nuts? Shake the branches and knock them down. These sheep have traveled a long way by the look of them. They need to refresh themselves."

The sheep ate the corn and the nuts, and then the Ogress led them to the stream, where they could drink.

"Baa," the sheep said quietly. Neither the Ogress nor the crows understood what this meant, but they could hear the desperation in their voices. One of the ewes pressed her flank against the Ogress's calf. The Ogress let her hands run along the animal's back.

The crows exchanged glances. There was no way of knowing what that infernal baaing meant. But there was no denying the feelings inside each baa.

It was a baa that appreciated kindness. It was a baa that was perfectly content to follow the Ogress wherever she went. And that's exactly what happened.

"Perhaps we should discuss this further," the crows cawed. "How will we know when there are too many of us on the farm? How will we know if there is enough room?"

The sheep moved into the barn that the Ogress had built. They ate corn and grass and what they were able to forage in the forest during their nightly excursions with the Ogress. In turn, the sheep provided milk, which was turned into cheese. The crows, as it turned out, were *terribly* fond of cheese. And the sheep kept the grass short, which made it easier for the crows to find bugs in the lawn. And also, the backs of the sheep made for a convenient resting spot that also allowed the crows to be carried from place to place. All in all, it was a useful arrangement.

The crows decided that the sheep could stay.

Soon, the crows could hardly remember what it had been like before the sheep arrived. "Ah!" they said. "Our lives are perfect. This farm is perfect. The Ogress is perfect. Thank heavens that nothing could possibly arrive to disrupt this best of all possible worlds."

And then, one day, the household increased again. By exactly one dog.

The crows met the dog before the Ogress did. As a rule, crows don't care much for dogs. Dogs lack the subtlety and mystery of crows. Dogs bark and scratch and drool. They howl at the moon, and yip at nothing, and dig holes for absolutely no reason. Dogs sometimes chase and snatch crows when crows are not looking.

And then there was *this dog*. Right here. Sniffling under the mulberry trees. These mulberry trees belonged to the crows. The crows puffed out their feathers and prepared for the worst.

They kept very still and watched, waiting for the dog to do something wicked. But the dog didn't seem to notice them. It kept its nose pressed to the ground. *Sniff, sniff, sniff*. It didn't look up. *Sniff, sniff, sniff*. It cocked its head from time to time, as though listening. Once, it pressed its ear to the ground. The crows had never seen a dog that didn't attempt to chase and catch crows at the slightest provocation. And here this dog was, snuffling about right below them. One crow flew very close to the dog. It blinked its milky eyes. It didn't bark or even flinch. What kind of dog was this?

"Caw!" the crow demanded. "State your business immediately."

The dog jumped back. It could not speak Crow, of course, so it merely whined.

"Caw," the crows shouted. "Caw, caw, caw, caw, *caw*!" They filled the air with sound. The dog's whining intensified. The dog moved this way and that, disoriented and afraid. It curled its body tight and pressed its rump against a mulberry tree. It wet the ground where it stood.

"What's all the fuss?" the Ogress said as she emerged from her house just as the sun set. The crows alighted on the Ogress's head and arms and shoulders, prepared to defend her if need be.

"Caw!" The crows warned. "Monster!"

"Alert!" they added. "A possibly dangerous dog is skulking about! Run for your life!"

The Ogress's face lit up when she saw the dog, shaking under the mulberry tree.

"Oh!" she said. "Welcome, my friend!"

The dog reared back with its tail between its legs. It whined and showed its teeth.

"Caw!" the crows said. "You see? Dangerous. You should probably run away while we menace the creature with our wings and claws and beaks!" The crows would face any danger in the world to keep their ogress safe.

Much to the crows' disappointment, the Ogress did not run away. She crouched down, resting on her heels, and spoke gently. "Come now, dear one." Her voice was as soft as a breeze in a field of wheat. The crows could feel the very air rippling with it. They started to calm down along with the dog. The dog inclined his nose, flaring his damp nostrils, breathing in the scent of her. It blinked its white, watery eyes. The Ogress smiled. "I can see that you can't see me, my love, but your ears are sharp and your nose is fine. You're safe here. We are friends here. You may come home with us and stay as long as you'd like."

Nothing more happened, not for several moments. The crows held themselves very still. They could hear their own hearts beating. Then, slowly, the dog approached the Ogress. He sniffed her hands. He sniffed the nut cake that she offered. He pressed the top of his head firmly against her knee and held it there for a long, long time.

This was how the dog came to live with the Ogress. The crows decided that the dog could stay. What was one more, really, among friends? They didn't communicate their decision to the Ogress, since they knew in their hearts that she already understood.

They decided to name the newcomer Dog. He came every time they called.

Over time, Dog knew the farm by heart, every stone and plant and divot in the earth. Sometimes, it was hard to tell that he was blind at all, so adept was he at finding his way around. He could navigate his way to the Ogress by smell, even if she was over a mile away. He stood at attention to the crows and bowed his head each time they spoke. He was the most polite dog that the crows had ever seen.

After Dog had been living at the farm for a full four seasons, he and the crows began to rely on one another in unexpected ways. Dog had an excellent sense of smell and an intimate understanding of the forest. He always knew where the Ogress was and could anticipate the geographic irregularities of the forest terrain, to keep himself from getting injured or lost. A group of crows stayed near him at all times—partially to keep him from wandering too far afield, and also because they worked together to find treasures to bring back to the Ogress.

Sometimes, the crows would see something glinting on the ground and would call Dog to come and dig it up. Sometimes, Dog would catch the scent of something that the crows would not have seen on their own, and one of the crows would fly it home. The crows praised themselves for having had the forethought to allow Dog to stay at their farm and become part of their family. Truly, they were the most excellent and forward-thinking crows in the world!

And then, on one of their nightly excursions, Dog came skidding to a halt. It was a new moon, and the night was a darkening deep, with bright stars spangled across a velvety sky.

He had been running through the twisted trails of the forest, navigating by sound and smell and the touch of the earth—and other senses that the crows couldn't even imagine—when all of a sudden, he stopped, barked, and then whined. The crows looked down. Dog barked again. The crows could not see what Dog was barking at, but they could hear the alarm in his voice.

"Caw!" the crows reassured him. "Do not be afraid, Dog! We are coming to rescue you!"

The crows landed delicately on the ground. The fur on Dog's back stood straight up in sharp points, but he held his head low and his tail between his legs. The crows had never seen Dog so scared. They peered at the thing that Dog had found. They clucked and murmured and squawked a bit. "Well," they muttered nervously. "Beats the heck out of me."

The Thing was largish. And floppy. It was the shape, they supposed, of a person. If the person had been deflated. Or if the skin of a person no longer had any actual person inside it anymore. It wore clothes with shiny buttons and buckles and other bits and bobs that glittered in the thin starlight. The crows might have been tempted to help themselves to the shiny treasures—since whoever owned both the clothes and the skin had clearly discarded them here on the forest floor—but they didn't want to get too close. It had a shock of bright, beautiful hair, along with a face that looked uncannily familiar—or may have, if the crows could have stood to look at it for long. They shivered and looked away.

There was something *wrong* about this thing, and the wrongness of it seemed to infect the very air in their lungs.

"What on earth are we looking at?" the crows asked, a sense

of panic rising in their throats. Dog whined. He swung his head from side to side and drooled.

"This thing smells like smoke and ash and money," the crows said. In response, Dog made a guttural growl. He rubbed his rear end on the ground.

"Dog does not like this Thing, either! Dog is strong and virtuous—the best and bravest of all dogs! If he is upset, then this Thing is very dangerous indeed!" The crows conferred and decided that the best course of action was to flee. They rose in a great murmur of wings, and Dog followed in their wake.

Normally, when Dog ran, he was quite careful in his footsteps and mindful in his movements. But not today. Dog panicked as he ran as fast as he could. He fell twice and, once, went crashing into a tree. The crows kept closer, warning him, to prevent more harm.

They arrived at the Ogress's farm, frazzled and exhausted. "Why, there you are!" the Ogress called, wrapping her arms around Dog and holding him close. She held out a hand for a crow to land upon. "Tell me what you saw in your travels. Tell me what you discovered in the woods!"

Dog trembled. The crows shook. They didn't want to speak of the Thing in the woods. They didn't want to mention the glittering buttons. They didn't want to mention the shock of hair. Or the way it draped on the ground. It was too unsettling. It was too *wrong*. They couldn't tell her.

"Caw," the crows said, avoiding her eyes. "Nothing. Nothing at all."

The Reading Room

Night fell on the Orphan House. The Littles, along with Dierdre and Elijah, piled around Myron in the parlor, listening with rapt attention as he read them stories, while Matron sang to the toddlers in the dormitory. Anthea checked the list of tasks in her ledger, which she always kept in her pocket.

√ *Mix the bread dough and set it to rise.*

√ *Strip the beds.*

√ *Hang out the washing.*

√ *Reattach the broken trim.*

√ *Fix the pump (again!).*

√ *Fold the clean diapers.*

√ *Make the Littles do their mathematics lessons (try not to yell this time!).*

Organize the Reading Room.

She had check marks next to everything . . . except for the last item on the list.

In truth, the last entry was just a ruse. The Reading Room never needed to be organized—it took care of that all on its own. Once Anthea had finished her earlier tasks, she simply said, loudly, that she couldn't help anyone completing whatever they needed help with because there was still an entry left on her list. And no one could argue with a list.

"Our work is never done!" she said as she hurried up the stairs. "Busy, busy, busy, rush, rush, rush!"

She shut the door behind her and breathed a sigh of relief. The Reading Room, and all of its many books, seemed to sigh with her.

The Orphan House's reading room had wide windows that had once looked out onto the old library. Indeed, the design of the Reading Room was meant to be a reflection of the Library in miniature, as both structures were built at the same time, by the same person, who felt that it was important for children, in their time of need, to have a quiet, beautiful place of their own, while remaining connected to the World of Ideas as well as the Life of the Mind that awaited them when they Grew Up. They were built during a time of great Civic Responsibility, with well-funded projects for the Public Good, when people often put their Grand Ideas in capital letters.

Those days were long gone, and it didn't look like they would be coming back any time soon. Now the windows in the Reading Room looked out onto a pile of rubble and ash. Instead of connecting the children of the Orphan House to the World of Ideas, or even the Life of the Mind, it simply reminded them that anything can go up in smoke—families, towns, dreams, even a library.

Anthea closed her eyes for a moment and listened to the quiet. The tightly packed shelves seemed to whisper. So, too, did the beams on the vaulted ceiling and the deep cushions on the window seats. The whole Reading Room crackled with secrets.

Which was a good thing. Anthea was hunting for secrets.

She pushed the ladder up to the tallest bookcase on the far wall and climbed up to the highest shelf. She ran her fingers along the spines, squinting at the titles. She wondered if the books she was looking for would be in today. The Reading Room and the books it contained all had minds of their own. She pulled down several volumes of fairy tales and set up a stack on the table, marking the relevant pages. She found volumes on animal folktales, and ornithology, and biomechanics. These, too, she marked and stacked. There was one more book she needed. She climbed back up the ladder.

Comparative Ethics and You! she read.

Conifers: Nature's Silent Colonizers.

Crocodile Smiles and Other Mysteries.

And then . . .

"Crows!" she hooted triumphantly, and she pulled out a book called *Crows: The Most Wonderful Birds in the World!* Anthea had read it before, a long time ago. It was so overly complimentary of crows that Anthea suspected that a crow might have actually written it. Which, frankly, wouldn't have surprised her, given crows and their nature. She heaved the book off the shelf. It was thick and heavy, and landed on the table with a thump.

She had a theory about the crows. She just needed more proof. Unfortunately, she couldn't get close enough to a crow to even ask the question. Which she could have done—*ask*, that is. In addition to being conversant or fluent in Latin, Greek, Sanskrit, Sumerian, Quechua, Mongolian, Old Norse, French and Swahili (there were books in the Reading Room written in every one of those languages), Anthea had *also* become fluent in Mouse, Dolphin, and Crow. The orphans, as I mentioned before, were curious children. And the Orphan House's collection was surprisingly large—there were more books than the space seemed to allow.

This is not unusual. Books, after all, have their own peculiar gravity, given the collective weight of words and thoughts and ideas. Just as the gravitational field around a black hole bends and wobbles the space around it, so, too, does the tremendous mass of ideas of a large collection of books create its own dense gravity. Space gets funny around books.

Time, too, unspooled differently in the Reading Room: the more time the children spent there, the more time they seemed to have.

The windows in the Reading Room faced west, and the light was already drifting from deep red to dark purple. Soon, the stars would appear. But not yet. Inside, the lamps glowed and the candles flickered. Anthea opened the book and began to read. She took notes in her ledger.

Bartleby and Cass burst in, each with a baby on their hip.

Anthea glared. "Excuse me," she said. "I'm in the middle of organizing, and I can't be disturbed."

Bartleby arranged his face into a skeptical expression. His mismatched eyes twinkled. "It doesn't look like you're organizing. It looks like you told everyone you were organizing so that you could have the room to yourself for some evening reading." He grinned. "Not that I blame you."

Anthea's glare sharpened into a scowl. "I can do both, *Bartleby*," she sniffed. "I am clearly organizing as I read. *Ergo*, this is a *both ways* situation."

"Sure," Bartleby said cheerfully. "You don't have to be so grumpy. Mind if we join you?"

"I do," Anthea said coolly, but both Bartleby and Cass ignored this. The babies wriggled and whined to get down. The two older children obliged, and Cass got on the ground as well, crawling as the babies shrieked with delight.

Bartleby looked at the book open on the table as Anthea pored over its pages. "Oh!" he said happily. "I mean, caw!" Which meant "Are we going to practice in Crow?" Bartleby's grasp of the language of the crows was passable, but he didn't have the same vocabulary or precise pronunciation that Anthea possessed. He tried to manage this shortcoming through sheer enthusiasm. "Caw," he added, which was supposed to mean "Excellent," but what he actually said was "Muffins." Anthea let this slide.

"Not right now," Anthea murmured, writing more words down in her ledger. She slapped her hand over her writing when she noticed Bartleby peering over.

He frowned. "What are you doing, Anthea?"

Anthea shook her head. "N-nothing," she said. "It's just . . . I have a theory. About the crows."

"I love theories," he said. "Tell me what it is."

Anthea wrote something else. "I'm not entirely sure," she lied. "But I'll know it when I see it." She added three more items to her notes. Then she closed the ledger with a slap. "Don't mind me," she said. "I'll help with the babies in a little bit." She thought they would take the hint and leave.

They didn't. Both Bartleby and Cass sat down on the window seat. They let the babies sit and play as they watched Anthea hunt through the stacks. She did her best to ignore them and not be annoyed.

The light outside vanished entirely. The Reading Room seemed to vibrate and shift. The books in the cases, while not in motion, seemed to alter themselves, or reveal new volumes, or rearrange their order, every time Anthea flicked her eyes to a shelf. The bookcase that was entirely stacked with ancient atlases (some with maps of worlds that no longer existed) suddenly became crowded with old-fashioned novels and stories of romance. Another shelf arranged itself with a delightful collection of books on architecture. The Reading Room's vast holdings of books on the study of insects were suddenly proudly displayed on the whole back wall. It wasn't that the books moved: that's ridiculous. But no one expected them to stay in the same place all the time, either. The children were accustomed to this sort of thing, and didn't question it overmuch. They simply accepted the Reading Room and its various quirks.

One of the babies (Nanette? or perhaps it was Orpheus) began to giggle at nothing at all. The other (Orpheus? or perhaps it was Nanette) curled around Cass's feet with an entire fist shoved into a drooling mouth. Finally, Bartleby couldn't stand it anymore. "So?" he said, folding his arms across his chest and grinning. "Are you ready to tell us what you're looking for?"

Anthea shrugged. "It's just . . . I have a theory."

"About the crows," Bartleby said. "Yeah, you mentioned that. So spit it out already."

Four cats stalked in, looking for mice. They leaped lightly onto the window seat and surged around Cass first, because she was everyone's favorite—especially the cats'. She picked up the smallest one and held it in the crook of her arm. She looked expectantly at Anthea.

Anthea glanced through her ledger. She thought about Elijah, on that terrible day at the butcher shop, when he had told her that the orphans would save the day. But *which* day would they save? And how?

The clock on the wall clicked loudly. *Tick, tock,* the butcher had said. Summer was ending soon, and autumn would sweep in, and she was to turn fourteen, whether she wanted to or not, and, oh, what was to happen to her then?

"Fine," Anthea began. She sighed. "Look, you already know about crows. How they collect things that delight them and how they decorate their homes. How they have language and stories and grand ideas. How they remember their enemies and make tools and mourn their dead." She checked her ledger again. It was a crazy idea. She knew this. And *yet* nothing else made sense.

One of the babies began to cry. Bartleby scooped one into each arm and started swaying back and forth. The baby's eyelids began to droop. "I'll put them down in a minute," he said. "Keep going."

Before Anthea could continue, there was another sound, this time coming from outside. Anthea ran to the window and knelt on the seat. She pressed her hands against the glass. She opened her eyes wide toward the darkness on the other side. The nighttime air was filled with the sound of crows. Anthea swallowed. "I've been taking notes," she said. "And tracking the days. Every evening that we hear the sound of the crows swooping nearby is followed by a morning that the benefactor leaves us a box of vegetables—and whatever else the benefactor thinks to give us. If it's a quiet night and we hear nothing, then the next morning there is nothing waiting for us on the front stoop. The crows are connected to the deliveries."

"Is this true?" Bartleby said.

Anthea opened her ledger to the neatly drawn calendar she had made. "Every time we hear crows at night, I put a little crow symbol on that square. And on the mornings when we find a box of food outside, I draw a star on that date. Look. Here is every single delivery date from this whole year. Each one is preceded by a night filled with crow calling. It's not just *sometimes*. It's *every time*."

Cass held the ledger, running her fingers along the strings of days, while Bartleby tipped his head and looked at Anthea for a good long time. "You've been thinking about this for a while," Bartleby said.

"I have," Anthea said simply.

Bartleby closed his milky eye and read with his hazel eye, focusing on the corners and edges of Anthea's handwriting. He frowned. "Why is there a sad face on your birthday, Anthea?" he said.

"Never mind that now," Anthea said, shutting her ledger quickly and tucking it under her leg. "The point is this. We know that Stone-in-the-Glen isn't a good town. We've helped out at Market Day. We've gone with Matron or Myron on errands. We've seen how they behave. Have we ever met anyone besides Matron and Myron who we would describe as *generous*? No. We haven't. *But* there is someone in town who does this incredibly generous thing for us." She closed her eyes and swallowed. "I don't think the benefactor is any person in town." She paused again. "I think it's the crows. Bringing the food. And growing the food. They are capable of so much more than people give them credit for. It *has* to be the crows."

Bartleby and Cass exchanged a worried expression.

Anthea powered forward. "Look. I know what you're thinking."

Bartleby folded his hands very tightly and pressed them to his chin. "I don't think you do," he said slowly.

"Just because something is improbable doesn't mean it's impossible," Anthea said primly. "Look at it logically. Point: The people of Stone-in-the-Glen are not kind. Counterpoint: One persistent and unexplained act of kindness occurs on the steps of our very home. The Orphan House receives the occasional box of food, and this act of kindness comes from an unknown benefactor. If we agree that the *people* are unkind and we agree that this action *is* kind, then it follows that the person who is responsible for this action is not a person at all. Ergo, our benefactor is *an animal*. Or a bunch of animals. My position is logically sound. I believe it is the crows. I don't see why not. Why would people write stories about helpful and crafty crows unless they had observed crows being helpful and crafty? I also don't know what other explanation you have for why we hear them every night before a delivery. Why only then? Why would they come near our house *only on those nights*?"

There was a long silence. The cats purred and meowed, demanding attention. Anthea looked outside, listening to the crows. She opened her calendar again, to mark the day, but the sad face she had drawn on the square for her birthday faced upward. Her gaze fell on the square for a moment. She winced and looked away.

At that very moment, the babies began to fuss and rub their eyes. Bartleby sighed. "Just a minute," he said, swaying his body back and forth. "I'll put Nanette and Orpheus to bed and then we can keep talking."

But that wouldn't happen, and both Anthea and Cass knew it. Bartleby would go, cuddle, and fall asleep with a baby in each arm. This sort of thing happened a lot.

Anthea looked back outside. The crows were loud and insistent. She heard a phrase in Crow—"The more you give, the more you have"—again and again. She had heard them say this phrase before. *How much more proof do people need?* she wondered.

Cass took Anthea's hand and held it next to her cheek for a good long while. With her other hand, she placed a finger on the calendar, where Anthea had drawn the sad face. Cass raised her eyebrows. Anthea closed her eyes, keeping all her tears inside. "There's this rule," she said. "About what happens to orphans when they turn fourteen. Matron and Myron love me. They love all of us. I don't think they would ever want to send any of us away. But how can I stay? Look at this place. The Orphan House isn't getting what it needs from the town, and so everyone suffers. Our whole family. If I stay, I'll just be taking away from everyone else. But, Cass, where will I go?"

Cass wrapped her arms around Anthea as Anthea wept on Cass's shoulder. There was no answer, of course. The cats curled onto the girls' laps, purring loudly. Outside, the crows called: "The more you give, the more you have." But it didn't make any sense.

Market Day

As the sun rose on Market Day, Anthea, Bartleby, Cass, and Myron arrived at their stall in the Center Square with their boxes and bundles. They set out their wares—blocks of soap, mostly. Matron was famous for her soap made from the ashes of the old library and tallow she bought cheap from the butcher, scented with flowers from their garden. They had other things to sell as well: jams, cordials, cut flowers, and a few precious lumps of fresh goat cheese, wrapped in linen. They also sold a special paint that Myron made from pine resin mixed with a clay and a mineral deposit harvested from the forest. The paint was often in high demand due to its resilience. The recipe was a closely guarded secret.

Anthea reviewed their inventory in her ledger, and Bartleby and Myron discussed the philosophical implications of soap, while Cass arranged everything *just so*.

Thin clouds stretched across the sky and a weak gray light trickled over the cobblestones. Anthea shivered and pulled a blanket tightly around her shoulders. From far away, she could hear the calling of the crows, but they were too distant for her to make out what they were saying. The Orphan House stall was off to the side, a good distance from the main walkway—not great for business, but it was the best they could afford. Once a month, they operated a stall for Market Day—first to sell, then to buy. Each penny was precious, the children knew, and how well they would eat that month rested heavily on their abilities to effectively sell and savvily negotiate at the end of the day.

Anthea felt her anxiety set its teeth on her stomach and clamp down tight. *Will it be enough?* she asked herself over and over. She hoped it would.

There were new signs around the Center Square—pasted up on abandoned buildings and tacked onto the unused light posts. MIND YOUR BELONGINGS, one sign pleaded. YOU DON'T KNOW WHICH OF YOUR NEIGHBORS ARE THIEVES. Another sign said REMEMBER THE FIRES? THE CULPRIT IS STILL AT LARGE. And there were an uncountable number of signs wherever Anthea looked that said A LOVELY TOWN BEGINS WITH YOU! GIVE GENEROUSLY TO THE MAYOR'S FUND!

Some of the signs had a silhouette of the Mayor's smiling face at the bottom. Anthea watched as people paused at the signs, taking a moment to place their hands tenderly on the image of the Mayor's face and then almost immediately cast a suspicious look at a nearby neighbor.

Bartleby stood close to Anthea. "You know," Bartleby said, as they watched one young man stare at a sign for a full minute, his hands pressed to his heart, "people certainly have a lot of big feelings in this town."

"Keep your hands to yourself!" the young man shouted at a passerby who was nowhere near him. The passerby jumped, then clutched her own purse close. Both hurried away from each other, glaring as they departed.

"Yeah." Anthea shook her head. "They really do."

The three children finished setting up, and when the sun inched over the tops of the buildings, they were ready to sell. "Soap!" Bartleby called out.

"Smart soap!" Anthea added.

"The smartest of soaps!" Bartleby finished, not to be outdone.

Despite the fact that this particular Market Day was the last one of the summer months, the weather was dreary and cool. Anthea rubbed her hands over her goose-pimpled arms and took a quick look at the broken clock just above the Town Hall. If time could stop for that clock, could time pause for everyone else? Autumn was just around the corner. And then it would be her birthday, and she would be fourteen.

Tick, tock, the butcher had said. If she could stop time, she would.

Still, neither Matron nor Myron had mentioned it. *So was it even true?*

The sky was the color of ashes. The square itself was the color of a bruise. The flagstones hadn't been washed in years, and it hadn't rained in weeks, so dust kicked up whenever anyone walked by, clouding every movement. Everyone coughed into filthy handkerchiefs and sucked at their teeth to clear off the grit. As the morning stretched on, Anthea, Bartleby, and Cass stood shoulder to shoulder, looking out into the thin crowd. People came by. They picked up the soap and smelled the soap and put down the soap. Twice, someone attempted to pocket a bar, but Cass was there like lightning, with a swift kick to an unsuspecting shin.

"Oh!" the offender said each time, flushing deeply. "My mistake."

The butcher arrived at midday, turning over each bar and eyeing the price with a sneer. "Seven?" he asked. "Have you gone quite mad?" He threw the soap down on the counter in disgust.

Cass quietly crossed her arms over her chest and narrowed her gaze. But Bartleby tried to explain. "Well, certainly for a lower quality of soap, seven would be insane. But most soaps dissolve quickly and are gone in a matter of weeks. And, worse, they either leave an oily sheen on anything you try to clean with them or they are so harsh that they take your skin away. Our matron's soaps are dense and solid. Just feel how heavy this one is. And smell how delicately she scented it. Soap that works and doesn't hurt? Amazing! There is no finer soap in the world." He flashed a winning smile. His mismatched eyes twinkled.

The butcher glared at Bartleby, but then his gaze fell on Anthea. "Oh," he said with venom in his voice. "It's you."

Anthea flushed but said nothing. The butcher's mouth twisted unpleasantly.

"And look," he sneered. "It's nearly autumn. A new age, one might say."

Anthea's cheeks grew so hot she thought they might melt. But she met his eyes and refused to look away. She stuck out her chin and glared.

"You know darn well how much it's worth," she said, point-edly ignoring what he had just said. "It's seven, and not a penny less. Move along if you're not interested." She gave a loud har-rumph. She looked to the passersby. "Can you even *believe* him?" she said loudly. The butcher was not a well-liked man in Stone-in-the-Glen. A few people stopped and nodded, and cast hard looks at the butcher, just because.

"I should report you to the Mayor," the butcher muttered. But he paid the full price anyway. It was good soap, after all. As he left, he made sure to lean close to Anthea. "Tick, tock," he said again, quietly enough so only she could hear. "Tick, tock." He slithered into the crowd and disappeared.

"What did that man just say to you?" Myron asked as Anthea's shoulders slumped and her arms wrapped around her middle, as though keeping herself from breaking in half.

"Nothing, Myron," Anthea said, forcing a smile onto her face and desperately attempting to remove the shake from her voice. "Nothing at all."

The Mayor arrived midafternoon and took up his place on the dais to give his Market Day address. The shoppers quickly made their way over, each jostling against everyone else to try and get the best view. Myron pressed his mouth into a tight line and narrowed his eyes. He didn't say anything, but Anthea noticed.

On the days when Matron came to Market Day, she could hardly contain herself the moment the bells rang announcing the Mayor's arrival in the Center Square. She would stop what she was doing and look with envy at the other townspeople hurrying over to claim their spots and sit in the Mayor's glow.

Matron could not, because doing so would leave the children unprotected. Their stall was too far away to see the Mayor, so Matron would stand on their makeshift table, shading her eyes and squinting, trying to catch a glimpse while she listened to his oddly amplified voice ringing across the Center Square.

Not so with Myron. Anthea noticed Myron's grim expression as he watched the people in the crowd, their faces shining and their eyes seeming unnaturally wide. He turned away and looked over Anthea's ledger with a frown. He shook his head and looked down at the table. "I'm afraid we haven't sold nearly what I hoped we would, my dears. And everyone tends to clutch their purses tight after the Mayor speaks. Perhaps we should close up now and make our purchases and be home before supper."

"Don't be silly, Myron," Bartleby said. "There's still hours before sundown. Surely we'll fill our own coffer by then. I can feel it in my bones."

Myron disagreed but relented.

By the time the final hour of Market Day rolled around, they had little to show for the effort. Half the soap remained unsold, along with most of the jam. They would have to make their own purchases soon—assuming they had made enough for that. Anthea had lost count, and Myron was holding the money.

The Mayor exited the dais and left the square as the sun sank even lower. People in the market began to move more quickly, their movements abrupt and uneasy, and their eyes darting toward the faraway, crow-heavy trees.

The woman in the stall next to the orphans' was admonishing her daughters as they boxed up their unsold wares. "Hurry up, will you?" she chided.

"Your mother's right," a large man said, unprompted, as he walked by. One of the daughters rolled her eyes. "You don't want to be out and about after dark. The Ogress will get you. And who will save you then?" He stopped and leered at the two girls, who wrinkled their faces in disgust and looked away.

"Well, that's a stupid thing to say," Bartleby said, more loudly than he meant to.

Myron covered the boy's mouth with his hand and quickly shoved Bartleby under the counter.

"Who said that?" the large man demanded, looking up at the sky, as if the clouds themselves had disrespected him. "Who called me stupid?"

Myron merely shrugged, and both Anthea and Cass busied themselves with organizing the stall. Eventually, the large man stalked off.

"Ouch," Bartleby said, rubbing his head under the counter.

"Serves you right," Anthea said.

"People fight here sometimes," Myron whispered to the three children, anxiously wringing his hands. "And those fights can get mean. And you are all smaller than you think."

"Am not," Bartleby said, but Anthea waved him off.

"Myron, we should make our purchases and get home," she said. She looked back at the crows.

"Soon," they seemed to caw.

But *was* it soon? Maybe this meant that there would be an overstuffed box on their stoop the next morning. Anthea closed her eyes and listened hard, searching hard for clues. *Is it you?* she wondered. *Is it?* She glanced at the broken clock. She shivered in the growing cold.

Cass packed the unsold soaps and jams. She held out her hand to Myron, who handed her the money belt without her having to say a thing, and she and Anthea counted it out. Cass's face became grim.

"Not to worry," Anthea said lightly. "It will be enough." She thought about how much flour might be ground from a peck of grain, if she was careful about it. She thought about how they might portion out a half peck of legumes and water down the soup, making everything last until *next* Market Day, when, hopefully, they could sell more. She thought about how she would be happy to go hungry for a night or two, or even three, if it could help make this whole thing work. Surely, that would be fine.

"Well, let's see what we can afford, shall we?" Myron said. His face was pale. His hands shook.

Anthea hooked her arm in his, placing her free hand under his elbow to steady him.

As it turned out, they weren't able to afford very much. The sellers had increased their prices from the month before. The sellers all shrugged. "Mice," said the grain man as he handed Anthea less than half a peck of wheat berries and an even smaller bag of oats.

"Locusts," said the bean lady as Anthea collected a third of a peck of lentils.

Their combined weight was a comfort. It felt like full bellies and a contented family. Enough for now. Anthea felt her stomach muscles relax, just a bit.

"I think the Ogress sets them on us," said a third vendor, from across the way, his face folded into a sneer. "Out of spite. Typical ogres."

"That doesn't make any sense," Anthea began, exasperation fraying the edge of her voice.

"Of course it makes sense," a shopper said with obvious menace. Cass stood between the shopper and Anthea, crossing her arms and jutting out her chin.

"I'm just saying what everyone else is already thinking," the vendor said. "Everyone knows that ogres are prone to wickedness."

"*No one* thinks that, because it's nonsense," Bartleby said. "And anyway, what on earth would make the Ogress even consider doing something like that?" he added. "Mice? Really? Locusts? Come on! It's a crazy notion. Your hypothesis lacks logic and is devoid of common sense and, if I'm being honest, seems unnecessarily unkind and ignorant."

Bartleby gasped, and clapped his hand to his mouth. He saw Myron rest his brow on his open palm and shake his head. "*Oh dear*," Bartleby whispered under his breath.

One man rose to his feet. A woman clenched her fists. Their eyes narrowed and gleamed like the blade of a knife. Anthea's eyes grew wide, and she took a step backward. "Say that to my *face*," the sneering man said.

"But," Bartleby said, honestly confused, "I just did."

"Time for us to go," Myron said, pulling the children's sleeves and moving to the side.

"Typical orphans, spouting hogwash," the butcher spat. He leaned against his makeshift table, looking for a moment like he might snap it in half. "You probably poisoned the jam. Sounds like orphan behavior to me."

Myron pulled the children even closer. "We don't want any trouble. And we certainly didn't poison any jam!" The sun had sunk almost all the way down. The sky had erupted in color. The crows' voices were louder now. "Soon," they seemed to call.

"Just take your purchases and walk away," the woman at the grain stand said. "I wouldn't have done business with your kind if I had known beforehand."

"Kind?" Anthea said, feeling her cheeks start to flush.

"Off we go," Myron said, tugging harder and pulling the children away.

"You heard me," the woman said. She glanced upward at the crows and the deepening colors in the sky. Her mouth curled unpleasantly. "Typical orphans."

Anthea felt these words like a kick to her guts. Her ears rang, and time seemed to get very slow.

Bartleby screamed, "*You take that back.*"

Myron said, "*Bartleby, no!*"

A man yelled, "*I'll teach you some manners, you sniveling little—*"

"*Don't bring these kids around here anymore,*" a woman said. "*I can't stand the sight of them.*"

The large man from before approached them at a run. Anthea noticed the way his muscles bulged with each step. The ground seemed to shake as he approached.

A woman threw a tomato at Myron's head. Or maybe it was a rock.

And somehow it was Cass who seemed to launch herself over her brother's shoulders and slide through the air as quick as lightning. She hit the man full force with both feet right in his solar plexus, making him spin, lose his balance, and fall. As the great bulk of him pinwheeled to the ground, his arms flailed and flapped. He hit Anthea on the side of her face, causing *her* to fall to the flagstones, face-first and hard.

The next thing Anthea understood clearly was the smell of dust on the ground and the reek of a donkey relieving himself on the other side of the stand. This was followed by the startlingly metallic taste of her own blood in her mouth. She had a broken nose. A bloody lip. A black eye and a deep cut on her cheek. Her soft tissues were beginning to swell. And there was a deep chip in her front tooth.

Even worse, everything that she had been carrying—the wheat, the oats and the lentils—was now spilled out over the filthy ground, much of it landing on a pile of donkey droppings. There was nothing they could save.

Myron began to weep. "Oh, my child," he sighed. "Oh, my beautiful child."

"I'm sorry, Myron," Anthea said, looking at the ruined grain. "It's all my fault."

"See what you get?" the woman said. "Just be glad we didn't set the Ogress on you. She'll grind your bones for her terrible bread! She'll eat your eyes so her wicked mouth is the last thing you'll ever see! Just you wait."

"*Enough!*" Myron spoke in a voice louder than Anthea had ever heard him use in her life. "I've lived in this town since the day I was born. I've known all of you since you were children. I knew your parents and your grandparents, too. And I'm ashamed of the lot of you." He didn't wait for a response. He helped Anthea to her feet and gathered what was left of their things and walked with the three children across the square.

Anthea's eyes felt hot, and her face was dripping wet. Tears and blood. She couldn't tell which was which. She thought her face might shatter from the pain in the bridge of her nose and her cheekbones. The bins in the larder were nearly empty, and now there was nothing to fill them. Soon, there would be no flour. No porridge. No bread. She could go hungry, but what about the littler children? And, yes, sometimes they received a box of beautiful food from their anonymous benefactor, but what about the days when there was nothing waiting for them at the front gate?

She looked back at the people in the stalls, who should have been packing up. Instead, they just watched the orphans and Myron limp away, their arms folded across their bellies. Their eyes were lit with the last rays of the sun. Their mouths were in shadow.

Cass slipped her arm around Anthea's waist and held on tight. They stayed quiet as they walked across the filthy square onto the darkened street, toward home.

And Then There Was Elijah, Who Loved Stories

The days following the incident at Market Day were a particularly gloomy period in the Orphan House. Anthea's face was bloody and swollen. Someone was supposed to sit next to her at all times, with clean rags and a bowl filled with ice chunks and water, to keep a cool cloth resting on her puffs and wounds and bruises. This was Elijah's task at first, but after two days, Anthea sent him away. His fingers were clumsy, and his touch was too rough. She needed a steadier hand to mind her injuries. Also, he would *not stop talking*.

"I love you, Elijah," Anthea told him, "I really do. But if you stay in this room for another second, my skull will actually explode, and then who will clean up that mess?"

Elijah tried not to take it personally.

He spent the next few days helping Dierdre mind and milk the goats, but she told him that his incessant chatter was making them moody and less productive, and then he spent the next week with the twins and Matron, making several extra vats of soap, which Matron was planning to sell on the sly at a make-shift booth in the Center Square.

"But isn't that illegal?" Elijah asked at last. It had only just occurred to him.

Matron's face settled into a flat, grim line. "Off you go," she said. "Why don't you see if Bartleby can stand your constant questions, my angel."

Bartleby had his hands full in the Reading Room, giving the Littles their lessons, and welcomed Elijah's help. At first. They covered spelling and geography and grammar and arithmetic, but the Littles got bored so easily it was hard to keep them focused and on task and in line. So Elijah did what Elijah did best. He began to tell stories. He paused briefly before he spoke, his eye drifting upward toward the beams on the ceiling, like he was listening.

"Once upon a time," Elijah said at last, "there was a dragon who disguised himself as a crow."

"You already told us that one," Iggy said.

"Fine," Elijah said, undeterred. "Once upon a time, there was a dog who had been blinded from a terrible beating by his cruel master. After wandering the land, lost and alone, he was rescued by a murder of crows."

"You told us that one, too," Hiram said.

"I like the end of that story," Justina mused, "but the beginning is too mean. Tell us something else."

"Once upon a time," Elijah said, "in the Library before it burned, there was, at the very center of the building, a book that told the true story of the past, as well as an accurate foretelling of all possible futures. But no one ever bothered to read it. You see, when a group of people live in an already-lovely town, they can't imagine that their home would be anything other than lovely forever, and surely all possible futures would simply be all possible versions of loveliness. This, of course, was a terrible mistake."

"I think we have that book," Iggy said, squinting at the overcrowded shelves.

"We don't," Elijah said. "Believe me. I've *looked*." He glanced up at the ceiling again and frowned, like he was now listening to a story he didn't like. He shook his head briefly, then said, "All right. What about this one: Once upon a time, there was a stone who fell in love with an oak tree. It spent a hundred years working up the courage to say hello, and another hundred years resolving to at last declare its love for the tree. But each time it attempted to say something, the stone found itself distracted by the dazzling whisper of the oak tree's beautiful leaves as they danced with the breeze, or the melodious creak of the tree's wide limbs. The stone loved the tree for its dappled shade and its welcoming embrace. But mostly, the stone loved the tree for its stories."

"Do oak trees really tell stories?" Justina asked.

"Of course, silly," Elijah said. "Oak trees tell the best stories. Everyone knows that. Anyway, the stone decided it had waited long enough. It readied itself to declare its love as soon as the morning light shimmered through the branches, brightening the glen. Instead, in the morning, the stone heard the bite of an axe. In short order, woodcutters removed each branch, each pretty leaf, and the dear curve of that oak tree's beautiful trunk. The stone watched in horror as they took the beloved oak away. The forest shook from end to end. The woodcutters fell to their knees as the ground lurched. They thought it was an earthquake. Or the end of the world. How could they know that what they were actually feeling was the stone's great heart breaking in two? Eventually, the shaking stopped, and the glen grew still. The woodcutters shrugged and made their way home, and they didn't look back. The end."

Hiram, Iggy, and Justina regarded Elijah for a long time, their arms folded across their chests, their eyebrows knitted together. "That story is too sad," Iggy complained.

"But look," Elijah said, pointing at the wood beams holding up the vaulted ceiling of the Reading Room. "It's all around you. We are sitting in the shelter of that very oak. If you listen very carefully, you can hear her sigh for her long-lost friend, the stone. She's still telling him stories, even now."

"I don't hear anything," Hiram said.

"Me neither," Justina said. She looked up and frowned. "Also, that story is *definitely* too sad."

"Elijah!" Bartleby called from the other side of the room. He was working with Kye on his short *i* words—*bit, lip, sit, hit*— and it was slow going. "Stop making the Littles sad!"

"Fine," Elijah said, sulking. He reopened the book of arithmetic drills. Hiram and Iggy responded with pitiful groans.

This lasted for less than a quarter of an hour, until Elijah launched into yet another story.

"Once upon a time," Elijah told them, "there was a young ogress who bid farewell to her mother and father and went out into the wide world to seek her fortune. She journeyed for a long time, exploring forests and fens and even the whole ocean until one day she came upon a tumbledown castle, with a magnificent laboratory. She thought she had found the home she had been looking for all her life. Unfortunately, there were two trolls already living there. And the trolls were *mean*."

"Elijah!" Bartleby admonished. "What on earth do ogres and trolls and castles and laboratories have to do with teaching long division to the Littles?"

Elijah was about to reply, but Hiram put his hand on Elijah's arm and gave Bartleby a withering expression. "Literally *everything*," Hiram said loftily. "And anyway, I love this story." He turned back to Elijah. "I want to know how it ends, so you should finish it."

Elijah also had several stories that he told to his family about the Ogress—whether or not they wanted to hear them. They had wide-ranging titles, such as "The Day the Ogress Learned to Speak Whale," or "Swamps Make Terrible Houses," or "The Dragon Who Swindled the Ogre Village and Burned Everything Down."

"How do you come up with these things?" his family asked again and again.

Each time, Elijah would shrug. "I'm just a good listener, I guess," he would say. Then he'd change the subject.

Later that evening, Matron and Myron cuddled the babies, and Cass and Dierdre read stories to the toddlers, and Bartleby wrangled the Littles into their pajamas while Fortunate and Gratitude sweetly sang lullabies in harmony, and once again Elijah found himself with nothing to do. He wasn't good at soothing babies, and sometimes he made the toddlers cry without meaning to, and even though he tried to tell stories as a way to calm the Littles down, half the time they were more energized by the end than they were when he had started. And when he sang, he sounded like a frog. Which wasn't so bad, really (he liked frogs), but once again it left him without a purpose.

He cleaned his teeth and washed his face and started staking out a spot to sleep. That was when he realized with a start that Anthea was not in the room. He frowned and started looking for her. The cats followed. The cats would follow Elijah anywhere. They liked his stories, too.

He found her, as usual, in the Reading Room, sitting in a corner all by herself. She had several stacks of books strewn about the floor. Her face was blotchy, and her eyes were red, as though she had been crying. Or maybe her face just looked like that now, after what happened at Market Day. Elijah wasn't entirely sure.

Two cats snaked through his legs and sidled up to Anthea, sliding their foreheads under her elbows and pawing their way onto her lap. Anthea barely seemed to notice them. She was too busy reading. She sniffed deeply. Her eyes leaked. She furiously wiped her tears away. She ignored Elijah.

Elijah shifted his weight and fidgeted, keeping his eyes fixed on the ground. He wasn't exactly sure what to say. Usually, Bartleby handled this sort of thing. Or Cass. Elijah wasn't typically at a loss for words or jokes or stories—in fact, he often had more than he knew what to do with—but this felt different. He felt the stress of the moment like the prick of a pin stuck into the center of his brow.

Finally: "Um," he managed. "Are you okay, Anthea?"

She didn't respond, which Elijah appreciated. They sat like that for a long time. The cats went from Anthea's lap to Elijah's lap and back to Anthea, purring with conviction. The room was quiet, save for the occasional turn of the page.

And another sound, too. Elijah could hear it. Anthea could not. He looked up at the beams on the ceiling and glared. "Shh," he said.

"What?" Anthea said.

"Nothing," Elijah said. "I wasn't shushing you. I was just . . ." He didn't say anything more; he just let himself look at Anthea's face, even though it hurt to do so. Her lower lip had a crusty scab where it had split, and a lopsided bulge on the left side. Her tongue kept going to the diagonal gash where part of her tooth had chipped off. And both the lump on her nose and the black eye had deepened to a sickly shade of green. It all looked like it hurt. "Seriously, Anthea, are you okay?" Elijah asked.

Anthea looked back at the books. "I'm not sure that any of us are okay, to be honest." She gently curled one hand over the side of her face and regarded Elijah. She frowned. "How hungry are you right now?"

Elijah had also noticed how thin tonight's dinner was. He had given most of his portion to Kye, who looked as though he was going to cry. "I'm not hungry at all," he lied, just as his stomach growled.

"Thought so." Anthea nodded grimly and then shook her head. "It's not supposed to be like this." She gestured to the books. "I've got the whole history of this town right here. None of this is supposed to be like this. The Orphan House used to have all the resources it required, and was the place where anyone, at any age, could get help when they needed it. The Library was for everyone's curiosity, and the House was for everyone's generosity. The whole town. And it just worked. Until it didn't. What happened?"

The cats purred. Elijah rested his chin on his knuckles. "There's an old story . . ." he said slowly. He glanced up at the wood beams and glared. Then he closed his eyes, letting his face relax. "I mean, it's *really* old. But that doesn't mean it happened a long time ago. Stories don't always stay in their own time. But it's about a dragon who once burned down a library."

"Why would a dragon burn down a library?" Anthea asked. "Why would *anyone* burn down a library?"

Elijah swallowed. He *hated* this story. "Who knows," he said. "Maybe he hated learning. Maybe he wanted people ignorant, because ignorant people are easy to control. Maybe he just loved the way that fire burns—all its heat and light and terror. All I know is this: In stories, a person can be terrible *just because*, but in real life, I don't think that is true. In real life, people are terrible because they are broken, or people are terrible because they are lonely, or people are terrible because they want or need something they can't have and they justify all sorts of crimes in order to get it. And sometimes, people are terrible because they are afraid."

His eyes flicked again to the wood beams. He forced himself to focus on Anthea. He wanted to cover his ears. "I think that what happened to you was awful, Anthea. Just awful. And I know you want to look backward at what you think Stone-in-the-Glen used to be like because it comforts you. But maybe that's a mistake. Maybe we shouldn't be thinking about what this town was like before, or even what it is now. Maybe instead, we should think about what it *could* be. And what our lives could be. Outside Matron and Myron's walls. You know, for all of us together, once we're all too old for the Orphan House."

Anthea leaped to her feet, her expression changing in a flash. Storms brewed in her eyes. "*What did you just say to me?*" she snarled. Her cheeks turned deeply red.

Elijah didn't understand why this was a Wrong Thing to Say, but it clearly was. He tried to press on. "I mean . . . because we will all grow up. You know. Because of . . . time."

Anthea nearly choked on a sob. She pressed her hand to her mouth and looked away.

Another Wrong Thing, Elijah realized.

"Tick, tock, you mean." Anthea's voice shook. Tears poured down her face.

"No?" Elijah ventured. Another sob. "I mean, maybe? I don't know what I'm supposed to say."

He couldn't fix this. Anthea left the Reading Room in a huff, the cats trailing behind her with their tails pointed high into the air (one looked back over its shoulder and gave Elijah an unmistakable *pfft!* as it hooked into the hallway).

"Sorry?" he called out. He wasn't entirely sure what he was sorry for. He had thought it might comfort Anthea to be reminded that they would all still be a family once they were All Grown Up, whatever that meant. He couldn't imagine a life that didn't include Dierdre and the twins and the Littles and everyone else. He couldn't imagine a life that didn't have Cass's helpfulness or Anthea's inventions or Bartleby going on *way too long* about philosophy.

Once upon a time, the ceiling beams whispered, *an ogress didn't see the danger in her own backyard until it was too late.*

Once upon a time, murmured the mantelpiece, *a dragon swindled an entire town. It was far easier than he ever thought possible.*

Once upon a time, breathed the floorboards, *a beloved community became a little bit less so.*

"Later," Elijah said. "*Please.* I can't listen *all the time.*" He covered his ears and breathed through his nose, trying to quiet his thoughts and focus. There must be a way to help his family. He just needed to find it.

The Orphan House was one of the oldest houses in town. The wood beams were ancient, some of the first trees ever cut down in Stone-in-the-Glen. Elijah had been hearing them whisper since before he could talk. Sometimes, he appreciated the stories. Sometimes, they got in the way.

He stood. He looked at the ceiling. He crossed his arms and tilted his head. "Just a request," he said out loud, "it would be nice if you could give me something that was, you know, *useful.*"

The house grew quiet. Elijah listened to his breath go in and out, in and out. Then:

Once upon a time, sighed the trusses.

Elijah shook his head. "No," he said. "Not a story. What I need is information. Do you have any actual information?"

Once upon a time, whispered the wainscoting.

Elijah shrugged. "Still not helpful." He glared at the beams and gave the floorboards a hard look before heading to the door.

The twins, far down the hall, were still singing in harmony. Their music drifted through the house. Elijah followed their voices toward the dormitory and crawled into bed.

A Visit to the Mayor's House

It was a chaotic morning in the Orphan House, but that was nothing new. Dierdre and Elijah had both contracted some sort of stomach illness, and, after spending all night bent over bowls and moaning, they were now on the downstairs sofas, in the sweaty, pale, restless sleep that sometimes befalls the sick.

Cass tried to feel sorry for both of them—and she did, mostly—but their illness meant there were two fewer pairs of hands available to make the work light. Cass, Anthea, and Bartleby, along with Fortunate and Gratitude, scrambled to strip the bedding, put clean diapers on the babies and toddlers, and give the upper floors a good airing and sweeping and wiping, in hopes that the other children wouldn't go the way Dierdre and Elijah did.

It was a lost cause. In short order, both Bartleby and Anthea went a bit yellow, and Hiram and Iggy fell asleep in a corner— something that *never* happened. Hiram, in particular, only ever fell asleep when he was tricked into doing so. Meanwhile,

Fortunate and Gratitude, who were always partially crabby, were far more irritable than usual.

Cass didn't slow down. She helped Matron and Myron haul in the box of vegetables that the benefactor had left that morning (a miracle!) and began sorting and peeling and chopping before being asked. She stoked the fire in the cast-iron stove in the kitchen and set out the wood next to the outside boiler in preparation to wash the bedclothes. Both Anthea and Bartleby moved through the morning like confused slugs. And poor Fortunate gathered the eggs but ended up on the wrong side of a chicken's beak and ran inside in tears, while Gratitude got dizzy and nearly fell down the stairs. All the while, Cass kept working.

"You should rest," Myron said, putting his hand on Cass's shoulder. Myron's tissue-paper skin crinkled around his wrists, and what was left of his hair wisped about his head like feathers. His scars had become flushed and livid. Cass hugged him around his middle—he was very thin, and his bones were light, like a bird's. Cass had to hug gently. She removed his hand from her shoulder, gave it a little squeeze, and hurried to the next task.

Matron had been spending the morning at her desk, looking over her ledgers and trying not to cry. Cass could always tell when Matron was trying not to cry—her hands would fidget, and her back would go rigid, and her shoulders would slowly inch upward. She would curl her lips between her teeth and press them together hard. Cass didn't exactly know why the ledgers hurt Matron so, but she made sure Matron had a mug of hot tea in arm's reach whenever her breathing started to rattle, and she made sure that the other tasks were done before Matron had a chance to wonder about them.

Finally, at lunch, with only Matron, Myron, Cass, the toddlers, and the babies sitting at the table, as everyone else was sick in bed, Matron seemed to come to a decision. She looked at Myron and took his hand.

"You're right, my love," she said. "Of course you're right. I will go and see the Mayor this very afternoon."

Myron nodded. He curled his fingers over Matron's hand and held them there. He leaned close and kissed her cheek. "You know I'd do it in your place, my darling, but in the end it's your house and your family's work and legacy. The town made a promise long ago to fund the Orphan House, and that promise has been broken. Surely, the Mayor will do the right thing if he is made to realize his . . ." Myron frowned. "I mean, I'm certain that this was just an oversight." Cass thought he looked like he had a bad taste in his mouth. He pressed his lips together, as though he wanted to say something more but thought better of it.

"That must be it." Matron gave a gentle smile. "A simple mistake. Easily rectified. The Mayor . . ." Her face became light, and her eyes glittered, just a bit. Cass couldn't understand it. "Well, our mayor"—again, the glitter in her eyes!—"is right about so many things. We are so lucky to have him. Especially in these difficult times. I'm certain that all we have to do is ask."

"I'll go with you, if you'd like," Myron said.

Matron shook her head. "You're so pale. It's only a matter of time before you get sick, along with the others. I'll help you put the toddlers down for their naps, and the babies, too, and then I'll walk down."

Lily and Maude banged their spoons on the table in protest,

but both of them blinked their drooping eyes, trying to glare their own sleepiness away.

Cass didn't need to be told twice. Or even once. She wiped their faces with a cloth and carried an only vaguely protesting Maude upstairs to bed, followed by an already-sleeping Lily. The babies had to be transferred to bassinets in the living room, where Myron settled into a comfortable chair with an old book and promised that he wouldn't fall asleep as well, though it was clear he would.

Matron gave Cass an assessing glance. "Perhaps you should come with me, dearest," she said. "The Mayor has never actually met any of the orphans in the house. Perhaps this is why he forgot us. The mind is funny in that way."

Cass tried to keep her face as neutral as possible and tilted her gaze to the ground. She shrugged, as though it really didn't matter either way, and then, as casually as can be, curled her fingers around Matron's hand and hung on tight.

"All right, then," Matron said brightly. "Together it is. I will appreciate the company."

Matron put on her best hat and her nicest shawl and insisted that Cass wash her face and comb her hair. Matron packed a basket with her handmade soaps and a tub of goat's butter (even though she needed it at home) and a clutch of eggs from the henhouse (also needed—there were so many bellies to fill) and a bouquet of flowers, picked from the garden and bound with a ribbon. At last, Matron was ready. "Come along, my darling," she said, offering Cass her hand.

As the two left through the gates of the Orphan House, Cass took in a breath that felt as though it were as big as the sky. She and Matron picked their way through the streets of Stone-in-the-Glen, past potholes and debris. People hurried this way and that, hauling carts full of deliveries or trash, on foot or on bicycle. There were carpenters looking for work and metal-workers looking for work and housecleaners and gardeners and farmhands looking for work. A long line of men and women waited outside the blacksmith's shop, which had a sign in the window: SEEKING PART-TIME HELP. VERY PART-TIME. INQUIRIES ACCEPTED TODAY ONLY. The line went down the block and around the corner. A woman and her children sat on the cobblestones near the Center Square, covering their faces with one hand and reaching out with the other, in hopes that someone might place a coin or a bit of food in their open palms.

Matron stopped. "*Oh!*" she whispered. "Oh, here it is!"

They stood in front of the charred facade and partial shell of a building that had burned long ago. The window had melted in the fire, and some of the old glass remained in lumpy mounds clinging to the stone sill. Light and shadow rested in soft angles inside. Someone had written several rude words on the brick wall facing the street, and the wind whooshed through the gaps in the broken windows.

"It was a toy shop once upon a time." Matron pressed her hand to her heart. "Oh, you should have seen it, Cass, darling. Back in its day. Every shelf held marvels."

Cass's frown deepened, but Matron smiled. She pressed her hands together like a prayer and held them next to her heart. "You know," she said, her face suddenly wistful, "our Myron, after he spent two seasons at the house, and after my father found a family to love and raise him, still came by whenever he could. Almost every day. To pay his respects. To spend time with his friends. And he was sweet on me even then." She blushed, and Cass felt her embarrassment hit her like a wave.

The thought of Matron and Myron holding hands and courting was almost too much to bear, but Matron didn't seem to notice Cass's discomfort. She peeled away from the abandoned toy shop and crossed the square, a strange, faraway look on her face. "Of course, back then, we were all encouraged to wander the town. Visit neighbors and make new friends. Everyone loved children in those days. And wherever we went, we were welcome and cared for." Her eye scanned the sad street, the creases in her forehead growing deeper. "Not like now."

Several bicycles whizzed by, each one old and rusty and mended again and again with a welding iron until the frames were lumpy and multicolored, but they seemed to do the job fine. One of them was pedaled by a boy who looked about the same age as Cass. His woolen pants were covered in hand-sewn scraps of fabric, and he carried a bag filled with loaves of bread. Did he also feel cramped at home? Cass wondered. And did he enjoy the sensation of wind and sky on his face? Did he ever feel like pedaling and pedaling and never stopping?

Matron continued. "We used to come by the toy shop in those days. Just to look. Everything was expensive, but the toy maker was a kind woman with a magical mind and clever hands. There were windup toys of every description. Toy soldiers that could really fight and mechanical horses that could gallop and rear and neigh. There were windup birds with iridescent wings that only had to be wound once a month and, when you least expected it, would open their throats and sing the most beautiful song you ever heard. They had toy mice that scurried and toy puppies that hurried and dolls that would open their eyes and tell you they loved you in a way that made you feel like they really *meant* it."

Cass gave Matron a sidelong glance to see if she was pulling her leg. This toy shop seemed too lovely to be true. Matron's face remained wistful and happy. She didn't *look* like someone who was making a joke. Maybe this sort of thing happened to very old people—maybe their memories got a little bit tangled.

Matron sighed. It didn't seem that she noticed Cass's skepticism. "There was this one day," she said, her cheeks brightening. "I had just turned eighteen. This was years before the fire in the Library, so everything in town was still as lovely as can be. I was about to go off to school far away, and Myron didn't want me to. He saved and saved and saved, and the day before I left, he brought me to the toy shop and presented me with a windup butterfly. It was the prettiest thing I've ever seen. It had cut-glass eyes that sparkled in any light and wings that were made from a thread that glittered in the dark." Matron's eyes were shining. She wiped her face with the back of her hand. "He told me that the toy maker had taken a tiny sliver of his heart and put it in the center of the butterfly. And that every time his heart beat, the wings would flap. He told me to put my hand on his heart." Matron blushed deeply. "And so I did."

Cass's stomach fully turned. She made a face and pretended to gag. *If she tells me that they kissed I will actually vomit, and then she will be sorry*, Cass thought.

Matron's face looked as though she were gazing at something beautiful in the far distance. "And sure enough," she said,

"I could feel Myron's heart going *beat-beat, beat-beat, beat-beat* against my hand, while the butterfly, in perfect timing, went *flap-flap, flap-flap, flap-flap*."

Cass raised her eyebrows. Matron shrugged. "I know it's silly to think there might actually be a piece of his heart in the toy. How would the toy maker even get it? And why would it still beat? Obviously, it's a mad notion. But"—she grinned and her eyes twinkled—"I still have the butterfly. It still flaps its wings with each of Myron's heartbeats. When he sleeps, the fluttering slows. When he wakes, the wings quicken. And when he was so sick last year and his pulse raced and we feared the worst, the butterfly nearly broke its wings it fluttered so fast. So you tell me."

Cass didn't know what Matron expected her to say or what to even make of it. So she just kept hold of Matron's hand as they turned the corner and walked toward the Mayor's house.

The Mayor lived in a mansion in the nicest part of town. Every surface gleamed. Instead of a lawn, the mansion was surrounded by a stretch of small, shiny stones, raked smooth and arranged in different patterns according to color. The yard looked more like a painting to be looked at than anywhere pleasant to play or sit or read. There were several statues—mostly of the Mayor himself—with fountains underneath. A sign hanging over the front gate said A FUNCTIONAL TOWN RELIES ON A GENEROUS CITIZENRY! BUT ARE YOUR NEIGHBORS GIVING ENOUGH? At the bottom, in very small letters, it said THEY PROBABLY AREN'T. "What fine taste our mayor has!" Matron said. "How lucky we are to have him as our mayor!"

Are we? Cass wondered. Matron fanned her face.

A clowder of cats stalked the edge of the Mayor's yard, pacing back and forth. They kept their gaze pinned on the front door, and their ears tilted forward. The cats didn't set foot on the yard. Cass counted at least thirty of them, patrolling the perimeter. They arched their backs and prickled their fur as Cass and Matron walked past, but didn't make any sound. They didn't even turn their heads. Cass had never seen cats behave in that way before. She and Matron made their way up the long walkway and stepped onto the porch.

The house was too tall and too wide. It had gilded carvings along the lintels and plump angels adorning the eaves. Wind chimes hung from each corner, and the windows were polished so meticulously that they shimmered (not that it mattered, Cass noticed—the curtains inside were all pulled tightly closed). Over the front door, in scripty golden letters, were the words

It is a Marvelous Day to be your Mayor!

Matron knocked on the door.

"My word, that's hot," Matron said, shaking her hand. Her knuckles were quite red.

Something heavy moved inside the house. A rumbly, jangly, creaky sort of heavy. Cass felt it in her feet. The porch shook. The whole mansion groaned. For one panicked moment, Cass worried that the whole thing might collapse, but then she looked at Matron's calm, enthusiastic face and began to second-guess herself.

"Who is it?" said a voice from inside. It was an excellent-sounding voice. It had resonance and gravitas. It made the small hairs on Cass's arm stand on end. Matron looked positively ecstatic, and her words tumbled out in a rush as she tried to explain why they were there.

"If it's not too much trouble," Matron stammered, "I wanted to talk about . . . well, the missing support money . . . for the Orphan House." Matron's voice cracked a little. "For the children."

There was more tinkling inside the house. Like the sound of breaking glass. Or the bright rattling sound that a pile of chains makes when you drop it. The whole house creaked. "Very well," the voice intoned. Cass could feel it vibrating the floorboards under her feet. "We can chat, I suppose. Go out to the patio and sit on the chairs. I will meet you there presently."

There was no shade on the patio, and the sun beat hard on the bleached stones. Light bounced everywhere—a harsh, startling, searing whiteness. Several statues of the Mayor loomed about—one with a crown and another looking piously at the sky and another where he was petting a bear with one hand and creating a perch for a bird with the other. Fountains gurgled on either side. Both Cass and Matron sat down and shaded their eyes with their hands, and even still they had to squint. It was difficult to see with so much light. The Mayor came out with a pitcher of lemonade and one glass. He sat across from them and poured himself a drink, knocking it back in one gulp. He smiled. "Ah," he said. "Refreshing."

Matron nodded. "You are so right. Lemonade is *so refreshing*." She gazed approvingly at the Mayor. "It is so calming in these difficult days to have a mayor who is so very right about every single thing nearly all of the time." She sighed a happy sigh.

Cass grimaced. There was too much light on the patio. All this squinting was giving her a headache, but the light didn't seem to bother the Mayor at all.

"Agreed," said the Mayor, glittering. He wore a long coat the color of butter and boots so polished they practically made their own light. He had burnished skin and a bunch of diamonds at his throat, and a watch with a clockwork dragon that curled its way through the hours, scale by shining scale. The Mayor smiled. His teeth were so white they nearly blinded the eye.

A silence fell. The Mayor adjusted the drape of his coat. He admired the shine of his watch. He pulled out a small mirror and beamed at his reflection. Cass wondered if he had forgotten that she and Matron were there at all. At the edge of the yard, the cats stalked silently. Finally, Matron cleared her throat. The Mayor raised his eyebrows as though startled.

Matron explained that for many generations, her family had managed the Orphan House. It was their mission, going back to the very founding of the town. Every year, the town sent money to the Orphan House for the children's upkeep: food and clothing and medicine and education and music, as well as for the maintenance of the house. But ever since the fire, and the other fires, and the sinkhole, and the persistent crop failures, and the floods, the amount of money that the town provided each year had been getting smaller and smaller and smaller.

"It's been harder, every year, to make ends meet. Then, last year, we waited for the annual payment. We thought that you were going to get to it. We thought that you wouldn't forget us. But it never came. We made do, but it was a struggle. And now we wait for this year's assistance. I do my best. I try to be industrious. I sell what I can, and make adjustments where I must, and I teach the orphans how to stretch, repurpose, and fix, and the value of thrift."

"Well, splendid!" the Mayor exclaimed. His smile glittered. Matron's face and shoulders relaxed. "I am a firm believer in making do! And thrift! And industry! My goodness! What a role model you are! What a marvelous citizen! Look at all the good that you do, just from your own know-how and elbow grease! If only the whole town could follow your example in all that they think and do. Why, the town would be back on its feet in an instant!"

"Thank you, so much, dear Mayor." Matron steepled her fingers and pressed them to her mouth. She closed her eyes, and tears leaked from the corners. "I knew you would understand."

"I do," enthused the Mayor. "I stand in awe of your service and fortitude. I can't imagine that you need my help at all!"

"Well, actually . . ." Matron began.

But the Mayor interrupted her. "Can you imagine if everyone in Stone-in-the-Glen was as industrious as you, my good woman? Well! We would be a lovely town again in a matter of minutes! Perhaps seconds! You are a credit to your generation! And you, young . . . *person*." He squinted at Cass. "Well, you are a credit, too. You are by far the most fashionable orphan I have ever seen."

"Oh!" Matron said. "You've met one of the orphans before?"

"Never in my life! And now perhaps I don't need to. I have clearly met the very best one." He gestured magnanimously and patted Cass on the head.

She stiffened. She *hated* it when people touched her head. She looked to Matron to see if she noticed, but Matron's eyes reflected the Mayor's light. She no longer shaded her brow. The brightness didn't bother her anymore.

"Well, after this conversation, I feel so much better, my dear, dear Mayor," Matron said, her voice soft and easy. The Mayor sparkled in the sun. "We are so lucky to have you as our mayor." Out on the street, one of the cats yowled.

"Are we?" Cass said out loud. No one seemed to hear her.

"You certainly are!" The Mayor stood. "I must get back to my work. You know how it is! Busy, busy, busy, rush, rush, rush. Alas. I long to be like one of your orphans, with their carefree days, counting butterflies and examining the grass. Ah, childhood!"

"Indeed," Matron enthused. "What lucky children."

"In the meantime, be sure to keep an eye on your neighbors. I'm afraid there have been more reports of liars and thieves. And tax cheats. The town coffers are dangerously low. People don't pay what they owe, and they don't give when they can. It is a sorrowful situation. Scofflaws! Misers! Don't they know that donations and taxes are for the town? The more you give, the more I have—I mean, we. We have. Of course I mean *we*. We're all in this together!" And with a sweep of his buttery coat and a click of his boots, he strode over to the rock lawn and onto the porch. He paused, turned, and bowed toward Matron and Cass with a flourish.

"Thank the Antelope for you, my good, good woman!" he said in a booming voice.

Matron, for the first time, was shaken out of her amazement. She blinked. "Thank the what, sir?"

The Mayor blanched, but it only lasted a second. "I apologize. I misspoke. I meant to say 'Thank the skies for you, my good woman.' Thank the very skies. The lucky skies!" And with that, he flowed through the front door, shutting it behind him with a small slam.

Matron stood still for a long time. The cats on the road continued to pace. One hissed. From very far away, Cass could hear the cawing of crows. She watched Matron's face go from adoration, to awe, to introspection, to confusion, to worry, to resignation. Matron met Cass's gaze for a long moment. Then she slumped into a shrug.

"Well," she said. Her voice was tired. "I guess we tried. We'll just have to think of something else." The walk home was a silent one, which Cass appreciated. She had a lot to think about.

$$\sim$$

Back at home, the rest of the family remained ensconced in their sickbeds, sleeping deeply. Neither Matron nor Cass wanted to disturb them, so they sat down for supper, alone. Vegetable soup, again. No bread. There hadn't been any bread since the incident at Market Day, because there was hardly any flour, and there wouldn't be any more flour until the next Market Day, and then only if Matron and Myron were able to sell anything. It shouldn't be like this. The town was supposed to be generous, and it wasn't. Why was it so hard for the people of Stone-in-the-Glen to give to others—except for that one generous benefactor who sometimes left them vegetables? Without whom they would surely starve. Where was everyone else?

Cass tried not to let her thoughts take her to dark places. She smiled at Matron, who took her hand and told her what a wonderful girl she was. Myron wandered in, wearing his nightclothes and robe. He was still impossibly pale. Cass felt her worry expand in her throat, hard and sharp. She tried to swallow it down.

"Hello, my dears," Myron said. "Any luck in today's efforts? Did the Mayor come through?"

Matron stared at her bowl. Her expression flickered between light and shadow. "Everyone loves the Mayor," she said. "He . . ." She stopped. "Certainly, he must know what he is doing." She pressed her hands to her face and started to cry.

"There, there, my love," Myron said. "Cass, dearest, could you clean up? Matron needs to rest. She has had a taxing day." And with that, Myron curled his arm around his wife's shoulders and guided her away.

Cass went to work. She milked the goats and filled the bottles and chased the chickens into the coop. She swept the front room and washed the dishes, and then climbed out the kitchen window and shimmied up to the roof of the porch to watch the sun set. She sat there for a long time. It wasn't often that she could be entirely alone in a house with that many children. She watched the light shift from brightness, to color, to dimness, to shadow. She watched the stars wink. There was a wide world outside the Orphan House. Outside Stone-in-the-Glen. She stared into the darkness and tried to imagine it all.

Eventually, the night became cold, and she slipped through the window, landing on the kitchen floor in silence. The whole house was dark. Matron and Myron slept in a small bedroom just off the kitchen, separated from the pantry by an alcove with a desk and a chest of drawers for documents and ledgers and a shelf for important things. Cass stood, and realized with a start that a sound was curling from under Matron and Myron's bedroom door.

Matron was crying. Cass felt a deep pinch in the center of her heart. She froze in place.

"Hush, now," Myron said, his voice like the darkening shadows—soft, quiet, and deep. "We'll find a way. We always find a way."

"It was never supposed to be like this," Matron said. Cass could tell that Matron's hands were over her face. Her voice was muffled by her cupped palms. "There were never supposed to be this many. And never for this long. Even if we were able to find a home for one of them—just one!—it would make a difference in what was available for everyone else. But how? Where could they go? Who would love our dear, dear children? We can't just turn them out—they're all too young! But we can't go on like this, either."

"We have always found a way," Myron repeated. "Eventually," he added.

Cass felt her cheeks start to flush. She had heard Myron's worry in that *eventually*.

"It would have to be Anthea, if we followed that stupid rule. I *hate* that rule." Matron's voice shook with swallowed sobs. "In the old days, we at least had options for our bigger children—apprenticeships or the university fund, but there's none of that anymore. How could she possibly support herself? She's too little to be all alone."

Myron was silent for a long moment. "I can't imagine what this family would do without our Anthea. I can't imagine what the children would do. We love her so. Everyone loves her so. I'm sure . . ." He paused. "I'm sure no one in town remembers that rule. And we certainly don't have to mention it. In any case, I don't see how their opinion would matter, since they don't give us a cent anymore. I'm certain that we will find another way. Let's not fret, my love."

Matron wept. Myron wept. Cass stood still for a long time as she considered the problem. She weighed the possibilities. She evaluated the variables. She added, subtracted, and divided the difference. Blowing a kiss at Matron and Myron's bedroom door, she tiptoed out of the kitchen. Her footsteps were as light as shadows on the floor. She crept into the dormitory and stood in the middle of the room, looking at her family all sprawled around her, their faces soft and their limbs draping randomly over whomever was nearby.

The Orphan House is good, she thought. *And the people in it are good.*

Cass held herself very still, listening to the sound of her own breath and the beating of her own heart. She knew how to fix this situation. She could see it as plain as day. Matron and Myron were right—the Orphan House couldn't function without Anthea. They needed her. But the arithmetic of their situation simply didn't add up. The only solution was a subtraction.

Cass was a *doer*. And she liked being helpful. And this would help. She wouldn't ask anyone what they thought. She wouldn't say a thing. She just needed a few days to plan.

And then she'd be gone.

The Crows Notice Something

That night, after the mushrooms and the nuts and berries and honeycombs had been gathered in the forest, after the sheep had eaten their fill of grass and were content to remain in their pasture under the stars, and after the pies and cakes and breads and cookies and vegetables and cheese had been loaded into the cart, the Ogress made her way through the town. The dog kept close to her, following by sound and smell. The stars glinted overhead, lighting their path. No other creatures stirred in the nighttime—the doors were locked and the shutters latched and the curtains drawn. Every house seemed to sleep, all breath and sigh and quiet dreaming.

As they reached the Orphan House, the crows landed on the wall, their beaks pointed toward the garden. The Ogress stopped and looked up. A tiny bit of light leaked from a window on the side of the house. Just a flicker of candlelight behind a curtain. Someone was awake. The Ogress had never been observed in her giving, and even though she could see no one about, the possibility unnerved her. She found herself fidgeting.

She flattened her grassy hair. She crossed her large arms across her chest.

What was it like to be *seen?* she wondered. She knew her neighbors caught glimpses of her from time to time, but this felt different. She always did this work in secret. What would happen if someone saw her?

The Ogress shrugged and laid a box of vegetables and cheese on the ground. She turned the cart around and began to walk toward the Mayor's house . . . and then she stopped. The crows kept their eyes on the Orphan House, their eyes fixed on the tiny bit of flickering light.

The Ogress tilted her head. "Is everything all right?" she whispered. The tiny bit of light continued to flicker. The curtain stayed closed. If someone was up, it didn't look like they were planning on coming out. "Come on, then," she said. "The sheep will wonder where we are."

"Caw," one crow said. "Someone's crying."

"Caw," said another. "Someone's heart is breaking in two."

"Caw," said a third. "Maybe we should give something more. Do we have anything more to give?"

There was only the pie for the Mayor. But the Ogress didn't want to miss that. He must be so lonely, after all, in that big house by himself. There was nothing worse, the Ogress knew, than loneliness. The large family in the Orphan House had one another to comfort them.

"We don't today, but I will be sure to bring extra tomorrow. And more cheese. I am confident that will solve whatever is crushing their spirits." And just by saying so, the Ogress felt certain it must be true. She knew from her observations through the periscope that everyone in the family loved one another very much and held one another in deep care. Morning was coming, after all, and the sun would rise and the winds would blow, and you never know what sort of goodness was waiting around the corner. Things would get better, the Ogress told herself.

She was sure of it.

Things Don't Get Better

There was something wrong with Cass. Anthea noticed, but didn't know what to make of it. First, she found Cass in the pantry, her hands over her face, her eyes wet with tears. "What's wrong, Cass?" Anthea asked. Cass wouldn't explain.

The day after that, Anthea found Cass in the Reading Room, looking through maps and taking extensive notes in a ledger, which she slipped into her pocket the moment that Anthea walked through the doorway. "What are you working on, Cass?" Anthea asked. Cass wouldn't explain.

On that same day, Anthea noticed Cass giving her possessions away. She gave the doll that Matron had made her when she was little to Lily, and her favorite set of tools to Hiram. She gave her bag of marbles to Elijah and a brand-new set of pencils to Dierdre (she had been saving them for over a year after she found them untouched in the junk pile).

"Don't you want this anymore?" Anthea said as Cass gave her a sweater she had knitted from the yarn she had salvaged from a cast-off bag of mismatched wool socks. It was very soft and quite colorful. Cass wouldn't explain. She just hugged Anthea as tightly as she could. She left without a word, leaving Anthea wondering.

And the day after that, Anthea found a book under the bed where Cass and Bartleby had slept the night before, open to a page titled "How to Make a Compass." Anthea didn't bother asking. She knew Cass wouldn't explain.

"Something's wrong," Anthea said to Bartleby that night. It was getting late. Matron and Myron were already in bed, utterly worn out from the day. Anthea felt her worries prick at her skin, like needles.

"There are many things that are wrong," Bartleby said. "Too many to list. Which thing are you referring to?"

"Cass," Anthea said.

Bartleby frowned. "What do you mean, *Cass*?" He shook his head. "Cass is perfect."

"*Obviously*," Anthea said, starting to seethe. Bartleby could get under her skin more than anyone else. She forced herself to calm down. "But I'm worried anyway. She was crying the other day. In the pantry."

Bartleby swayed from side to side. The toddlers had both fallen asleep in their carriers. He patted Lily's head. "She probably just had a stomachache."

"I don't think so." Anthea went on to explain the other things. How Cass had started giving away her possessions. How Anthea had seen her in the middle of the night, sitting by the window and pressing her hands to the glass.

Bartleby waved these concerns away. "Cass is just generous," he said, walking to the dormitory to put the toddlers to bed. "And sometimes *you* sit by the windows in the middle of the night. Should I be worried about you?"

"No," Anthea said quickly. Then she shrugged. "Maybe. Maybe we all need to be a little bit more worried about one another." She looked out the window. It was fully dark. The leaves were dry and rustled in the wind. Soon they would all fall to the ground. Soon she would be fourteen. *Tick, tock.* She shivered. She wrapped her arms around the whole of herself and pulled in tight. "I'm worried about Matron and Myron right now." She remembered being called *your kind.* She remembered the swirl of activity and her face hitting the ground. Unconsciously, her tongue found the chip in her tooth. It was still sharp. She hadn't realized she was on the verge of tears, but the tears surged and fell all the same. She wiped her face with the sleeve of her dress as Bartleby put his arms around her and hugged her.

"I'm worried about everyone, too," Bartleby said. "Literally everyone. But I'm not worried about Cass. Cass is Cass. And Cass is forever. That is the only thing I will ever know for sure. It is my primary philosophy."

Downstairs, Cass sat in the window seat of the living room, darning socks. She was very good at it. There is an art to darning socks. It doesn't do to simply sew the edges of the hole together in a rigid seam, because it will render the sock uncomfortable and unusable from that day forward—it will always feel as though there is a stick inside the sock, which is a terrible way to walk through the world. No, a foundation must be laid, so that the remedy may be carefully woven in. The darning itself must be soft, compliant, and easy on the feet: a person's heel must not know that a hole was ever there.

Cass darned the socks while rocking the babies in their small cradles with her toes. The babies snored. The candle flickered. The wind whispered outside. There was no better place than the Orphan House. And no better family. But hopefully, she would leave enough of a foundation to make sure the thing stayed strong, and the mending held. Hopefully, she had been helpful enough and had planned carefully enough for the remedy to be woven seamlessly in, with no discomfort or fraying to show where a gap had been.

Earlier that evening, as bedtime approached, Cass had hugged every one of the orphans and kissed their cheeks. And then she had hugged Matron and kissed her tenderly, and hugged and kissed Myron as well. She had turned and walked out into the alcove and on to the kitchen. "Don't worry," Cass had said, very, very quietly. "Tomorrow morning, things will be better. I promise."

Myron thought Matron had said this.

Matron thought it was Myron.

Even when Cass spoke, her presence was quiet. And gentle. It didn't matter, she knew, who had said the words. It only mattered that they were true.

The next morning, the orphans stumbled into the kitchen. They milked the goats and gathered eggs and spread out a fresh cloth for the table. They worked together to haul in a new box of vegetables. They helped to dish out the porridge. They filled a bowl with raspberries and plucked a blooming lily for the table.

It wasn't until everyone sat down and grasped one another's hands to bow their heads in gratitude that they realized that Cass was not with them.

They got up, the whole family. No one spoke. Everyone realized that no one spoke, and the *wrongness* of the silence felt like its own kind of dread. They checked the henhouse and the shed and the cellar in silence. They peeked in the attic in silence. They looked under blankets and tables.

It was no use.

Cass was gone.

22

Again, the Dragon

Listen.

I still don't like talking about that dragon. But there is something else you should know.

Once upon a time, there was a dragon who angered his fellow dragons.

Dragons had been using the magic-infused skins (from animals who had lived full lives, both short and long, and had died naturally—as all dragons would be *very* quick to point out) for centuries. Millennia, really. Through their time in the skins of other creatures, entire generations of large and mighty dragons had learned what it could feel like to be as cunning and nimble as a small rabbit. As delicate as a cricket. As tender as a mother fox to her newborn kits. The skins were treated as holy objects—the Blessed Skins, dragons called them. Because of the skins, a dragon could experience the world through the eyes of an antelope, or a whale, or an arctic tern, or a jellyfish. They learned what it can mean to be vulnerable, like a butterfly resting for a moment on the face of a flower during an impossibly long journey. They learned what it felt like to be forgotten, like a rabbit trapped in a doomed warren after the farmer blocks every exit. They learned what it felt like to live on the margins, like a mouse hunting for scraps and dodging traps on a kitchen floor. By shedding themselves of their inborn size and strength, they discovered the tremendous value of understanding and connection. These were remarkable experiences for dragonkind, and they tried to use their wisdom in service toward others, for the good of all creatures.

Well, most of them did.

One dragon did not take with him the same lessons that his brothers and sisters had. Instead, he used the skins to swindle others. Or harm others. Sometimes, he did this simply for the challenge and to delight his own vices. For example, he once put on the skin of a humpback whale and used his honeyed tongue to convince other whales to beach themselves on a sandbar, where they perished, the whole pod. Just to see if he could. Another time, he made himself king of a colony of rats, and convinced his subjects to sneak into bedrooms and lockboxes and come back with coins or rings or diamond bracelets. These he collected in a brand-new lair, where he grew sleek and indolent on the work of his subjects, the most dragonish rat that ever was.

Across the globe, whenever he was caught using one of the Blessed Skins for a selfish or duplicitous purpose, the Dragon would be chastised by his dragon relatives, and punished with stern words and exasperated expressions. They hoped he had learned his lesson. They hoped their sincere disappointment would help to curb his outlandish ways. They hoped that the sheer power of their own good example would teach him to seek truth and understanding, rather than chaos and self-dealing.

But the Dragon did *not* change his ways. The Dragon did *not* learn from anyone's example. The Dragon was just getting started. He wore a dog's skin and took control of a leaderless pack, where he taught them the arts of thieving, scheming, and villainry—and violence, too.

He wore a carrier pigeon's skin and delighted in altering the text of the messages moving between nations, and manipulated hard feelings among soldiers in the field, enough to start a civil war. The Dragon loved wars. It made plundering so much easier.

He would stay in the skins for far longer than was normal— usually a dragon would regularly shed the Blessed Skin on the day before the new moon and return to their dragon-ness so as to replenish their magic and power from the sun and the moon's shadow under the wide sky. If they had more to learn, they would return to the skin; otherwise, they moved on to something else. This dragon, on the other hand, made it his habit to stay in the skins for months, or even years sometimes, milking his situation for all it was worth, depleting his dragon strength all the while. He found it a useful trick to slip away when he had shrunk and shriveled to a fraction of his size. He would slither out of the skin, wriggling into the shadows, unseen and unnoticed, and retreat to his beloved lair to replenish his magic and power at his convenience. Even his wickedness was lazy.

Misuse of any animal skin was a grave offense. A sacrilege, some dragons said. Multiple misuses was an abomination. So a Council was called, and wise dragons from around the world assembled to discuss the case. The Council confirmed that the duplicitous way in which the Dragon had used the Blessed Skins was a disgrace to the memory of the First Antelope.

"We find him guilty," the Council proclaimed. Some dragons wept when they heard the verdict read. They had never imagined they would see such a day.

The Council announced that this dragon was to be cast out of the fellowship forever. The Dragon listened to his sentence and merely shrugged. He was not, generally speaking, a *fellowship* sort of a person. But then they announced that the Dragon's lair would be confiscated and its contents distributed to needy creatures around the world. This would be a terrible blow for any dragon, one that strikes at the heart, for dragons' lairs are precious to them. He did his best not to show his hurt, while inside he raged and wailed and gnashed his teeth.

"Where should I go?" the Dragon said. He yawned dramatically, pretending he couldn't care less, even as he trembled with indignation and sorrow. He thought of the pile of gold left behind in his lair. *His* pile. *His* gold. *Mine*, he thought. *How dare they!*

"We do not care where you go," the Council said. "You can go to the mountains and cavort with ogres for all we care." Dragons, I'm sorry to say, carry a terrible prejudice against ogres and consider them to be "low" creatures, and not worthy of skin-wearing. It was and is an unfair characterization. In truth, dragons had never worn an ogre skin simply due to the inconvenience of obtaining one from among creatures who lived for thousands of years. When an ogre does die, its body is set out on a mountaintop at night. The ogre's corpse remains in the sun for a full day and then transforms into stone at the moment of the rising of the moon. Very few people have witnessed this.

(Listen. I have, obviously. But I'm a special case. And my experience is beside the point.)

Since no dragon ever had the opportunity to wear the skin of an ogre, dragons never learned to empathize with ogres. It was easier to think little of them—or even better, to think of them as little as possible—than to acknowledge the dragons' own limitations. Even wise creatures can be a bit . . . fuzzy about their own areas of ignorance.

The Dragon sighed dramatically. "*Ogres*," he said with great distaste. "*Really?*"

"By the Antelope, you shan't stay here!" the Council decreed.

So the Dragon wandered the mountains for more than a century, hunting when he felt like it, and lazily looking for a dry cave or an abandoned fortress to build a new lair. Nothing that would require too much effort, you understand.

One day, when he thought he would never again have a pile of gold to luxuriate upon and think his most dragonish thoughts, the Dragon chanced upon something unexpected.

He found a dead ogre.

The sun was high, and the sky was a startling blue. The ogre's corpse had been laid out on a hilltop covered from end to end with wildflowers. It was a beautiful resting place. Not that the Dragon cared. According to ogre custom, the body had been lovingly cleaned with fine-smelling oils and dressed in the ogre's best clothes. It lay on a bed of smooth, round stones. Flowers rested on each of the ogre's eyes, with a third blossom in the center of his mouth. Gold coins were heaped in his open palms.

"*Gold!*" the Dragon exclaimed. And he took all of it. He also ate the flowers. Dragons don't particularly care for flowers, but he figured, *Why should that dead ogre have something that I cannot?*

The ogre was dressed beautifully—in fine silks and gold brocades and silver jewelry. He had a diamond ring on each hand. He had golden buckles on his shoes.

The Dragon's eyes glittered at the gold rings in the ogre's earlobes, and the diamonds on his fingers. So many riches, and for what? He mused, *If ogres care so little for their gold that they cast it away on the bodies of their dead, just think how much more gold they must have in their village.*

The very thought made the Dragon dizzy.

And though he still believed that ogres were low creatures, that certainly didn't mean they weren't worthy of swindle. Gold is gold, after all. But something else tugged at his heart. It wasn't only the gold that called to him. It was the *game* of it, the *trick*. His paws tingled at the very thought. For to trick another creature—to give them a version of the world that was upside down and inside out and to then let it all come crashing down with delightful chaos—well, that was power indeed. Delicious power.

And the Dragon was hungry for it.

The sun began to sink lower in the sky. The ogre would be stone soon. If the Dragon was going to do it, he'd better do it. And so he did. By the time the sun had disappeared, the Dragon had taken the dead ogre's skin, imbued it with the proper amount of magic, and put it on. He whistled as he walked down the footpath to the ogre village. He practiced his most glittering smile.

Silly ogres, he thought. *Won't this be fun?*

The rest of this story, you've probably already guessed. In the guise of an ogre, the Dragon convinced the community that his death was a false alarm and his recovery was complete. He saw the ogres' joy at seeing one of their own returned to them, and saw their care for their once-lost friend, and used them to his advantage. He turned joy and care and compassion into weapons. He turned the ogres against one another. He made them stop trusting one another. He swindled them out of their livelihoods and then convinced them to blame one another for their suddenly altered fortunes. The more unhappy the villagers were with one another, the more he laughed and enjoyed himself.

When the ogres finally discovered his ruse, he behaved exactly as you might expect. He stepped out of his ogre skin, revealed his dragon-ness, and unleashed his magic and rage. He hadn't been living in the ogre village for very long. His magic had been depleted, but not by much. Even in this state, he was still a very powerful dragon. And dangerous. The entire village was lost in a torrent of explosive fire—each home burned, each building leveled, each orchard and each farm scorched and salted. Nothing could be saved. It would be years before anything grew on that land again. There was no choice but to leave. The ogres sadly bid one another farewell and set out into the world alone.

The Dragon watched the smoke rise from the ruins of the ogre village from a vantage point on a mountain peak some miles away. He had learned quite a bit from this experience. He did not bring his misbegotten treasure with him. Too heavy. And he was a lazy dragon. He carried only a single token from his time with the ogres—a pair of golden buckles to attach to his next pair of boots. He set out in search of another opportunity.

"Well," he said to himself. "That was terribly fun."

He smiled as he lumbered down the mountain.

"Let's do it again."

23

The Unexpected Unpleasantness of Running Away

Cass wasn't a bad child. She didn't want to cause anyone any pain. She was just good at math. One less mouth to feed meant more for everyone else. And Cass loved Anthea. The family needed Anthea. Cass could remove herself, she could take Anthea's place outside the gate, and then everything would be okay.

That night, after she had changed into her nightclothes, she folded her wool trousers and her one warm sweater neatly and stashed them under her pillow, and then waited until the whole house slept. The wind blew outside. The dry leaves whispered. Lily murmured in her sleep. Justina giggled at something in a dream. Bartleby threw his arm over his face and snored. Cass felt her heart tighten as though it were caught in a vise.

She slid into her warm clothes. She had saved her baked potato from dinner to quell her hunger come morning, wrapping it in paper and carefully putting it in her jacket pocket. It was still there, cold now, when she put the jacket on. She closed her eyes to steady herself, and then she tiptoed out of the dormitory, down the stairs, and through the kitchen. She shimmied out the window and into the yard. The moon was hidden by clouds and the wind packed a dull chill. Autumn had certainly arrived. Cass put on her hat and mittens and scarf (all made by Anthea). She stopped to bid farewell to the chickens (who didn't notice) and to kiss the goats (who did) on the way to collect her packed rucksack from the shed, where she had stashed it.

Once she had slung her bag across her shoulders, she paused for a moment to look at the Orphan House as it rested in shadow. The Orphan House was *good*, she reminded herself. And all who lived there were *good*. This was the right thing to do.

Behind the garden, raspberry bushes hid a gap at the bottom of the wall. It wasn't large. Cass already knew that she would fit through it—she had, unbeknownst to anyone else, snuck out from time to time. Not for very long, and she never went very far. But just to enjoy the sensation of being alone.

One of the goats bleated mournfully. Cass didn't look back. She shoved her bag through the gap with the heel of her boot and slid in after it. She stood in the center of the empty street. And then Cass started walking. Away from the Orphan House. She wrapped her arms around her middle, curling her fingers around each strap of her rucksack. She turned the corner. And just like that, the Orphan House was out of view, and Cass was alone in the dark.

It didn't take long for Cass to realize that maybe her plan wasn't as complete as she had earlier thought. She didn't know where she would spend the night. It was cold, and the air was starting to smell like rain. She would need shelter soon. The sound of her footsteps grew louder and more lonesome. The crows called to one another from far away at the edge of town. They had always sounded friendly to her before, but in the dark, when she was all alone, they sounded sinister. Cass started running.

Eventually, she made her way to the old creek bed. The abandoned mill, with its small donkey enclosure, stood nearby. Once upon a time, the creek had fed a little pond. Sometime after the fire, the creek had stopped flowing evenly. Now it was dry for half the year and a raging flood the other half, so the miller had left with his donkey for a more prosperous town with a more reliable water supply.

The old donkey enclosure didn't have much to offer—no hay, no old blankets to spread on the damp floor, no door that closed—but it did have a corner with a mostly intact roof. Cass had just entered it when the sky opened up and a cold rain began to fall. Cass curled into the corner with her thin, scratchy blanket wrapped around her shoulders and knees. She had several maps tucked into her bag. She was pretty sure she understood them. She also had packed a couple of candles and the small tinderbox that Matron didn't use very often.

She lit a candle and studied a map. Tomorrow, she would take alleys and back roads to travel to the far end of town, past the Ogress's house. She would take the trails through the forest, in case her family was looking for her. She'd cross the river at the stone crossing (surely the map was still correct) and then would join up with the main road next to the fen. And then there were other towns. She would find a job. She wasn't exactly sure how to do that, but she hoped it would be obvious when the time came. She was useful. She liked being useful.

The rain fell. The chill deepened. Even the crows stopped

calling. All alone, Cass shivered. She tried to sleep, but she couldn't. She rested her chin on her knees and waited for morning to come.

The next morning, as the light shifted from dark to dim to gray, Cass emerged from the donkey enclosure. Her legs ached and her back ached. She was shivering all the way to her bones, but her cheeks felt hot. She pulled the cold potato from her pocket but was strangely unhungry. No matter, she decided; she would save it for later. She headed down the footpath, a map clutched between her chest and her upper arm, keeping to the shadows and the lesser-used walkways and largely staying out of sight.

As it turned out, reading a map was one thing, but actually *following* it in real space was something else altogether. She traced the footpath as it snaked past decrepit buildings and abandoned farms. She reached the edge of town, where the trees still grew—sycamores, mostly, creaking in the wind. She saw the crooked house where people said the Ogress lived. She heard sheep baaing and crows cawing, and saw a pleasant curl of smoke rising from the chimney. She followed the river that kissed the corner of the Ogress's farm to the edge of the woods. She looked at the map again. The map showed a footpath through the forest, as straight as an arrow, which would bring her to the other side and eventually meet with the main road. What she saw before her was something else entirely: a curtain of green, and an absence of light, and a tangle of trails that intersected or wandered off or simply petered out into the undergrowth.

Cass felt dizzy. Her bones shivered. Her cheeks were hot. She was hungry . . . but not. The ground under her feet seemed to sway. She set her chin forward and began walking anyway and very quickly became turned around, discombobulated, and utterly lost. Branches moved like dancing girls, and vines moved like snakes. She looked at her map. It was useless. She looked up, hoping to get a sense of direction from the sky, but the roof of the forest obscured her view.

Cass kept going.

Hours went by.

Night fell.

She heard the hooting of an owl. She heard the calling of crows. She covered herself with her blanket and covered her blanket with the branches of a tree and shivered until morning. For another night she did not sleep.

The next morning, Cass was still in the woods. Still lost. She ate her potato, finally, but retched it up immediately. It must have gone bad. The world swam. Her mouth was dry. She would need to find a stream soon, but she had no idea how. She gathered mushrooms and berries and realized she didn't know which were poisonous and which were safe, and she found that it was much harder than she had thought to crack open the nuts that she had harvested from a tree. She looked at her map. It swam in her vision. Surely, she should have gotten out of this forest hours ago. Or even yesterday. Surely, she would have found a warm, dry barn to sleep in, one owned by a cheerful and accommodating farmer, whose smiling wife brought breakfast over on a tray, which is what happens all the time in books. She had no idea that books would betray her in this way. Or maps. The nerve.

Night fell again. Cass pressed her back against the trunk of a tree and stared into the darkness, waiting for the light to return. The next morning, she kept walking even as she stumbled. She kept walking even as she shivered in her muscles and bones, and her skin seemed to boil. The rain returned—not hard, but cold. And her belly was empty, and she was still in the thickest part of the forest, and she had no clue where to go next.

The darkness deepened, and the world seemed to spin. Cass fell to her knees and curled herself under a tree. She shivered. Her body hurt. She couldn't warm up, even as her skin felt as though it were blistering.

The moon rose, and with it came a thin, pale light. A crow perched on a nearby tree. It tilted its head. It regarded Cass with one bright black eye.

The world kept spinning. Cass had a hard time staying awake. She looked at the crow. It moved in and out of her vision. She wasn't entirely certain it was real. She was not as conversant as Anthea was in Crow—none of the other orphans was—but she could hold her own.

"Caw," Cass said, which roughly translated to "It was the right thing to do, and I don't regret it."

"Caw," she added. "I love them more than I love myself, and that's the way it is."

The crow didn't say anything. It hopped from branch to branch. It hopped onto the moss next to Cass and nestled close, making little murmuring noises as it did so. Cass had never seen a crow up close, and really had no idea what to expect in terms of crow behavior. But she certainly wasn't expecting *this*. She put her arms around the crow. The sudden closeness when she was feeling so wretched was a balm on her heart. Within moments, Cass fell into a feverish sleep.

That night, she dreamed she was suspended in a sky full of crows and flying away.

Things Get Slightly Worse

The cobbler had only just begun opening his shop for the day when he heard the sound of screaming. He stood and ran to the window and saw an old woman racing from the gates of the Orphan House directly toward his shop. He threw open the door.

"Why, Matron!" he cried. His hands were covered with beeswax and tallow. He did his best to wipe them off on his wool trousers, taking care not to cut himself on any of the tools in his many clever pockets. "Whatever is the matter? How can I help?" He ran outside.

The old woman called out a series of unintelligible words that were drowned in her overwhelming sobs. Somewhere in there, he could make out "She's gone!" and "Someone took her!" Everything else, he did not know.

He turned back toward the open door of his shop, cupped his hands around his mouth, and called as loud as he could, "My darling wife! Come quick!" The cobbler's wife was a sensible woman. Surely, she would know what to do. The cobbler reached Matron and embraced her in the street. The old woman collapsed in his arms, sobbing deeply, which nearly broke the cobbler's heart in half. He knew Matron well—he had lived in the Orphan House himself as a child, when his father had left the region to go look for work after his mother had died in childbirth. His time at the Orphan House was brief—only a couple of months. Both Matron and Myron were a young couple back then, filled with light and life and kindness. It was a terrible time in the cobbler's life, a time of heartbreak and sorrow—and yet he remembered the house with a tender fondness, as a place of love and care in the face of loss. He had tried to show the same care for others, ever since. He kept one arm curled around Matron's back as he led her into his shop and sat her down on a chair.

The cobbler's wife bustled in carrying a pot of tea and a blanket. "There, there," she tutted as she wrapped the blanket around Matron's shoulders. The cobbler pulled up two stools, and he and his wife sat, he with his hand on Matron's shoulder and she with her hands on the old woman's knees. "Just take a minute and let the tea do its work," the cobbler's wife said. "What is it that happened, my dear woman, and how can we help?"

They watched her hands shake as she brought the cup to her lips, and waited for her to speak.

"Our Cassandra," Matron managed, the words sticking in her throat. "She's been taken." Great tears rolled down her face, following the deep grooves around her eyes and cheeks. "We realized at breakfast. Sometime during the night, she was snatched from her bed. Without a trace." She put down the cup. "You must help us, Arthur," she said to the cobbler. "You must help us to find our baby."

The cobbler frowned. He knew the tenderness and warmth of the Orphan House very well. In his youth, he himself had not wanted to leave, and had to be persuaded to do so. There was no chance any child would leave willingly. He turned to the window, his face grim. "There has been over the years an unkindness growing in this town that did not exist when I was a child. Even still, this is a shocking crime. Who could have done such a thing? What sort of . . . creature . . . is capable?" His eyes narrowed.

"There could be several explanations," the cobbler's wife said, her voice brisk and pragmatic. "It doesn't do to jump to wild speculations. Fear won't find the child, but cool heads and keen eyes will."

The cobbler stood. "There's no time to waste. I'll go straight to the Mayor. He'll know what to do. This wickedness must be addressed." He went to the hooks and retrieved his hat and jacket.

His wife threw up her hands in exasperation. "What wickedness? We don't even know what happened. Only a fool rushes to conclusions without understanding the facts." She turned to Matron. "Don't let him worry you. We will find her safe and sound—you'll see. Despite what you might think, there is kindness everywhere in this town. More than people realize. Perhaps someone is already looking after her. Perhaps she sleepwalks. Perhaps something frightened her, and she's hiding. Perhaps she is playing a *very* naughty joke. Perhaps she got it in her head to run away—orphans sometimes do that sort of thing, I hear."

The air went suddenly cold. The cobbler gasped. Matron dropped her cup, splashing her tea onto the ground. Both turned very red and glared at the cobbler's wife. An uncomfortable silence fell hard in the center of the room.

The cobbler's wife flushed scarlet. She hadn't realized she was being rude. "I mean . . ."

The cobbler held up his hand and shook his head. He turned instead to the old woman in the chair. "Do not fear, my dear Matron. I'll get to the bottom of it." He gave his wife a hard look and rushed out the door.

On his way to the Mayor's mansion, he stopped at the constable's. The constabulary had burned down years ago, like so many other buildings. So ever since, whoever held the job of constable simply operated out of their house. The current constable had converted her old barn out back into a stockade for people to spend a night or two cooling off when necessary. The functions of the office all happened in a tent she set up in the front yard. It had been repaired so many times that it was now a mishmash of shapes and colors and textures—a faded, multicolored lump. The constable wore a silver star, which was how people knew she was the constable.

"Good morning, Arthur," she said as the cobbler rushed in.

"Constable, come with me, if you please, to the Mayor's. There has been a kidnapping." He explained the story, exactly as Matron had said. The constable leaned back on her chair and gave the cobbler a skeptical expression.

"Well," she said. "That is quite a story. Are you sure it's accurate? There are so many bad things happening in Stone-in-the-Glen. Every single day. Who can keep up? I can't go running after wild tales that might not even be true."

The cobbler felt his cheeks flush. "What on earth do you mean? The child is missing!"

The constable folded her arms across her chest. "But is she? Can we really trust the testimony of a very old woman who may or may not have all of her faculties intact? How is her eyesight? Can she see into the corners? Has she actually counted all the children? Does she even know how to count? So much illiteracy these days!"

"What kind of question is that?" the cobbler said indignantly. He took a step backward. "Of course she can count!"

The constable shrugged. "No need to get sore at me," she said. "I'm just asking questions. Nothing wrong with questions. So many people lie these days. Is it possible the matron is lying?"

"It is *not*," the cobbler nearly shouted.

"Well, does her arthritis even allow her to bend down so far as to check under the tables and chairs? My guess is no. This is the constable's office, my good man! We require evidence. We don't just upend the tranquility of this town on mere speculation." She let that sink in. She glared at the cobbler. "Come back with evidence, and then we can talk."

Grunting in frustration, the cobbler took his leave.

He stopped at the blacksmith's, who could barely hear him over the roar of the forge. After several tries, the blacksmith frowned. "Didn't one of the orphans violently attack a man at the last Market Day?" the blacksmith said. "I'm not sure they represent the most desirable element in this town."

"What?" the cobbler said. "What on earth are you talking about? This is a *child*. Who may have been *kidnapped*. In *our town*. I have no doubt that the Mayor will want to be involved.

I think we need to form a delegation. Create a plan for the whole community."

The blacksmith shook his head. "Have you talked to the constable yet? I'm not sure I like the idea of lawless orphans running about and causing mischief."

The cobbler left in disgust. He stopped to see his friend the butcher, who was kneeling in front of his shop, replacing a section of missing stones. All morning, the butcher had been hauling, shaping, and replacing rocks. Sweat dripped from his brow and soaked his shirt. He grimaced as he worked.

"Greetings, friend," the cobbler said. "I have upsetting news."

The butcher unfolded his body from the ground, his joints creaking loudly. He pressed his fists into his back, deep into the muscle. He was red-faced, and he winced as the cobbler told him the story.

"So what do you want me to do about it?" the butcher asked crossly.

"Well, I'm off to the Mayor right now," the cobbler said. "He needs to be apprised of the situation. But more importantly, we need to create a delegation, organize a community response and a search team to find the child." His resolve started to dwindle as he noticed the expression on his friend's face.

The butcher took a handkerchief from his back pocket and wiped his brow before blowing his nose. He shrugged. "I mean," he said slowly, "I guess."

"My friend," the cobbler said incredulously, "a child is missing. A *child*. We must all take action!"

The butcher cupped his hand over his mouth. Finally, he said, "Well, certainly. But . . ." He shrugged again. "I mean to say, there are so many children in that house. Too many. Is one less that much of a concern? Perhaps the child left of her own accord."

The cobbler had never heard anything so insulting in his whole life. He left without another word.

He spoke to the miller and the undertaker, the grocer and the seamstress. All agreed that it was terrible that a child was missing. But . . .

"Maybe it's for the best," the miller said.

"There's kind of too many people in this town as it is," the undertaker said.

"I heard orphans sometimes steal things," the grocer said. "I better not catch her here."

The seamstress, at least, showed real concern. "I'm a bit overwhelmed at present, my friend," she said. "But tell me what the Mayor says. And let me know what I can do to help. I lived in the Orphan House, too, for just a little while when I was a child. I know exactly what you mean. I didn't want to leave it, either." Her eyes shone behind her spectacles. "Poor Matron. Poor Myron. They're probably both worried to death. Let me finish these tasks, and I'll help with whatever you need."

With that small showing of support, the cobbler's spirits were buoyed a bit as he made his way to the Mayor's mansion. He knocked on the door, which was very hot, as though it had been sitting in the sun, even though the day was cloudy and cool. The cobbler shook his hand. His fingers were quite red, as though burned.

"Patience," came the sonorous voice of the Mayor from inside. The cobbler felt the voice everywhere—in his feet, on his skin, even in his hair. There was a great sound of rattling and shuffling inside—a tinkling, jangling cacophony of chimes, followed by the sound of something heavy moving across the floor.

The door opened, just a crack. The chain lock was pulled tight—it was shiny and polished, and gleamed as though it were made of gold. The Mayor's face appeared, shining in the gap. The cobbler had to squint. "If it isn't my favorite cobbler!" the Mayor said, smiling broadly, though he didn't pull the door open wider. "Thank you so much for stopping by!" And with that, he closed the door.

The cobbler assumed that the Mayor was simply organizing himself and would be coming out presently. He put his hands in his pockets as he stood on the porch. He rocked back on his heels. The streets were quiet. No children played and no dogs barked. A single thrush sang in a nearby shrub, but other than that, the town was silent. Even the cats, stalking back and forth at the edge of the yard, were silent.

The cobbler knocked again. Something heavy moved across the floor inside. The door opened just a crack, the chain lock still pulled tight. The Mayor's face, still filled with light, appeared in the gap. "Well!" he said brightly. "If it isn't my favorite cobbler!" He didn't pull the door any wider. He simply grinned through the crack.

"Sir," the cobbler began.

"Well!" The Mayor winked. "Thanks for coming by!"

But the cobbler was ready. He put his boot between the door and the jamb. The cobbler was very good at his job. He had made his boots himself, and they were sturdy and solid. Despite the force with which the Mayor tried to close the door, the cobbler's boot held.

The Mayor frowned.

"Listen," the cobbler explained, speaking quickly. "It's the Orphan House. A child has gone missing."

The Mayor pressed his lips together in concern. "There are so many children in the Orphan House," he said sadly, shaking his head. "Too many."

"That, sir, is beside the point," the cobbler said. "It is my belief, and the belief of the venerable matron of the Orphan House, that the child has been taken. If this is true, it is a serious and terrible crime, and concerns us all. I would like to organize a search party to look for her, and I would like official support in that effort."

The Mayor's frown deepened. "That is a powerful statement, my friend. Do you have any evidence as to who might have done this thing?"

The cobbler shook his head. He glanced west. There were crows massing in the far-off trees. "No evidence, sir. Just a feeling."

The Mayor smoothed his hand over his face. "Feelings are funny things. They feel like facts. Sometimes, it is nice to think that they might be facts. If I could transform my feelings into gold coins, I would stack them on my desk and call myself the richest man in the world." The Mayor trembled, just a bit.

They stood in silence for a long moment. The Mayor's wristwatch *tick, tick, tick*ed. The intricate dragon curled its way across the numbers, a little marvel of gears and know-how. Seeing the watch made the cobbler feel better. *Our mayor defeated a dragon. Isn't that marvelous!* It was dizzying, really. His eyes shone at the thought. Surely the Mayor would solve all of their problems. Even when it was difficult to remember what those problems were. It was difficult to think clearly in the face of all that shine. It was difficult to make connections in all that light. What even *were* problems anyway? the cobbler found himself wondering. What could they possibly find to complain about when they had so marvelous a mayor? The cobbler swayed back and forth, a half smile curling over his lips.

The Mayor inclined his chin indulgently. "My dear man," he said, "this conversation has helped me so much more than you know. Isn't it wonderful, really, the way we come together? As a town. Really, you must be feeling better already."

The Mayor had a *wonderful* voice. It made the small hairs on the cobbler's arm stand on end. He could feel it rumbling in his feet. Even the word *wonderful* seemed to take on new resonance. It was an intoxicating word. *Wonderful, wonderful, wonderful.* What a *wonderful* mayor! What a lucky town!

"Now that you mention it," the cobbler said slowly. "I rather *do* feel a bit better." He shook his head. *Wonderful*, he thought hazily, like it was the only word in the world. It was a big thought, the wonderfulness of the Mayor. It took up so much space in the cobbler's mind that there was hardly any room for anything else.

He shook his head.

Wasn't there something else?

The Mayor started to close the door. The cobbler remembered with a start. He blocked the door with his boot. "The child, sir!" the cobbler gasped, reaching for the thought as though it had fallen down a deep well.

The Mayor heaved a petulant sigh. "It is my fondest wish that the greatness of Stone-in-the-Glen can one day assert itself. Are there interlopers and saboteurs, thieves and miscreants, wandering our streets as we speak? Alas, yes. Do you not need a glorious mayor to keep them all in check? Of course you do. Is there a missing child? Well, you seem like an honest man and declare it to be so, which means I suppose I must believe it. Do you need your mayor to rid this town of its slinkers and snatchers, its backstabbers and swindlers and plunderers? Do you look to me, and me alone, to solve this? Why, yes, you do." The Mayor paused for a long time. "I'll tell you what, my dear fellow. In two days' time, I shall give a speech to the people of Stone-in-the-Glen. To raise their spirits. To show leadership. To bind us all together. You must lift your eyes to the heavens and gaze upon your glorious mayor, and all shall be well!"

The cobbler frowned. The Mayor set his head spinning. Finally, he fixed his thoughts on the image of Matron weeping in his shop, just this very morning. "A fine idea, of course," he said slowly. The cobbler blinked. It was difficult to think straight. "Another thought, though, sir, is that we organize a search party. And actually find her."

"Find who?" the Mayor said.

"The child, sir," the cobbler said. This was exhausting. He needed to sit down. He needed a good long rest.

"Ah, yes. Children. Dear, dear children. How we adore them all! How we insist on their being well behaved and silent at all times. An obedient child is a happy child, I always say!" The Mayor began to close the door. Very slowly. The cobbler didn't notice. Behind him the cats hissed. They yowled. They didn't come near the house.

"Well, then," the cobbler said. He rubbed his face. This was confusing. "I'll just . . . keep looking? I guess. Oh! And a search party. I will organize a search party. Do I have your permission to engage the constable?"

"We have a constable?" the Mayor said, slightly bemused. "Well, how droll. Just like a real little town. Fine, fine. Engage away."

The cobbler frowned. There was too much light. His eyes hurt. Why wasn't there any shade? "Well, sir, I'll be sure to keep you informed if we learn anything."

The Mayor smiled. "Do, my friend. Do."

And with that, the Mayor shut the door.

An Unexpected Treasure in the Woods

There was a crow named Harold.

Harold was not his actual name, of course. Crows typically don't name themselves, as they really don't see the point. A crow already knows who he is. But the Ogress liked to give each crow a specific name, just for her own use, as a way of telling them apart and to shower them with compliments, which the crows appreciated. When this crow was just a chick, the Ogress decided to call him Harold. Everything that little nestling did, the Ogress thought, seemed layered with foresight and portent.

Harold would never admit it to the other crows, but he actually enjoyed being called Harold. The Ogress had told him it was a prophetic name. A name that is unafraid to speak the truth when the truth needs speaking. This thrilled Harold all the way to his bones. He felt his name suited him.

The crow who both was and was not named Harold loved his flock and he loved the Ogress, but he also loved wandering out on his own. The woods were broad and deep and filled with treasures. The trees held firm to the forest floor, winding their roots deep into the earth. Harold didn't speak the language of the trees, but they made their meaning clear. The trees were storytellers. And the forest was thick with tales. Harold couldn't hear them, but he could *feel* them.

One night, Harold had one of those flights that crows often dream of—he swooped and fluttered and soared. He noticed the way the starlight glittered on the blackness of his feathers. He delighted in the rush of wind over his beak. He loved his family, and he loved his ogress and his sheep and Dog, but when he flew alone, each glide and loop felt lighter, faster, and more alive. Even his talons seemed to glint. How wonderful it was, he thought, how very, very wonderful to be this very crow.

And then he saw something lying on the forest floor.

His first instinct was to panic. And he did, briefly—his feathers stood out from his body like tree trunks, and his vision compressed to the size of a pinprick. *What if it was that Thing? That terrible, wrong Thing?* The Thing that once had frightened his whole crow family. They still never spoke of it. They still couldn't stop thinking about it. After all those years. He threw his wings wide and took a long curve at a steep angle and began to fly away.

But then he stopped.

What if the Thing truly was dangerous?

What if the Thing might follow him back and bring harm to the Ogress?

His name was Harold, after all. A brave name. Didn't he owe it to the Ogress who gave him that name to be brave and investigate? The truth of the matter sank in Harold's stomach like an overly large pebble, and nestled in his guts. He circled back, spiraled over the object on the forest floor, and landed at a safe distance, where he could get a better look. He held his breath.

It was not the Thing, Harold realized. It was a child. He hopped onto a closer branch. An *actual* child. He squinted. A *sleeping* child.

It was most unusual to see a child in the woods. He couldn't remember *ever* seeing one—or hearing reports of others seeing one. Certainly, not on its own, and *certainly* not in the dark. Human parents didn't allow that sort of thing. Harold moved closer. The child didn't stir. It was huddled on the ground, its legs pulled close to its chest, its head resting on its knees. He looked closer. The child seemed to be shaking.

Harold landed on the ground. Very cautiously, he hopped to the child. He murmured and clucked. The child opened its eyes with a start. Harold froze. The child didn't seem to notice Harold. Not at first. The child was quite pale. Even though it shivered, there was sweat on its brow. Harold moved even closer. The child blinked. Blinked again. The child met his eye.

They held each other's gaze for what seemed like a very long time.

And then she spoke. *In Crow.* He had never known of a human child who could speak in Crow.

Indeed, at first he thought he had imagined it. After all, the child was crying and coughing and didn't make a whole lot of sense. And her voice was as soft as the feathers of a newborn crow chick. Harold liked the sound of it right away.

"Caw," the child hiccuped. "I'm so sorry," it sobbed.

But what could the child possibly be sorry for? Harold wondered. It didn't seem the sort of person to throw rocks. And certainly, if it had wronged a crow, any time recently or long ago, he would have heard about it by now. Crows gossip, after all. And they have long memories.

"Caw." The child coughed again. "I didn't know what else to do." That didn't make sense, either. What was the child babbling about?

"Caw," Harold said. "There, there." And because he couldn't think of what else to do, Harold approached the child and nestled close. The child was warm. And comfortable. Harold nestled closer. He pressed the top of his head to the child's body, which is what his own crow mother used to do when he was a hatchling. The child put her arms around him, like a little nest. She lifted him up and held him close. He heard the beat of her heart and the swish of her breathing and the soft hiccuping sounds that she made. He liked the way she smelled. He made the soft gurgling coos that his crow mother and aunties used to sing to him when he was little, and soon the child was again asleep.

Harold found himself in a bit of a conundrum. Even though she was alone when he found her, it didn't feel right to leave her alone now. What if a fox came? Or a wolf? Or a swarm of angry bees? What if the Thing came back? He suddenly found himself anxiously imagining all manner of harms that might befall this sleeping creature holding him close. It felt nice, he noticed, cuddling close to this sleeping child. He wondered why he had never done anything like this before. She murmured in her sleep. She pulled him closer in her arms. Her breath smelled of celery and flowers, and warm bread cooling on a windowsill.

He liked her face. There were spots on her cheeks and a dimple in the center of her chin. Her skin was very different from the Ogress's—more like dense moss than rough stone. But warm. And not green. It was comforting to lean against.

He couldn't bear the thought of anything bad happening to this child. He needed to find someone. He needed to tell the Ogress. And the other crows. And perhaps the sheep. And maybe even Dog. Taking a moment to memorize the place where the child lay, Harold flew into the night.

When he arrived at the house, the crows and the Ogress and Dog and the sheep were ready to head into Stone-in-the-Glen and were not particularly keen to change their plans. Harold explained the situation, but the crows were skeptical. The night was slipping away. And the Ogress did not want to be out and about after the sun rose.

To make matters worse, the more Harold explained the seriousness of the child's plight, the more skeptical the other crows grew. "Caw. Children aren't allowed out by themselves in the forest at night," they chided. "Everyone knows that."

Harold shook his head. He described the child shivering on the ground. He described her tears. He spoke as bravely as he could, as bravely as one would expect of a crow named Harold. He spoke the truth.

The Ogress frowned. "Caw." she said, her voice faltering. "I'm not sure I understand."

Harold flapped his wings. After all this time, the Ogress's grasp of the Crow language was far from complete. Harold oscillated between wanting to praise her for her pronunciation and fervently trying to make her understand.

"Caw," she continued. She knitted her brow. "A lost some-one? A human? Very small?" she managed.

Harold nodded vehemently. "A child someone. All alone. And very sad."

"And cold," he added. "And coughing."

"Oh my goodness!" the Ogress breathed. She left her baked goods and her vegetables in her handcart, taking only her lantern. "Quickly, then!" she said, striding toward the forest. "Show me where she is. There is no time to lose."

Harold led the way, with the Ogress, Dog, the sheep, and the rest of the crows all following behind.

The child was just where Harold had left her, sleeping fitfully. Harold nearly collapsed with relief. The Ogress fell to her knees. She took a close look at the child. "I know you," she whispered, running her hand along the child's forehead, smoothing back her hair. "You are from that wonderful house. With the wonderful family. But what are you doing here?"

Harold alighted on the child's shoulder. "Caw," he said softly. "What should we do?"

The winds were picking up, and the temperature had dropped noticeably. It would be raining soon. Again. It always rained in the autumn. Heat seemed to pour off the child's body. The Ogress's face was grim. "I believe this child is sick with a fever. Who knows how long she's been wandering? We can't deliver tonight."

The Ogress paused, as though coming to a decision. "I will have to bring her to my house. She needs to be warm and fed. And out of the rain." The Ogress reached down and scooped the child into her arms, letting the child's head rest on her large, comfortable shoulders. The child stirred but did not wake. "Hush, now," the Ogress whispered. Her voice was as gentle as a breeze. "Hush now, and sleep."

The dog whined. The sheep baaed. The crows crowded and spun in the air, some alighting on nearby branches to get a closer look. They had never seen a child up close before. "Caw," the crows said. "Surely they don't all need to be carried."

"Caw," a few muttered, "Are you sure they don't bite?"

"Hush yourselves, you dolts!" Harold chided. "Children are marvelous!" The truth of it thrilled him to his bones. "Everyone should know this!" He gave a happy swoop in the air.

The Ogress didn't pay any attention. She just hummed as she carried the child back to the crooked little house. Keeping the child in one arm, she used her free hand to gather herbs from the garden into her basket, which she brought inside. The crows gathered on the windowsill and open door. They watched as the Ogress held the child in her rocking chair and fed her warm water with herbs and honey. They watched as she wiped the child's brow with a cool cloth. They watched as she sang to the child, low and sweet, a lullaby that the Ogress hadn't heard for hundreds of years, since her own ogre parents had once upon a time sung it to her. The child murmured and fussed. She rubbed her eyes. She coughed. And then, finally, she slept deeply in the arms of the Ogress.

Harold flew in. He landed on the Ogress's knee. He hopped onto the child's open hand. Onto her softly breathing middle. He nestled there, on the warmth of her jacket, and sighed as she curled her arm around his feathers. The Ogress sang, the child slept, and Harold understood, for the very first time, what it meant to be truly happy.

The Orphan House Was Never
Meant for This

The first day of Cass's disappearance, a sharp panic settled on the Orphan House.

Kye walked in circles in the kitchen, pinching himself, while Iggy sobbed under the couch. Fortunate and Gratitude checked the chicken coop no fewer than fifty times, while Hiram continually climbed onto the roof to see if Cass had somehow made her way up there in the meantime. "Just in case," he said in utter seriousness, leaving his crutches again on the ground. Anthea knew better, and eventually put him on door duty.

Matron had run out the door screaming and found the man who had all of the tools kept in those clever pockets, which Anthea thought was a sensible plan. Anthea implicitly trusted people who not only understood how tools worked but also devised useful places to keep them. Very quickly, however, Anthea began to suspect that perhaps her trust had been misplaced.

Matron returned, saying that this man, who Anthea learned

was the cobbler, had gone to the Mayor. Matron's face became light at the thought, even as her tears flowed.

"The Mayor?" Anthea said slowly. "Are you sure that's a good idea?"

"He defeated a dragon, you know," Matron said, blowing her nose. "Surely he will find our Cass. Indeed, perhaps he already has!"

The more Matron hoped, the more Anthea felt her heart sink. *We have to be practical*, she thought desperately. *Without logic, we are lost.*

The cobbler's wife rang the bell at the front gate midmorning, offering sympathy. Later, she came back with a vat of soup. An hour after *that*, she returned with bags of things the house might need—shoes and sweaters and mittens and day-old bread from the baker. Which was generous. But then the cobbler's wife *wouldn't leave*. She mentioned the thinness of the children. The chilliness and the draft. She lamented the lack of toys and wondered how on earth any of the children could be educated. She mentioned the disrepair of the furniture and the lack of insulation in the walls. She kept fussing over what she called "the state of things," which Anthea found rather rude. She tutted and exclaimed as she bustled from room to room.

Matron followed in her wake, wringing her hands, unable to finish a single sentence. "Thank you for your concern, Mrs.—"

"Oh, I insist that you call me Esmé. One cannot stand on ceremony at a time like this." She pulled out the measuring tape in her pocket and began measuring the twins. "These two are in dire need of warmer dresses, with winter coming soon. Does anyone have pencil and paper? I need to write this down." She scribbled numbers and started a list, first asking everyone to show her their shoes.

"We appreciate your—"

"And to think, you've been suffering deprivations all this time, and no one in town knew. What a disgrace!"

She checked the cupboards and added to her list. She noted with some alarm the sagging floorboards and the broken stair. She examined the larder and nearly fainted dead away. "This isn't enough!" she gasped. "This isn't nearly enough. These children are *growing*."

The children watched as she fluttered from room to room— a blur of alarm and activity.

"No," she muttered. "This will not do, this will not do."

"I think," Matron attempted, "what is needed is—"

"Volunteers?" Esmé, the cobbler's wife, said. "Yes. I heartily agree. I'll return with reinforcements as quick as I can." She hurried to the front door, readjusting her hat and shawl. "This town should be ashamed of itself," she said, looking up at the cracks on the ceiling, the bulge in the wall, the window patched with wood. "Absolutely ashamed. This problem must be solved, starting today. That is a promise." And with that, she left in a rush, her skirt fluttering in the wind. Anthea shut the door behind her.

"Does that mean she's coming back *again*?" Dierdre muttered.

"Can we change the locks?" Elijah said hopefully.

"I mean to say, her husband is out looking for the monster who stole our Cass," Matron said. "We will all do well to remember that."

Myron, pinned in place on the sofa, rested his head on his hands, while Matron couldn't sit still. She paced from the living room window to the kitchen window and back again. She opened the front door and went out. She paced the yard. She went back to the living room window. And back to the kitchen. Myron quietly wept. They asked themselves how they could have been so stupid as to let an evildoer into the house to steal a child.

Except that wasn't what had happened. Anthea was sure of it. Cass had given away her possessions. Cass had been acting strangely. Cass might have been saying goodbye. Anthea had even said that there was something wrong with Cass, but no one wanted to listen. She certainly couldn't say so now. And to make matters worse, *she had told Cass her fears about her birthday*. Anthea felt the weight of guilt and shame settle in the well of her belly.

Bartleby sat on the bottom stair, hunched over, holding his head, too miserable even to cry. The Littles sobbed in the corner, and the twins remained weirdly obsessed with the chicken coop. The only way to keep the house moving forward was if Anthea herself saw to it.

Anthea took out her ledger. She started making lists. *Step one*, she wrote. *Find Cass*. She glared at the paper. Perhaps there were other steps that needed to occur first. Perhaps she, too, wasn't thinking clearly. She needed to be logical. How could logic exist in the midst of so much panic?

Step two, she wrote. *The orphans save the day*. She wasn't sure how to accomplish that step, either. But Elijah had told her it was true, and it gave her some comfort to believe it.

Step three, she wrote. *Make sure everyone eats.* Well, *that* she could do. Perhaps it should be step one.

She saw to the babies, and changed their diapers, and put them in a carrier that she strapped to her back. She put Dierdre and Elijah in charge of the toddlers. She fed everyone the soup that the cobbler's wife had brought. It was delicious, she noted grudgingly. She checked on Bartleby. He hadn't moved from his spot on the bottom stair, his face still covered with his hands. She handed him a bowl of soup.

"Bartleby," she said, crouching down on her heels and resting her arms on her knees. Her eyes bored into Bartleby's, and she refused to look away. "You *have* to eat. We can't help one another unless we also care for ourselves. Eat. That's an order."

Bartleby wiped his nose with the back of his hand. He couldn't talk. A terrible sign. His body shook with swallowed sobs.

The cobbler returned later that afternoon with the seamstress, the butcher, the blacksmith, and the constable. "I spoke to the Mayor," the cobbler said slowly.

"Oh, thank heavens!" Matron said, throwing her hands in the air. "Has he found her already? What a wonderful mayor!"

"Well," the cobbler said, shoving his hands deep into his pockets. "No. Not exactly. But he intends to give a speech. In two days' time. He thinks that will help. Assuming we haven't found her first." He dropped his gaze to the ground, as though embarrassed.

Myron stared at them in a daze. "A . . . speech?" His face was slack and his expression hopeless. "Is that all?"

"Matron, may I say something?" Anthea ventured. But the cobbler cut her off.

"It is my hope that we will find her in the meantime. I have a search team. I'm hoping to recruit more people. But I tried to start searching with a team that has experience and know-how. Which is why I have the constable."

The constable wore canvas trousers and a wool coat with a silver star affixed to her lapel. Her hair hung in one long braid, and she wore a smart cap on her head. She gave a short bow to Matron. "Look. I find lost things all the time. Lost donkeys. Lost keys. Lost cats. Finding a child is no different." She ran her thumb across her silver star. "A constable's work is never done, but no matter! We will get her back in a jiffy."

Anthea stared, openmouthed. *Lost donkeys? Was she serious?*

The constable continued. "Was there anything, erm, *removed*, on the night in question? A door or windowpane or an entire wall or similar?"

Matron looked baffled. "Why, no," she said.

Of course not, Anthea thought. *Has everyone lost their minds?*

"Well," the constable said. She pulled out a folded piece of paper and began to scribble notes. "Was anything broken? Vases, chimneys, staircases, doorways, et cetera?"

Anthea rolled her eyes.

"No. Not at all," Matron said.

The constable wrote this down. "Well, had the child in question been acting strangely in the weeks leading up to the incident?"

Matron was about to reply, but Anthea interjected. "Yes. Yes, she had."

The constable turned to Matron. "Well?" she said, as though Anthea had not spoken.

Matron shook her head. "No. She was her regular self: helpful and kind and generous. Our Cass."

Anthea stomped her foot. "That's not right. She *was* acting strangely. She was crying at odd times, and she gave away her special possessions, and was making plans to . . ." Anthea began to cry. "I don't know what. But Cass had something in mind. She . . ." Her voice broke.

Matron took Anthea by the shoulders and guided her away. "Anthea, my love, you have experienced a terrible shock. Someone, or something, took your darling Cass away. Why don't you go and sit down next to Bartleby. There's a dear."

"But . . ." Anthea began.

"Now, dearest." Matron plunked Anthea down and went back to the adults. Anthea rested her head on the heels of her hands. This didn't make any sense. None of this made any sense. Anthea believed in facts. *Facts matter*, she told herself again and again and again. Still, she couldn't stop a creeping suspicion that maybe she was wrong. Maybe facts didn't matter, after all.

The constable continued to take notes. "Well," she said, "this whole thing was only a matter of time. We got ourselves an ogress—an actual ogress—living there at the far edge of town. Who on earth would allow such a thing? Dangerous situation, and haven't I always said so? To the Mayor and all. She might have him in her wiles, you know. Poor fellow. I've heard ogresses can do that sort of thing."

"*Wiles?*" Anthea snorted.

The constable didn't notice. "Anyhoo, we'll give the town a good look-see. Every abandoned building. Anyplace where a child might have wandered in and gotten stuck. We'll check all the wells. We shouldn't forget that old mill. And we'll search the forest. But we can't neglect that ogress's house. After all, the evidence is overwhelming."

"*What evidence?*" an exasperated Anthea howled.

"Bed," Matron said. "All children off to bed. Right now."

It wasn't even dark yet.

∞

The orphans went to bed that night all tangled together, except for the babies, who slept in their cradles. Bartleby still hadn't spoken. Anthea tucked him in, and Lily and Justina curled up, one on either side, and Kye wound around his feet. The rest of the children curled up, one after another, until they formed a large heap in the center of the room. The cats stalked in and found warm places to sleep in the crook of a knee or the hollow of an elbow, or right on someone's face. No one asked them to leave.

"You never know," Anthea said. "She could come back tonight."

Bartleby didn't respond. He just lay on his back, staring up at the ceiling. Anthea reached over and curled her hand into his, holding on tight.

"Look, everyone." Elijah said with a yawn. "You need to stop worrying so much. I already know how this story ends. The orphans save the day. I'm not exactly sure about the details. But I know we do."

One by one, the children fell asleep, until only Bartleby was left awake. He stared at the ceiling for a long time.

"But how?" Bartleby asked.

No one heard him.

The Return

Harold woke to the smell of baking. The Ogress had moved the child—and Harold, in the arms of the child—over to the cot in the corner. Harold blinked. The Ogress had her paints and papers set up on the table. And her rolls rising on the counter. And her pies cooling on the windowsill. The light poured in at the deep slant of late afternoon. Normally, the Ogress spent every spare moment looking through her periscope, gazing at the town she loved so much. Now she gazed at the child, who murmured in her dreaming. The Ogress smiled at Harold.

"You're awake," she said. "Lazybones."

Harold agreed. He *was* awake. He was the most awake he had ever been. Every detail presented itself with utter clarity— from the sensation of the child's lungs filling and releasing, to the afternoon light, to the gentle tilt of the Ogress's face as she gazed at the child. The child's body felt a little bit cooler than it had the night before. Still warm, and still comforting, but less hot.

"Is she still sick?" Harold asked, in Crow. He spoke slowly so that the Ogress would understand.

She nodded her head. "Yes, but she's mending well," she said in her own language. "Her fever broke about an hour ago. She woke briefly, quite disoriented. I gave her some juice and some water, and she went back to sleep. She needed to sleep. I don't think she registered very much. Fevers can do that to a person."

Harold nodded. He nestled close to the child. He listened to her heart beat. "Caw," he said quietly, with an ache at the center of his own heart. "Can we keep her?"

He knew the answer. The Ogress didn't have to say it. She gave Harold a loving pat on his head and returned to her work. Harold paid attention to this moment. The joy of being near the child. The grief that soon he would be saying goodbye. Both at once.

$\sim$

That night, the Ogress got a later start than she intended. The child slept easily, and the Ogress didn't want to wake her. Heaven only knew how long the poor thing had been wandering in the woods. She needed to sleep in order to heal. But mostly, the Ogress enjoyed having the child there. The softness of her. The quiet presence. If the child were to wake up, they could talk together or think together or count the stars together. When she sat with the child in her arms and rocked her . . . The Ogress shook her head. It felt like belonging. It *was* belonging. She only ever wanted to belong. Still, this child belonged with her family. That much was clear. And the Ogress knew what she had to do.

The half-moon rose. It was warm by the farm—it was always warmer than everywhere else. It would be cold in town.

The Ogress wrapped the child in a blanket. And then another blanket. Her heart sank at the thought of saying goodbye. She didn't know if she could bear it.

"Caw," Harold asked. "Must we?"

The Ogress nodded, turning her face away. "Yes, Harold," she said, her voice thick. "We must."

She finished filling her cart. She packed an extra box of vegetables for the Orphan House. And an extra round of cheese. If this child was any indication of the others—thin arms, thin cheeks, a belly with no give to it—it meant all the children in that house needed to eat more. The Ogress wished she had known.

The hours kept flowing past. Usually, the Ogress felt as though she had all the time in the world, but now she wanted to stop time altogether. Wait for the child to wake and then take a meal, or a walk, or just sit outside with the crows and the sheep and the dog. It felt good to not be alone.

The moon slid across the sky. The wind reminded her that morning was coming whether she liked it or not. She couldn't delay any longer. She carried the child in the crook of one arm and guided the cart with her free hand, and she walked toward the Orphan House.

What the Butcher Saw

The butcher paced his shop. His cleavers and knives, all hanging on the wall, had been sharpened and washed and placed just so, a picture of order and responsibility and moral rectitude. He glared, as though they were judging him. If there was one thing he couldn't stand, it was *judginess*. He turned away with a loud *harrumph*.

The butcher was not a bad man. But he was not a good man, either. Was it necessary, he wondered, to be entirely *good* or entirely *bad*? Surely, a person could live a perfectly acceptable life being *neither*.

A jug of wine sat on the counter. The butcher held an empty jar in his hand. It was late—far too late to be up. It would be morning soon. But he hadn't been able to sleep all night. His back hurt too much. He was *far too old* to be replacing a broken section of the road. He had been asking the Mayor to fix it for years, until at last he just did it *himself*. It had taken *days*. And he did it for *free*. Do bad men do this? No, he decided. They do not.

Well, so far it was free. It was true that the butcher had sent a bill to the Mayor's office, and, immediately after, put in a formal complaint that the bill had not yet been paid, since he assumed it would not be. But he wanted it to be official—that he, the humble butcher, had done this deed for his community with no hope of recognition or compensation. The whole town should know, he reasoned.

And now here he was. Injured. Awake. Pacing his shop to walk off the pain. And the cobbler—his best friend—had *looked at him in that way.*

He thinks I'm a bad man, the butcher thought, a mixture of petulance and indignation churning in his guts. *How dare he!* He grimaced at another stab of pain, this one traveling straight down his leg, making it feel as though he had knives in his feet. The butcher poured himself another jar of wine. And another.

Outside, the sound of crows rang through the streets. *Varmints,* he thought. *Pests.* It was another thing he complained about. It was another thing that the Mayor ignored. He opened his curtain to shake his fist at the night. And then he froze. Outside his window, in the light of the moon, stood the Ogress.

The Ogress!

He felt as though his heart had stopped beating. Time wobbled and slowed as the space around him seemed to rapidly swell, making him dizzy. His ears rang. She was—*oh, heavens!* He trembled at the sight of her. She was twice as large as the biggest man he could imagine. And yet so silent. Her heavy footsteps made no discernible sound on the cobblestones. If it weren't for the crows, she could sneak up on anyone, and for all he knew, she often did.

He pressed his hand across his mouth to stop his own screaming, and then pressed his other hand on top to hold the first in place. She was *so much bigger* than he'd thought she'd be. Her body appeared to be made out of stone. Her hair sprouted from the top of her head like shrubbery. The butcher's stomach clenched, and his knees went wobbly. He steadied himself with his elbow.

Above the Ogress's head, crows swirled and cawed, making their awful racket. One landed on her shoulder. Another landed on her head. It seemed typical that pests such as crows were drawn to the Ogress. Like pulls to like, as the saying goes. The butcher took another sip from his jar and scowled. He knocked it back and drained it dry. The wine swirled in his brain.

The Ogress pulled a cart behind her. She held something in one arm. Something with a head that lolled and an arm and a leg that dangled. The butcher adjusted his spectacles. He squinted.

The head had a face. A young face. Dead, or asleep? He had no way of knowing. The face yawned and resettled itself. Asleep, then. The butcher sighed. At least that.

"Well, I'll be," he whispered. "The child." So the constable was right. And perhaps the cobbler, too. The butcher grimaced. He disliked being incorrect. Still, this was enormous information. The Ogress was stealing children. Here was the proof. Everyone knew ogres were wicked, and here was one caught red-handed in the midst of the wickedest deed he could think of. The butcher went to his tools and pulled down his largest cleaver. He walked to the door. He stopped. He turned around and put the cleaver back. He stood at the center of the room, not knowing exactly which way to go.

The butcher was not a bad man. But he wasn't a brave man, either. His insides felt like water. His head swam. *Someone must save the child*, he thought valiantly. He ran to the door to open it, but then froze. *Open it and do what, exactly?* he asked himself. He couldn't confront the Ogress! Ogres are dangerous. They grind men's bones to make their bread. And anyway, he was half her size! *Well*, he thought, *maybe as much as three-quarters*. And he puffed out his chest and straightened his back to what he believed was his full height.

Still, he was only one man.

And injured.

Guilt gnawed at his bones. A fire lit in his belly. He *must* do something. This was a *child*, after all. Was he not a man? And yet . . . his feet were anchored to the ground. His hands were weighted to his side. He was unable to move. *What good could I do*, he thought reasonably, *if I were devoured by an ogre?* No, he would need his neighbors. The whole town, really. And they were all asleep, with locked doors and locked shutters to keep any evildoers out.

The butcher's heart raced. He paced. He looked back out the window. The child curled in the Ogress's arms. She rubbed her sleeping face with her hands. *She's alive, which is something*, the butcher thought. The crows cawed, which made his headache worse. His hands shook, and his breath rattled. He went to the far wall and retrieved his great meat cleaver. Then he put it away again. He was sweating, nearly drenched. The Ogress was so large, and his cleaver was puny. And anyway, he didn't really think it would work on an ogre. Their skin was too tough. It would probably just bounce off. Besides, he had never killed anything in his life that wasn't tied up first.

He definitely needed his neighbors. Lots of neighbors. It was not smart to go outside. He was smart, he told himself, to refuse to act. He was the bravest man he knew. He'd gather the townspeople at first light. They would all be heroes. What was the point of living in a town at all if you couldn't rely on your neighbors?

He sat in his chair, refilling his jar with wine. He planned what he would say. He was already enjoying the looks of admiration his neighbors would give him, once they knew. He watched the sky, patiently waiting for morning to come.

Bartleby's Strange Night

The orphans slept with Matron and her Myron, all crammed into their small bedroom off the kitchen. They couldn't bear another night in the dormitory without Cass.

They didn't all fit in the bed, mostly because Myron was delicate and couldn't be crushed. They brought the babies' bassinets down and put them in the corners. Lily and Maude shoved themselves between the old man and the old woman, and Dierdre and Elijah curled around the outsides like bookends. Justina, Iggy, and Kye all cuddled together at the bottom of the bed. Fortunate and Gratitude shared an overstuffed chair, their arms wound around each other and their heads on each other's shoulders, while Hiram occupied the top of the bureau, his arms and his leg draping off the sides, and his mouth open in a colossal snore. Bartleby and Anthea ended up on the floor. At first, Bartleby pretended to sleep. Anthea, seeing the ruse, pretended right along with him, and in this way they both finally sank into a fitful, uneasy slumber.

That night, Bartleby had a strange dream. In it, he sat on the floor of Matron and Myron's bedroom. Five of the cats sat at attention, watching him. Their ears stood tall atop their soft heads. Their tails lashed. Their eyes glowed in the dark. Bartleby stood and tiptoed out into the kitchen and up the stairs to the Reading Room. The cats followed solemnly behind.

The Altruria lay on the floor. One of the cats sat next to it—the large tabby with the scar on his ear—cleaning its paws. Its eyes slid sideways, watching as Bartleby picked up the book, opened it, and started reading aloud.

"What does it mean, then, to call a person Good?" the Philosopher asked the Ill-Tempered Grouse. "How do we know if a person is Good, or Wicked, or simply Indifferent?"

The Grouse scowled at the question. "I question your assumption that one might ask that question at all. A person is Good if they do not steal the eggs of an unsuspecting grouse! A person is Good if they would never consider doing so—and if they lack the capability of doing so. All foxes are capable of stealing my eggs. Therefore, no fox can be Good. If no fox can be Good, it follows that this fox cannot be Good."

"I disagree," the Fox said. "You forget the fallacy of expectations. You expect me to be Wicked, and therefore, in your estimation, I will only ever be Wicked. But if I spend my life doing Good, would it not then mean that I, too, am Good? If not, and if you insist on declaring me Wicked, then you must also accept that the Wicked are capable of Good Deeds, and, conversely, that Wickedness can be committed by the Good. In which case, declaring a person either Wicked or Good is arbitrary. Goodness and

Wickedness have no meaning if they are not defined by choices or actions. My friend, you must choose: either your definitions are incorrect, or your expectations are based on an error."

"Meow," the tabby said. Bartleby stared at the cat. The cat had said "meow," but it sounded strangely like "You should take that message to heart and stop worrying whether or not you are a good person. If you wish to be good, do good." Which would be a strange thing for a cat to say.

Bartleby put the book down. He reminded himself that this was a dream. He looked up and noticed the painting hanging above the bookshelf. He pulled a chair over to get a closer look. The painting of the Library, which took up the whole wall, was larger than he remembered it. The painted crows over the painted building were suddenly swooping and fluttering about, and the Library itself—indeed, the whole painting—seemed to exist in three dimensions.

Bartleby found himself, all at once, not outside the painting looking in, but *inside the painting*, looking around. He did not find this strange. Inside the painting, he began to walk around the whole of the Library and look up at the stained-glass windows. He waved at the crows, who did not wave back. He watched as a black feather fell from one of the crows' wings and fluttered to the ground. He bent down and picked it up, twirling it in his fingers before putting it in his pocket.

He laid his hands on the broad, ancient stones. When he pulled his hands away, they smelled like smoke. Bartleby appreciated the painter's attention to detail. Something soft brushed against his ankle. He looked down and realized that the cats all stood with him, inside the painting. Some stalked the grass near his feet. Others climbed on the old stone steps. Some sunned themselves on the windowsills, enjoying the heat of the day. Phyllis, the small kitten, climbed up the back of Bartleby's pants and sweater as though he were a tree, and fastened herself to his shoulder. She licked one paw as she regarded the building.

"You should pay attention to the stained glass," Phyllis said as she washed her face.

Bartleby was startled. He knew he couldn't speak Cat. He looked at Phyllis. "Wait," he said. "Do you speak Person?"

Phyllis nibbled on her claws. "Obviously," she said.

Bartleby frowned. "Have you always been able to speak Person?" he asked. He rubbed his face, trying to make everything make sense.

"Obviously," Phyllis said again.

"Honestly, we thought you knew," said the orange cat on the nearest windowsill. She flicked her tail lazily.

Bartleby shook his head. "I didn't. I'm sorry."

"Well," said the large gray tomcat. "You *should* be sorry. But you may make it up to us with cream and adoration, if you wish."

"Okay," Bartleby said. He looked up at the stained-glass windows. They were more detailed than he remembered. One showed a village entirely populated by friendly ogres. They smiled at one another and gave to one another and helped one another with tasks. It looked like a pleasant place—what a town *should* be like. A dragon hid in one corner. He held an ogre mask in one hand.

"The stones they used to build the Library were cut from the Stone at the heart of Stone-in-the-Glen. A long time ago," the tabby said.

"Were they now?" Bartleby said. "It must have been a large stone."

"It is," the gray tomcat said. "You have no idea." He licked his paws. "Well, we do, obviously. But we are cats." He said this as though it settled the matter.

"And the beams and timbers came from the fine old trees that stood near it," the tabby continued.

"You don't say?" Bartleby said. "I heard once that a stone fell in love with a tree who told stories. But I don't remember where I heard that. I also heard that stones have memories."

"Obviously, they do," the gray tomcat said. "Why wouldn't they? And the stained glass was made from the sand that once was part of the Stone. You should pay attention to where things come from and what they have to say."

"What should I be paying attention to now?" Bartleby asked.

"You'll know it when you see it," Phyllis said, curling her tail around the back of Bartleby's neck.

Bartleby walked around the perimeter of the Library. There was a window showing a group of people holding hands and bowing their heads in front of a dying tree. There was another showing a man sleeping on a pile of gold coins. Another of a very large, ogreish woman with crows on each shoulder as she tended a garden. Another of a tangle of children playing in a yard. And then of a girl with short hair and trousers riding on the back of a crow.

"Cass?" he said. The girl looked like Cass. It couldn't have been Cass, though. The painting was too old, and the stained glass in the painting was even older. But it looked like Cass.

Bartleby kept walking around the Library. He climbed up onto the building, standing on the ledge in order to get a better look. "Is that—" he started. He squinted. Everyone in the picture looked familiar.

"Is it you?" Phyllis said. "Well, it certainly looks like you."

"I thought you were the smart one," the gray tomcat sniffed. "You seem a bit slow to me."

"They're all a bit slow," drawled the tabby. "I've been here for hours, and no one has stroked me even once." She yawned, showing her teeth.

Bartleby stared at the stained glass. He seemed to be looking down on the scene in it, as though from a vantage point of a hovering bird. The top of one head definitely looked like his own—all flop and curl and curious tilt. The person next to him, holding his hand, looked like Anthea. Fortunate and Gratitude had their arms, as always, wound around each other. There was the bald head and unsteady gait of Myron. Fortunate's face was tilted toward the sky. And they all stood at the open gate, gathered around a figure curled on the ground, wrapped in blankets.

"Cass," he breathed. He felt his stomach drop. "It's Cass." He turned. The cats were gone. "It is, isn't it?"

"Meow," a cat said from very far away.

Bartleby blinked. Where did the cats go? He looked to his left. The Library was gone. And so was the painting. And he wasn't on the grass, or in the Reading Room, or on the floor of Matron and Myron's bedroom at all. He was outside the Orphan House on the walkway. He was standing in front of the gate. He shook his head. Anthea took his hand. Was he still dreaming?

"It's okay, Bartleby," Anthea said. "We'll figure everything out today. I feel sure of it."

Bartleby shook his head again. He felt as though his brain had been packed with sand. Myron patted his shoulder. *When did Myron get here?* he wondered. When did *he* get here? Myron opened the gate. The sky was pink and gold overhead. Bartleby had seen this. In a painting. Or in a dream. Or in a dream inside a painting, or a painting inside a dream.

"Cass," Bartleby said as the lock clunked into place.

Anthea squeezed his hand. "I know," she said. The chickens pecked for bugs, and the goats munched on the grass. Myron pulled the heavy gate slowly. The iron hinges moaned.

"Cass," Bartleby murmured. His voice seemed to be coming from very far away. He didn't altogether feel the inside of his own body. He must not have slept very well. Or maybe he hadn't slept at all. Or maybe he was still dreaming. He let go of Anthea's hand and helped Myron open the gate. The sun peeked through a gap in the houses across the street, flooding them with light. He squinted. It was difficult to see.

"*Cass!*" His voice jolted from his body as though it had been yanked out into the open. He fell to his knees. His sister lay on the ground, her body curled up tight like a snail's shell, her arm draped across a box heaped with vegetables. Her hair was spangled with leaves.

Later, Bartleby would remember that moment as though the whole world rang with Cass's name. It trilled out of the clouds and the trees and the cobblestones. It echoed through the grass and the bushes and the brightening sky.

He would remember how the box of vegetables tipped on its side.

He would remember his sister in the circle of his arms, and himself again inside the circle of Matron's arms, and Anthea's and Fortunate's and Gratitude's and Dierdre's and Kye's. He would remember the taste of tears and the sound of weeping and the smell of home.

And there was one more thing. It would take him several days to work out the meaning of it. But, in the corner of his eye, he saw something sitting a few feet to his right on a raggedy shrub—more stick than leaf. A single crow. It hopped from clump to clump. It winked one eye. And then the other. And then it said, quite distinctly, "Caw," which meant "There now. Isn't that better?"

Or, at least, that's what Bartleby thought he saw and thought he heard. But when he looked again, the crow was gone. And maybe it hadn't been there in the first place.

Several People Get the Wrong Idea

Cass felt many things that day. Guilt, for one. Confusion, for another.

She coughed, and coughed again. And then kept coughing. She didn't feel all that well.

Matron fussed and fawned. She set Cass on the couch and tucked her in. She boiled water and brought her tea and porridge. "Are you sick?" she said, with her hands pressed on Cass's forehead. She looked at Cass's throat and under the rim of each eye. "No fever—that's a relief. You either *are* sick, or are *getting* sick, or have *recently been* sick." Matron couldn't stop pacing. "Which is it?"

Cass had no words. The whole household had crowded onto the couch. She gasped under the weight of her family, under the weight of their love for her. No one wanted to leave the living room. No one wanted Cass out of their sight. They sat next to her or behind her, or cuddled on her lap or on each of her feet. The twins sang songs, and Elijah told stories, and Dierdre painted her portrait, and Hiram did tumbling tricks and feats of strength, and somehow, Anthea had already knitted a pair of socks. Bartleby kept his hands pressed to his belly as though he were in pain. And maybe he was. He kept his hazel eye and his milky-white eye fixed on Cass as though he were memorizing both her details and her shadows, so he might keep her close forever. He curled his arms around her and wouldn't let go. She closed her eyes for a long time, finally finding words deep inside herself. "I'm sorry," she managed. "I'm so sorry," she said again.

Bartleby waved her words away. "No need," he said.

No one was mad at her. Cass was astonished. She wanted to say something. She didn't know what to say. Maybe there wasn't anything that could be said in such a moment. She closed her eyes and tried to make sense of where she had been. She remembered holding something in her arms and being held in arms, and the sound of singing and the smell of bread. She remembered the rush of wings and the wagging of a tail, and something saying *baa* very sweetly in the distance. But it didn't make any sense. *Just a fever dream*, she told herself.

The bell at the front gate rang and rang. "Oh dear," Matron said. "They're back." She caught the eyes of Anthea and Myron and smiled. "Well, I guess we should give them the good news. I daresay they'll forget all about us by this afternoon." Matron left to get the door, and returned bobbing in the wake of the cobbler's wife, who was flanked by two other people Cass did not recognize. The cobbler's wife carried a large, steaming pot. The tall man to her left carried a basket full of bread, and the woman on her right carried a large box filled with clothes and shoes.

"We won't be but a minute," the cobbler's wife said as she streamed past the family piled in the living room. She blew kisses and went straight to the kitchen. "I've made you all some chicken-and-potato soup. It's nourishing for those who have experienced a shock." The man and the woman struggled to keep up. Matron followed, her hands twisting together.

"Thank you, Esmé," Matron said. "This is so generous. You should know—"

"I talked to a couple of the farmers. It's been another bad year, but they all said they would be able to send over a few bags of wheat. And the miller said he'd grind it for you—fancy doing it on your own, with all that you have to do all day! You poor woman, worked to the bone like this!"

"That's very kind," Matron said. "Really, it's no trouble. But what I'm trying to say is that we have excellent—"

"Imogene!" the cobbler's wife said to the woman with her. Neither seemed to register that Matron had spoken. "Why don't you lay out the clothes on that counter there, so Matron can see what is available for the children." She set the pot on the stove (moving aside the soup that Dierdre had already made) and stoked the fire. She sighed. "Well, strike that off the list. So much to do!"

"Always," Matron agreed. She had never met anyone who talked as fast as this woman did. It was disorienting. "What I'm trying to say is—"

"And of course my husband noticed the state of the children's shoes," the cobbler's wife said. "I just wish we had known earlier. I am truly sorry for it, my dear, dear woman. And I promise you that I will make it my mission to rally the efforts of the whole town in making this right. We must all make sure that the support for your work here at the house remains at top of mind. The Orphan House is a community responsibility. The shoes in the box are worn, and there's certainly not enough for everyone, but they are sturdy. Children grow so fast. Once we get to the other side of this calamity, you can send the children over to the cobblery to get their footwear mended properly."

"That sounds wonderful," Matron stammered, "but—"

"Eustace!" the cobbler's wife admonished. "What on *earth* are you doing? That is the entirely wrong knife for your task! Honestly!"

With an expression of shame, the man—Eustace, apparently—put down the knife he had been using to slice the bread.

"Let me see . . ." the cobbler's wife began as she rummaged through the bins and drawers. "Here. Use this. And slice *generously*, please! These are *growing children!*" She gave Eustace a hard look.

"Of course," Eustace said, his cheeks growing red. "How insensitive of me." He arranged thick slices of bread into neat stacks and set them on a plate.

The cobbler's wife did not slow down. She ladled the soup into bowls, talking all the while. "I don't want to frighten you, my dear, dear woman," she said, dropping her voice to a whisper, "but the butcher saw something terribly alarming last night. After all this town has endured—our calamities and bad luck—well, I mean, what I'm trying to say is that you don't have to do a thing. Your town is working on your behalf. We have rallied the troops and screwed our courage to the sticking place. You, meanwhile, can eat soup and mind those babies, which is a tremendous task. We have formed search teams, and we are sending a delegation to the Mayor's speech this very afternoon, to marshal his great wisdom and power to do what we must. All will be well. I promise."

"It's just that—" Matron attempted. But it was no use.

"Well, this task is done. Lunch is ready for whenever you want to feed those children. Eustace! Imogene! We must be off! I must now go cook a feast for the searchers." She enveloped Matron in a hug. Matron's mouth was pressed against the cobbler's wife's thick shawl, making it impossible to say a thing. "Never fear! We shall solve this—and everything! You'll see!"

The cobbler's wife, along with the man and woman, flowed out of the kitchen and swirled through the living room on their way to the door.

"She's back," Bartleby said, leaping to his feet as they hurried by. "She came back. My sister. No need for searching. She's no longer missing."

"We had no idea how big this problem was," the cobbler's wife said as she readjusted her hat. She hadn't seemed to notice that Bartleby had spoken. "But now we are all coming together. As a community. Isn't that marvelous?"

"But—" Bartleby said.

"I always knew this was a special place. I am ashamed of my neglect these past years. I'm ashamed for my town. Please forgive me, and us. I will do what I can to make it right!" In a whirlwind of scarves and blown kisses and excellent intentions, the cobbler's wife and the man and the woman all blew toward the door, and were gone.

Matron and Bartleby stared at the stack of sliced bread and the bowls waiting for the soup, which bubbled on the stove. Bartleby shrugged. Matron twisted her hands together as though she were wringing out a sponge. She looked at Bartleby. "I don't think she heard you," she said.

After lunch, Myron brought Anthea and Bartleby with him to the cobbler's shop. His original plan was to bring Cass, to show to the cobbler and his wife that Cass was home and fine, and that the world was now as it should be, but Matron wouldn't hear of it. Cass was still coughing. Still pale. Cass wasn't going anywhere. Bartleby and Anthea needed a bit of persuading—they didn't want to leave Cass's side, either—but they remembered that Myron was a timid man. And fragile. And they didn't want him to go alone. They walked quickly down the road toward the cobblery, holding tightly to one another's hands.

"Oh dear," Myron said as they rounded the corner and saw the shop. There were so many people crowded inside. Others had spilled out the door and into the street. Some had climbed halfway up the side of the building to listen through the transom windows to what was happening inside. Myron pressed his lips into a grim, straight line. "Come on, children," he said as they prepared to push their way in. It took some doing—mostly with Myron offering several iterations of "Pardon us" and "Excuse me" and "Oh dear, was that your foot?" but eventually they made it to the center of the shop. The butcher stood on a stool, his face livid. Anthea gulped. *What was he doing here?*

"As big as a house, she was. I could feel the rumble of her fell footsteps a full league away. I ran to the window and saw her hulking hideousness—so big she blocked the moon and the stars. Her eyes were red, and her sharp teeth were bigger than a man's foot. I stood there, all on my own, trembling with fear. I thought to run and hide like a mouse. But then I saw in her clawed clutches—the child! She has taken the child! Not a runaway, like some unkind townsfolk might have been muttering—yes, I know who you are! No! That good girl was taken by the wicked ogress!"

Everyone gasped. A woman burst into tears. A man fell to the ground in a dead faint. The butcher wiped his face with his handkerchief and held a serious expression, but Anthea could see the way his eyes shone.

"Didn't I always say so?" the constable added. She stood in the corner, taking notes in her ledger. "How many times have I told the Mayor to make an example of that ogress. But he is just so tenderhearted, bless him."

"So," the butcher continued, casting a hard look at the constable. "Let me finish. Thinking fast, I grabbed my largest cleaver!" He held his right hand high over his head, as though about to rush into battle.

"Pardon me," Myron said.

The butcher startled briefly, put his hand down, then scowled at Myron. "Why must I be constantly interrupted?" he asked.

Myron kept the children close, with one hand on Anthea's shoulder and the other on Bartleby's, and he squeezed the two together, like bookends. Myron smiled nervously at the butcher, which only made Anthea even more anxious. "Really, I am so very sorry," Myron said. "I don't want to be rude. Your story is truly captivating. I would just like to know which child you are referring to. The one who was in the clutches of that . . . well, a monster, I suppose."

The butcher's face became a mask of incredulity. "Suppose?" he scoffed. "You *suppose*? What *is* an ogress other than a terrifying monster? How have we allowed this danger to fester at the edge of our once-lovely town for this long, I ask you? Why must you come here and waste our time with the foolish questions of a foolish old man?"

"Jonathan!" the cobbler admonished. He pushed his way through the tightly packed crowd and put his hand protectively on Myron's shoulder. "Show some respect! This family has suffered a terrible blow."

"Oh, but you see, that's exactly why we've come," said Myron. But the butcher was intent on finishing his story.

"*Fine*," he said. "*The Ogress*, I meant to say. That terrible ogress who has been ruining our lovely town for a generation, and now! Now she is no longer content with destroying our prosperity and causing our crops to fail and our milk to sour and our buildings to dilapidate, but now—*now!*—she is stealing children. She stole that child from the Orphan House, and *I saw the crime with my own eyes*. Is there anything more wicked than that?"

The room vibrated with murmurs.

"Well," Myron said. "Of course that would be *very wicked*, but you see, no one has stolen anyone at all. Our Cass was returned to us. This morning, we found her right outside the gate. A little frightened and with a bit of a cough after being lost in the woods, but nothing too terrible."

Everyone stared at Myron. Myron cleared his throat. He pressed on.

"So you see, this is *good* news. This story ends happily. It is a good day for Stone-in-the-Glen."

The room fell silent.

For a moment.

And then everyone spoke at once. "Well," the constable said, "that can't possibly be right. The butcher saw the Ogress, plain as day. I have it right here in my notes. And I signed it and everything, and that makes it official, so it must be true. That's the law."

"The poor butcher went to do battle with the Ogress," the seamstress said. "And look at him now! He's injured! His back is twisted, and his hands are cut. How else would that have happened?"

"I don't want my bones to be ground into bread," the black-smith said.

"And has anyone noticed how she's always accompanied by a murder of crows?" the rag seller said. "Did we not hear their infernal cawing outside our windows just last night? Did we not toss and turn in our beds due to their sinister cackling?"

"But wait," Bartleby said.

"Children should be seen and not heard!" the butcher said. "I thought that the Orphan House was raising those children right. Well, it appears I was mistaken!"

"But Cass is at home!" Anthea said. "She's with Matron this very minute! Why would we tell you something that isn't true? There is no logical reason."

The cobbler held up his hands. "Good neighbors, good neighbors!" He stood at the center of the room with his arms wide and his palms out. He had no need for a stool—the cobbler was a very tall man. He quieted the room. "There are answers to everything, my friends. Our beloved mayor is addressing the town this very afternoon. We will bring our concerns to him then, and he will solve our problems once and for all." He turned to Bartleby. Everyone turned to Bartleby, who felt himself begin to flush. "You say, son, that your sister returned to you. Well, surely she has told you the story of her ordeal. Of the hands that snatched her in the night. Of her brave escape!"

Bartleby felt the collective eyes of the crowded room bore into him. His skin was damp and his mouth went dry. "I . . . I mean, no. She—"

"Did anyone else witness the kidnapping?" the constable said from the far corner. She was waiting to take notes in her ledger.

"What?" Bartleby said. "No. That's what I'm trying to say. Before she disappeared, my sister had been acting . . . I mean, Anthea noticed it. I didn't want to see. And then we woke up, and—"

"So you're saying you all were in a trance, then," the constable said. "Like a magic spell. I've heard of this. Ogres have special abilities. It's not magic, per se. But it's close." She wrote this down.

"No," Bartleby said, "you see . . ." But he didn't know how to explain it. He wished Elijah were here. Elijah was the story-teller. The jostling crowd started murmuring at once.

"So," the cobbler said, "if I'm understanding you, you're say-ing she *could have been stolen*. But she's simply traumatized and can't speak."

"That's not what he's saying at all," Myron said.

"There are other ways of communicating," Anthea said. "Cass never says much. But she still communicates a lot."

The butcher threw his arms out wide. *"Don't you see what this means?"* His voice was at a fever pitch. "We don't know how deep this goes. We don't know how many times the Ogress has done this terrible thing. There are families who may have simply assumed that their children ran away to seek their fortunes—because why wouldn't they, given that the Ogress has ruined the prosperity in Stone-in-the-Glen—but no! They may have instead landed in the clutches of the most wicked ogress to ever live!"

"*Oh dear*," whispered Myron.

"This is completely illogical," Anthea attempted. "You have no evidence for any of this."

Bartleby said nothing. He felt as though he were made out of wood.

"My cat went missing last month!" the apothecary said. "And a month before that, my favorite goat vanished."

The butcher slapped his knee. "You see? The Ogress. I am *sure* of it!"

"My wife and children disappeared last year," a man leaning against a corner said. "Granted, she did tell me that she was going to leave and then she left a note saying she and the children were going to live with her sister on the coast, but it could have been the Ogress copying her handwriting in an evil ruse!"

"*But that doesn't make any sense*," Bartleby roared, finding his voice.

"*No more of these children*," the butcher roared back. "We've heard quite enough from them. They belong indoors, doing their lessons. There are dangerous ogres about. All children should be kept under lock and key!"

The crowd murmured its assent and looked at the children with narrowed eyes.

"Go," Myron whispered. "Off we all go."

Anthea, Bartleby, and Myron slid through the crowd. The chanting crowd barely noticed.

"No more ogres!" the butcher called.

"*No more ogres!*" cried the people in the room.

"*No more ogres!*" shouted the people outside. "*No more ogres!*" Again and again and again.

"Oh dear," muttered Myron. "What a ghastly collection of boors and blowhards. They do love hearing themselves speak, don't they?" He gripped Bartleby's and Anthea's hands. As they hurried home, a grim silence settled over them.

"Myron," Bartleby finally said. "What are we going to do?"

"How are we going to fix this?" Anthea asked, her voice small and desperate.

Myron said nothing for a long moment. Then he pressed a firm smile onto his creased face. "Don't spend another moment worrying about any of it, my darlings," he said, his voice overly bright and brittle. "After a day or two, this will all blow over. People lose interest in nonsensical things after a bit. Cooler heads always prevail!"

Anthea leaned back, catching Bartleby's eye from behind Myron's back. They held each other's gaze briefly, their faces communicating the same thing: *He doesn't believe a word that he's saying. He's just as scared as we are.*

Arriving at the entrance to the Orphan House, the three went in. Myron paused as he locked the gate. He checked it once, twice, three times, as though making sure that the lock would hold, making sure they would stay safe inside.

Have I Mentioned That Everyone Loved the Mayor?

The Mayor was vexed.

He rubbed his stomach. It ached something terrible. He was prone, alas, to dyspepsia, which was then made worse by annoyance, anxiety, or, in this case, general agitation—something that he had largely been able to avoid and minimize in his fairly charmed life since he had come to Stone-in-the-Glen, ever so long ago now, first as its famous dragon hunter, and then soon after as its mayor.

He stepped out onto his veranda. The sky was a brilliant blue, and not a single cloud interrupted the pour of the light. He lifted his chin and opened his eyes, gazing at the full brightness of the sun. He luxuriated in this way for a long moment, as a cat luxuriates in a sunbeam on the floor. As if on cue, one of the cats along the perimeter of the yard stood at attention, stared at the Mayor, and hissed.

It should have been a marvelous day, one of an endless stream of marvelous days. Everyone in Stone-in-the-Glen loved their mayor. This was right and proper. After all, he loved the people of this town . . . didn't he? Or, perhaps if he was to say it properly, he did so love being loved by the people of Stone-in-the-Glen. After all, isn't that what being mayor is all about?

He took a moment to admire himself in the shine of the window. He had polished his golden buckles moments previously, and he did so love the deep glow of the gold, just as he loved the smart, heavy tread of his boots. He adjusted the drape of his cloak and swept his golden hair from his eyes in a decidedly beguiling manner. His face shone—not from his skin, exactly, but from within. It was his very own, very special beauty secret. One that he would never divulge, except to say, "For most people, their beauty is only skin-deep. But I, as you have probably guessed, am not most people." And then he would wink. He made the people in town dizzy. How he loved making them dizzy.

He placed his hat on his head. He looked marvelous. Of course he did. He adjusted the fit of his skin, making sure it was just so, and flashed a grin at himself in his reflection. Even more marvelous. He pressed his hand onto his belly, quelling yet another dyspeptic gurgle. He allowed himself one very brief, very hot belch—aimed away from the house, just in case. He placed his hand on the exterior wall of the mansion and let it rest there, a feeling of tenderness washing over his heart like a wave.

Such wonders were contained within the mansion. Time was, in the days of earlier mayors, the building kept its doors open from sunrise to sunset, when any resident could come to see earlier mayors to express concerns or to offer ideas or to file complaints or to simply have a chat. These mayors held forums and symposiums and concerts and debates. There once was an entire gallery space dedicated to displaying the art of local children.

But the Mayor put a stop to all of that business on the very first day. "How can I expect my dear citizens to keep their own homes safely locked and shuttered and guarded if I, your beloved Mayor, am not perfectly willing to do the same." People saw the wisdom in this statement. The Mayor was very good at convincing people that his own wisdom was self-evident. It was one of his gifts.

And it had worked. Everything had worked.

But now . . .

There was something in the cobbler's visit the other day that nagged at the Mayor. The cobbler had put his foot in the doorjamb to prevent the Mayor from ending the conversation and retreating indoors. His *foot*. The Mayor couldn't entirely remember *what* the man's problem was. It was difficult to pay attention when there were more attractive things to occupy one's thoughts. The man hadn't mentioned once how marvelous the Mayor was, or how lucky the town was. The Mayor frowned. He didn't like it a single bit.

But that was why giving a speech to the town was such a genius idea. It used to be that he gave speeches in the Center Square nearly every day. Back at the beginning. It was how he'd convinced the citizens of Stone-in-the-Glen to love him. In those days, people saw a terrifying dragon lurking in the woods quite often. Once a month, more or less. Always on the day before the new moon. And then they witnessed their mayor—their marvelous mayor—emerge from the woods, victorious, without a dragon in sight. But over time, the dragon sightings dwindled. And their love for him . . . well, it didn't dwindle *exactly*, but it was all a bit much for them at first, poor things. He was *too* beautiful and *too* wise and *too* erudite. He shone too brightly. In truth, his tenure as mayor might not have lasted very long if those feelings had continued.

Then there were those beautiful fires. One after another. His stomach hurt at the thought of them, but his eyes glittered at their memory. So much light crowding out the shadows! So much power unleashed with a single breath.

How they needed him then! How they *depended* on him. He told them then that he, alone, could solve this problem and he, alone, could fix it, and what a thrill it was—a deep and profound thrill—to see in the shine of their faces and the glaze of their eyes that they utterly *believed* him. How pleasurable it was in those days, going from yard to yard, alley to alley, chatting, commiserating, redirecting, convincing. They were all just *so easy* to convince. He cleared his throat and did a few vocal exercises to warm up his voice.

And if a speech didn't work this time, well, then . . . another building could burn. Or a whole block. Or the whole town, if need be. It had worked before, after all.

The bells atop the Town Hall began to ring, which meant the citizens would begin to gather. He crossed the yard. The cats snaking the perimeter paused. They sat at attention, their ears tilted forward, their tails extended upward, like spears.

"Hello, *cats*," he said derisively. "I'm not sure if you noticed, but I'm still here."

The cats hissed as he walked by.

In the Center Square, the Mayor stepped onto the dais and faced the assembled crowd. He gulped. He adjusted the flounce of his coat. Unconsciously, he brought his hands to his throat and adjusted the fit of his skin to make sure it clung just so. He flashed the crowd a brilliant smile. He saw their eyes crinkle as he did so, readjusting to the light. Strangely, his smile didn't have the desired effect. *What's happening?* he wondered.

The crowd astonished him. He had forgotten how many people actually lived in Stone-in-the-Glen. Surely it couldn't be this many! He frowned and wished with his whole heart that he were back in the mansion, with all the wonders contained therein. He closed his eyes to imagine it.

"Sir," a voice said. The Mayor cracked open his eyes, and saw a man step onto the dais and stride across. People were always *wanting* things, the Mayor grumbled silently. He was very tall, this man. And he wore wool trousers, and a wide-brimmed hat, shading his face. The Mayor frowned. He detested shade.

"Pleasant sun, don't you think?" the Mayor said indulgently.

"Thank you for doing this, sir," the man said. "As we discussed earlier—"

"Earlier?" The Mayor shook his head.

"Yes," the man said, "when I came by two days ago."

"Ah," the Mayor said. This was the man who had started all this mess. He did his best to force his frown away. "Yes. Earlier. I am excellent at recognizing people. One of the very best," he enthused. "But, of course, you knew that."

"We, um . . ." The man hesitated. "There has been some discussion in town. About how to proceed. About what the community's concerns are. If it's all the same to you, sir, we thought it might be best if you heard directly from your constituents."

"Constituents?" the Mayor said, bafflement creasing his face.

"Yes. The people who voted for you would like you to hear them out. If it's all the same to you. You know. A listening session."

Well, then, the Mayor thought, relaxing. *Listening is much less work than giving a speech. All a person has to do is affix a benevolent expression while thinking about something else entirely!* This would be easy. He clapped the man on the back. The man pitched forward and stumbled. "Marvelous," the Mayor said. "Simply marvelous. Let's begin, shall we?" The man bowed curtly, and the Mayor faced the crowd.

"Ah, my good people!" He beamed at everyone in the square. "My dear, dear citizens of Stone-in-the-Glen. I'm so glad you could all gather today. There are . . . well, there are more of you than what we normally see." His voice, needing no amplification, boomed through the square and echoed through half the town. He looked out at the crowd. They stood elbow to elbow, their brows knitted together in expectation. They crossed their arms and pressed their mouths into thin lines. It was unnerving. He cleared his throat. "Perhaps some of you would like to sit down?"

No one did.

The Mayor paused for a full beat. Then another. "Very well. I shall begin. It has reached my attention that the citizens of my beloved town are unhappy. That they are worried. That they feel unheard. It devastates me—truly devastates me—that this is true." He bowed his head and pressed his hands to his chest, closing his eyes. He snuck a peek. Normally, even the passing thought that something had made their mayor slightly sad would send the residents of Stone-in-the-Glen into a full panic. But not today. How perplexing. He straightened up and clicked his boots together and stood at magnanimous attention. He flashed a winning smile. No one's face became light and adoring. There was no response at all.

What is going on? The Mayor couldn't understand it. He cleared his throat. He readied his voice. He tilted his face toward the sun, enjoying the angle of the light. Surely this would take only a moment. "I would like to begin, my dear citizens, by saying—"

"Excuse me, Mayor," a woman at the front of the crowd interrupted. Had he ever been interrupted before? He couldn't remember a single time. He didn't know if he should be aghast or fascinated. "There is an ogress—as in, an actual ogre—living *right there* at the far side of town. She's been living there *for years*. It is much too dangerous having her here. You *must* make her leave."

The Mayor nodded. "It is my duty to listen, but it is also my duty to assuage fears. Ogres are low creatures, after all. Dull. Slow. Dreadful conversationalists. Barely worth thinking about. I certainly never do. They are not nearly as interesting as, say, dragons. Which, well, as you know, I defeated a dragon. Several, actually." The Mayor let that sink in. He gazed at the crowd, waiting for hints of adulation in their faces. None came. He cleared his throat. "The world we live in is treacherous and terrible and full of dangers. What a time to have such a powerful mayor on your side to defeat those dangers. I am so happy we are of the same mind on this subject."

He gave the woman an indulgent smile. She squinted back.

A man toward the back spoke. "We lock our doors out of fear. We are afraid to go out in the dark. A child was taken. We are afraid for our children. You must make the ogre leave!"

People murmured in agreement.

"Again," the Mayor said, "there are so many dangers everywhere. Very *interesting* dangers, you understand. Much more interesting than ogres. Have I mentioned that ogres are low creatures? It's hard to really think that a dullard such as—"

"How many more children must go missing before we take any action?" a woman from the middle shouted. The Mayor nearly stumbled in shock. The woman raised her fist. No one had *ever* raised a fist at the Mayor before. "When can we, as a town, say, 'No more ogres'?"

"NO MORE OGRES!" cried out a group sitting on a dilapidated bench.

"NO MORE OGRES!" echoed a group gathered at the right.

The Mayor pressed his hands to his chest. He paid close attention to the swell of chanting coming from the assembled square. After his initial bafflement, he realized that there was something *thrilling* in the way everyone was speaking. Worrisome, too, of course. He knew from personal experience that things don't typically go well for mayors when the people get riled. And these people were *riled*. He took special care to layer in a little something . . . extra into his voice. It wasn't magic, exactly. But it was close.

"My dear citizens," the Mayor said in a soothing tone. "I am sensing a pattern. Do you all feel this way?" He inclined his chin. His face was full of light.

"WE DO," the people said together.

"I must say, I have never heard of an ogre who steals children, and I have traveled this whole earth before arriving here, in this very town, the most wonderful in the world. Ogres are . . . well, they're rather oafish fellows. Easily—" He suppressed a smile. "*So* easily swindled." He cleared his throat. "I mean, I've *heard.*"

"OGRES DON'T BELONG HERE," bellowed a woman standing on a donkey cart.

"NO ONE ASKED HER TO COME HERE," shouted a man standing on the rim of a dry, trash-filled fountain.

"OUR CROPS FAIL EVERY YEAR, AND WHOSE FAULT IS IT?" cried a woman in the center of the crowd.

"THAT OGRE," shouted the people of Stone-in-the-Glen.

"Our children aren't safe."

"Our animals aren't safe."

"The trees died."

"The school burned down."

"Our library is in ruins."

"It used to be a lovely town before she *came here."*

There was a moment of silence. "NO MORE OGRES!" a man began chanting.

"NO MORE OGRES! NO MORE OGRES!" the crowd joined in.

Their voices swelled. The buildings surrounding the Center Square shook. The sun continued to sink. The last rays of the day fell on the faces of Stone-in-the-Glen, making their skin gleam like a town full of miniature suns. It was the most beautiful thing that the Mayor had ever seen.

But worrisome, too. Discord and division could be beautiful things—and lucrative—but they could also be difficult to control. Best tread lightly. The Mayor lifted his right hand, palm out, and bowed his head. The chanting ebbed and finally ceased. The people looked to their mayor with quiet expectation. They uncrossed their arms and clasped their hands over their hearts. This, he felt, was a hopeful sign. "My dears and my darlings," he said, carefully measuring his words. His enlarged voice was low and sonorous, rumbling gently through the crowd. "First things first. We should all put our money where our mouth is. Where is that tall man from earlier? The one with the hat."

"Here, sir," the cobbler said, waving his hand. "We've met many times, you know. My name is Arthur. I made you those boots?"

"Of course, of course," the Mayor said vaguely. "Why don't you take off that . . . *marvelous hat* of yours and take up a collection. This problem will definitely need money." The man took his hat off and almost instantly people dug into their pockets and filled it with whatever they had. The Mayor's cheeks flushed. *Well*, he thought, *today is going simply splendidly*.

He smiled as the hat moved through the crowd, growing heavier with every moment. "It seems to me that we have come to an agreement. No one wants to continue having an ogress—*an ogress, I tell you!*—endangering our safety and tranquility by living as bold as brass on the far edge of our beautiful town. Of course not. It isn't fair. You work so hard! Does the Ogress work hard? Not that I've seen. Not that you've seen. She sits there from sunup to sundown inside her crooked house, while you work hard *all day long*. That sounds like laziness. I can't abide laziness. She is stealing the days of rest and indolence that rightfully belong to you! I can't abide stealers!"

"NO MORE OGRES!" the people chanted. "NO MORE OGRES!" Their voices echoed against the empty storefronts and dilapidated buildings. "NO MORE OGRES!" Their voices scratched against the afternoon sky.

The Mayor lifted his hands again, quieting them. "Yes, yes, of course we all agree. But you must trust your mayor, my dear citizens. Trust me, and all will be well."

The townspeople nodded. Their faces shone. Even as the sun slipped below the lip of the buildings surrounding the square, casting them all in shadow, their faces still glowed like flames. The Mayor's heart skipped a beat. He had forgotten how lovely rage can be.

"I just hope," he said with a grin, "*that nobody breaks the law.*" He let a hiss slither into his voice, all honey laced with poison. "This is important, my friends, my compatriots. I must be emphatic about this. I hope that no one throws eggs at her house, or rocks at her windows. Really, I—" *Oh!* the Mayor thought. *This feels delightful!*—"I hope no one posts threatening signs in her garden. Or defaces her walls. *Terrible.*" He shivered at the thought of it. "I hope no one tries to steal her ridiculous sheep. I hope no one throws rocks at her infernal crows. Because *that* would be against the law. No one should break the law. I repeat, *no one should get caught breaking the law.* Thank you for joining me today, dear citizens. I think we all have learned a lot."

And with that, he exited the dais, the boards groaning under his feet. He walked through the crowd. The people shuddered as his hand grazed their shoulders and wept as he passed by. They reached out to touch the hem of his garment. They curled their fists. The veins on their necks bulged, and their cheeks flushed. Their narrowed eyes, gleaming like the edge of a blade, slid to where the Ogress lived.

Never had he been so proud, so very proud, to be the Mayor of Stone-in-the-Glen. He couldn't wait to find out what would happen tomorrow.

Nothing Blows Over

Anthea, Bartleby, and Myron had returned from the cobbler's shop in a state of worry but were gratified to find that not everyone in town had joined the crowd there. The cobbler's wife, true to her word, had not let up on her quest to improve conditions at the Orphan House. In a single day, she had brought over six loaves of bread, two pots of soup, four bundles of clothing, nine pairs of shoes, a basket of yarn, and a box of medicines. She bustled in and out, cheerfully meting out marching orders to a team of assistants, who followed her around in a state of bafflement and breathless activity. At the moment, two of them were climbing up and down ladders, measuring window after window, making plans to replace some of the rotting sashes. Matron again attempted to explain that the search could be called off, because Cass had been found, and again found herself interrupted by an avalanche of big plans and kind attention. She couldn't get a word in edgewise.

"She certainly is good at convincing people," Anthea remarked to Matron. "She's not great at listening, though."

"I mean," Matron said helplessly, "surely she'll just *notice*. Won't she?"

"This way!" the cobbler's wife trilled to two elderly women who trailed after her. She streamed past Cass in the doorway, paused, cupped Cass's face, and tutted, "Oh! So thin! Someone please put butter on the supplies list! These children need more butter!"

"But," Anthea said. "Don't you see, Mrs.—"

"So much to do," the cobbler's wife said. "There are two carpenters coming by tomorrow to fix the stairs, and I asked the veterinarian to pop over later this week to take a hard look at your goats. One of them has a sore on her leg that I don't like at all. And we might as well give the chickens a checkup while we're at it, *don't* you think? We do want them all to be mothers in the spring!" And with that, they flowed out of the room. Outside, two more volunteers had arrived with tools and supplies, and a third promised to bring his rooster by to help facilitate the arrival of spring chicks.

Anthea shook her head. There was no doubt that the cobbler's wife was doing good, despite her poor listening skills, and expanding on that good. It was remarkable, Anthea thought, how it took only one person *deciding to do good things*, and then convincing others to join in, to create a cascade of good deeds, each one sparking the next. Just think if *everyone* decided to do good. Just think if *everyone* decided to do so *every day*. Or, if not everyone, what if *some* did, and it still expanded? This was a whole new kind of arithmetic. How long would it take for those good deeds to compound? And what would the town look like then?

These thoughts churned in Anthea's mind for the remainder of the afternoon.

They ate an early supper—a casserole and a salad and more bread that a neighbor had brought over at the insistence of the cobbler's wife. Matron had begun to fuss that there wasn't nearly enough room in the icebox. But she must have said this in earshot of the cobbler's wife, who returned within the hour with the local secondhand dealer, who brought an old but still serviceable icebox, and the ice seller, who brought with her a block of ice packed in burlap and sawdust. They set it up in the cellar. Matron sent them home with jars of jam and bottles of elderflower syrup and bars of her famous soap. Everyone smiled as they waved goodbye.

Once the meal had been eaten and the dishes washed, Matron and Myron took the toddlers and babies upstairs for their baths, while Elijah told the Littles their bedtime stories and Dierdre and the twins put clean sheets on all the beds, because it was their turn to do so. Anthea looked out the window and saw Bartleby and Cass standing outside. Listening. Anthea stopped. She heard it, too—a voice, oddly amplified. It seemed to vibrate in the very floorboards.

"What on earth?" she muttered.

She went outside, and stood shoulder to shoulder with Bartleby and Cass in the yard, and listened. Then, without saying that they were doing so, the three went to the wall closest to the burned library. Bartleby grabbed the ladder from the toolshed and braced it on the wall, and they began to climb. The three sat together at the top of the wall, looking over the Library ruins and on to the Center Square. They couldn't entirely tell what was going on, but they certainly did see a large crowd present to hear the Mayor.

They listened for a good long while. Bartleby shook his head. "I don't understand it. Why are they so angry at the Ogress? Cass is home. And she's safe."

Anthea rested her chin on her fists. "I have no idea. It doesn't make a tiny bit of sense."

Cass knew, though. It was like when a pile of dry brush becomes a bonfire. The pile could be growing for years, resting without incident, layer upon layer, kindling upon kindling, yet it only takes a single spark to make the whole thing burn. She thought about what had happened on Market Day—people's anger and desperation and frustration. They wanted someone to *pay*. There wasn't enough for everyone, and the less each person had, the less *everyone* had. Until that feeling of *less* was everywhere, all the time.

The people in the square were chanting. Bartleby frowned.

"Are they saying what I think they're saying?" he asked.

Anthea swallowed. "No," she said, as the words *no more ogres* drifted overhead. "They couldn't possibly . . . Oh dear."

They heard the booming voice of the Mayor saying, "I just hope that *nobody breaks the law*." They heard the slither and the hiss inside his words. They knew that someone surely *would* break a law. They saw people raising their fists.

Bartleby took his sister's and Anthea's hands. He held them tight. "This isn't right," he said. "She didn't do anything wrong."

"The Ogress isn't safe," Anthea said. "Someone needs to warn her."

Cass had opened her mouth to reply when she was interrupted by a clucking sound nearby. All three looked down. There, on the ground, was a dog looking up at them.

"Arf," said the dog. He had milky eyes and a patient expression. He wagged his tail.

Perched on the dog's head was a fine-looking crow. It turned its beak and fixed one bright eye directly on Cass. The crow bowed slightly. "Caw," said the crow, which meant "Hello, Child. I believe we've met."

Cass stared for a full moment, her mouth wide open. Then she leaped to her feet, throwing her arms out for balance. "Oh!" she cried. She pressed her hands to her mouth. Her eyes flowed with tears. "I remember now." Her voice filled the yard. Bartleby raised himself onto his knees, his eyes on his sister. He put his hand on her arm. Cass turned to her brother, her face wet, her eyes shining. "I remember it all," she said.

And the crow flew from the head of the dog into the arms of Cass. "Caw," the crow cried joyfully. "Caw, caw, caw, caw, caw."

"Yes," Cass murmured to the crow. "I love you, too."

Harold and Dog Strike Out on their Own

After the Ogress and the crows had left the child outside the gate, Harold had spent the next day brooding.

What if the child was lonely? fussed Harold.

What if they had left her at the wrong house?

What if she got lost again? He couldn't bear the thought. The nights were getting longer. And the frost was already starting to set in here and there, which meant that winter would soon follow, which meant that it was more important than ever to make sure that everyone stayed safe. Harold thought it might be a good idea to check on the child.

The memory of nestling close to the child, feeling the warmth of her and the breath of her, and holding her particular smell deep in his feathers, felt to Harold to be the most precious memory of his whole life. He observed Dog to see if Dog felt the same way. Dog sniffed the ground. Dog scratched his chin. Dog tilted his face toward the sky. Dog nibbled at a flea and then began cleaning his nether regions before setting out to find some sort of snack.

Yes, Harold decided. Dog *definitely* felt the same way. They were simpatico about most things, he and Dog. And so Harold and Dog journeyed back to the place where they had left the child. Along the way, they found themselves crossing the Center Square, where many of the townspeople had gathered, and they stopped to see why. Dog sat next to a largish stone, which was hidden slightly by a pile of trash and debris, and Harold sat on Dog's head, listening.

None of the people standing about noticed them. They were too busy looking at the man on the platform on the other side of the square. Harold sniffed. He supposed one *could* pay attention to that man, but really, wouldn't they rather admire handsome crows, such as himself?

Apparently not. No one gave him a second look. Harold tried not to take it personally.

Why was it, Harold wondered, that the man on the platform looked so familiar? Harold was fairly certain that he had never seen the man before. But that coat rang a bell, somewhere in Harold's crowish mind. And so did the buckles on those boots. He felt unsettled all of a sudden. And discomfited. But he didn't quite know why.

The man spoke to the people. The people began to shout.

"Caw," Harold whispered to Dog, which meant "I do not like the sound of all of this anger. It cannot be safe for dogs or crows!"

"Arf," Dog said, which of course meant nothing.

Dear, dear Dog, Harold thought. He pressed his forehead on the fur between Dog's beloved eyes.

"Caw," Harold said, "It's okay that you don't understand me, Dog. I love you anyway."

"Arf," Dog said, which was as close to "I love you" as he was able to do, and Harold appreciated it. Dog stood up and began walking away, taking care to move behind the crowd and not in front of it. Even he seemed to know that it did not do to stand in front of an angry crowd.

(Harold didn't notice the Stone as they walked away. No one ever noticed the Stone. It was a pity. Had he looked closely, he might have seen a small, nearly worn symbol that looked *just like* a crow roosting upon the head of a dog. And he might have noticed that the crow looked a bit like Harold. And the dog looked a bit like Dog. And I believe this would have pleased him. Ah, well. So it goes.)

Dog kept his nose to the ground, following the scent. Finally, he stopped at the bottom of a very tall wall. He whined a bit. He thumped his tail. He tilted his face upward and said, "Arf."

Harold looked up. And then Harold saw. And he felt his heart leap.

There she was! Sitting on the high wall. *The child!* Harold trembled with joy. He didn't know what he would do if he couldn't see her again. If he couldn't one more time see her face. It seemed to Harold that the world was now *more* of itself, now that the child was in it. He took a deep breath, to center himself. And then he uttered a tremendous squawk.

The children sitting on the wall were startled.

Harold bowed low and addressed the child. And very soon, he returned to her arms. He felt his heart lift, expand, and break, all at once. How long did that moment last? A second? A hundred years? Time was funny when one loved this much.

But everything changed suddenly when the other child spoke. This one had black hair that was pulled into two swinging ropes. "Caw," she said, in perfect Crow. "Thank you so much for coming."

Harold regarded her with one eye, and then the other.

"Caw," the girl continued. "I have wanted to speak with you for a long, long time." Harold was delighted. Did all children speak Crow? Or was it only these children? He had so many questions.

"Caw," the boy said. "Were you the one who brought my sister home?"

"And is it the crows," cawed the girl, "who bring us the food, or is it the Ogress?" She paused. "In either case, thank you," she added primly.

Harold hopped onto the beloved child's knee. He focused one bright eye on the other girl and one on the boy. He planned his words carefully, just to make sure they understood. "Our lady ogress grows the food and bakes the food and gives it all around town. We thought you knew."

The girl with the braids shook her head. "We did not," she said in Crow. "And it's not just us? Well, then, no one knows. No one speaks of it. It has been a great mystery."

Harold cleared his throat and paused again to make sure he was understood properly. "Caw," he continued. "We crows all help. We do this because we are crows, which means 'wonderful.'" He held himself still and tall, to give a good impression. The boy and the girl looked at each other and nodded. Harold puffed up his feathers in delight.

The dark-haired girl held up her hand. She was less enthusiastic than Harold would have guessed at the news of how wonderful crows were. "Do you live with the Ogress? Can you carry a piece of paper in your beak? Because we need to get a message to her right away. She is in danger. Someone needs to warn her."

The girl was gone in a flash.

Harold looked at the child, worry settling in his bones. "Why must my ogress need warning?" he cawed.

In response, the boy and the child looked out at the crowd in the square, their faces grim.

He understood what they meant immediately. "Oh dear," murmured Harold.

34

Ogres Can't Read

Something didn't feel right, but the Ogress wasn't entirely sure why. She fed the sheep under the multicolored sunsetting sky and touched their faces. She went out into the garden and planted new rows of spinach and parsley and chard. She shook the mulberry trees to release the late-season overripe fruit onto the sheets she had lain on the grass below. These she would boil and boil until they became a thick, sweet syrup that she could use in a number of delicacies. She detasseled the corn and repositioned the squash and pinched the basil and plucked the lavender flowers in great bunches. She filled a bushel basket with tomatoes and another with beans. And then she leaned back on her chair to watch as the first stars began to wink in the sky.

The crows munched their dinner. They were quieter than usual. The Ogress could see that they kept their heads cocked and raised. Their top feathers stood at attention. They were listening. *But for what?* She didn't know.

"Caw," the Ogress said to the crows. "Where is the dog?"

The crows didn't answer. The Ogress folded her hands. She lifted her face to the sky. More stars appeared. And a few planets. Why weren't they answering? "And where's Harold? He never misses a meal."

Again, the crows said nothing. It was quite unlike them. What a strange night! The Ogress regarded her crow friends in silent contemplation and then gazed about her farm, listening to the sounds of the coming nighttime. She looked out toward her neighbors. Normally, the farm next door and the farm across the road would have some amount of activity—someone locking up the plow or bringing in the horses or cajoling the cows into the barn. But now there wasn't a sound. "Caw," the Ogress said quietly. "Does tonight feel odd to any of you?"

The crows didn't answer, and the Ogress gave up. She stood and went to her house. She paused at the door to blow the sheep and the crows twenty kisses each, and she disappeared inside. The oven was filled to bursting. Her pies were nearly done. And at least one of the cakes. She still needed to put in the cookies, and she would set the bread to bake while she went into the forest to gather more nuts and mushrooms. So many treats for her neighbors. So many ways that she could fill their stomachs with kindness and love. How she loved this work!

Moments later, Harold and Dog arrived at the farm. Harold held something in his mouth. The crows stood at attention. Sometimes, Harold went on secret missions, just he and Dog. This the crows found absolutely unfair. Harold was being a Dog hog, and the other crows resented him for it.

The Ogress had given all of the crows individual names, but none of the crows had ever used them to refer to themselves or anyone else. Except for Harold. He *called* himself Harold, and the other crows did too, in spite of themselves. Harold had set himself apart. And so the crows, too, set Harold apart. They gave Harold a hard look.

Harold carefully placed the piece of paper in his mouth on Dog's head and held it in place with his foot. "I have news from town," Harold said. "The unkindness of Stone-in-the-Glen has grown into something ugly and fearsome. And it is now aimed at our ogress. We must protect her. She cannot go back into town. I spoke with the children at the house she likes, and they agree. Our ogress is in danger."

The other crows stared at Harold for a very long time, without a click or cluck or coo. The only sound came from the rustling of the sycamore leaves and the calling of frogs and the chirp of the crickets.

Finally: "You spoke to the children?" the crows said. "No. We don't believe you."

Harold stared at his family. "Whyever not?" he said.

"Children don't speak Crow."

"The Child we found in the woods spoke Crow. Plain as day." Harold's heart swelled at the very thought of her.

"According to you," the crows said. "We did not hear her."

"Well, she did," Harold insisted. "And the other children do, too. They are very well-educated children. And well mannered. Polite to crows, if you understand me."

The crows exchanged glances.

Harold was baffled. Here was the very thing they had been worried about.

"It's just that sometimes you make things up," one of the

crows said. "And give yourself airs. It is tiresome, and we are weary of it." The other crows sniffed.

"I never!" Harold puffed himself up. "Are you ignoring this only because I am the one saying it?"

"It is *so like you* to say something like that," one crow sniffed.

A very large crow hopped close to Harold. "Listen," she said. "We are weary of your wild tales. Your uncrowishness is irksome. And frankly, I don't like your tone. Don't trouble the Ogress with your foolery. I forbid it." And with that, the crows turned their backs on Harold and continued pecking at their dinner.

Dog whined. He thumped his tail on the ground. Dog did not like discord.

"Caw," one of the crows said. "Don't worry, Dog. Look what we found for you behind the butcher's shop in town!" The crow flew over to the sycamore tree and returned with a bone, dropping it in front of Dog with a heavy thunk. All of Dog's worries were gone. He fell upon the large bone.

Harold tried not to take it personally. It wasn't the first time his crow family didn't believe him. He clucked. He clicked. He cooed. He even whistled. But none of the crows turned around. *Fine*, he thought. And he placed his piece of paper back into his beak and flew over to the window. He tapped on the glass. The Ogress beamed and opened the sash.

"Hello, my friend!" she said, in the language of people. But then she caught herself. "I mean, caw," she clarified in Crow, which meant "Please make yourself at home."

Harold fluttered over to the table. He set the piece of paper down. He turned his head so he could look the Ogress in the eye. "Caw," he said, "I know I wasn't supposed to, but I went into town today to see the child. I wanted to see if she was okay."

The Ogress listened carefully. Harold wasn't sure if she entirely understood him. He pushed forward. "Caw," he said, which meant "I spoke to the children. They are worried about you. The unkindness in town grows and grows. They say you aren't safe."

The Ogress pinched her eyebrows together and grimaced. Was she understanding? Harold wasn't sure.

"Caw," he concluded. "Look. They wanted you to have this. It is a Paper. One of the children told me it contains Information."

With one talon, Harold flicked the scrolled paper and let it roll toward the Ogress. She clapped her hands with delight. "Caw," she said. "From the children?" Harold bowed his head.

The Ogress flattened the piece of paper. At the top were words. At the bottom was a carefully drawn picture, showing all of the children in the Orphan House, along with the very old couple and a few cats along the edges. In the center, with her arms around the children, was the Ogress herself. All of the figures were smiling.

The Ogress was curious what the words said. But how could the words matter as much as this picture? She felt her heart swell and nearly burst out of her chest. No one had ever given her *anything*, which made it the most precious thing that she had ever received. The Ogress pressed her hands to her eyes. She wept happy tears. She scooped up Harold in her hands and held him close. "Caw. Thank you."

Harold was concerned. "Caw," he said. "Do you understand?"

The Ogress trembled with joy. This was perhaps the happiest day of her life.

"Caw," she said. "Yes. Oh, dear Harold. I understand. I understand perfectly."

(Listen.

She didn't.)

∾

As the Ogress pushed her cart from house to house that night, she thought about the picture that the children had given her, now hanging prominently over her hearth. It wasn't just that the children had drawn her; it was that they had drawn *all of them together*, her arms around the children, and the children's arms around her. *Belonging.* The word repeated in her head as she laid tarts on one doorstep. *Belonging,* she thought as she placed a round of cheese on another. *All I've ever wanted was a place to belong,* she thought as she brought scones to one house. And bread to another. She had thumbprint cookies and nut clusters and hand pies and muffins. Each gift she gave with a new purpose, a new sense of importance. She let her fingers run along the old stone wall as she walked, marveling at the patterns and texture. *I belong here,* she said to herself. *This is my home, too.* The thought rang through her heart, like a bell.

She stopped at the Orphan House. Dog whined and thumped his tail. The crows went closer to the house than they had ever dared. Harold went all the way to the window. It was dark in the house, but the window was open. Harold peeked his head inside. He stayed there for a long time. He clucked and clicked and cooed. "What wonderful children," the Ogress murmured outside, her hand lingering on the gate.

They arrived at the Center Square in the darkest part of the night. The moon had set and the stars were so bright it hurt to look at them. Trash was scattered across the flagstones and heaped in corners. The Ogress looked up. It was hours before dawn. She had time. And so she started picking up the trash and putting it into her handcart. She figured she could burn it in her fireplace and keep her house warm.

Her gaze drifted to the large building at the head of the square, the one with a large platform in front. On top of the platform was a very large sign. The Ogress tilted her head. The sign was bright red, with large white letters written across it. It was a sign that meant business. It was a sign that shouted rather than spoke. It was a sign that insisted that no one look away. It was a sign that meant trouble. "Caw," she said to the crows. "What a large sign. I wonder what it says."

"Caw," Harold said desperately. "It doesn't matter. It isn't safe for you here."

"Don't be silly," the Ogress said. "This is my home. Of course it's safe."

"Caw," he pleaded. "The children were very clear. And how could they be wrong?"

"Hush yourself," the other crows admonished. "Don't vex the Ogress."

And so Harold was quiet. He didn't say anything the whole way home.

He didn't look back at the town as they turned away from the Center Square.

He didn't see the brick shop with the dingy window and a man holding a candle inside, watching them.

He didn't see the man come outside to watch them go.

And he didn't hear the man say, "Just wait."

Stone-in-the-Glen

The cobbler's wife woke to find a lovely loaf of bread and a heavy round of cheese waiting for her on her doorstep.

"Oh," she said. "So kind. So very, very kind. I knew there were still good people left in Stone-in-the-Glen! I knew there was still loveliness here, and haven't I always said so?" There was a little card next to the cheese. It had a small painting showing a dog, sitting at attention. There was a crow on his head. It was, the cobbler's wife had to admit, a rather odd little picture, but sweet in its way. And lovingly painted. She pressed it to her heart and then set the card on the mantel, next to the other cards she had received over the years. Humming softly to herself, she sat at the table and sliced the bread and the cheese. Her husband would need the nourishment. He was so upset about the Ogress he was hardly himself. His eyes were weary, and his cheeks were nearly hollowed out.

"Strength for another day," she told him as she handed him a sandwich. He took her hand and kissed her fingers.

"Thank you, my darling wife," he said, and ate the sandwich gratefully.

Across town, the former teacher received berry custards in pastry cups, each one fitted with a bit of maple sugar spun into the shape of a butterfly.

"Oh," she said, lifting her face to the sky. "Thank you."

The blacksmith received a small box of nut clusters. It wasn't much, but it was breakfast for his children when there was nothing in the larder and all the cupboards were bare. He didn't say anything, but he pressed his hands to his face in case anyone might catch him crying.

"Thank you," he whispered to no one at all.

The lady who made a living fixing broken contraptions received a plate of apple turnovers.

"Thank you," she whispered. "Thank you, thank you, thank you."

The constable received a sweet-potato cake. She took out a piece of paper and wrote *Thank you*, across the top, pinning it to the door for the next time a stranger thought to give her something.

The apothecary received cookies in the shapes of birds. She could barely bring herself to eat them, they were so pretty.

"Thank you," she said, marveling at the buttery wings.

There was another pie on the Mayor's doorstep that morning, but he did not have time to stop and have a slice. He did pause, just for a moment, to bring the pie to his nose and take a good long sniff. Pear with dried cherries, if he wasn't mistaken. Sweetened with honey. Delicious. It would have to wait for later. He had large rolls of paper under his arm. The Mayor's mansion had, in the basement, an ancient printing press and art studio. It had been there since before he had come to Stone-in-the-Glen and long before he ever became mayor.

(How long? No one could say. Except me. But no one asked me.)

He had spent another evening making signs to hang up around the Center Square. NO MORE OGRES, one sign said. SAFETY IN, OGRES OUT, read another. MAKE OUR TOWN LOVELY, said yet another. Each sign had crisp white letters. The paper was red, like the center of a flame. Each sign was excellent, he told himself. He was an excellent mayor. All was right with the world.

Anthea's Plan

Cass had never spoken so many words in her life. First, she explained it to Anthea and Bartleby. It took several tries before they fully understood. "Why didn't you tell us before?" Anthea said. Bartleby glared at her. He was right: there was too much reproach in her voice.

Cass shrugged. "It all felt like a dream. I didn't know which parts were real, or if any of it was."

"We need to tell Matron and Myron," Bartleby said. "They'll believe you. I just know it."

They didn't.

"You spoke to a crow?" Matron said. "Impossible. People can't speak Crow."

"But we can!" Anthea said. "Many of us can. There are several books in the Reading Room on the subject of crow linguistics."

"I never saw such a book," Matron sniffed.

"It's true, though," Bartleby said. "For example, if I say 'Caw,' it means 'It is an honor to make your acquaintance.'"

Myron looked skeptical. "You can't just say the word 'caw' and have it mean any old thing that you want."

"It doesn't, though," Anthea said. "What you just said means 'Beware of cats.' It's all about the intonation. We've gotten good, I promise."

Matron and Myron exchanged a look, throwing up their hands.

"These children!" Matron exclaimed.

"I think everyone might be a little overtired," Myron said, trying to soothe her.

"It is true, though," Cass said, grimacing. "I was lost in the woods, and cold and sick. The crow found me and stayed with me until I fell asleep. Later, I was in the Ogress's house—"

"The Ogress!" Matron's face became pale. "Banish the thought! Little children don't just wander into an ogre's den. They are snatched and probably eaten. Ogres are *dangerous*."

"I don't think they are! *She* isn't," Cass insisted. "She took care of me. She wrapped me up and rocked me. It's true—I know it. And then she brought me home. I didn't escape, and I didn't wander back. I was carried. Didn't you wonder where the blankets came from?"

Matron and Myron exchanged a stricken expression. Matron shook her head. She held up her hand and closed her eyes. "No," she said. "This is the fever talking. And trauma. You may never know what really happened, and maybe that is for the best. Rescued by an ogre! What a ridiculous thought!"

Matron sent the three eldest to bed—no ifs, ands, or buts—as she was certain they were all suffering from brain fever. Cass wept silently, her fists balled up in frustration, and Bartleby tried to compose philosophical arguments, muttering dialogues to himself in hopes that the next conversation would be more useful.

Anthea, on the other hand, pulled out her ledger and started taking notes. There was an answer to this problem. She just needed to find it.

∽

Later that night, after the Littles had finally gone to sleep, Anthea sat on the floor with Bartleby and Cass and laid out her plan. The next day was Market Day. It was the perfect opportunity.

"I'm not convinced," Bartleby said. "Why do you think anyone will listen to us?"

Anthea dismissed this concern with an exasperated wave. "You saw what those people were like. If we can't convince *everyone*, maybe we can inform the Mayor. If people won't listen to us, then maybe they'll listen to him. He has the loudest voice in town anyway. The Mayor is . . . odd, but it's not his fault that the people in this town are so terrible. Look at all the good the cobbler's wife has accomplished, just from deciding to do good and pulling everyone else along with her. If we can convince the Mayor, maybe he can persuade everyone else."

"I'm *not convinced*," Bartleby said, raising his voice slightly and going a little red.

Anthea was about to say something meaner than she should have, but then she noticed that Cass had curled her fingers around Bartleby's arm. She gave him a *look* that said, with utter clarity, that Bartleby was to set his reservations aside, and that was that.

Bartleby locked eyes with his sister. He looked at her closely. "Are you sure?" he said. "Remember last time?" Instinctively, he grasped Anthea's hand and Cass's hand, and pulled both siblings close. "I don't want anyone to get hurt again." His eyes were shiny and wet.

Cass nodded. She was sure.

It took some doing to convince Matron and Myron to allow the three eldest to accompany Myron to Market Day. They had convinced both Dierdre and Elijah to fake stomachaches as a precaution. After much fretting and hand-wringing, it was settled. Anthea, Bartleby, and Cass breathed a sigh of relief as they passed through the gates with Myron. That relief vanished the moment they reached the Center Square. They stopped and looked up. The square was filled with signs:

WE DON'T HAVE ROOM FOR OGRES, one sign said.

PROTECT OUR CHILDREN, KEEP OGRES OUT, over the butcher's shop.

MAKE OUR TOWN LOVELY AGAIN, draped across the Town Hall.

WHOSE CHILD WILL BE NEXT? written in chalk on the ground.

SEE WHAT HAPPENS WHEN WE LET OGRES IN? draped over the tumble of stones where the Library used to be.

IT USED TO BE A LOVELY TOWN, BUT THEN THE OGRES TOOK IT, fluttering from the statue standing in the center of the old fountain.

Sign after sign after sign.

"What on earth," Anthea whispered.

"This is bad, Anthea," Bartleby sighed. He shook his head. "I'm not sure your plan is going to work."

Anthea held her hands up. "It will work," she said. As though saying it was true would make it so.

Cass rolled up her sleeves and started setting up the market stall. A defunct lamppost stood next to their space. It had a sign on it that said RALLY AT THE END OF MARKET DAY! MAKE YOUR OPINIONS KNOWN. Cass waited until no one was watching. Then, in one quick movement, she snatched the sign from the post and folded it quickly, shoving it into her back pocket. She nodded grimly. And then she returned to the task of setting up.

Anthea couldn't stand still. She glanced up at the dais. No one was there. She looked toward the road that led to the Mayor's mansion. She saw several people on bicycles and an old man walking an even older dog, but she saw no sign of the Mayor himself. No matter, she told herself. There was still time.

Her eyes drifted toward the Library ruins. She tried to imagine what it must have looked like. Wide doors. Wide windows. Crows lounging on the sills and ledges, listening to the hubbub within. *Why is it still ruined?* she asked herself. *Why didn't they rebuild? Why give up and do nothing? It isn't rational.*

The butcher made his way past the stalls and stopped in front of Myron. He had his arms folded across his belly and pressed inward, as though it bothered him. His mouth curled into an unpleasant pucker. "I apologize, Myron, for my outburst the other day. I should have been more kind, considering. Sorry about your loss."

Myron smiled. "Oh, my good sir, you are mistaken. Nothing, and no one, has been lost. We had a child who went missing. But look!" He put his arm around Cass. "She found her way home! Isn't that marvelous! All is well, but thank you for your concern."

The butcher's arms pressed deeper into his belly and his sour expression darkened. "That's not what I heard. And that's not what I seen. That ogress is taking children, is what I know. And we're gonna stop her. Just you wait." He flared his nostrils and glared, like a bull. "I don't know why you want to lie about it," the butcher said.

Myron flipped his hands slowly, exposing his palms to the butcher. He spoke calmly and gently, the way a person might speak to a dangerous animal. "No one is lying at all, my dear, dear friend. All I am saying is that this, here, is the child who went missing. And this, here, is the child who returned. I can see you are feeling very concerned about what the Ogress may have done. I do not know either way. But maybe you might feel better after a nice, long, relaxing soak in the tub. Would you like to buy some soap?"

"Humph," the butcher said, gesticulating in exasperation, and he stomped away. He didn't buy any soap.

Myron and the children stood very still for a long time after that. Finally, Anthea said, "What is the use of truth when people refuse to believe verifiable facts?"

"I do not know, my love," Myron said. Myron was trying to keep his face very blank, but Anthea could see the worry in his eyes. She reached over and took his hand, giving it a little squeeze.

Bartleby frowned. "Our favorite philosopher says that anger is just fear in disguise." He paused as they watched the butcher make his way down the row of stalls, frowning and yelling and throwing his hands up to anyone he met. "I wonder what that man is actually afraid of?"

Cass cleared her throat. She glared. And then, very quietly, she said, "I would like to kick that man." If the other three hadn't been listening closely, they might not have heard it.

"Me too, Cass," Bartleby said, putting his arms around his sister. "Me too."

∾

The morning slid past, and the Mayor still hadn't arrived. The day was overly bright, and the light was searing, even though it was still windy and cold. Bartleby called out the praises of their wares, and Cass counted the money, while Anthea fussed over Myron. He looked pale, so she brought him some water. He had a cough, so she gave him some lozenges she had made from boiling herbs and raspberry seeds in honey until they'd hardened into little nuggets. He looked cold, so she insisted that he wrap himself in the thin blanket they had brought. He squinted in the glare, so she made him a sunshade. She saw that he was shifting his weight from one leg to the other and pressing his fists into his back.

"Myron," she said, the truth of the matter suddenly dawning on her, "you need something to sit on."

He waved her off. "No, dearest. I'm fine, I'm just—"

"I'll be right back!" Anthea grabbed her tools and ran past the market stalls and through the expanse of the Center Square, squinting in the harshness of the light.

In the center of the Center Square sat a stone that no one noticed. No one had noticed it for ages. Even when they paused near it or lingered next to it or set their bag on top of it to give their shoulders a break for a moment or two, they *still* didn't really notice the Stone. It was drab, after all. And nondescript.

There was a bunch of old wood strewn about it. And because it was already messy, people didn't notice themselves leaving a sack of old, rusty hinges, for example. Or a bent metal bar. Or a broken table. Or the splintered leftovers of an ancient school desk. Or the remains of an old handcart that had long ago pushed its last load.

Over time, the junk pile grew, dwarfing the Stone. The pile was so high that, at the time that Anthea walked over, the Stone sat in a little bit of shade, which was a relief. Despite the shade, the Stone was still quite warm, as though it had been sitting the whole morning in the sun. Anthea rested one hand on the Stone, and then the other, marveling at its delightfully radiant heat. She figured it must have been sun-warmed for hours.

(Listen.

It wasn't. The Stone was always in shadow. And the Stone was always warm.)

Anthea sat on the Stone, observed what was available in the junk pile, and assessed the possibilities. In her mind, she began designing what she might build, given the available resources. There were old nails littering the ground—most bent, but some straight and true. That was a good start. She pressed her hands against the warm stone. Its nubbly grooves and notches felt nice to touch. Her mind started to wander. If her hand drifted a little to the left, she started thinking about the Ogress, and a little farther still to the left, she had, quite suddenly and clearly, an image of a whole village of ogres living happily with one another, not noticing that a dragon was lurking nearby.

Anthea shook her head. She lifted her hands off the Stone. The image in her head disappeared. "What a strange thing to think about," she said out loud.

She took a step back. She looked at her hands. Her hands had been touching something. She had been thinking about something. *But what was it?* She shook her head. "Focus, Anthea," she said, and reoriented herself to the task of building a stool.

She pulled out bits and pieces of wood, as well as some mismatched but functional brackets. The top of an old desk made a fine seat, and she found four fairly even and sturdy bits of lumber to act as legs. She leaned against the Stone, her palm flat on the warm surface, as she fitted the brackets onto the makeshift seat and readied her hammer.

She found herself thinking about a dragon who swindled a village full of ogres. The dragon wore shoes with golden buckles and a smart cape and an actual ogre's face and spoke with a glittering smile. The image startled her. She removed her hand and rubbed her face. She must not have gotten enough sleep last night. Why on earth was her mind wandering so? Also, how would a dragon wear an ogre's face? Almost instantly, the image began to fade from her mind.

What is happening? she thought. *Oh*, she remembered. *The stool. I have only been thinking about the stool.* She re-adjusted her seat as she tested the stability of the stool. She leaned her back against the Stone. And she thought about those shoes with golden buckles. Or maybe they were boots. And she wondered if a dragon could wear an ogre's face, could he wear any other sort of face as well? Then she saw in her mind's eye a dragon taking off a man's skin and setting off to do dragonish things. Like hunting small animals, and creeping along the side of a stately old building, and unhooking its wide, glittering jaws and unleashing an inferno into a quiet night.

Anthea yelped. She jumped backward, shivering. Her skin crawled. What had she been thinking about? She couldn't remember. The thoughts crowding her head had vanished like smoke. She looked up and down the square. No one came over to this section. Too much garbage. People had forgotten it was there.

She walked away from the Stone. She shook her head to clear away the distractions. Why was she so foggy today? She needed to take the stool to Myron. She walked away with a nagging, unsettled notion that she had forgotten something important. It buzzed in her ear, like a persistent mosquito. She batted it away.

"I made you this," she said when she arrived back at the stall. "Because your back was hurting."

Myron clapped his hands together. "Well, my Anthea! How very clever! But where on earth did you find the materials?"

Anthea frowned. She looked behind her. Something was bothering her, but she couldn't quite pin down what it was. It was a vexing sort of question mark. She tried to ignore it. She looked back at Myron. "Oh, you know," she said vaguely. "There is always a little bit of cast-off trash in Stone-in-the-Glen."

Myron nodded. "Indeed."

For the rest of the day, Bartleby called out to customers, and Cass minded the cashbox, and Anthea kindly informed people when they were wrong about something, which happened pretty often. Anthea kept her eyes on the dais, waiting for the Mayor to arrive. She would tell him the truth, and then he would tell other people the truth, and then things would be okay. She was sure of it.

"Soap!" Bartleby called. "Excellent soap!"

"And elderflower syrup and raspberry cordial and jam!" Myron added.

Cass counted the money. She glared at anyone who might try to cheat them.

The afternoon light blared. People shaded their eyes, trying to get a little bit of relief. They squinted and peered through an ever-narrowing view. Anthea pressed her hands hard against her eyes. It was too bright, which made it hard to think. When she had sat by the junk pile, her mind had wandered, and the places it had wandered to were . . . strange.

The Town Hall bells rang.

The Mayor arrived.

Anthea looked around. People from town were streaming into the Center Square. Some had homemade signs. All wore scowls on their faces. "I think it's time to go," Myron said. He started packing their unsold wares into boxes.

The Mayor held his hands up high over his head. His hair and smile gleamed in the sun. He shone like a torch over the crowd. "Be right back!" Anthea said, and before Myron could say anything, she snaked through the crowd at a run.

Anthea ducked and dodged through a sea of elbows and boots and wooden signs. Some people chanted, "*No more ogres!*" while other people chanted, "*Take back our town,*" getting louder all the time.

The Mayor smiled. He scooped his hands upward, again and again, as though asking people to raise their voices. And the gesture seemed to work. Some people raised their fists. Anthea saw how their mouths became hard. She saw how their eyes began to glitter.

Surely, facts would matter. Wouldn't they? Anthea pushed her way to the front. The Mayor stood before her. The boards of the dais groaned and shuddered each time he took a step. The Mayor lifted his face toward the low sun and smiled slightly, like he was enjoying the angle of the light. His hair shone, his skin shone, and even his eyes seemed to glow. The Mayor dazzled the eye. The dramatic sweep of his coat sparkled in the sun. The golden buckles on his boots flashed, so bright it hurt to look at them.

Golden buckles, Anthea found herself thinking, like the memory of a memory. She shook her head, to clear it.

"Mr. Mayor," she called out.

He didn't hear her. "My dear townspeople," he said to the gathering crowd, his voice oddly amplified. "I am so happy to see that so many of you could come. I must say, I expected more, though. Perhaps if you all chant louder, more people in Stone-in-the-Glen, or maybe every single person in Stone-in-the-Glen, will come and pay attention to me—I mean, they will come and pay attention to this serious, serious concern. Raise your voices, my friends."

"Mr. Mayor!" Anthea shouted. She knocked on the dais. She waved her hands. He didn't look down.

"Keep your hands to yourself!" a woman on her right said.

"Children today have *no manners*. No wonder the Ogress wants them. Oafs love oafs. That's logic, that is. Ogres have no taste at all!"

Anthea ignored all of this. "*Mr. Mayor!*" she roared.

The Mayor frowned. He scanned the crowd. Anthea knocked on the boards by his feet, but it took him a long minute before he thought to look down. He gave Anthea a quizzical look. "Are you a child?" he asked mildly.

Anthea blanched. It was not the question she was expecting. "Yes?" she said.

"Ah," the Mayor said, his face unfurling in a magnanimous smile. He opened his arms in a grand gesture, letting the fabric of his coat ripple splendidly in the light. "I've met children before. It is one of my many attributes as mayor."

A woman next to Anthea swooned as the pressed crowd of adults nearby burst into applause. Anthea turned around and glared. "Stop applauding!" she ordered. "What's the matter with you? *All of you* have met children before!"

But the Mayor wasn't listening, and neither were the people nearby. "I should be hearing more chanting, my good neighbors!" the Mayor said, and people chanted more.

"*No more ogres!*" the crowd said, again and again.

Anthea pounded on the boards. The Mayor looked to his left and right, and once again slowly turned his gaze down and registered Anthea's presence with a slightly surprised smile. "Oh!" he said. "Are you a child?"

"Yes," Anthea said acidly. "We've already discussed that. *You need to listen to me.*"

"I've met children before!" the Mayor enthused.

"*No more ogres!*" the crowd said, again and again. They pressed closer to Anthea's back. They smelled of dust and work and sweat. The Mayor looked up and admired the crowd. He smiled broadly. He was saying something softly to himself, but Anthea couldn't hear it. From the shape of his mouth, it looked as though he was saying, *Mine, mine, mine,* but that didn't make any sense. None of this was logical. She felt like tearing her hair out by the roots.

Anthea pounded on the boards. The Mayor looked down with mild surprise. "*You have to listen*," Anthea yelled. Her voice had begun to rasp. "The Ogress doesn't steal children. Everyone has made a mistake. A child from the Orphan House *ran away and got lost in the woods*. The Ogress found her and *brought her home*."

The Mayor's face became indulgent. "Children are so funny when they are wrong," he said.

"*I'm not wrong*," Anthea said as loud as she could. "You need to tell everyone. People do stupid things when they get riled up. They do stupid things when they believe something that is untrue. They make mistakes that they later regret! Someone could get hurt. It isn't logical to allow falsehoods to spread!"

The Mayor looked out at the crowd. "Whose child is this?" His voice carried so far it seemed to shake the buildings and the flagstones of the square. He glittered in the sun. His golden boot buckles were too bright to look at.

Anthea shaded her eyes. "And another thing!" she said. "The Ogress has been leaving food for the Orphan House. And probably other houses, too. She's been doing this for *years*. The crows told me so!"

"Silly child," the Mayor said. "Crows don't talk." He looked out into the assembled townspeople. "*This is not a place for children*," the Mayor boomed. People looked up admiringly, pleased to have a mayor who could so command a crowd. "Will whoever owns this one please remove her at once?"

Anthea turned desperately to the adults near her. "You don't understand!" she said to the woman on her right. "Please listen to me," she begged the people behind her. "The Ogress didn't take anyone." She said to the man on her left, "*The Ogress brought our sister home.*"

The Mayor didn't look down. "Remove her," he said with a wave of his hand. He smoothed back his golden hair. The crowd went wild.

At once, a man picked Anthea up by the waist. "Shh, child," the cobbler said. "I have you. You have been making quite a fuss. This is *no place* for a child! Let's go someplace safe, shall we?"

Anthea kept talking desperately. "Sir," she said, "you have to understand. Everyone has the wrong idea. The Ogress is kind. She helps the Orphan House. She's been helping us when no one else in town would. We wouldn't have survived without her. She brought Cass home. You have to *listen.*"

The crowd chanted. The Mayor asked for more cheers and was rewarded every time.

The cobbler set Anthea down next to Myron. The cobbler had a kind face, and Anthea knew he was a kind man, but he didn't look at Anthea or Bartleby or Cass. He looked only at Myron. "You need to take these children out of here right now," the cobbler said.

"Sir," Bartleby said. "You need to make the Mayor understand what Anthea is saying."

"I absolutely agree," Myron said to the cobbler. "I have never seen people so riled up."

"Cass *ran away,*" Anthea said. "And the Ogress *brought her back.*"

"Do you need help carrying your supplies?" the cobbler said to Myron.

277

Bartleby was in tears. "Kindness exists! Can't you see? And it makes more kindness! Look at what has happened at the Orphan House just in the last few days. Why don't you understand?"

"No, no," Myron told the cobbler. "We are fine. I think your leadership is needed here. Cool heads must prevail." Myron attempted to lift one box, but his face twisted in pain.

Cass swooped over and grabbed it herself. She stepped in between Myron and the cobbler and tried to make herself look taller. "This is my fault," she said. Her voice was loud and clear, like a bell.

The cobbler seemed to melt a little bit. He was a tall man, much taller than Myron, and towering over Cass. He knelt down on the ground and looked Cass in the eye. "No, darling. Never say that." He put his large hand on her shoulder. "This isn't anyone's fault. What you're seeing here is many years' worth of worry and frustration and pain. Go on home and have a good meal and get to bed early. Don't blame yourself for any of this." With that, he stood and strode toward the crowd.

After a moment, he paused briefly and called over his shoulder. "And anyway, the only one at fault here is that ogre. She never should have come here." Then he disappeared into the din.

It wasn't a long walk back to the Orphan House, but Anthea felt it seemed to take a thousand years.

How could reason fail her so?

How could facts have no meaning?

Every step she took echoed through the empty street, and every echo seemed to be saying, *You failed, you failed, you failed.*

Humph

The Ogress threw open her door as the sun set and greeted a
sky full of color.

"Hello, my friends!" she said to the crows. "Hello, my dears!"
she said to the sheep.

Her cooling racks were heavy with baked goods: Hand pies
with hearts carved in the crust. Bread loaves sweetened with
honey. Éclairs filled with custard, and cookies bursting with
nuts. Nut-filled pies and fruit-filled pies, and pies made from
sheep's-milk pudding layered with honeyed rose petals.

She fed the sheep and watered the garden and filled her basket full of apples from the tree.

"Caw," the crows warned. "Something isn't right."

"Caw," they said. "Let's not go to Stone-in-the-Glen tonight."

Harold said nothing. He knew they wouldn't listen to him
anyway. Instead, he went over to the Ogress and perched on her
shoulder.

"Why, Harold," she said, inclining her cheek toward his

shiny feathers. "So lovely to have you here. Is there something you wanted to tell me?"

Harold knew that the other crows didn't want him frightening their dear ogress. He knew that they thought he had made everything up. And now, even when they, too, could sense something was amiss, he knew that they wouldn't like it if he spoke up now. So instead, he said, "Caw." Which meant "I have nothing to say that will vex or upset you. I only want you to know that I love you."

The Ogress beamed. "Why, Harold!" she said. "Of course I love you, too." She gave him an affectionate tap on his head. "Come, my friends. Let's see what the forest has for us." And she walked toward the road, the sheep behind her and the crows rushing ahead.

She saw a group of men and women in dusty coveralls and heavy boots walking toward her. This was unusual. Most people in Stone-in-the-Glen were indoors by sunset. And she never saw people traveling in groups. She waved and smiled.

The faces of the men and women, already hard, became like sharp stones thrown from a fist.

"Humph," a man said. He held up a sign.

"What?" the Ogress said.

"Humph," said a woman. She, too, had a sign that the Ogress couldn't read.

"Good evening," the Ogress said.

Another group approached from the left. There were so many people in one place. The Ogress suddenly felt dizzy.

"What's the matter with you?" a woman said. "Can't you read the sign?" She held it over her head.

The Ogress stepped backward. The sheep crowded around her. They were part wild, those sheep, and they tilted their horns forward, making sure everyone could see how sharp they were. "Baa," the sheep said. No one knew what this meant.

"Caw," the crows called, which meant "Let's get out of here this minute."

"Caw," Harold whispered. "There's more of this to come. Get ready."

The Ogress looked at the woman who had spoken. She wore plain woolen trousers and tall boots and a leather work coat that was much too big for her. The woman's hair was tied back in a black kerchief. She glared at the Ogress.

"I'm sorry, but no," the Ogress said, not knowing what else to say. "I can't read the sign at all."

"Don't talk to her," said a man whose face was crumpled in the center like a wad of paper. "You don't have permission. Move along."

The crows landed on the shrubs and nearby trees. Some circled menacingly overhead. The sheep showed their horns, and the dog growled.

"I'm sorry?" the Ogress said.

"*We don't want you here,*" a man yelled, holding up a sign.

"*Go back where you came from,*"· a woman said, holding up her fist and stepping back.

"But I live here," the Ogress said, feeling herself beginning to cry. Each of their words hit her face like a slap. "I belong here."

"*Humph,*" said the man near her.

"*No more ogres!*" said another.

"But . . ." the Ogress said, trying to catch her breath, "but why?"

"*You will never belong,*" a man roared. He reached down and picked up a rock, reared back, and threw it. It landed hard on the Ogress's shoulder. Humans are not as strong as ogres. Or as dense. The rock didn't hurt her the way it would have hurt a person. But it shocked her all the same. Another man threw a rock. And another.

The crows had seen quite enough.

"Caw," the crows shouted as one. There is no translation for that particular word. It is the oldest phrase in the whole Crow language. It is part screech, part ululation, part wild, brave cry. It is the call of war, a call of justice, a call of holy love. Even people who don't speak Crow know exactly what it means. The people on the road saw a rush of wings and the glint of beaks and the pitiless razor-sharp tips of oncoming talons, and they ran for their lives, screaming.

The Ogress stood on the road in perfect stillness for a long time. The sheep kept close. The dog kept close. The crows alighted softly on the ground nearby. Harold carefully climbed from her shoulder to the upper pocket of her apron and nestled himself next to her heart.

The Ogress sank slowly to her knees. She put her large face into her larger hands. She cried so much that a great pool opened up before her, deep with tears. She did her best to dry her eyes before she accidentally washed out the entire road, and then where would everyone be?

The Ogress wiped the sadness away from her cheeks and looked at the crows, who all stood at attention on the ground, looking at her. They didn't move a feather. The sheep stood at attention. They didn't move, either. Only the dog moved. He sniffed the ground. He made his way over to the Ogress. He lay down and leaned against her, resting his snout on her knee, and whined, just a little bit.

The crows said nothing. They loved the Ogress so, so much. They scanned the roads for signs of danger. They quietly resolved that if anything like this were to happen again, they would go for the eyes.

The Ogress looked up at the crows, as though hearing what they were thinking. "No, my friends. Crows are brave and noble. Violence isn't brave. And retaliation isn't noble."

The crows protested, but she held up her hand. "I know they started it. And I don't know why. This isn't just anger—I've seen anger. It's something bigger and sharper and meaner. The antidote to anger is tenderness, and the antidote to discord is reconciliation. I have lived longer than all of you, and I can tell you that this is the only way. I have seen this town behave with secret acts of kindness and connection for a long time. I know they are better than this, and I will prove it to them. I will show them what their best selves can look like."

She stood, smoothed out her dress, and headed back toward home. She had racks full of delicious food to give to the town. She trusted in generosity. And no one was going to stop her.

Back at the crooked house, the Ogress paused for a moment to take in the sky. She was a large creature in comparison to the crows or the sheep or the cat or the dog or the people in town. She had large hands and a broad brow and heavy feet. But in the face of the world and in the light of the universe, she was a tiny thing indeed. And yet . . .

The great universe still delighted in tiny things. She knew this in her bones. And even a tiny act of kindness and generosity still mattered.

She pushed her cart, heaped with gifts, toward Stone-in-the-Glen, under the glittering stars.

Enough

The next morning, the Mayor found pie, and the cobbler found an excellent cheese, and the carpenter found a plate of blackberry muffins. The butcher found a basket of rolls, which he thought surely would only aggravate his indigestion, so he threw them into the trash. Then he thought better of it and pulled them out again and ate them. He grudgingly admitted that they were delicious.

Indeed, all around town, people noticed that, for some reason, this morning there was more of everything. Their gifts were larger, sweeter, more wonderful than usual. The former teacher marveled at the arrival of apple pie *and* a custard tart *and* a plate of cheese turnovers. The former street sweeper couldn't take his eyes off the massive mound of cake on his doorstep. The town doctor deeply appreciated the acorn bread—filled, as she knew, with both protein and minerals, and excellent for good health. The whole town was given something more than usual.

They stopped and marveled. What was the reason for this abundance? And who was responsible? And in their stopping and marveling, they forgot to be suspicious. They forgot to hide their good fortune. They stood on the stoops and steps and streets, holding their gifts up in the light, taking in the scent of butter and honey and melting crumb.

And then they noticed one another marveling. "You too?" the doctor asked the street sweeper.

"It's not just me?" the former janitor said to the lady who used to light the lamps.

"But who? Who did this?" the apothecary asked.

"Not me," said the blacksmith.

"Nor me," said the cobbler, with his mouth full.

The cobbler's wife gave an exasperated shrug. "You sillies! It doesn't matter who did it," she said to anyone who would listen. "The thing that matters is that it *happened*. The thing that matters is that this act of kindness and generosity could have been done by anyone. Anyone at all! The world is filled with goodness, and our response should not be silence and suspicion. You have a responsibility to be *grateful*. You have a responsibility to do *good* as a result. Be good and do good. That's the lesson." And then, with a decisive nod, she bustled back and forth to the Orphan House, scolding anyone who didn't come with her to help.

Anthea, Bartleby, and Cass were outside with Myron, harvesting the last of the tomatoes, turning the earth and covering that section of the garden with mulch, when they heard a loud group pass by on the street, just on the other side of the wall. Some in the group slurred their words. They whooped and huzzahed.

"You shoulda seen her face when the rock hit her," one man howled. "She cried like a little baby. Wah! Wah!"

Myron's face creased, and his eyes became grim. The children stopped their work to listen. Another man laughed until he coughed. "Well, the bigger they are, the harder they fall. Like a tree in the forest—*timber!* I'd like to see it when it happens."

"Can you believe a monster of that size has no fight in it?" a woman scoffed. "She was the size of a big bear standing on the shoulders of a bigger bear. She might be big, but she's weak."

"You know," yet another said. "That house is a tinderbox. One match, and poof!"

"Serves her right. Bloody ogres. This is *our town*. She can buzz off."

"I keep rocks in my bag, just in case."

"I always keep my flint and steel. Opportunity waits"—the man hiccuped—"for no man."

They laughed and hooted and stumbled away, their voices echoing against the far buildings.

Anthea turned to Myron. She folded her arms. "Someone needs to warn the Ogress," she said. "She did nothing wrong."

"You don't know what you're talking about," Myron said. "You're just a child."

"The Ogress found Cass in the forest and brought her home," Bartleby said. "She's the one who brings us the vegetables. Don't you see? We owe her."

"Cass was delirious and has no idea what she actually saw," Myron said. "And don't even start with the crows. You children can't speak Crow!"

"There is an entire section on the Crow language in the Reading Room," Anthea roared. "Myron, what's the matter with you? How can you not do anything? You are supposed to be one of the good ones!"

Myron knelt down onto the damp grass. He took Anthea's hand. "Don't you see? This isn't a good town. They will *always* do bad things. You're too young, and you haven't seen what I have seen. We *can't* get involved. Did you hear those men? Imagine if they took it in their heads to talk about the Orphan House that way. We have too much to lose. All we can do is lock the gates and keep ourselves safe and love one another with everything that we have. The Ogress is bigger than us and stronger than us. She can take care of herself."

"But, Myron," Bartleby began.

"There are creatures on this earth that are capable of terrible things. Things I can't even speak of," Myron said, getting creakily to his feet. "You can't possibly know." His face grew cloudy, and Myron looked away. Unconsciously, he rubbed the scars on his hands and arms. "Clean this mess up. I have to go inside." He hurried in, without looking back.

The wind stirred the trees. The leaves were just starting to turn new colors, and there was a chilly bite in the air.

Anthea turned to Cass and Bartleby. "We have to go. We have to warn her. Tonight, if we can."

That evening, after everyone in Stone-in-the-Glen had finished their dinners and cleaned their dishes, some turned their gazes toward the Ogress's crooked house.

It used to be a lovely town, people grumbled.

But then that ogress moved in, they said, seething.

And who does she think she is?

The wind blew the limbs of the sycamores. Even from the center of town, people could hear those trees creaking in the breeze. Even inside their homes, they could hear the crows starting their infernal racket. How could a person hear themselves think with those crows about? How could a person feel safe with that ogress about? Somebody needed to do something.

In the waning light, some houses in Stone-in-the-Glen heard a knock at the door. Some people peeked through the keyhole and saw the butcher standing there. "Our town is a shadow of what it used to be," the butcher told them. "The ruins of our beloved buildings still lie in heaps on the ground, and the smoke from the fires is still in the air. Look at what we've become! Do you remember our streets before the blight? Do you remember the park before the sinkhole? Do you remember our beautiful library? Someone is responsible, and you know exactly who it is. Don't you think it's time we stand up for ourselves?"

One by one, people came out of their houses. One by one, they gathered in the street.

"Let's go," the butcher said.

The last remnants of the day's light slanted deeply through the mulberry trees and dappled the garden. The crows snoozed in their nests, deep in dreams. Inside the house, the Ogress pulled six pies out of the oven and set them on racks next to the breads and honeyed nut loaves to cool. She had finished decorating the cakes, but still had final touches to put on several dozen cookies, each one depicting the smiling face of a person in town, carefully painted in frosting colored with pulverized flower petals. This was her most abundant baking day yet, an avalanche of treats to delight, comfort, and nourish. This was what her community needed most. Someone to care about them. Someone to share with them. This was how they could remember who they truly were.

She didn't hear the footsteps on the road. She didn't see the people creeping along the gullies and ruts, staying out of sight of the sleeping crows.

She had just finished the face of the constable when a stone flew through the window, spangling the pies with broken glass. As she whirled around, the dog put his tail between his legs and hid behind her massive boots.

She ran to the door. Several figures approached, silhouetted by the setting sun. She squinted, and retreated into the shade. She couldn't see how many there were. "Hello?" she said.

An egg hit her open door.

Another hit her apron.

Six rocks hit the wall next to where she stood.

The crows rose up in a cloud. "Caw," they screeched. "Danger," they meant.

The Ogress held up her hands. "Stand down, all of you. Surely this is a misunderstanding." The setting sun glared. She shaded her eyes. It was difficult to see clearly. "Excuse me?" she called. She smiled broadly, her large hand unconsciously smoothing back her prairie-grass hair. "Hello! I don't think we've met. Please, come inside. I have so many things to share. After all, the more we give, the more we—Oh, please don't hurt my plants!"

Five men stood in her garden, stomping on the squash and tearing plants out by their roots. They ruined the tomatoes and the beans. They smashed the melons.

The crows screamed and the dog growled, his hackles up.

The Ogress stood in the square of shade on the veranda, afraid to move. She squinted to see better. "Please," she called. "I don't understand. Why are you doing this? We're neighbors."

"No, we're not," one man said.

"No one asked you to come here," a second man added, throwing another rock.

Someone threw a rope over the top of the periscope and pulled it down from the roof. Someone hung a banner between the mulberry trees. It said OGRES, GO HOME, but the Ogress could not read it.

The crows refused to wait a second longer. They raised themselves up in a great black cloud overhead. "*Caw*," they screamed. "*There are more of us than there are of you.*"

The men began to scatter.

"*Caw*," the birds cried as they dove into people's faces. Their arms. Their backs. Their necks. "*We will not be merciful.*"

"Let's get out of here!" one man yelled, protecting his eyes.

"They don't call them 'murders' for nothing!" replied another as they scrambled back to the road.

"*Caw!*" They nipped people's cheeks and arms and rear ends, each time drawing blood. "*Never come back.*"

The butcher peeled away from the crowd. His lantern swinging, he charged around the far end of the ruined garden toward the barn.

"*Not my sheep!*" the Ogress cried. She ran into the light of the setting sun, ignoring the burning sensation on her skin, the dog following close at her heels. "*Please don't hurt my sheep.*"

The man swung his right arm in a wide arc and let the lantern fly through the open window. It landed on a pile of hay, which ignited instantly. Flames encircled the posts and spread across the walls, curling over the roof.

The Ogress ran across the yard, toward the burning building. "There are lambs in there!" she yelled. "And two mothers who just gave birth yesterday. How could you?" Tears streamed down her stony cheeks as she raced into the smoke.

The butcher went pale. "Lambs?" he gasped.

There was no other choice. He ran after her into the barn. The fire roared. The sheep screamed. Smoke pressed into his eyes and mouth, disorienting his vision and making him choke. He threw his arm across his face as he stumbled to the pens. He opened the gates and grabbed the four infant lambs, coaxing their mothers to follow him to safety. The Ogress was able to gather five or six full-grown sheep at a time. Very quickly, they were all accounted for and safe. The butcher fell to his knees, checking each lamb—their eyes and gums, and listening to their lungs. Making sure they weren't injured.

The Ogress sank to the ground next to the butcher, watching the fire devour the barn she had built. The flames were bright and angry. It hurt to look at them. The butcher cradled a lamb in his arms, stroking its head, soothing and shushing it like a baby. The sun sank low, and the shadows grew long. The Ogress turned and looked at the butcher, who was a little less than half her size. He lifted his face and looked back at her and then down at the lamb in his arms. He shrugged.

"Thank you," she said. "For them. Even though . . ." There wasn't much to say after that. She returned her gaze to the burning barn.

The lamb, content in the butcher's arms, began to snore. "I grew up with sheep," he said. "Had a pet lamb when I was a boy. Can't abide harming them. I won't touch them in my shop. A sheep is a creature who couldn't possibly hurt anything else." He looked at the barn. "Sorry about the fire." He looked at the Ogress and frowned. "I thought . . ." he began. Then he swallowed.

Inside the barn, the loft collapsed. There was no way the structure could be saved. The butcher looked behind them at the ruined garden. He held the lamb a little closer. "I thought you couldn't go into sunlight," he said. "I thought it would . . . you know."

"Kill me?" the Ogress said. There was resignation in her voice.

The man hung his head, rubbing the back of his neck.

The Ogress pressed her stony lips together. "That's not how sunlight works." She didn't take her eyes off the barn. She put her arms around several sheep. "It gives us a rash and sometimes a mild burn. It hurts. But it doesn't hurt as much as the thought of losing my sheep." She tilted her face away so he couldn't see her crying.

The sheep pressed against the Ogress, tenderly leaning their faces on her arms and torso. The lamb in the butcher's arms had fallen fast asleep. It felt warm and soft and safe. The butcher cleared his throat. "Well," he said. He set the lamb down.

"Well," he added, just because. He turned without another word and walked away.

The crows watched him go, letting him pass without incident. He had helped to save the lambs, after all. The crows gathered on the backs of the sheep and on the shoulders and hands of their beloved ogress, keeping close.

The fire raged. They stayed there together, watching the barn burn down.

∽

Anthea, Bartleby, and Cass snuck out of their beds a little after midnight. Together, they tiptoed down the stairs. They went to the drawer in Matron's desk where she kept the keys. It was empty. Then they noticed that the door to Matron and Myron's room was open, and neither one of them was in their bed.

"What on earth?" Bartleby said.

They tiptoed to the front door. Matron and Myron were sleeping in cots blocking the exit. They both had keys in their hands. Myron had put a small sign next to his pillow. NICE TRY, it said.

∽

In the butcher shop, several townspeople were washing their cuts and binding their wounds. The butcher arrived a little bit after the rest. He didn't explain why.

Some of the lacerations from the crows' beaks were deep and required stitches. It was a miracle that no one lost an eye.

The people had known that crows were wicked, but they'd had no idea they were *this* wicked. Their clothes and hair and skin smelled of smoke from the burning barn. With any luck, they thought, the house would burn, too, and the Ogress would have nowhere to go.

"Will it be enough to make her leave?" one man asked.

"It's enough," the butcher said.

Consequences

The Ogress knelt on the ground, silently gaping at the horror of it.

They stayed together—ogress, crows, sheep, and dog— until the sun rose. The Ogress remained in place for as long as she could stand it, even as her arms erupted in rashes and her cheeks burned red, but eventually she stood and went inside. The animals heard her heavy feet treading carefully through the broken glass. They heard her collapse into her chair. And they heard her make a sound—a deep, guttural, lonely sound, and the saddest thing they had ever heard.

Have you ever heard an ogre cry?

I hope you never do. It might break your heart forever.

The crows spent the day on the windowsills and on the roof. They gathered on the branches near the front door. They pressed their wings against the walls. The sheep arranged them- selves in a circle around the crooked house, their faces pointed inward. The dog sat by the front door and howled.

They waited until nightfall. But even then, the Ogress didn't come out.

That night, after the stars returned to the sky, the Ogress did not go into the forest. She did not gather berries or nuts or mushrooms. She didn't look at her garden. She didn't look at the smoky remains of her barn. She didn't bake. She didn't go into town. She didn't leave a single treat for anyone. She threw everything from her racks and tables into the compost heap. She didn't come out of her house for the rest of the night.

Or the next night.

Or the next.

The crows worried she would never come out again.

The Mayor went to the front door with a song in his heart. The rallies had been going *very* well. Day after day of them. And it turned out he had a great talent for making signs! Who could have known? He wondered what other obscure tasks he was secretly excellent at. He made his way through his house, through the mounds and mounds of treasure—oh, what treasure is to be had by those who do not share! After all, the more you have, the more you have! *It is the best sort of magic*, he thought. Every coin, every jewel, every tiny bit of value gathered and swirled around his feet. The floorboards groaned under the weight.

It had been some time since he had left his beautiful mayor skin behind and wandered the forest as . . . *himself*. His beautiful, dragony self. Months. Maybe even years. What is time, really when one is so excellent a mayor?

(Listen.

It was a little over five years since he had last removed his skin. Since he'd last replenished his power. I knew this, obviously, and could have told him so, if he had ever asked me.

He never asked.)

It was a thing to be attended to every once in a while—every new moon, supposedly, but that seemed like such a bother. Truly, though, his magic was depleting. It was difficult to know how much, exactly, since he hadn't taken his skin off, and he didn't know how small his dragon self had gotten. Wearing the skins was a slow, inexorable siphon for one's magic and power and size. He needed to walk under the sky as a dragon to set it right again. He used to do so regularly, sometimes setting a fire or two, just for old times' sake, to remind himself how good it felt to be great and powerful and dangerous. He also loved the sensation of lying on his pile of treasure in the Mayor's house on his own dear scales, luxuriating in the shine of his skin and the shine of the gold and the tinkling of the coins in his claws. But it was a lot of work taking the skin on and off. And he was a lazy dragon.

"Soon," he told himself, yet again. "I'll do it next new moon. Whenever that is."

It had been a week—*a whole week!*—since there had last been a pie waiting for him on his front steps. The wrongness of the situation itched at him. Surely there would be a pie *today*.

Mine, he thought in happy anticipation. *Mine, mine, mine.* He went out to the front door and opened it, sure in his skin, and in his other skin, and in his deep, dragonish bones, that there would be a pie waiting for him.

Mine, mine, mine.

He opened the door. Nothing was there.

"*No pie*," he cried in astonishment, a sudden wave of sorrow crushing him flat. The first day had felt like a fluke, and the second day like an aberration. A week without pie was an eternity. He couldn't bear it.

The Mayor felt his sorrow and hopelessness swell like a wave. He thought it might take him away entirely. The pies had felt like a friend. His only friend. And now he had no one else.

Down the road, the constable opened her door, hoping there would be tarts to be had. It had been a week, after all. "*No tarts*," the constable wailed.

The lamplighter walked to her front gate, looking for bread. "*No bread*," she cried.

And the man who swept the streets hurried out to look for cookies. "*No cookies*," he sobbed.

All through the town, people cried out.

"*No buns!*"

"*No rolls!*"

"*No croissants!*"

"*No galettes!*"

With each passing day, the hole left by the lack of these acts of generosity began to feel more like an abyss.

In the Center Square, the blacksmith tore down a NO MORE OGRES sign. *Who cares about the Ogress?* the blacksmith thought.

The treats are gone.

The streets are in shambles.

The school is closed.

The lamps aren't lit.

The crops have failed.

Nothing matters.

In the house next to the old library, a very old man and a very old woman opened the front gate with a loud creak. They looked right and they looked left, to make sure the coast was clear. And then they looked down.

No box.

No vegetables.

Nothing for the children.

"What shall we do?" Matron said.

"Hopefully, we can continue to rely on the town," Myron ventured.

Matron scoffed. "Soon they will forget us, as they forgot us before. Has our benefactor forgotten us, too? Are we truly alone?"

The early autumn frost grew deeper each night. Matron and Myron covered the garden as best they could to keep the plants going, but they knew that soon all growing would cease. And then what? "How can we feed these children once the town moves on?" they asked each other. They spoke in low voices. They didn't want the children to hear.

But the children sat by the window, holding their breath. And they heard everything.

Rope

The orphans, all fifteen of them, sat in the dormitory, slumped and dejected.

"I thought for sure they would listen," Bartleby said.

"I thought for sure they'd believe us," Anthea said.

"Children should be seen and not heard, *my eye*," Cass said, looking for something to kick. It was satisfying saying things out loud, she realized. Not *all* the time. But sometimes.

"Do you know the way to the Ogress's house?" Elijah asked suddenly.

"Of course," Bartleby said. "I mean, in theory."

There was a long pause. Elijah pressed his lips together. He squinted one eye, as though listening to something.

"So," Elijah said slowly. "We could, you know . . . just go there. And talk to her. All of us together."

"Sneak out, you mean?" Anthea said. *Was he joking?* He didn't seem to be. "Even though Matron and Myron are on to us? Don't you think we'll get caught?"

Elijah shrugged. "I mean, maybe, but there's always another way in stories. A secret door. Or an alternate route." He frowned. "Is it possible that Matron and Myron *won't* be sleeping next to the door tonight?"

Cass shrugged. "I doubt it," she said.

Several cats stalked among the orphans. The kitten named Phyllis curled up on Bartleby's lap.

"There are so many books in the Reading Room . . ." Fortunate offered.

"Surely one of them has a recipe for a sleeping potion," Gratitude finished.

Anthea folded her arms and shook her head. "We are *absolutely not* going to give a possibly poisonous sleeping potion to a very old woman and a very old man." She made an exasperated face. "I mean, they have become our parents. What would we do if something happened to them?"

Iggy began to cry. "I don't want people to be mean to the Ogress."

Justina started to cry as well. "Playing outside at night when we're not allowed to sounds *very* fun, and I will be so sad if we can't do it."

Bartleby shook his head. "This is going nowhere. I mean, if we had some rope, that would be something. They never lock the dormitory window. You know Matron and her thoughts on fresh air."

Hiram grabbed his crutches and stood up. "Oh!" he said. "I have rope. Just a minute."

He was gone in a flash. He returned in seconds. With rope.

It was handwoven of tightly knotted pieces of fabric, tied so thick it was the width of Bartleby's upper arm.

"Where did you even get this?" Anthea asked.

Hiram shrugged. "I made it. When Cass was gone. I thought I would go out and look for her."

"*By yourself?*" admonished Dierdre.

"*Without me?*" demanded Justina and Iggy and Kye.

"How dare you," Iggy said.

Hiram raised his open palms in a question mark. "Sorry?" he said.

Bartleby and Dierdre examined the rope. It seemed sound enough.

"How did you even figure it out?" Anthea said. "I mean, people don't just *know* how to make rope."

"I found the instructions in a book," Hiram said. "In the Reading Room. But then I didn't need it anymore, because Cass came home."

"Okay, then," Anthea said. "Rope it is."

The children of the Orphan House were good. They worked hard to be helpful, and to follow the rules. That night, Elijah milked the goats while Dierdre gathered in the chickens and Bartleby cleaned the kitchen with Hiram and Iggy. Anthea read stories to the toddlers while Cass put the babies to sleep, and Justina cuddled with Matron and Myron as Fortunate and Gratitude sang a duet.

It was a normal evening in the Orphan House.

Or mostly normal.

Bartleby offered both Matron and Myron a second cup of chamomile tea. "To soothe your nerves," Bartleby said.

Anthea kept the toddlers calm, and Cass made sure the babies never made a sound. The twins sang as sweetly as nightingales, their voices soft and soaring. Matron yawned. Myron rubbed his eyes.

"I think it's time for bed, my loves," Matron said, heading to her cot by the door and collapsing upon it.

"My thoughts exactly," Anthea said.

They put the babies to bed, and the toddlers, too. They swept the floor and kissed both Myron and Matron good night, and then they went upstairs.

The orphans did not put on their nightclothes.

They did not wash their faces or brush their teeth.

They threw open the window as wide as it would go and let in the night air. They stopped up the gaps around the dormitory door with blankets to keep the draft from spreading through the house. They knew they would have to bring the babies and toddlers with them. It was too cold to leave them in the dormitory with the window open. They would cry and wake up Matron and Myron, and then everyone would be in a pickle. Anthea had designed and sewn secure carriers to bind the littlest children onto the bodies of the biggest. Dierdre strapped Orpheus to her body, and Cass buckled in Nanette. Bartleby took Maude, and Anthea took Lily. The carriers had straps that crossed and looped and cinched. The little ones were quite secure.

Fortunate and Gratitude used the knot book from the Reading Room to tie a complex knot onto the drying rack, which was bolted onto the wall. And they threw the rest of the rope out the window. The orphans peered outside. They gulped.

"I hope this works," Bartleby said, who suddenly wished he were reading this in a book, rather than having to experience it himself.

"It's easy," Hiram said, throwing his crutches out the window without hesitation. He grabbed the rope in one hand and started rappelling down the exterior wall, as quick as a mouse.

The orphans watched him with open mouths.

"How did you know how to do that?" Bartleby said.

Hiram shrugged. "Books," he said, as though it was obvious.

Justina went next. Then Anthea. Then Elijah. Then Cass. Bartleby hesitated. He watched the door. "I'm just making sure we don't get caught," he said.

Kye climbed down. Then Fortunate and Gratitude. Then Dierdre. Bartleby looked at Maude, fast asleep in her carrier. "Well," he said, kissing the top of her head. "Here we go." And he descended into the dark.

Hiram had made another rope, which he kept in the shed next to the chicken coop, and also had produced a makeshift ladder, which he had hidden behind the tea bushes.

"How on earth did you learn how to do all of those things?" Anthea marveled.

Hiram shrugged again. "I already told you. Books."

"Then why did you make reading lessons so unpleasant," Anthea muttered, but she said this well under her breath, and she was pretty sure that Hiram didn't hear her.

Hiram set the ladder against the wall and climbed up, hopping from rung to rung on one leg while using his hands to steady himself. Justina held Hiram's crutches and handed them up when he reached the top. Hiram tied the rope to the metal rod, threw the rope over the side, threw his crutches next, and then leaped over with a wave.

"*See?*" he called. "*It's easy!*"

Anthea wasn't so sure, but she did it anyway.

Eventually, all fifteen orphans were on the wrong side of the wall. It wasn't entirely dark yet, and people were about, though not on their block. The *clip-clop* of donkey hooves and the bells of bicycles echoed through the streets, though they couldn't see the actual donkeys or bike riders.

"It's easy to get turned around," Cass said. "Let's hold hands and stick together."

And so they did. No one seemed to notice them. The other passersby kept their eyes tilted to the ground. They wore a worried expression.

Anthea looked down as well. Tattered, dirty flyers for last week's rally against the Ogress littered the cobblestones.

The children moved in a mass, holding on to one another.

"I can't believe we're out here," Iggy said, bouncing a bit.

"By ourselves," Justina said, hardly able to contain her excitement.

"Pssh!" Hiram said dismissively. "We're not by ourselves. We're with one another. That's the opposite of alone."

They followed the road past the Center Square and up along where it started to curve and lift, where the nicer houses were. At last, they stopped at a house with no grass and no plants—just a yard of carefully raked rocks on which stood several statues. The edge of the yard was lined with cats. The cats watched the house, their eyes flashing in the waning light. "Hi, kitty," Bartleby said, reaching down. The cat ignored him. It watched the house, a low yowl rumbling in its belly.

"Our cats don't act that way," Dierdre said.

"That's because our cats are better," Elijah said. One of the cats hissed, as though it understood, and Elijah instantly felt ashamed. "Sorry," he whispered to the cats.

There were signs everywhere now, of every size and color. They lined the fence around the Mayor's yard, and adorned the porch. Some hung from the trees, spinning slowly in the dark. The signs nearest to the perimeter had stains and stinky splotches from where the cats had unceremoniously peed on them. The children didn't bother reading them. It was all nonsense anyway.

Cass stopped and pointed. "The Mayor," she said. They could see him through the curtains, moving about.

"Come on," Cass said, and she ran around to the back of the house and peeked in through the window. Anthea and Bartleby looked at each other. They shrugged.

"Well," Bartleby said. "At this point, why not?" And the rest of the orphans followed Cass.

Not only had the orphans climbed out a window on a make-shift rope, but they were, apparently, about to trespass. And spy. What a day. They tiptoed to the window, braced their feet on the foundation, and looked inside.

The Mayor sat at his desk. The desk chair bowed under his weight. Gold coins were heaped across the desk surface. They were piled on the floor. They covered the sofa and the chairs. There were no books on the shelves—only gold. Gold on the side table. Gold in the corners. Gold filling the fireplace. Coins and jewels and crowns and chains. There were no lanterns or candles burning—and yet, the room was full of light, and the gold glittered. The Mayor glittered. He let the gold coins run through his fingers. He rubbed the gold against his cheeks. He closed his eyes at the tinkling of coins and sighed with pleasure.

The orphans slid back into the shadows. They frowned as one. "I thought there wasn't enough for the Orphan House," Anthea fumed.

"I thought that people in town hadn't been generous," Bartleby said. "Looks to me like they're more than generous."

"I would like to kick him," Hiram said, and Justina, Iggy, and Kye all agreed. "May we?" he asked.

"Not right now," Anthea said.

"Maybe later," Cass said very quietly, but not everyone heard it.

"Let's keep going," Bartleby said.

Under the light of the moon and the glint of the stars, the children walked to the far edge of town, where the roads wound and the thickets tangled and the heavy limbs of the sycamores creaked in the wind.

They followed the sound of crows. They followed the smell of smoke. And eventually, they found the Ogress's house.

As It Turns Out, the Crows Discovered, Children Are Wonderful

The Ogress hadn't left her house for over a week. Every once in a while, the crows heard the sound she made—a low, rumbling, sorrowful sound—and they felt their hearts begin to crack. Sometimes, she wept, and her tears ran out the door like rivers, gushing and tumbling until, without warning, they would suddenly cease.

Indeed, it turned out that the *lack* of weeping, when the Ogress's sorrow became so great that all she could feel was nothing, was more alarming than the weeping itself. The sheep bellowed and baaed as the crows pecked gently at the sides of the house.

Harold, to his credit, never once said *I told you so.* He never gloated. He was simply out of his mind with worry. He fixed himself on the sill by the broken window, careful of the glass shards, and kept his eye trained on the figure of the Ogress, slumped next to the cold fireplace. He clucked and cooed—the same sounds his mother had made for him when he was a tiny chick. It didn't matter. The Ogress didn't move.

The door was slightly ajar. Only Dog went in and out of the house—mostly to relieve himself in the gully or to help himself to the discarded treats in the compost heap. The crows did their best to supplement his meals with items they had stolen from the local farms. (Crows, as I have mentioned, are very moral creatures and never steal. Or, they almost never steal. In this case, however, they made an exception, both in order to see to Dog's needs and also to stick it to the people in town. Indeed, they stole with a song in their hearts.)

Dog's milky eyes couldn't see much of anything, but his capacious heart saw much more. Each day, he greeted each sheep and each crow. Each day, he sat on the floor next to the Ogress, leaning his full weight against her leg, his tail gently thumping on the ground.

As the moon rose over the eastern trees, a cold, thin light fell on the ruined garden, making it sparkle like silver. Normally, the Ogress's love and care kept the garden's soil warm and the plants thriving long after the nearby farms succumbed to the killing cold. It wasn't magic, exactly. But it was close. Now, the Ogress's sorrow had drained the warmth away, and the garden, or what was left of it, had given way to frost. The crushed squash and smashed melons glinted with new-formed crystals. The beans were scattered, the ground-cherries utterly obliterated, and the tomatoes—oh, those beautiful tomatoes!—had been reduced to an acrid lump of pulp and juice and shredded vines.

Never had the crows seen such a ruin! The poor garden! The poor ogress! They were beside themselves with grief.

"Caw," they called at the windows.

"Caw," they called at the door.

"Caw, caw, caw," they crooned at the chimney. They nestled in the roof and thatch, and they cuddled close to the eaves. With each caw they said:

"We love you."

"We are here for you."

"We will never betray you."

The sheep baaed and bleated along with the crows. The crows had no idea what the sheep were saying, only that each baa was layered with love. The crows could feel it in their bones.

On the eighth day, afternoon slid toward evening, and evening softened into nighttime. The Ogress did not come out. The sheep bleated and the crows clucked. The moon climbed toward the roof of the sky and its light spilled onto the winding road. Dog tipped up his snout and howled, all high and thin and lonely, into the rustling trees.

Hours passed.

Suddenly, the crows stood at attention. They readied their wings. Shadows, long and strange, moved their way up the road. Several crows murmured, wondering if it was a monster. Harold left his perch on the windowsill and alighted on the ground, a little way off from the rest of his crow family. He cocked his head. He recognized that smell—or part of it anyway. Dog lifted his nose and sniffed. Then he thumped his tail on the ground.

The other crows murmured and rattled and clicked. They did not yet venture a boisterous caw. They didn't know what, *exactly*, was approaching. The sheep stood shoulder to shoulder with the crows. They lowered their horns.

Finally, from the strange shadows on the road, a voice called out—loud and clear and sweet, like a bell.

"Caw," the shadow hailed. "We are here to help."

Harold turned and faced the rest of his crow family. He did not say *I told you so.* But he thought it.

The rest of the crows inclined their beaks and narrowed their eyes. They didn't know that a shadow could speak Crow. They didn't know that any other creature—except for the Ogress, and in her case, not very well—could speak Crow. Except for what Harold had said in his lunatic ravings. But they were accustomed to disregarding Harold.

Harold spoke first. "Caw!" he said. "Hello, my friends!"

He gave another sidelong glance at his family.

The shadows grew nearer. Fifteen children approached the mulberry trees, their faces inclined toward the crows. Their skin shone in the moonlight. The crows had never seen this many children at once. Or this close. They hardly knew where to look first. One child with long dark braids stood slightly apart.

She bowed very low—so low that the top of her head nearly touched the ground. She motioned to the rest of the orphans to do the same. She intoned a soft and sonorous caw, deep in her throat, which meant "Greetings, beloved friends."

The crows stared at the girl. The girl who *spoke Crow.* For the first time in their memory, every single crow was silent. If the children appreciated the oddness of this fact, they didn't say.

"Caw," the girl continued. "We know you love the Ogress. And she loves you, because you are wonderful crows. We would like to join you in friendship. And we wish to help her as she has helped us."

The crows were profoundly moved. They had never seen such polite or well-educated children. They had no idea such a thing was possible.

"Caw," Harold said, which meant "You see? Children are wonderful." And he left it at that. Harold fluttered toward one of the other children and settled himself into her arms.

It was all the rest of the crows needed. They landed lightly on the ground and began to speak at once.

"Caw! Caw! Caw! Caw!" Their voices tumbled over one another in a wave.

"Look at the garden!"

"You won't believe what they did to the barn!"

"The poor sheep!"

"And look at poor Dog! He's beside himself!"

"We had to drive them away! Oh, the treachery of the townspeople!"

"And, oh, our poor, poor Ogress! And, oh, her broken heart!"

The girl with the braids knelt down next to the crows, and the crows fell silent. The other children knelt down with her. The night was deep and still. Only the crickets called. The sheep pressed shoulder to shoulder and stood near, their nostrils flared, taking in the scent of the children. Harold continued to say nothing, which moved the other crows deeply. He had every right to gloat. Instead, he relaxed in the arms of the child, clucking and tutting all the while.

"Caw," said a boy with two different kinds of eyes. His grasp of Crow was not as good as the girl's. After a few hesitating attempts, he explained that a man in town—a big man with golden hair and golden buckles on his boots (the crows trembled with a memory that they preferred not to think about)—had been deceiving people. For years, probably. Taking what he should not take and telling people to live with less and less, so as a result the townspeople had begun looking for someone to blame.

"This man," the crows cawed. "Does he take off his skin, by any chance?" They had to repeat themselves several times before Bartleby understood what they were saying.

"His skin?" Bartleby cawed. "Why, no. Or not that I've seen. That's not a thing that usually happens with people."

"Oh!" Elijah said, his eyes suddenly wide. "There's a story about this. You see—"

"No one wants to *hear* it, Elijah," Anthea said. "Not now. Focus, please!" She rolled her eyes.

"Caw," said the child holding Harold. "We have been told since we were small that the bad people outnumber the good. But I do not believe that is true. We have seen in the Orphan House recently that it only takes some people doing good to encourage many people to do good. One good person can inspire other people to do good things. Good is not a number. Good is more than that. With good, the more you give, the more you have. It is the best sort of magic."

The crows nodded. They had heard that sort of logic before.

"Caw," the girl with the braids asked. "May we have your permission to see her? We think we can help."

The crows regarded the orphans. They were not what the crows had expected. They did not yell or jeer or throw rocks. They didn't call them varmints or pests.

The night winds whispered, and the mulberry branches creaked. The crows took in the smell of the children—wheat and corn and green leaves and the smell of play and care and togetherness. There were other smells as well—worry, for one. And ancient heartbreak. But those scents were subtler. The crows cocked their heads. They murmured to one another. The crows decided that they liked the look of these children. They had kind faces. The thin moonlight slicked their hair. Their eyes were full of stars.

After a bit, the eldest crow spoke. "Caw," she said. "The Ogress is inside her house. You may see her if you wish. Perhaps you can help."

And so, under the light of the moon and under the glint of the stars, the orphans stood. They bowed again to the crows, who bowed back. Then they knocked on the door of the crooked little house.

"Dearest Ogress," the girl with the braids said. "May we come in?"

First Impressions

The door to the Ogress's crooked house was very large. Anthea had to stretch her hand far above her head in order to reach the handle. They pushed the door open and peeked inside. The Ogress sat in her chair by the hearth, her face in her hands. She was enormous—astonishingly so. About twice the size of a large bear.

Even though everything in the house was outsized—the chair, the hearth, the workbench, and the shelves full of tools—the Ogress still seemed too large for the space. Even seated in her chair, her head was awfully close to the ceiling, and if she had stretched her long arms out from side to side, she would have touched each end of her house.

Anthea cleared her throat. "Excuse me, dear Ogress," she said. "Please forgive our intrusion. We wanted to see if you are okay."

The orphans stood close to one another, looking up at the Ogress. They liked her right away. They liked her large, stony hands. The liked the coppery sheen of her bright eyes. They liked the flowers growing in her grassy hair. They liked the uncountable pictures hanging on the walls, with even more fluttering on clotheslines strung across the ceilings throughout the house. They liked her face. They liked the dog, whose milky eyes gazed at nothing, but whose tail thumped happily on the ground. The dog could see them with his nose, and he could see them with his ears, and he could see them with his heart. The children could tell.

∽

The Ogress liked the orphans right away, too. Of course, she knew she would. She had been observing them for a long time. She knew their kindness and helpfulness and joy. Now, as she watched them come in, one after another, the littlest children carried by the biggest, she felt her heart leap.

Oh! she thought. There was the serious girl with the long braids. The one who hid sometimes in the shed. The one who worked harder than she should and whose face had recently become careworn.

And, oh! There was the boy whose eyes were two different colors. Who thought deeply and who spoke so quickly his words outpaced his thinking and his face twisted up until he could right himself.

And look! There was the girl with short hair and large eyes. Who quietly cleaned or soothed or fixed. The girl that she had cradled in her arms and taken home, even though it broke her heart to leave her behind. The Ogress cupped her hand over her mouth, holding in a sigh.

And there was the girl with the bright eyes and the large smile, who drew and drew and drew, and there was the boy with a big mouth and a bigger voice. The Ogress had never heard him, but even through the periscope, she could tell that he was loud. And that he rarely stopped talking.

There were the twins who looked nothing alike and yet were impossible to tell apart.

There was the fast, agile boy with the crutches, and the littler children who tried to keep up and follow him everywhere, even to places where they could not reach without his help.

There were the toddlers, asleep in their carriers, and the babies, sighing in their dreams.

They were all *here*. Her favorite family in all of Stone-in-the-Glen.

She didn't say anything. Not at first. She was too afraid. So many terrible things had been happening lately. She gripped the arms of her chair and held her breath. She didn't dare blink, out of fear that she was only imagining it. She didn't want the children to disappear.

∽

Harold knew exactly what to do.

He readied himself in the child's arms and flew up in an arc over everyone's heads, spinning a brief pirouette in the rafters before landing gracefully on the table. He shook his feathers and bowed to the Ogress.

He cleared his throat. "Caw," he said gallantly. "My precious ogress. I would like to introduce you to your friends." And he bowed to all in the room.

The children bowed, too.

Anthea smiled. "I hope it is all right that we came by for a visit. I feel it is long overdue."

The Ogress folded her hands together, unable to speak at first. Her eyes were dry, but the orphans could see she had been crying. They could see the tear tracks on her stony cheeks. They could see the pools on the ground.

"We didn't realize it was you," Bartleby said. The toddler in his carrier whimpered a bit, so he started bouncing and swaying back and forth. He kissed the top of the child's head. "We would have thanked you long ago if we had known. We are so sorry. You kept us fed. We would have gone hungry without you."

The rest of the children nodded. They could see that the Ogress was afraid. They kept their voices soft and their movements slow. They didn't want to startle her. But they were helpful children. They looked around and saw that the house, thanks to the cruelty of the town, was a bit of a disaster. Broken glass spangled the floor and the counters. Rocks had smashed through the thatching on the roof in two corners, leaving heaps of debris. Smashed tomatoes and onions and squash oozed along the back wall. The mess was atrocious, but the children knew what to do with messes.

"It's a bit cold in here," Elijah said, noticing the dying embers in the fireplace. "Let me fix that." He crouched next to the fire, banking the coals, heaping the wood shavings, and tenting the kindling. Some of the logs were too large for him to carry, and the iron tools next to the fireplace were a bit unwieldy (he felt a little like a knight at a jousting competition), but he made do. Within moments, a bright fire roared, cheering up the room. "Should I tell a story?" he asked.

"Maybe later," Hiram said with a yawn. It was late. And he was tired.

"The glass on the floor is dangerous," Dierdre said. She grabbed a broom—it was twice her height and about her width, and she had to lean the heavy handle on the fulcrum of her shoulder in order to wield it—and started sweeping. Fortunate and Gratitude stood on stools and used rags to gather up the glass particles on the table, carefully depositing them in a bucket.

Kye and Justina helped with the dustpan—it required both of them to lift, and even then it was a struggle. Hiram stroked the dog. Anthea's eyes drifted to the Ogress's workbench, with a spot for sewing, a spot for papermaking, a spot for building, a spot for painting, each tool in its place. It was the most perfect workbench she had ever seen.

Bartleby could only take his eyes off the collection of telescopes, all made lovingly by hand, to examine the diagrams the Ogress had drawn of the sky.

Cass had a sleeping baby harnessed to her back, and a crow in her arms. She approached the Ogress and held out her hand. The Ogress responded by laying her large hand on top of Cass's tiny one, palm to palm. Finally, Cass spoke. "I thought I dreamed you," she said. "That terrible night. All I knew was that I fell asleep in the woods and woke up with my family. Thank you for bringing me home."

And then Cass climbed up onto the Ogress's chair, leaned over, and hugged her.

The Ogress had never been hugged before. Not by a child. Not by another ogre. Not by anyone. It felt as though she held the whole world in her arms. Her heart felt light and limitless. She closed her eyes and hugged the child right back.

The boy with the mismatched eyes laid his hand on the Ogress's forearm. The girl with the braids put a hand on her knee. The boy with the crutches inserted himself into the center of the hug. Followed by the littler children who always followed him. The boy with the loud voice joined in. And the girl with the giant smile. And Harold. And a few other crows. And the dog. Were all hugs like this? The Ogress couldn't possibly know. She allowed the moment to paint itself at the center of her mind. She'd keep it with her, always.

Later, Anthea stood at the workbench, thinking hard. Her whole life she had found ways of making use of otherwise useless things, making sense out of seemingly senseless things. She looked at the stack of handmade papers. At the mesh screens and basins for papermaking. At the paints and the set of brushes. At the collection of sturdy needles and thick, brightly colored threads. She noticed the wide array of useful things. Shiny contraptions and clever tools. A silver spoon. An ancient locket. A carved whistle made from a very soft stone. A broken teacup. A pair of binoculars. A letter opener. A compass. A strangely shaped pair of scissors. A small pressboard and several stamps, and a leader pin for a scroll. A deckle box, and several brushes and a stitching awl with handles carved out of bone.

She turned and looked at the Ogress.

"Pardon me, madam," Anthea said. "Please don't think me rude. I am admiring your workbench. Where do you get your supplies?" She couldn't imagine the Ogress simply walking into a store.

The Ogress smiled. "The crows, mostly. I have found things here and there in the rubbish heaps in the forest. But usually it is the crows who notice what I like and bring it back." Her bright penny eyes became a bit brighter. "But only that which has been cast off, you understand."

Anthea nodded. "I'm glad to know that the crows are every bit as clever as I thought they were." She paused a moment. "So, if they can gather, can they deliver as well? Nothing too large, you understand. A small something. To a person's house?"

The Ogress looked over at the two crows sitting on the window-sill and blew them a kiss. "Of course. They do all the time."

Bartleby regarded Anthea with narrowed eyes. "What are you thinking of, Anthea? Another theory?"

Anthea ran her hands along the stacks of paper. She appraised the nibs and quills and tubs of ink. She considered the tools for folding, stitching, and binding up. She shook her head. "Not exactly. More like a solution. I keep thinking about the Library. Everything went wrong when the Library burned. The Library was what held the whole town together. Maybe people have to remember what that felt like." Her eyes found Elijah. "I think we are going to need that story, Elijah. In fact, I think we might need a few of them."

The New Plan

The next day, people in town woke up to find that someone had carefully placed an object on their doorsteps. Or on their kitchen tables. And, in a few cases, right into their hands as they slept. A tiny hand-stitched book. Each one was meticulously inked with tiny brushes, and contained painstakingly detailed illustrations showing dense forests or grand castles or the churning waves of a stormy ocean. Each one was astonishing—a small, lovely little marvel.

Listen.

I should clarify.

It wasn't that the people in Stone-in-the-Glen hadn't seen a book before. Of course they had! And many had shelves or stacks of old books in their homes. But the Library had burned so long ago. And there hadn't been any stalls with booksellers at Market Day for years. It had been such a long time since they had read anything new. And it was even longer since they had discussed what they were reading with anyone else.

The books delivered to the different homes were not all the same. The constable, for example, read a story about a puppy who wanted nothing more than to love his master, but his master drove him away with a large and terrible stick, hitting the puppy so hard that he was rendered quite blind. She wept at the injustice of it.

"Oh!" she cried as she read the story over breakfast. "That poor puppy! What a terrible owner! Anyone who harms a defenseless animal must be punished immediately!" She read on, following the story as the puppy lived by its depleted senses and sharp wits as it grew into a dog, how it traveled over hill and dale through terrible tribulations until it found a home in the arms of a friendly ogress, who loved it forever and ever. The end.

"Well," she said, holding the story to her heart. "That was the most lovely story I've read in a long time. What a marvelous gift! Now who gave it to me?"

The cobbler's wife read her book out loud to her husband as he started working—a story about a young man who put a portion of his heart into a mechanical butterfly for the girl he loved. And how it beat and beat and beat, no matter how far away they were from each other, until one day, when the young man was quite old, the butterfly beat its wings for the very last time. And then he died.

"Oh my goodness!" The cobbler's wife burst into tears. The cobbler folded her in his arms. "This is the saddest story I've ever read!" She blew her nose.

"Are you quite all right, my dear Esmé?" the cobbler asked. "I can throw the book away, if you wish."

"Nonsense," she said. "Having a good cry is an excellent way to start the day. Feelings are important, after all. And love, even when it ends tragically, still matters. I can't wait to read it again." And with that, she walked out and went straight to the first neighbor she saw and gave them a hug. She had six casseroles in the oven—two for the Orphan House, one for another family, whose children's cheeks were thin, and three to be divided among several elderly neighbors, who looked as though they might enjoy a meal that they didn't have to cook themselves. "So much to do," the cobbler's wife said breathlessly. "This broken world isn't going to fix itself, after all."

The butcher read a story about an innocent young ogress who lived with two mean trolls, who coped with their meanness by learning to build and invent and study the stars.

"Well," he said with a knowing nod. "Trolls are *terrible*. I've always said so."

The blacksmith read a story about a wicked king who hoarded the treasures that were supposed to be used in service to his kingdom and his people, and kept it for himself instead. And how his greed and grasping slowly made him go mad. "Hmm," he said, his eyes drifting over to the Mayor's mansion. "Interesting."

The next day, there were more books. People found them on their front steps, or in their gardens, or even on their easy chairs. There were books on the windowsills and on the eaves.

The former teacher read a story about a person at the far end of town who planted a garden to help the needy and shared her heaps and heaps of vegetables under the cover of night so that her identity might not be discovered. She gave without desire of recognition. She gave for the sake of giving.

"Yes," the teacher said, wiping her eyes. "That's the way it's supposed to be."

The seamstress read a story about a murder of crows who left gifts for people just because. Right away, she started work on a dress with a crow appliqué adorning the skirt. She wore it out that very day. "Don't you think that crows are wonderful?" she asked everyone she saw.

The baker read a story about a flock of feral sheep who wandered the earth until they finally found kindness in an unlikely place. "Oh!" she said. "What happy sheep!"

The next day, more books appeared, stacked on garden walls and piled in unused birdbaths. An entire curb became a bookshelf.

The cobbler read a story about a beloved library that burned to the ground, and of the brave and valiant actions of a town working together to save what they could—their last, great act of neighborliness. It ended with the townspeople, exhausted and sad, holding hands next to the smoking rubble and declaring that they would rebuild.

"What happened?" he asked anyone who would listen. "What happened to us?"

The cobbler's wife looked around. So much needed to be done. She watched as neighbors chatted over their fences, showing one another what they had just read. She watched as people's faces lit up as they discussed their stories. How gently they held those books in their hands.

This could be useful, she found herself thinking.

Then she went further. *Once upon a time*, she thought, *before the Library burned, we all used to do this. We gathered in the shade of the promenades and public parks, to discuss literature or philosophy or poetry or art.* It had been such a long time since any of this had happened. For some reason, people had stopped talking and stopped trusting one another. She could barely remember why. Every time she tried to think about it, her mind went fuzzy.

"Well," she pronounced. "That's all in the past. I know what to do now." She started knocking on people's doors. "Book swap," she said cheerfully. "This very afternoon. Right there in front of our house. Bring something to share, or just bring yourself. We'd love to hear what you're reading! Spread the word!"

And they did. They came. The cobbler's wife made cookies. She handed one to everyone, whether they wanted it or not. People shared the books they had received. They listened to others share their own books. And they found themselves remembering the Library. Even the people who were too young to remember the Library found themselves remembering. They remembered that a story, in the mind of the reader, is like music. And discussing stories among other minds and other hearts feels like a symphony. They remembered how ideas make their own light, and how words have their own mass and weight and being.

More people came outside. They made makeshift benches. They spread out blankets. They squinted and covered their eyes. Without their trees, there was no shade on the street, so they sat under the shade of umbrellas instead. They hugged neighbors that they hadn't hugged in . . . well, it was difficult to say how long.

And then, they started talking.

And once they started, it was difficult to stop.

In the mansion, the Mayor paced back and forth, back and forth, the floorboards groaning under his feet. His gold coins tinkled as they were brushed aside by his incessant moving.

That morning, with all the hope and faith that befits a man (but was he a man?) of his stature and bearing, he had flung open his door, fully anticipating that the previous days were merely a fluke and that there would be, as was right and proper, a pie waiting for him on the front steps.

A pie.

Did he, after all he had done for this town, deserve anything less? No. He did not. He deserved a pie and he should get a pie, just as he deserved his gold and he should get his gold, and he deserved the golden buckles on his feet and the delightful shock of golden hair on his head, and the skin he wore that had been so distasteful to him once upon a time but had begun to feel as much a part of him as anything else. He might never shed it, he thought. He might remain mayor forever. He couldn't go back and live with the dragons, after all. And after several miscalculations when he had lived with those wretched ogres, he'd had to burn down the village in order to save himself.

But *here.*

Well, Stone-in-the-Glen was *home.* Since he had dispatched with that library, of course. The wood beams had been on to him. And after he had covered up that ridiculous stone, as a precaution. Human beings are interesting creatures, the Mayor knew. Easily swayed. They don't believe what's right in front of their eyes if a clever person tells them not to. The Mayor loved living among humans.

And he deserved a pie.

He had waited long enough. He opened the front door and looked about. The cats, as usual, lurked at the edge of the yard. They didn't come close. They didn't dare. They just wanted him to feel bad about himself. Which was rude, if you think about it. *Cats*, the Mayor decided, *are rude*. He looked down to the front step. Once again, there was no pie.

Once again, there was something else. He picked up his book and went out onto the patio. Surely the statue of himself looking noble and honorable would soothe his rumpled spirit.

It did not.

The new book told of a mad king who spent his days counting his wealth. The Mayor read it once in curiosity, a second time in bewilderment, a third time in a blind rage. The carefully painted illustration of the king depicted a fine-looking fellow with a marvelous shock of golden hair, an excellent coat, and a pair of smart boots with gold buckles.

"*Who has done this?*" the Mayor roared.

He decided to take a walk through town. Surely the fawning looks of the townspeople would ease his worried mind. Surely the light in their eyes at the sight of his glittering smile would fill his soul with gladness. The cats hissed as he passed, but he didn't let that dampen his optimism.

He walked to the Center Square and was surprised by the proliferation of umbrellas. He frowned and looked up at the sky. It was blue from end to end. Not a cloud threatened shade.

Thank goodness. But there was no hint of rain, either. So why on earth were so many people huddled under umbrellas? He walked closer to investigate.

On a makeshift bench in front of the apothecary's shop, people leaned against one another, reading handmade books. They read while resting against the warm walls of the blacksmith's. And at the cobbler's. Three people were sitting on that infernal stone with books in their hands. They lounged with books in their hands on the mostly collapsed wall next to the remains of the Library. And in an unused donkey cart. Everyone was *reading.*

The Mayor marched home to make more signs. Later that afternoon, he removed several signs about the Ogress ("Who even *cares* about that ogress anymore?" he asked himself petulantly) and replaced them with BOOKS ARE DANGEROUS and DON'T BELIEVE EVERYTHING YOU READ and PERHAPS SOMEONE SHOULD BAKE A PIE. That last one he made with soft, inviting letters. Like pie. He was quite proud of himself.

He hung the signs and walked home sure that he had finally solved his problem. He closed and locked his front door and began to count his money. Every single coin.

The Very Old Woman and the Very Old Man

Matron woke to the sensation of something pulsing in her hand.

Beat-beat.

Beat-beat.

Beat-pause-beat.

Beat-beat.

Beat-pause-pause-beat.

She opened her eyes and smiled. Someone had placed the butterfly in her left hand. The butterfly that Myron had given her . . . oh, a lifetime ago. She brought it close, delighting in its clever construction. It glinted in the morning light. It was, after all these years, a marvel of craftsmanship and beauty. She never had to wind it or mind it. It just beat of its own accord.

Myron had told her that it had a piece of his heart at its center.

But Matron was a realist, and of course it was foolish to think that was true. And yet how many times in their long marriage had she held the butterfly in one hand and placed her other hand over her husband's heart, and felt them beating in tandem? And lately . . . she could hardly bear to think about it . . . but lately, the butterfly's wings had been pulsing more erratically than they used to. She couldn't bring herself to check her husband's heart. Myron was *fine*, she told herself. The butterfly was just old—that's all. Sometimes, toys break. Matron did her best to force her worries away.

Matron brought the butterfly to her lips and gave it a quick kiss. The fluttering increased. Myron turned on his cot to face her and smiled.

"Good morning, dear wife," he said sweetly.

"Good morning, my Myron," she murmured back. And then she noticed her other hand. She frowned. "It looks as though I've gotten another one. Have you?"

Myron showed her a small handmade book, with a carefully painted picture of a crow with a gold coin in its mouth on the cover.

Matron sat up in her cot, and Myron sat up in his. It had been an uncomfortable night, leading to a more uncomfortable morning. Their bones were old, after all, and creaky, and it would have been better for both of them to sleep in their actual beds. But the children had been acting so strangely lately. After what had happened to Cass, they didn't feel right leaving the door unattended.

They had gotten their first books the morning before. Myron's was about a little girl who became lost in the woods and was rescued by a crow, then a dog, and then an ogress. It seemed an improbable tale. And yet he found himself weeping at the end of it.

Matron's story was about a mad king who had taken what he should not and left his people to struggle and starve, until it was only by coming together—sharing and coordinating, and standing as one—that they were able to topple his rule.

This story, too, felt . . . improbable. And strange. And yet reading it made Matron's heart lift and her mind wander. It made her think about what the town was like once upon a time, when everyone's doors were as open as their hearts, and when neighbors would spend all day chatting with neighbors, sharing ideas and garden bounties and suppers. She thought about Bartleby—was he right? Were they wrong to lock their gate and shut the town away? Were they wrong to think that the bad outnumbered the good?

Matron looked at Myron. He sat quietly absorbed in his new story. There was a picture of a small dog with milky eyes and a crow perched on its head. Myron sniffed and wiped his nose with the back of his hand. The lower rims of his eyes were slicked with tears. Matron patted his knee. "Come on, you softhearted old man. Let's wake the children."

As they had been the day before, the babies and toddlers were bright-eyed and eager as they sat in their beds. The rest of the children slumped and staggered like the newly awakened dead.

"What has gotten into you children?" Matron asked.

"Are you sick?" worried Myron.

"Nothing," Anthea mumbled as she moved through her chores as though still sleeping.

"Nothing," Bartleby yawned as he headed out to the yard with Cass to gather eggs.

"Nothing," murmured the twins.

"Nothing," said Dierdre.

"I have a story about that," said Elijah. "Let me sit here and collect my thoughts, and I'll tell it to you." The moment he sat down, he fell asleep.

Matron shook her head. It wasn't like the children to lie. They were good children. They followed the rules. Didn't they? And yet something wasn't adding up. "Come, my love," she said to Myron. "Let's go and see if there is anything at the front gate."

They went out into the light, shading their eyes so they could see. The sky was a shattering blue. Occasionally, great lumbering clouds, each one like a dollop of cream, moved across the sun to provide shade. Matron and Myron turned the key in the gate and stepped out onto the street. There was no box of vegetables. Again. Instead, they saw something even more surprising.

Their neighbors were out. Some had put together makeshift benches. Others had dragged chairs from their homes onto the street. One man had a tureen of coffee and a stack of paper that he was folding into cups and offering a sip to people as they walked by. Two women spoke in animated tones, their hands louder than their mouths. They held books. They pressed books to their hearts. They swapped books. They read from books out loud.

"Well," Matron whispered to herself. "Well, I'll be."

The cobbler's wife came bustling over. "Oh, Matron, I'm so happy to see you. Make sure to leave your gate open today. Several neighbors will be arriving shortly with breakfast and lunch for the children. Here. We collected some more clothing. I hope at least some of it fits." She handed Matron a basket heaped with children's clothes. Matron had to put her book in her mouth in order to hold it. She tried to say thank you around the pages clamped between her teeth.

"Oh!" exclaimed the cobbler's wife. "You received books as well! That's wonderful! I hope you're sharing them with the children. It's always a good day for a story! I was hoping to organize a read-aloud in the Center Square today or tomorrow. I'll make sure to let you know!" And she fluttered away, the edge of her skirt flapping in the wind.

Matron looked at Myron. He was just as confused as she was. They looked down the street in one direction. They saw people sitting on the curb, or leaning against a wall, or lounging on an ancient stump. And reading. They saw the same thing looking the other direction.

Above their heads, hanging from windows or hastily pasted onto the walls, were signs—in bright colors with white, crisp letters—saying things like DON'T BELIEVE EVERYTHING YOU READ or ASK NOT WHAT YOUR MAYOR CAN DO FOR YOU BUT WHAT YOU CAN DO FOR YOUR MAYOR or WHO HAS TIME TO READ WHEN THERE IS WORK TO BE DONE, but no one seemed to pay them any mind. Their attention remained with the books in their hands.

"What on earth is going on?" Myron muttered. Matron had no idea.

45

The Stone

Anthea had noticed on that first night at the Ogress's house how time got . . . *funny*. Squishy. And stretchy. Less like a mountain to be climbed, and more like a rubber band that could be pulled or snapped or tied up in knots. It was like the Reading Room, but more so. The children had time to complete tasks that should have taken hours and hours or days and days. And yet, they returned home with time to spare. Enough to sleep a little bit. Not enough sleep, of course. But a little. And it helped.

The second night, the stories in their books were longer, the illustrations more detailed and precise. The Ogress set the table up outside so they could work under the stars, and so that the little ones could sleep on cushions and blankets next to the fire. Anthea had studied astronomy. She knew that the stars rose in the east and set in the west from precise and predictable points on the horizon, and that their timing and position was so dependable that sailors relied on it to chart their courses and keep from getting lost in the wide-open sea.

The stars should *not* have slowed down in the sky.

And yet they certainly seemed to.

Was it magic? Anthea wondered. There was no way of knowing. So she got back to work, feeling grateful for the unraveled time.

The Ogress couldn't help with the writing, but she was a gifted artist. And she was able to understand how things *worked*. She quickly ascertained the mechanics and processes for large-scale bookmaking. She helped to streamline everyone's efforts, separating each task so they could be completed like clockwork. On the third night, they wrote more, and drew more, and painted more, and accomplished more. The books seemed less like a project undertaken by children, and more like . . . *books*. Everyone was proud of what they had done. The crows delivered the books, and the orphans stumbled home.

Climbing back into the house with Hiram's rope was more difficult than climbing in, but they managed it without injury and collapsed into bed.

Morning, once again, came too fast and too soon. The orphans spent the rest of the day as though they were in a dream. "What has gotten into all of you lately?" Matron said, utterly flummoxed.

"Are you sick?" Myron said, reaching out and touching forehead after forehead.

"Um," Elijah said slowly. "Yes?" He rubbed his eyes and yawned. "Yes. Very sick. We should all go lie down." He yawned again. "You know, so we can get better." And the orphans returned to the dormitory and collapsed onto their beds.

On the fourth night, the Ogress set out a feast of the most delicious foods the orphans had ever eaten, and sewed them jackets and slippers and sleeping caps. She embroidered cushions with their faces on them and blankets with fanciful animals for the littlest children and showed them how to use the telescope to observe planets and asteroids and stars. She baked them cookies in the shape of crows, and cakes in the shape of sheep. She gathered apples and pears and nuts from the trees and heaped them into bowls for the children to snack on during the night. The crows had found pages of gold leaf, and the children were using it to illuminate the borders along the edges of the books, and the grand lettering at the beginning.

Anthea shook her head. Facts matter, she knew, and these were facts that didn't seem to make any sense. Where did the crows find gold leaf? "Is this magic?" she asked the Ogress.

"Is which part magic?" the Ogress asked.

Anthea pinched her eyebrows, trying to piece together her own thoughts. "Time, I guess. Is time magic with you? I feel as though there are more minutes when we come here. Or, that each of our minutes is longer. I've noticed this sort of thing before. In our Reading Room, for example. Is that magic, too?"

The Ogress smiled. "Magic?" she said. "No. Not really. But I suppose it's close."

This made Anthea remember something. "Lady Ogress," she said, because that is what the crows called her, "there is a large stone off to the side of the Center Square. Have you noticed it before?"

The Ogress frowned. "Can't say that I have. But that doesn't mean it's not there. Stones are funny that way. Sometimes, you don't notice them unless they want you to. Perhaps I should stop and say hello."

Well, that certainly didn't make any sense. Anthea pressed on. "A funny thing happened to me when I sat on that stone. I . . . saw things. Not with my eyes, but inside my head."

The Ogress nodded. "Well, that is the best sort of seeing, of course. Our eyes deceive us all the time! If we want to know what's true, we need to look with our minds. And then, if we want to know what is vital, we need to look with our hearts."

Anthea rubbed her face with her hands. "Are you sure?" she said.

"If that stone had something to say, I think it's a good idea to listen. Stones are very old, you know. And their memories are long. I once met a stone that was so old it remembered the future."

"There's a story about that, you know," Elijah said.

"Of course there is," Bartleby said in a soothing voice. "Write it down. We still have more to do."

Anthea patted the Ogress's hand. She had only known her for a matter of days and she already loved her—despite the fact that some of the things she said didn't sound exactly logical.

The half-moon had set and the night was rich and deep when the orphans had finished. Stacks of beautifully bound books crowded the table, and the crows began the difficult work of carrying each one to its destination.

Anthea shook her head. *How was any of this possible?* Her thoughts returned to the Stone. What had she seen, *really*? And would the other children see the same thing?

While the crows dropped each of the books at the home of its intended recipient, the orphans paused in the middle of the Center Square, their faces tilted toward the spangle of stars and the soaring birds. It was colder in town than in the Ogress's yard. The wind blew harder. They pulled their coats tightly around their shoulders.

"I'm tired," Justina said, starting to cry.

"I know, honey," Bartleby said, picking her up, even though he already had a toddler strapped to his back. "Anthea, I don't know how much longer we can do this."

Anthea turned to her family. "I know we're all exhausted, but will you please come with me for one more thing? There's something I want to check." She brought them to the Stone.

Bartleby stared. "Where did this come from?" He squinted. "Has this always been here?"

"Look," Anthea said. "We are going to have to explain to Matron and Myron what's going on. We can't keep sneaking out. And we can't do this on our own. We do actually need some grown-ups to help. Matron and Myron love us, and they trust us, but we have to show them in a way that they can understand. And I have an idea. That last Market Day, when I went to build a stool for Myron, I sat on this stone, and . . . well, my mind went all funny. I saw things that I shouldn't have seen and remembered things that I shouldn't remember. And then I forgot the things I had seen. Just like that, my mind went blank. But bits and pieces have come back, and I feel as though they are important. Maybe I need other people to help me to work it all out. Maybe if all of you touch the Stone, you'll see the same things I did, and maybe together we'll understand. And maybe Matron and Myron will too."

"Oh," Elijah said. "You mean like what happens in the house sometimes?" He looked closely at the Stone.

Anthea tilted her head at him. "The house? What do you mean?"

Elijah shrugged. "The wood beams tell stories. The oak, specifically. At least to me. For as long as I can remember." His cheeks flushed scarlet. "I mean," he added, "not every day. Just sometimes."

The Stone seemed to vibrate a little bit. Bartleby and Dierdre looked closer. "Look," Dierdre said, narrowing her eyes. "That little carving in the Stone looks like the Orphan House."

"And look," Bartleby said. "That one looks like a dragon burning a library."

"And look at that one," Elijah said. "It looks like the Ogress."

Everyone knelt close to the Stone. It felt strangely warm, despite the cold night. "Put your hands on it," Anthea said. "And close your eyes." And the orphans did. All of them together. They closed their eyes.

And they saw. A dragon in a man's skin. A swindle of an entire town. A trail of destruction with an insidious purpose. The whispers in ears that made eyes narrow and mouths twist and neighbor turn from neighbor. A man with a dragon inside his skin who slept each night on a pile of gold as the rest of the town went hungry.

"Oh," Cass said. "*Oh.*"

And they understood. The children hurried home. It was time to wake up Matron and Myron. They needed to come right away.

46

Introductions

It was still dark when several sets of knuckles rapped on the door. Matron, in her cot in the front entryway, woke in a panic. She thought that Myron's heart would stop beating. She thought that *hers* would. "Run, darling!" she cried, reaching for her husband. "Run for your life."

"Stop," Myron said, grabbing her hand. "It's the children's voices."

It didn't make any sense. The children were in bed, of course, because the children followed the rules. Out? At night? All of them? *Impossible.*

She opened the door, fully prepared to be incandescent with fury. Instead, the looks on the children's faces stopped her cold.

"We know you're probably angry," Anthea said. "But we need you to listen."

Matron's head swam. The children—*her children*—had *snuck outside at night.* That sentence didn't even make sense. It was as though words themselves suddenly had no meaning. How could such a thing be true?

"Please," begged Dierdre.

"Please, please, please." Bartleby's eyes were large and desperate.

"We're not tired anyway," Hiram insisted.

"For me," Cass said quietly. "Please come for me."

Matron looked at Myron. They were defeated. Matron put her hand on Anthea's cheek and looked into her eyes. Myron held on to Cass's hand. Matron and Myron looked at each other and nodded. "I'll get the coats," Myron said.

The Ogress sat by the fire, knitting socks for the children. Next, she would knit mittens and hats and scarves. Winter would come, as it does, and winter is more bearable with warm ears, she knew. She couldn't bear the thought of the children being cold. She hummed happily as her needles clicked and danced in her hands.

She heard the crows making a ruckus in the mulberry trees and felt the uncomfortably familiar grip of fear. But only for a moment. She recognized the word for *friends* and the word for *child* in the cacophony of crow voices. She smiled as someone knocked.

There, outside the Ogress's crooked house, were the children she loved so much. And also a very old man and a very old woman. She stood, suddenly self-conscious. She was so much bigger than everyone else, and she noticed, with some trepidation, the way in which she occupied space. Her heavy feet trod quietly across her floor and onto the threshold. She thrust her broad hands into her apron pockets, hiding them from view.

She walked outside under the wide nighttime sky. The fallen leaves rustled and scattered across the lawn. The Ogress recognized the couple, of course. But she had recognized the people who had gone on to do horrible things to her home as well. Who could she trust now?

The old woman pressed her hands to her heart and bowed. "Hello," she said, her face tilted upward and shining in the moonlight, "my dear, dear neighbor. I have so much to thank you for. And I feel so honored to finally make your acquaintance." And with that, the very old woman ventured close to the Ogress. She extended her hand. The Ogress knelt down on the frosty grass, which crunched under her knees.

The crows held their breath. The old woman's eyes were surrounded in soft crinkles and folds. They sparkled in the light of the early-morning stars. The Ogress opened her great arms and gently surrounded the matron of the Orphan House in a large, stony hug, as though the two were old friends who hadn't seen each other for a long, long time.

Anthea Hatches Another Plan

After the initial rush of joy and togetherness (and of course an overwhelming doling out of snacks and treats, because the Ogress couldn't bear to see anyone hungry), after the full bellies and the keen interest in the various contraptions and the broad praise for the hard work the children and the Ogress had already accomplished, there was still much to be decided.

Matron said, "No more sneaking out. It isn't safe, and it isn't healthy, either. You are children, and you need to be awake during the day and sleeping at night. And that is that."

Myron said, "What we need is a schedule. With all the comings and goings in the Orphan House, we need to make sure that some of us are there at all times, holding down the fort. I don't think people are ready to understand what it is that we're doing here with our dear ogress. But we also need to make sure to keep the work going. We can help clean up the garden, and eventually we'll need to start dreaming up plans to build something for the poor sheep. With winter coming soon." He looked at the stacks of papers and paints and pencils and a long, narrow sheet that said *Elijah's List of Simply Amazing Story Ideas* at the top. "And of course, there are the books. Everyone in town is reading them. Whatever it is you children are doing, it certainly seems to be having an effect on people."

"But we *like* sneaking out at night!" Justina complained.

"Can't you just pretend that you don't know, so we can continue with our ropes and open windows and hijinks?" Hiram inquired. "I'm quite good at all of it, and everyone else is perfectly fine."

"Ropes are fun!" said Kye.

But Matron insisted and the Ogress agreed, so Anthea gave herself the task of setting the schedule, taking great pains to be impartial and fair and to make sure that no one had to spend too much time managing the cobbler's wife when she bustled in with her whirlwind of necessary supplies and baffled volunteers and unrelenting helpfulness. It wasn't that everyone in the family wasn't grateful—they were—but it was difficult to get a word in edgewise when Esmé was on a mission.

Over the subsequent days, Matron, Myron, and the children divided their time between the Orphan House and the Ogress's cottage. When they were home, they helped the volunteers replace shingles on the roof, and repair the broken stairs, and shore up the sagging joists to better hold up the floor. They joined large canning parties organized by the cobbler's wife, and soon the pantry was stocked with tomato sauce, beef stew, applesauce, and precooked beans, all preserved in large sealed jars.

At the Ogress's cottage, they wrote and illustrated stories and bound them into books. Once again, time stretched and unraveled and unwound. The more time they used, the more they had.

Matron sewed old sheets together, and Myron constructed a set of tent poles. From these they created a large, shaded ramshackle porch, so that the Ogress could come out of doors and sit with her new friends during the day, safe from the sunlight's assaults on her skin. The garden had been mended and replanted, and already a new crop of hardy winter greens grew vigorously toward the sky. Even some of the squash mounds had been salvaged. The potatoes, safe underground, were fine, and could be dug up any day now. The Ogress's farm was warm again—ever so much warmer than the rest of the town—and produced with gusto.

The crows, for their part, had discovered the marvels and delights of sitting on a child's lap, cuddled and close, and they often argued over whose turn it was. A child's lap, they'd decided, was better than the finest nest in the world. (Harold never argued, of course. Harold always had a place on Cass's lap. That was a given.) Every night the crows delivered books to the people of Stone-in-the-Glen.

The children played with the sheep, and they played with the dog, and they played with the crows when they were at the Ogress's house, and they played with the chickens and the goats and the cats when they were at home. They were in constant motion, back and forth, back and forth.

But how long would they have to keep on like this? That was the question. No one seemed to have the answer. The children looked to Anthea, of course, but Anthea had grown curiously quiet. She often wrote notes in her ledger. She didn't show them to anyone.

∾

One day as the children sat in the shade of their makeshift porch and painted illustrations for one of Elijah's stories, Bartleby looked up. "What is a neighbor?" he asked.

"I don't understand the question," Anthea said. It sounded suspiciously like philosophy, which made her instantly annoyed. Also, she was busy painting a tree.

"Can someone please hand me a new pen. This one's broken," said Elijah, whose stories flowed onto the page. He didn't look up. He just waited for a pen to appear and then continued.

He wrote, Cass wrote, Dierdre and the Ogress drew, Matron helped with the sewing, and Myron minded the little ones.

Many minutes passed. Anthea thought that Bartleby had forgotten his question. "No, seriously," he persisted. "What is a neighbor?"

"Use a dictionary," Anthea said acidly. She had moved on to writing a story and had inexplicably found herself deep in a long-winded description of different sorts of drill bits. She shook her head. Why was this so much easier for Elijah?

Bartleby was undeterred. "No. I'm not talking about dictionary definitions. A definition lives on the surface. Think like a philosopher—look at the thing from *within*. What is the essence of neighborliness? What does it mean to be a neighbor?"

Anthea put her pen down. She frowned. "I'm not sure what you're getting at," she said.

Bartleby sighed. "We are giving people these stories, and they are making a difference. But they need something more, something bigger. In the end, people will only change their behavior and bad ideas through big changes in their thinking. And thinking starts with questions. That's how philosophy works. So, how do we get people to start asking questions? The town didn't only fail at being a neighbor to our Ogress. They failed at being neighbors to one another. Maybe it's time that they start asking themselves what being a neighbor actually means."

Anthea shrugged and returned to her work. "I question your assumptions," she said.

"I question your face," Bartleby returned. And then he let the matter drop.

But Anthea kept on thinking.

As she walked home with Bartleby and Cass, along with the babies snoozing in slings (and Harold on Cass's shoulder), Anthea paid close attention to what she saw on the way. Bartleby was right. The books were helping. She could tell. Everywhere she looked, doors and windows had been thrown open. People had brought their books outside to read. The blacksmith had set up chairs for impromptu discussions and, as a result, had taken on two young people as his new apprentices. The constable, because of the constant flow of people in and out, had brought out pitchers of cider or tea and offered a spot of conversation.

The children crossed the Center Square. The Mayor's signs were still up, but people mostly had stopped paying attention to them. His flyers collected in heaps in corners. If anyone noticed them, it was just to help clean up debris and throw refuse into the trash. Off to the side of the square, a young man had set up a story hour with a pod of children. They all held umbrellas to make a little shade. The young man told the story of a kind fox and an ill-tempered grouse and a philosopher who didn't always understand the truth of the matter and kept making silly mistakes. The children laughed and laughed.

Anthea paused a moment and took in the scene. She tilted her head. "Hmm," she said.

Later, Anthea sat alone on the stone step at the Orphan House's open gates, and watched as people walked by. She took notes in her ledger. People waved and greeted one another by name. They even knew *her* name. She waved shyly back.

Anthea considered the other changes she had observed since the books first appeared. Chats had become discussions, which had become gatherings, which had become potlucks. People had stopped hurrying. They smiled at each other. They grasped each other's hands, or touched an arm, or even hugged. The cobbler's wife had organized a town-wide garden swap, so that people could trade bags of green tomatoes for boxes of bulbs or a bag of excess squash.

The Orphan House, too, had begun to change. Someone had built a small fence to keep the goats and chickens in, so that Matron and Myron could unlock the gate in the morning and leave it wide open all day. Myron had decided to open up the Reading Room to the community and had set up a checkout list. People now came and went with books to borrow or books to return. The shelves adjusted themselves and never seemed to empty. No one questioned this. Townspeople bustled in with casseroles and extra shoes, and left with homemade soap or jam or raspberry cordial as a parting gift. But the children didn't tell their neighbors that they had been going back and forth to the Ogress's house. They didn't think the town was ready to understand.

After a bit, Bartleby and Cass sat on either side of Anthea. She didn't stop writing things down in her ledger. They sat that way for a long while. Finally, Anthea paused and looked up. A pair of women with tool belts and ropes had arrived to inspect the chimney. Inside the yard, a man on a ladder was fixing a window, while two children from the neighborhood, who had come with their mother to play with the Littles, were feeding the chickens by hand and squealing with delight.

Anthea turned to Bartleby. "Seriously, though, what *is* a neighbor?" she asked.

Bartleby grinned. "You see? Philosophy isn't so bad once you get the hang of it. Shall we organize a symposium?"

"No," Anthea said flatly. She looked back to the street. A group of neighbors had set up chairs in a circle at the end of the block and sat deep in conversation, exchanging books and snacks. They all smiled at one another.

"Or maybe," Anthea amended. "Something like that. I have a plan, you see."

"Does it have to do with philosophy?" Bartleby asked. Cass rolled her eyes. She removed Nanette and Orpheus from their slings and took them with Harold to visit the children feeding the chickens.

"I think it might," Anthea said. She wrote one last sentence in her ledger. "Mostly, I'm pretty sure you're right. People do need to ask big questions if they want to make big changes. We need to get everyone asking the same big question." She circled something in her notes and drew several lines under it.

"How will we do that?" Bartleby asked.

She smiled. "We are going to make a very large sign."

Possible Solutions

Those infernal books kept coming. The Mayor was in a lather.

Where have they been coming from?

And why are people ignoring my beautiful signs?

There were signs that said YOUR MAYOR KNOWS WHAT'S BEST FOR YOU and signs that said OGRES ARE DANGEROUS and signs that said PERHAPS WE SHOULD BUILD A WALL TO KEEP HER OUT. The signs were plastered all over the town. They hung from clothes-lines. They fluttered from flagpoles.

And yet . . . they didn't seem to be doing any good.

The Mayor remembered those earlier days, ever so long ago, when he'd first arrived in town and the people of Stone-in-the-Glen regularly lounged in the shade reading books and discussing books. He grimaced at the thought of it. Poets stood in the dappled light under apple trees back then, reciting epics and odes. Philosophers came to lecture and debate at forums in the square. Librarians sat on the grand front steps to do story time with hordes of grubby children. It was *terrible*. Even the memory of it was repellent. Burning down the Library was the best thing he could have done for this town. And had anyone thanked him? No, they had not.

Oh, the Mayor realized with a start. *That was a secret, wasn't it? Well. Good thing I didn't say it out loud.*

The difference between *secret* and *not secret* was a bit fuzzy to him every now and again. He blamed time. It was one of the problems with living as long as he had—time had a tendency to loop and twist and wobble. And this made the difference between *truth* and *lies* even fuzzier than normal. This, the Mayor felt, was not his fault. Should things not be true simply because he said they were? It certainly felt that this should be so. Being mayor was a lot of work, after all. And he asked for so little.

He walked through the town, looking resplendent with his sweeping coat and smart boots and magnificent shock of hair. He flashed a glittering smile to all he passed. The citizens of Stone-in-the-Glen didn't notice. *How odd*, thought the Mayor. *What on earth is going on?*

He tried it again. He clicked his smart boots together. He gave a gallant bow to a group of women who were hurrying by with books under their arms. He smiled so brightly it could have shattered glass. The women kept walking by like he wasn't even there. They all spoke quickly, urgently, their cheeks flushed with ideas and complicated *thoughts*.

And none of those thoughts were about their mayor. He could tell. The Mayor felt himself awash with an emotion that he had not felt in a long, long time. The Mayor, there was no doubt about it, felt glum. He continued, glumly, on his way to the center of town.

People had set up sunshades in the streets and in the square. They had brought out blankets and chaise lounges and rugs to sit on. There were discussions and readings and debates. They were *everywhere*. People were gathered on the weedy edge of the muddy pond in the old sinkhole that used to be the park. They sat on the tumbledown stones in the ruins of the Library. They gossiped in the shade between buildings or in the doorways of shops suddenly bustling with activity. Someone had written poetry in chalk on the flagstones. The Mayor detested poetry.

"Hello," he enthused at people as he walked by. "Hello, hello. It is I. Your beloved Mayor." It was such a lovely word. *Mayor*. It was the most wonderful word in the world. Normally, he said it to people and they looked at him with indulgent and adoring eyes, which was his favorite part. But now? They were too busy with their books. They didn't notice him at all.

The bells in the Town Hall rang, and it was time for another speech. He would give everyone a chance to air their grievances about the ludicrous ogress, and they would forget their books and their problems, and once again everything would be as it should. Tempers would rise. Rancor would fester. He would make more signs! People would chant! A glorious wave would crash over the whole town.

He approached the dais with a song in his heart. His boots clicked, and his hair shimmered, and his golden buckles flashed in the sun. He waited for the applause. No one applauded. The people in the square had their noses in books. They murmured in groups. They had barely registered his arrival.

"Ahem," the Mayor said gallantly. Still nothing. "Now, my dear, dear citizens, what speeches I have ready for you today.

And listening! So much listening! It is important for grievances to be aired, after all. Especially if they are about"—he winked—"*certain someones.* You know. Who live at *the far end of town?*"

A woman approached the dais. The Mayor relaxed. *At last, we are getting somewhere,* he thought.

"Mr. Mayor, I do appreciate this," she said. "Honestly, I do. And I appreciate your . . . sudden willingness to listen to the town. That is a nice change. I don't so much have a grievance to be aired so much as I would like to offer a solution."

He beamed at the crowd and indicated the woman with a gallant gesture. "You see?" he said. "This is what I just love about Stone-in-the-Glen. We are a problem-solving people. How grand! Tell me your solution, my dear!"

"Well, you see, sir, after the loss of prosperity, many of our former citizens simply left for good, and there are several abandoned homes in Stone-in-the-Glen. There are also several capable folks who are out of work. I propose we all work together to make at least one thing in town better. Why don't we salvage what is useful from the abandoned homes and use it to build a new school? The children desperately need it." The woman inclined her chin expectantly at the Mayor.

The Mayor stared at the woman, his mouth slightly open. "I'm sorry, what?" he said. She wasn't talking about the Ogress at all. What on earth was going on? To make matters worse, several people now crowded around her, *nodding their heads.* The people with their noses in books, the people who hadn't been paying attention at all, suddenly rose to their feet. They slapped one another on the back and shook hands. Several began to cheer wildly. The woman who had spoken, an obvious busybody, started walking around with a sign-up sheet. The Mayor was baffled. Since when did people just walk around carrying sign-up sheets? That had never happened before.

This was not going well. The Mayor had to think fast. "Yes, yes, that is all very nice. Does someone *else* have anything that they would like to share? A problem, for example, that I, alone, can fix?"

A man approached the dais. "You know," he said, "the sinkhole is a fixable problem."

"What?" The Mayor guffawed. "No it certainly is not! If only the people of Stone-in-the-Glen were more generous in their donations to the town! But they are not! It is too sad!"

"No, sir," the man persisted. "I have several books in my house about civil engineering. My father checked them out from the Library right before it burned, and we have held on to them ever since, thinking that we would return them when it was eventually rebuilt. I'm certain with just a little organization and—"

"*Does anyone else wish to speak?*" the Mayor roared.

"Ahem," a small woman said. She held an open ledger full of numbers.

Oh no, the Mayor thought. *Not an accountant!*

"It seems to me," she said, "that the problem in Stone-in-the-Glen is not one of a lack of generosity, but one of improper distribution. If we all pay our taxes, then where does the money go? I truly believe that we can start to solve our problems if we apply some basic arithmetic. Could you please elaborate on your knowledge of the town's finances?"

The Mayor sputtered and swore. "Well!" he huffed. "Finances! The very idea! I don't believe I like your tone! I mean, just look at the beautiful signs!" He pointed overhead and only then saw that one of them had been vandalized. Instead of NO MORE OGRES, it said NO MORE GREED. What had gotten into everyone? "And also!" the Mayor continued. "How many ogre attacks have occurred today? That's right, none! Have you thanked your mayor? Have you sent him something wonderful—a pie, for example, with a note that says 'Well done, Mayor!' No. You haven't."

Several groups approached. They did not look happy. A man in an apron stepped forward to say, "I would like to point out that the streets in town are—"

"*Fine!*" the Mayor interrupted, stomping so hard that the wood platform cracked under his boots. "The streets are *perfectly fine*," he roared. "Everyone in this town has gotten *so picky* these days!"

A woman with knitting needles in her hair spoke up. "It seems to me that there are too many citizens going hungry. Let's create a surplus shelf, where people can share their extras with those who have nothing." She smiled.

"For crying out loud," muttered the Mayor.

"With all these extra books, we need a community structure to house them, so that we might share stories and ideas with one another," a man said. "You know. A new library."

"*Well, that is just—*" But now the Mayor was interrupted.

"When I was a girl, there were community picnics. I think it's time to bring those back."

The Mayor lifted his eyes to his beautiful signs. He had worked so hard on them. They lined the entire square. His gaze drifted along the lot of them, but the last one stopped him cold. He hadn't made that one. He squinted.

What, he read, *is a neighbor?* The Mayor frowned. He turned back to glare at the crowd. "What is a *neighbor?*" he said. "Who put that sign up there? I certainly didn't. It's barely even a question. Everyone knows what a neighbor is." He looked at the words again. *What is a neighbor?* Who would dare ruin his work with an unsanctioned sign?

Clouds rolled in, and a light rain fell. The Mayor hated rain. It made his skin bubble and itch. The citizens of Stone-in-the-Glen didn't seem to mind the rain at all. They tilted their faces to the sky.

"Well, that's enough for today!" the Mayor said. No one indulged him. No one applauded as he tromped down the stairs. He left in silence and walked home by himself, his thoughts racing. He would cover up the renegade sign. He would make more signs. He would ban books. He would end their questions. He would make the people hate the Ogress. By any means necessary. Everyone would love him again.

Everything would be as it should.

Even if he had to burn the whole town to the ground.

What Is a Neighbor?

The next day, when the citizens of Stone-in-the-Glen woke up, they each found, once again, a brand-new book. This time, each person received the exact same thing, the prettiest book yet. It had carefully drawn pictures and hand-painted lettering, and pressed flowers in some of the pages. It smelled like mown grass and fresh air and turned earth and hard work. The title of this book was *Neighbors*.

What is a neighbor? the book asked under an illustration of the schoolteacher.

"People keep asking that question," muttered the citizens of Stone-in-the-Glen.

Is a neighbor simply an accident of place—I am near you, and therefore we are neighbors? the book inquired.

People thought about the question as they admired the carefully painted illustrations of the streets of Stone-in-the-Glen—not as they were now, but as they once had been, when the town was lovely.

Or is it something else? the book went on. *I may claim as my neighbor a person who lives in my town. Or perhaps on my block. Is the person who lives in the house next door to mine any more my neighbor than the person with no place to go, who sleeps on the cobblestones right outside my door? Who is my neighbor, really?*

The people in Stone-in-the-Glen kept reading. They lingered on the illustration of the apothecary sitting down for a meal with the constable, even though everyone knew those two hadn't spoken in a decade. They smiled at the picture of the cobbler and his wife, each with a crow resting on an open palm. They skipped breakfast. They wandered outside and sat on the curb. They didn't take their eyes from the pages.

What is a neighbor? the book asked again. This page showed a picture of the young man who lived in a hand-built shack under the bridge, who made his living doing odd jobs.

Your neighbor lives, the book went on, *in the house down the lane. Or in the lean-to shelter in an abandoned yard. Your neighbor lives in the farm between the forest and the town. Your neighbor lives by the park. Or in the park. Your neighbor lives in the Orphan House. Your neighbor lives where the roads wind, and the thickets tangle, and the heavy limbs of the sycamores creak in the wind. Your neighbor, you see, is anyone. A person. A person who thinks and breathes and worries and loves. That person is your neighbor.*

The cobbler and his wife sat side by side under the sunshade next to their house. The cobbler pressed the book to his heart. Esmé reached over and took his hand. The blacksmith ran outside and said hello to everyone in sight, while the constable walked straight over to the apothecary and hugged her.

What is a neighbor? the book asked, yet again. *A neighbor is similar to you. Or they are different from you. Or they are equal parts similar and different. A neighbor shares all your values. Or some of them. Or none of them. A neighbor is someone you care about anyway. A neighbor is someone who helps you for no reason at all. They help because you are a person, and because they are a person, and people help one another. A neighbor is someone who shows up* just because.

An image of the Ogress smiling with her crows, her dog, and her sheep decorated this page. The people of Stone-in-the-Glen thought about the crooked house. They shifted uncomfortably where they sat. Because she was a neighbor. Of course she was.

There was a time, the people in Stone-in-the-Glen knew, when neighbors helped one another. When neighbors showed up for one another. Why did it go away? they wondered. Why did the neighborliness stop? And then a smaller, sharper question itched at the backs of their brains: What do I owe to my neighbor?

What is a neighbor? the book asked. There was a painting of the lamplighter. Followed by a painting of the butcher. Followed by a portrait of the old man and the old woman who ran the Orphan House. *A neighbor exists without condition—if I were to declare that* this *person is my neighbor and that* person *is not, then it is I, and not they, who have failed at neighborliness. It is only by claiming all as your neighbors, and behaving as though all are your neighbors, that we become good neighbors ourselves. The act of being a good neighbor must always begin with* us.

The people of Stone-in-the-Glen thought about the many times that they had passed by the Ogress's house and didn't say hello. How they didn't offer her welcome when she arrived. They thought about the NO MORE OGRES sign, and they felt ashamed. They thought about the BOOKS ARE DANGEROUS sign, too, and they started to wonder.

One by one, the people of Stone-in-the-Glen looked up. They looked one another in the eye. They waved. They noticed for the first time there was a bit of a ruckus near the center of town. The sound of children laughing with one another. The sound of crows calling and calling and calling. One by one, the people of Stone-in-the-Glen stood and followed the sound.

What is a neighbor? the book asked. *A neighbor is someone who brings soup. Or bread. Or open arms. A neighbor is ready to help with the roof that has caved in, or the garden that needs turning, or with safe shelter during a terrible night. A neighbor looks out for you, worries about you, laughs with you, stands up for you. Doesn't that sound lovely?*

The people in Stone-in-the-Glen found themselves standing in the Center Square, openmouthed and amazed. They hadn't intended to come. And yet the seamstress waved at the former teacher, who waved at the trash collector, who waved at the greengrocer, who waved at the undertaker, who waved at the butcher, who waved at the cobbler and his wife.

"So nice to see you," their neighbors said.

A flock of sheep milled about. And what sheep! They were muscular and agile and wily. And their wool was the softest that anyone had ever felt. A flock of crows swooped and murmured overhead, and they seemed to be playing with children and the obviously blind dog. Even some of the sheep had joined in. The children laughed, and the crows cawed. And then the crows laughed, and the children cawed. They ran and flew and jumped and twirled like there was nothing more fun in all the world. *Do crows usually play with children?* the citizens of Stone-in-the-Glen wondered as they scratched their heads. Maybe. Who was to say?

There was the matron of the Orphan House and her husband, Myron. They were both upstanding members of the community. They were well respected and highly regarded. And there they were—standing with the Ogress. Matron and the Ogress had their arms around each other, despite the difference in size. The Ogress and Myron were laughing together. The Ogress wore long sleeves and long gloves. She held an umbrella over her head, shading her face. She hadn't turned into stone. Or ash. So that made two stories about ogres that were clearly not true. What else wasn't true?

What is a neighbor? the book asked. *A neighbor is the lady with tools and skills and know-how who stops by and helps you to mend what is broken. A neighbor is the man who tells stories late into the night. A neighbor is the one who sees you coming around the corner and waves and waves and waves.*

The children of the Orphan House moved like worker bees. They made a table using the cast-off pieces of lumber from the junk pile next to that old stone. They set out treats, pulled from a handcart one at a time, pies and cakes and rolls and cheese. The littler children carried sunflowers and zinnias and mums in their arms, which they scattered about.

One of the orphans, a tall, serious girl with long dark braids, tied a sign to the makeshift table. PICNIC TODAY, it said. FROM NEIGHBORS, FOR NEIGHBORS. ALL ARE WELCOME HERE. The table was heaped with fresh-baked breads. And intricately crafted cookies. And thick pies. And shining rolls.

The townspeople wandered about the square, as though in a dream. They greeted Matron. They greeted Myron. They greeted the Ogress, too. They craned their necks to look her in the face. They marveled at the flowers in her prairie-grass hair. They grinned at the way her stony skin crinkled around her shiny-new-penny eyes every time she smiled. They shook her large hands and were surprised at how soft and warm they were. They liked her. In spite of themselves. It felt *good* to greet her. It felt good to shake her hand.

"Are you hungry?" the Ogress said.

And, yes. They were.

"Thank you," they said.

Again, Neighbors

She knew all of their faces. She had known all of their faces for a long, long time. She had been watching them through her periscope.

Look, the Ogress thought. *There is the woman who builds birdhouses for the swallows who live in the swamp that filled in the sinkhole where the park used to be. Each birdhouse is tiny and detailed and perfect. Each one is painted with a stain that she made herself. Each one is padded inside with old pieces of soft fabric.* Because everyone deserved a lovely place to live—even though the woman herself hadn't had a roof over her head in years and slept each night in an old barn on the other side of town.

And look! She smiled. *There is the man who had a bakery that went out of business. Who once lost two fingers in a bread slicer. Who holds his hand to his face as though it still hurts.*

And there! The former organist, still grieving his departed spouse.

And there! The apothecary.

And the harried doctor.

And the cobbler and his fast-talking wife.

But it was a very different thing to see someone up close rather than from far away. Up close, their faces told all sorts of stories. The Ogress could see love. And loss. And scars. She could see disappointment. And worry. And sorrow. The Ogress could tell right away which people were good at telling jokes and which ones were good at numbers and which ones would always be ready with a box of tools and a head full of know-how.

As the day went on, the people of Stone-in-the-Glen noticed the depleted platters on the table. "I'll be right back," said the woman who fixed bicycles.

"I think I have something to share—just give me a minute," said the blacksmith.

They brought jars of applesauce and bowls of plum compote. They brought wine from their own vines. Even the butcher brought a ham. A small one. And only reluctantly. A pot of coffee arrived. A tray full of mugs. A pitcher of milk. A bowl of scrambled eggs. A bowl of salad. A basket of raspberries. A vat of soup.

People who didn't have food to share brought other things to the square. Sunshades. Chairs. A group of older children hauled an ancient sofa over and set it down next to the Stone.

"I'm sorry," one neighbor said to the Ogress. "For everything. I don't know what got into us. Can you forgive us?" She had brought bells for the sheep so they wouldn't get lost, and a bone for the dog.

"I'll stop by later to fix the window," another neighbor said.

"A group of us could help with the garden," offered another. "Many hands make the work light."

"How did you make cookies look like birds?" a neighbor asked.

"What is your recipe for the nut cakes?" asked another.

The Ogress answered their questions about her food and told stories about her life—her time swimming with the whales, and in the castle with the trolls, her time in the swamp, and in the ogre village. She told them how she had come to Stone-in-the-Glen, because she knew a thing or two about loss.

"In fact," the Ogress said. "Look there. On that stone." She tilted her head and squinted. "If you look at it right, it looks *just like* my old village." She frowned. "What I learned is that a dragon came in disguise and swindled everyone and then burned the whole place to the ground. But how could a dragon disguise himself in an ogre village? It doesn't make any sense."

"Oh!" Elijah said. "I know! I read all about it."

And so Elijah told the whole town about the dragons. And the skins.

Anthea didn't interrupt him. Not even once. He told the story all the way to the end.

The Picnic

The Mayor stepped out of his mansion and immediately noticed that something was off.

He frowned.

His house looked normal. His yard was untouched. The statues of him looking regal still glittered in the sun. So what had changed?

His magic was quite depleted, which likely explained how difficult it was to convince the townspeople lately. He had been foolish, he realized, to remain this long inside his mayor skin. As far as he could remember, he had never stayed inside a skin for this long before. Indeed, it was unlikely any dragon ever had. When was the last time he had shed his mayor skin? He wasn't sure. But it was just so much work, and he was *such* a lazy dragon. He would have been the first to admit it.

It shouldn't have been a surprise, then, that his situation was in such a state. No one got dizzy as they marveled at his beautiful voice. No one glittered in his presence. No wonder— not with this little magic. No matter, he decided. The new moon was approaching, and just before it arrived he would march himself straight into the woods and enjoy his marvelous dragon-ness. Once upon a time, he did so every month, like clockwork. But that was long ago, when there were buildings to burn and towns to swindle and he needed to be in top form. He had been getting too used to indolence. It was time to dragon up. If not this new moon, then certainly the next one. If he was feeling up to it.

He had a stack of signs rolled up under his arm. He walked out the front door, the porch groaning under his feet. Today, he decided, was going to be better. Today, he was going to get to the bottom of the mystery of the books. Today, he was going to direct the town's misery in the proper direction, and then . . .

He stopped at the edge of his yard. "Oh," he said.

Nearly all the cats were gone. Only one remained—an ancient ginger cat with a missing eye. She flicked her tail. She stared right at the Mayor and didn't blink. Well, this was strange, the Mayor thought. There had *always* been cats surrounding his house. So many infernal cats. Watching. Waiting. Staring at him. He didn't know why. Well, he did. Cats and dragons never got along. But it had been *so long* since he had really thought of himself as a dragon. Being mayor suited him so. He had never particularly gotten along with other members of dragonkind. As mayor, the only person he needed to impress was himself. And he found himself *terribly* impressive.

"Well," he said to the cat. "Looks like you lost your little friends."

The cat said nothing.

He shrugged. "Guess you're not that powerful after all."
What was he even saying? Cats could never be as powerful as
dragons. He stalked away in a huff. The ancient cat didn't move.

He marched back to the square, doing his best to forget the
nonsensical behavior of inconsequential cats, and focus instead
on his own marvelous self.

He had, under his arm, a sign that said

NO MORE OGRES.

Which was fine, as signs go. And another that said

DON'T LET STRANGERS TAKE
WHAT IS YOURS.

Which was okay but didn't have quite the ring he was looking for. And another that said

WE CAN'T ABIDE LAZY STEALERS.

Which was far and away his favorite.

He fully intended to see if any layabouts out of work would
be willing to hang the signs for a coin or two—he always kept
a couple of counterfeits in his pocket for just this purpose. The
fake coins disappeared at sunset, a marvelous bit of magic.
Which depleted him even more. No matter. He'd fix that soon
enough.

As he turned onto the square, the Mayor was met with a
shocking sight.

The Ogress. Right there, in the square. Sitting on an old chair. *During the day.* Under a sunshade that someone had set up. The Mayor *hated* sunshades.

And look over there! People were sharing food. He *hated* sharing.

And look over there! People were petting a dog. Or snuggling sheep. And someone was *hugging the Ogress.* He vowed to make a new decree outlawing hugging. And petting. And, *ugh,* snuggling.

The crows looked up. The Mayor glared at the crows. The crows glared right back. And then, without warning, the crows leaped up and rushed at the sky, streaking over the buildings and out of sight. The children watched them go until they disappeared.

"Good riddance," the Mayor said under his breath. "Varmints." He scratched his arms. He scratched his face. He had been in the rain for far too long the day before. He had been itchy all day.

He marched to the center of the square. "*What is the meaning of this?*" the Mayor roared.

"Would you like a cup of coffee?" the constable asked. She had a wide smile. Did she always have a wide smile? The Mayor didn't think so. Normally, the constable was rather dour.

"No," the Mayor huffed. "I do not want coffee. I want order! And laws! I want to take this town back, from . . . all of this!"

Everyone was smiling. *This is all wrong,* he thought desperately.

"Would you like some soup?" said an extremely old man.

"Or some scrambled eggs?" said an extremely old woman.

"I made cookies," said the Ogress. "Unfortunately, the pie has already been eaten. I do know how much you love your pie, my friend."

The Mayor's head swam. He couldn't believe what he was hearing. "*I do not want soup or eggs or cookies, and I am very upset about the pie.*"

The people of Stone-in-the-Glen covered their ears. His voice was oddly amplified. It shook the sky.

The Mayor felt his skin shift. He adjusted it. It had been shifting *so much* lately. One of his cheeks seemed to lose its plumpness. One of his shoulders felt as if it were deflating. People seemed to notice. They backed away from the Mayor. Their eyes became wary, and their cheeks lost their color.

The Mayor cleared his throat, embarrassed. He concentrated, drawing on the deepest depths of his magic reserves. He needed to dazzle the town. He needed to use the last dregs of power to really wow them. He scratched his arms. He scratched the back of his neck. He was *so itchy*. "Does anyone," he said in a much softer voice (was it working? he hoped it was working; he cursed himself for not powering up his magic), "want to help me distribute these signs?" He gave the Ogress a hard look, and then returned his gaze to everyone else. "They are regarding," he dropped his voice to a whisper, "*you-know-who.*"

"No, thank you," the former schoolteacher said. "We are having a wonderful picnic with our wonderful neighbors."

The Mayor closed his eyes. He imagined stores of magic deep within himself, like a precious spring at the bottom of a deep, deep well. He imagined the magic expanding, bubbling up, taking all the space it needed inside this precious and beloved skin, this mayor self that had become so much a part of him that he couldn't imagine being anything else. He visualized the magic shining forth, billowing in his body. He prepared to use magic to amplify his voice, layering in intoxicating sweetness, making it impossible for anyone to listen and not be utterly entranced. He cleared his throat. But at that very moment, the air had become thick with crows.

Crows with something shiny in their beaks and in each talon.

"What on earth?" the Mayor said to himself. He squinted, trying to get a closer look. Then he gasped. "Oh," he said when he realized. "Oh no."

The Crows

It had been five years since the crows found the Thing—that deflated skin on the ground of the forest. The skin with a shock of golden hair. Even the gleam of the golden buckles—right there for the taking!—didn't tempt the crows. They didn't touch them. They did not want to get close to the Thing. And later they did not speak of the Thing. They didn't want their thoughts to linger there. It was too unsettling. Too *strange*.

But Harold thought about the Thing a lot. *What kind of creature leaves its skin behind?* There was an old story among crows about a dragon who lived in a crow's skin for a time. But that dragon was good and benevolent and wise. Nothing like the Mayor. Still—the hair, the buckles, the coat. Once he had noticed it, Harold couldn't *un*-notice it.

Later, when Harold learned about the Mayor and his house full of gold, he was convinced.

Dragons hoard, after all. Just like the Mayor.

The night before the picnic, Harold conferred with his crow

family and discovered that they, too had come to a similar conclusion. *Something had to be done about that dragon.*

The crows knew that the Ogress and the children and the old man and the old woman all had some sort of plan. Something about neighbors and togetherness and so forth. Which sounded lovely, but the crows were realists. It was fine and good to share stories and to discuss ideas, but does that help when there is a lying, ruthless dragon in town? No, the crows decided. It does not.

The children weren't going to deal with the dragon. And the Ogress was blinded by her affection for the so-called mayor. No, this was a very large problem, and the crows, alone, could solve it. Clever, brave, and handsome crows. They tossed their heads proudly at the very thought of it. They puffed up their feathers in the quiet knowledge of what excellent and neighborly crows they were.

And so the crows helped deliver the books about neighborliness to every lousy neighbor in Stone-in-the-Glen. "Caw," they whispered as they made their deliveries, which meant "You don't really deserve this, but here you go."

The crows helped assemble the food into the handcart. They nuzzled the Ogress, and they cuddled the children. Even the old man and the old woman gave them snacks and affectionate taps on their attractive crow heads. The crows played with the children in the square as the rest of the town arrived. They puffed up their feathers. They readied themselves for a fight. Instead, everyone had a lovely time. The townspeople apologized. They hugged the Ogress. They bent their heads in sorrow and shame. This was all very appropriate, the crows felt, but certainly not enough. They still regarded the townspeople warily.

And then the Mayor came.

"Now," Harold called out in a loud voice.

In a great rush of wings, the crows crowded the skies. Their feathers shone like ink. Harold spun and dove. They were so beautiful, his family. They were so, so *beautiful* when they flew as one. "This way!" Harold called out. And they flew, with one purpose and one mind, to the Mayor's house.

When they arrived at the house, they noticed the single ancient ginger cat seated at attention at the edge of the yard. The crows fluttered down to face the cat. They bowed low. "Caw," the crows said, which meant "Greetings, cat. We are here to steal the treasure of the dragon who lives in disguise in this house. Please grant us safe passage."

Crows do not speak Cat. They never have. Cats, on the other hand, do speak Crow, as they have the ability to speak in several languages, but they prefer not to. Communication is vexing. Cats speak as they please. "Meow," said the cat, which meant "My compatriots are waiting in the square. We have been watching his magic deplete, and we believe that now is the time to make our move. If you want to steal the treasure, this is an excellent time." And with that, the cat slunk away. The crows had no idea what she had said, but it was clear that she didn't much mind if they stole what they could.

The crows flew toward the mansion and in through two open windows, where they landed on a mountain of coins. The Mayor had separated the piles according to type—copper coins were heaped in hills and valleys in the kitchen and the pantry, an avalanche of silver coins spilled down the stairs, and a mountain range of gold stretched through the living room. The crows could see paths worn through the money landscape, and depressions where the Mayor sometimes lay down for a nap.

It was the shiniest sight that Harold had ever beheld in his whole life. He was dizzy with it. He shook his head to clear it. "Caw!" he called out to his family. Which meant "There is more here than we can take at once. No matter. A coin in the beak, two coins in each claw, and we will fly to the square."

The first wave of crows plucked their coins from the piles and flew out of the mansion, over the houses to the square, where they let the coins rain down on a crowd of astonished faces.

The Town

Listen.

This is a story, as I said, about a town. But the story is incomplete. This story that you have been reading has a beginning, a middle, and an end. But these things are arbitrary, don't you think? A story begins at a place in *time*, but the place *itself* existed before the story ever started. And the story ends in a place in time that is convenient for the teller, but the *place itself* persists. And the people in that story persist until they shrug their bodies off at their life's end and go on to their next story, their next adventure. Perhaps a story is simply a reminder to the reader that time is a funny thing: It stretches and snaps. It bends and wobbles. And it slows down when you move too fast.

It is true that there was a place called Stone-in-the-Glen, and that it was built, once upon a time, after the original townspeople cut down a grove of trees. It is also true that the Stone who loved those trees wept and wept with the grief and loss of it—and weeps still. It is also true that those early citizens of Stone-in-the-Glen did try their best to build a beautiful and just and fair town. A beloved community. Sometimes, they succeeded. Sometimes, they failed. It is also true that a beautiful Library was built during a time when the citizens of Stone-in-the-Glen attempted to share things like knowledge and wealth and public good and civic responsibility. And it is true that the Library burned and that the people of the town watched, wretched and powerless, and that they were marked by the horror of it.

Was it a lovely town, once upon a time? I suppose it was lovely enough. And good enough. And kind enough. Was it perfect? Oh, heavens, no.

The town of Stone-in-the-Glen had a mayor who wasn't the man he said he was. Indeed, he wasn't a man at all. In addition to enthralling the citizens of Stone-in-the-Glen with his pretty lies and manipulating them with his devious half-truths, the dragon in the man suit who called himself the Mayor had been stealing from the town for years. Letting the public good go bad. Standing by while the notion of neighborliness shriveled and died like an unwatered garden. Encouraging the people to cultivate grievance and petulance and isolation and to reject reconciliation and community. The dragon was not entirely at fault, of course. There was blame to share all around. But the town's failures didn't mean that they couldn't choose to do better. The Ogress knew this. So did the orphans. And eventually, so did the rest of the town.

This is what the town saw that day:

The sky grew dark with crows, and the people were afraid. But then a woman pointed and said, "Look!" That was when the crows released their coins. Coins covered the ground. Some crows flew low and stashed coins in pockets and satchels. Others gently placed coins in the hands of children. Back and forth the crows flew, bringing coin after coin after coin, until there were no more to bring. Dropping coins in the fountain. Coins on benches. Coins in the gardens. Coins *everywhere*. For everyone.

The Mayor fell to his knees. He couldn't stop scratching his arms. He clawed desperately at himself. The magic that had once infused his skin was almost entirely used up. He didn't notice. He tried to gather his coins into his hands. "*My lovelies,*" he cried. "*Don't touch it. This is all mine.*" His voice was hoarse. Smoke came out of his mouth. He gripped his belly.

Cats of all sizes and colors began to snake through the crowd. Not just the cats from the perimeter of the Mayor's yard—it seemed that every cat in town had made its way to the Center Square.

"With all due respect, sir . . ." Anthea said primly.

The crows chortled happily. They had come to love Anthea's prim little voice.

"Those coins don't belong to you at all. Ergo, this money is *ours*. The town's. It's supposed to help everyone. All of us, together."

The Mayor stared openmouthed at this insolent child. He looked to the adults in town to set her straight, but they, too, were nodding, like this was the most obvious thing in the world. The cats crept closer.

"This is exactly what we need to reopen the school," the constable said. "'Bout time, too. Been saying so for years."

"This is exactly what we need to fix the streets," the butcher said.

"This is exactly what we need to replant the fruit trees," said the old schoolteacher. "And maybe a town garden as well."

"There is so much that is broken," said the former street sweeper. "It will be difficult to decide what to fix first. But I think we'll manage."

The Mayor cursed and swore. He kicked the table and sent the beautiful baked goods flying. A cat sidled close to his leg. The Mayor didn't notice. And then, with a vicious swipe of his paw, the cat tore open a seam in the Mayor's trousers and cut into the skin as well. But the Mayor didn't bleed. He didn't cry or even blink. There seemed to be nothing under his skin. The wound just flapped and stuttered, making a noise that sounded a bit like a fart.

"Say 'Excuse me,'" said Anthea.

Another cat reared on her hind legs and swatted the Mayor on his middle, cutting deep into the skin. Again, there was no blood. Just an empty, dark space. Air blew from the wound.

"*Stop it*," the Mayor roared, swinging his fists wildly. "*Get away, you infernal cats.*"

Another leaped up and clawed at the Mayor's arm. Another cut, still no blood. This time, people could see a dull glint from scales, as though shining from a very great distance. The Mayor's stomach hurt. His skin itched. His thoughts panicked and swam.

"Are you okay?" asked the Ogress. "Perhaps you're just hungry. We have so much to share."

The Mayor made a guttural cry. He recoiled from the Ogress as though she were covered in something vile. The townspeople gave the Mayor a hard look. Another cat leaped up, adhering itself to the Mayor's back. Another rip. Another cut. No blood.

Something moved inside the Mayor's skin. "*I . . . don't . . . want . . . sharing,*" the Mayor spat. "And certainly not from an *ogre*. My kind doesn't think highly of your kind. Ridiculous ogres. Weak. Dull. Low creatures. Dragons would *never* trouble themselves with *ogres*." And with that, the Mayor lunged at the Ogress.

Or he tried to.

He felt as though he were moving through syrup. He attempted to call up his magic—for strength, for fire, for anything. There was nothing to be had. But that didn't matter to the sheep, who only saw a bad man with floppy skin threatening their beloved Ogress.

"Baa," the sheep bellowed as they lowered their horns.

At that, a small, wrinkly creature crawled out of his Mayor's skin with great effort, like a hatchling limply heaving itself through the just-pipped hole in an egg. He gasped and grunted from the strain of it.

It was definitely a dragon. But he had been in that skin for so long that his body had shriveled to barely the size of an undernourished mouse. His scales were patchy, and they no longer had their magnificent sheen. His tail kinked, his wings drooped, and his arms had no muscle at all. His milky eyes squinted in the light, as though it hurt him. He looked more like a waterlogged snakeskin than a dragon. And worse, he smelled like old socks and swamp gas. Some people made a face.

"*What are you looking at?*" said the dragon. "*I am magnificent! And handsome! Look out or I will burn you the way I burned your ridiculous library.*"

This made even the Ogress gasp.

In any case, it was an empty threat. There was no fire at all in his belly. And he didn't have enough magic to fly away.

"Meow," one cat said. Which meant "We have been waiting for this day for a long, long time."

"Meow," said another cat. Which meant "I daresay you will give me indigestion, but I believe it will be worth it."

The Dragon didn't speak Cat, but he knew enough about communication to deduce what they were saying. He ran as fast as his weak, spindly legs could carry him, down the road and toward the forest. The cats followed in hot pursuit, their yowls echoing against the cobblestones, growing quieter and quieter, and farther and farther away, until the sounds of pursuit vanished altogether.

Did the Dragon escape? Was he eaten? Did he continue to shrink and shrivel and diminish until he was absolutely nothing at all? Listen. I don't know, and I can't say. All I know for certain is that he was never seen again.

The Ogress and the Orphans

Many months later, when winter settled over Stone-in-the-Glen with deep, deep snow, the Ogress walked out of her crooked house, toward the Orphan House. She pulled a heaping load of cookies and treats behind her on a sled. The crows sped ahead. Dog walked with the Ogress, thrilled as always to be included. The sheep were safely ensconced in their brand-new barn, munching happily on hay.

As she walked, the Ogress veered out of her way and went to the Center Square. The whole square had been decorated for the various winter feasts and holidays. The lamps were lit and glittered like stars, each decorated with a winding ribbon and a bow, one of the new mayor's projects. Esmé had given up her work helping her husband at the cobbler's shop and had run for mayor. She was elected in a landslide. And she was good at it—efficient, empathetic, and fair, with big ideas on how to make things better. Right away, she had gotten to work organizing and beautifying, employing local people. The school was nearly done. The new library was set to open come spring. She put up a sign on the Town Hall that said THE PUBLIC GOOD MEANS THAT THE PUBLIC IS GOOD. I BELIEVE IN YOU!

And, yes, the Ogress figured, Esmé probably did. Some people are gifted not only in seeing the best in people, but in convincing those people to see the best in themselves. Good for her.

The Ogress admired the square as she walked. People called out to her and waved as she went by, and she waved back. She stopped at the Stone.

(Listen.)

She looked at it for a long time, and then (oh, then!) she sat down.

People hurried past, carrying packages or platters of food. Most greeted her kindly. Some did not; some people will never change. There was a freedom in accepting this. She let her hands drift to the Stone's surface and rest there. The Stone shivered. The Ogress closed her eyes and smiled.

"Hello, Stone," she said.

"Hello, Ogress," I said.

"You could have said something, you know."

I didn't answer right away. Time works differently for stones. And ogres. But I will admit it: I was lonely. It was nice to have someone to talk to. "You could have stopped by before today and said hello," I said more petulantly than I should have. "I mean, I can't exactly come to you."

This wasn't exactly true. No one knew how deep the Stone went. Or how wide. I did, obviously. But it's nice keeping some things to myself. We remained just so for a good long while, telling each other stories. Ogres and stones have a lot in common, you see. More than you might think.

After a while, Dog began to whine. "I must go, my friend," the Ogress said.

"Oh, I know," I said. "I already know how this story ends. And the next story. And the one after that."

The Ogress laughed. She patted the surface of the Stone, my very face, with her lovely, stony hands.

"Come back and see me, will you?" I said hopefully.

(And she did. But that's another story.)

The Ogress stood and walked away under the darkened sky, her feet touching gently upon the ground, pulling the sled behind her until she arrived at the Orphan House.

The Orphan House wasn't exactly built for a creature of the Ogress's size—she had to move very carefully from room to room, ducking in doorways and turning her broad shoulders sideways in order not to crack the walls. The family in the Orphan House did their best to accommodate her. Anthea built her a special chair, and Cass made sure she had a blanket for her lap, because it was cold out, and Dierdre made sure she always had a stack of mechanical drawings to look at, and Elijah was quick to tell her a new story, and the twins would sing her duets at the drop of a hat, and Bartleby was always ready to discuss the newest philosophical concept that he had discovered in his books. Hiram wanted to climb on her, and Justina offered to wrestle with her, and Iggy and Kye made faces and told jokes, hoping to make her laugh.

I wish I could tell you that everything was perfect now in Stone-in-the-Glen and that the Ogress was accepted by everyone and that all of these problems were solved. Unfortunately, Stone-in-the-Glen is a real place. Filled with real people. And real people aren't that simple. They make good choices and bad choices, and are sometimes fair and honorable and good . . . and sometimes they are not. But the Ogress knew who her friends were, and knew whom she could trust, and knew whom to avoid.

Some people from town were true to their word and helped her rebuild the barn (they were amazed at what they could accomplish in so little time), and they were surprised to see that their help wasn't needed in fixing the garden. The Ogress became quite famous in the area for her cheeses—so famous that youths in town who were interested in the trade of cheese making knocked on her door asking to be her apprentices. And they were good, these young people. Hardworking and inventive. Kind to the sheep. They would make excellent cheese makers one day.

After the meal, and the gifts, and the endless discussion, and the stories, and the songs, the older children started getting the younger children ready for bed while Matron saw to the babies, and the Ogress relaxed on the sofa with Myron. Myron was looking a little bit worse these days. Paler than usual. More tired. His skin was almost translucent. His scars stood red and livid, on his neck and hands and cheek. He held a little windup toy in his left hand. A butterfly. Its wings pulsed unevenly, taking long breaks sometimes. *Beat-beat, space, space, beat-space-beat, space, space, space.* Myron stared at it with grim fascination.

"What is that?" the Ogress asked.

"A reminder," Myron said with a sad smile.

"A reminder of what?"

"Of how much I have loved in my life. And both how much and how little time I have left." His gaze drifted toward the door. The children made a terrific ruckus. "They are wonderful, aren't they? The children. They are the best thing in my whole life. I sometimes wish I had all the time in the world. Or that I could take each individual moment and expand it to infinity."

"Time is a funny thing, for ogres, you know," the Ogress said. "My feet have walked this world for . . . ever so long. You humans think of time as a thing that passes. But that's not true. Time simply *is*. If a person leaves Stone-in-the-Glen on a long journey, we know that Stone-in-the-Glen still exists. And we know it can be returned to. Why should time be any different? A moment is a concrete thing, separate from other moments. It doesn't leave. It doesn't pass. It simply exists on its own point on the axis. Take this moment, for example. Why on earth would you think the universe would work so hard as to create this moment if only to let it slide away to oblivion?"

Myron laughed. "Don't let Bartleby hear you talking like that," he said. "The poor lad's head is liable to explode." He coughed. And coughed again into a handkerchief. He quickly shoved the handkerchief into his pocket. The Ogress placed her large hand on his.

"We don't have all that many moments together, you and I," she said. "My life is long, after all. Ever so much longer than any of yours. This is why I hang on to each moment. Each is a jewel, bright, hard, and precious. A thing to be treasured. A thing to be shared. So much more valuable than any coin in that ridiculous dragon's lair."

The butterfly stuttered and shook. Then it continued to beat—irregularly still, and faintly. But it didn't stop yet.

"Well, then." Myron coughed. "I look forward to the moments yet to come. I'm glad I get to spend some of them with you. And I'm glad you'll be spending even more with these darlings of my heart after I am gone. I think even the moments we *don't* ever get to see are precious, too. Don't you?"

Anthea, Bartleby, and Cass appeared in the doorway. The other children massed behind.

"We can't possibly go to sleep yet," Anthea said.

"It's too beautiful out," Bartleby added.

"Shall we?" said Cass, offering the Ogress her hand.

And so they did. The Ogress, the orphans, and the dog walked out into the bright snow beneath the dark sky, where the crows waited for them. The trees creaked and the wind blew, but they barely noticed. They lay down on their backs, sinking into the soft snow, and stayed there together for a long, long time, to watch the stars.

ACKNOWLEDGMENTS

This book would not have existed, were it not for the following
people:

• Tracey Baptiste, Martha Brockenbrough, Kate Messner,
Olugbemisola Rhuday-Perkovich, Laura Ruby, Laurel Snyder,
Linda Urban, and Anne Ursu, who read the first, nascent,
shadowy draft of this story—the first thing I had written in
a long, long time—and told me: *Yes. This is a Thing. Go find
out what it is, and also maybe show it to your agent.* Remember
when I thought I was writing a picture book, ladies? Well, ha
ha, joke's on me.

• My agent, Steve Malk, who is able to see what I am trying
to do before I ever can. I'm so grateful for your generosity and
perspicacity. Thanks for sticking with me, Steve, for real.

• My editor, Elise Howard, who is basically the Mary Poppins
of editors. Thank you for your intelligence, vigor, and insight.
And for everything else. What would I do without you, Elise?
What, indeed?

• The members of the Wyrdsmiths—Eleanor Arnason, Naomi
Kritzer, Theo Lorenz, Lyda Morehouse, and Adam Stemple—
who read the early chapters in the Dark Days of a Certain
Administration, when we were only just learning about a deadly

epidemic rampaging in countries far, far away, and we didn't yet know the kind of upheaval and devastation that was about to descend on our dear nation. The conversation we had that day—about generosity, about baking when we don't know what else to do, about the purpose of kindness, about neighborliness, and what might make a broken community beloved again—impacted me deeply. This book is more of itself because of you.

• And to my family. You're in this book, all of you, though you may not see yourselves at first. You are my most precious treasures, my darlings. I wish all of our moments together were infinite.

But mostly, the person I want to acknowledge above all is *you*. The Reader. My task as the writer is to provide you with the necessary materials—stones and bones and places and faces. The *stuff* of the story. But I am not the one who builds the story. The person who builds the story is the Reader: it's *you*. I hope you had fun with it. I hope you were able to build something beautiful. I hope you discovered things, or created things, or realized things, that I could never have expected or imagined or planned. A story is always so much bigger than the author. It is always so much bigger than the words on the page. A story is an experience. Or, no, that's not right. A story is a *process:* it bends time, expands space, and allows the universe to invent itself, and re-invent itself, again and again and again. It is through stories that our world becomes new. A story can't become what it's meant to be without a Reader to read it. Without a Reader to give it breath and life and soul. You did that. You did that all on your own. So thank you.

Read on for an extract from
Kelly Barnhill's Newbery Medal-winning novel,
The Girl Who Drank the Moon

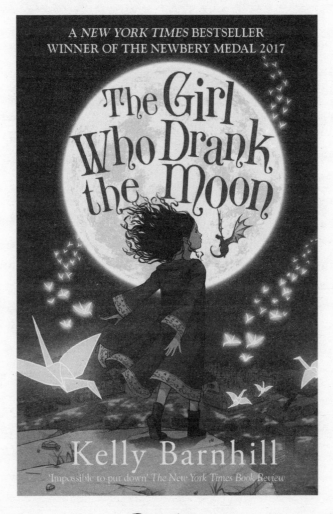

A *NEW YORK TIMES* BESTSELLER
WINNER OF THE NEWBERY MEDAL 2017

The Girl Who Drank the Moon

Kelly Barnhill

'Impossible to put down' *The New York Times Book Review*

Piccadilly
PRESS

1.

IN WHICH A STORY IS TOLD

Yes.

There is a witch in the woods. There has always been a witch.

Will you stop your fidgeting for once? My stars! I have never seen such a fidgety child.

No, sweetheart, I have not seen her. No one has. Not for ages. We've taken steps so that we will never see her.

Terrible steps.

Don't make me say it. You already know, anyway.

Oh, I don't know, darling. No one knows why she wants children. We don't know why she insists that it must always be the very youngest among us. It's not as though we could just ask her. She hasn't been seen. We make sure that she will not be seen.

Of course she exists. What a question! Look at the woods! So dangerous! Poisonous smoke and sinkholes and boiling geysers and terrible dangers every which way. Do you think it is so by accident? Rubbish! It was the Witch, and if we don't do as she says, what will become of us?

You really need me to explain it?

I'd rather not.

Oh, hush now, don't cry. It's not as though the Council of Elders is coming for you, now is it. You're far too old.

From our family?

Yes, dearest. Ever so long ago. Before you were born. He was a beautiful boy.

Now finish your supper and see to your chores. We'll all be up early tomorrow. The Day of Sacrifice waits for no one, and we must all be present to thank the child who will save us for one more year.

Your brother? How could I fight for him? If I had, the Witch would have killed us all and then where would we be? Sacrifice one or sacrifice all. That is the way of the world. We couldn't change it if we tried.

Enough questions. Off with you. Fool child.

2.

IN WHICH AN UNFORTUNATE
WOMAN GOES QUITE MAD

GRAND ELDER GHERLAND TOOK his time that morning. The Day of Sacrifice only came once a year, after all, and he liked to look his best during the sober procession to the cursed house, and during the somber retreat. He encouraged the other Elders to do the same. It was important to give the populace a show.

He carefully dabbed rouge on his sagging cheeks and lined his eyes with thick streaks of kohl. He checked his teeth in the mirror, ensuring they were free of debris or goop. He loved that mirror. It was the only one in the Protectorate. Nothing gave Gherland more pleasure than the possession of a thing that was unique unto him. He liked being *special*.

The Grand Elder had ever so many possessions that were unique in the Protectorate. It was one of the perks of the job.

The Protectorate—called the Cattail Kingdom by some and the City of Sorrows by others—was sandwiched between a treacherous forest on one side and an enormous bog on the other. Most people in the Protectorate drew their livelihoods from the Bog. There was a future in bogwalking, mothers told their children. Not much of a future, you understand, but it was better than nothing. The Bog was full of Zirin shoots in the spring and Zirin flowers in the summer and Zirin bulbs in the fall—in addition to a wide array of medicinal and borderline magical plants that could be harvested, prepared, treated, and sold to the Traders from the other side of the forest, who in turn transported the fruits of the Bog to the Free Cities, far away. The forest itself was terribly dangerous, and navigable only by the Road.

And the Elders owned the Road.

Which is to say that Grand Elder Gherland owned the Road, and the other Elders had their cut. The Elders owned the Bog, too. And the orchards. And the houses. And the market squares. Even the garden plots.

This was why the families of the Protectorate made their shoes out of reeds. This was why, in lean times, they fed their children the thick, rich broth of the Bog, hoping that the Bog would make them strong.

This was why the Elders and their families grew big and strong and rosy-cheeked on beef and butter and beer.

The door knocked.

"Enter," Grand Elder Gherland mumbled as he adjusted the drape of his robe.

It was Antain. His nephew. An Elder-in-Training, but only because Gherland, in a moment of weakness, had promised the ridiculous boy's more ridiculous mother. But that was unkind. Antain was a nice enough young man, nearly thirteen. He was a hard worker and a quick study. He was good with numbers and clever with his hands and could build a comfortable bench for a tired Elder as quick as breathing. And, despite himself, Gherland had developed an inexplicable, and growing, fondness for the boy.

But.

Antain had big ideas. Grand notions. And *questions*. Gherland furrowed his brow. Antain was—how could he put it? *Overly keen.* If this kept up, he'd have to be dealt with, blood or no. The thought of it weighed upon Gherland's heart, like a stone.

"UNCLE GHERLAND!" Antain nearly bowled his uncle over with his insufferable enthusiasm.

"Calm yourself, boy!" the Elder snapped. "This is a solemn occasion!"

The boy calmed visibly, his eager, doglike face tilted toward the ground. Gherland resisted the urge to pat him gently on the head. "I have been sent," Antain continued in a mostly soft voice, "to tell you that the other Elders are ready. And all the populace waits along the route. Everyone is accounted for."

"Each one? There are no shirkers?"

"After last year, I doubt there ever will be again," Antain said with a shudder.

"Pity." Gherland checked his mirror again, touching up his rouge. He rather enjoyed teaching the occasional lesson to the citizens of the Protectorate. It clarified things. He tapped the sagging folds under his chin and frowned. "Well, Nephew," he said with an artful swish of his robes, one that had taken him over a decade to perfect. "Let us be off. That baby isn't going to sacrifice itself, after all." And he flowed into the street with Antain stumbling at his heels.

◆ ◆ ◆

Normally, the Day of Sacrifice came and went with all the pomp and gravity that it ought. The children were given over without protest. Their numb families mourned in silence, with pots of stew and nourishing foods heaped into their kitchens, while the comforting arms of neighbors circled around them to ease their bereavement.

Normally, no one broke the rules.

But not this time.

Grand Elder Gherland pressed his lips into a frown. He could hear the mother's howling before the procession turned onto the final street. The citizens began to shift uncomfortably where they stood.

When they arrived at the family's house, an astonishing sight met the Council of Elders. A man with a scratched-up face and a swollen lower lip and bloody bald spots across his skull where his hair had been torn out in clumps met them at the door. He tried to smile, but his tongue went instinctively to the gap where a tooth had just recently been. He sucked in his lips and attempted to bow instead.

"I am sorry, sirs," said the man—the father, presumably. "I don't know what has gotten into her. It's like she's gone mad."

From the rafters above them, a woman screeched and howled as the Elders entered the house. Her shiny black hair flew about her head like a nest of long, writhing snakes. She hissed and spat like a cornered animal. She clung to the ceiling beams with one arm and one leg, while holding a baby tightly against her breast with the other arm.

"GET OUT!" she screamed. "You *cannot* have her. I spit on your faces and curse your names. Leave my home at once, or I shall tear out your eyes and throw them to the crows!"

The Elders stared at her, openmouthed. They couldn't *believe* it. No one fought for a doomed child. It simply wasn't *done*.

(Antain alone began to cry. He did his best to hide it from the adults in the room.)

Gherland, thinking fast, affixed a kindly expression on his craggy face. He turned his palms toward the mother to show her that he meant no harm. He gritted his teeth behind his smile. All this kindness was nearly killing him.

"*We* are not taking her at all, my poor, misguided girl," Gherland said in his most patient voice. "The *Witch* is taking her. We are simply doing as we're told."

The mother made a guttural sound, deep in her chest, like an angry bear.

Gherland laid his hand on the shoulder of the perplexed husband and gave a gentle squeeze. "It appears, my good fellow, that you are right: your wife *has* gone mad." He did his best to cover his rage with a façade of concern. "A rare case, of course, but not without precedent. We must respond with compassion. She needs care, not blame."

"LIAR," the woman spat. The child began to cry, and the woman climbed even higher, putting each foot on parallel rafters and bracing her back against the slope of the roof, trying to position herself in such a way that she could remain out of reach while she nursed the baby. The child calmed instantly. "If you take her," she said with a growl, "I will find her. I will find her and take her back. You see if I won't."

"And face the Witch?" Gherland laughed. "All on your own? Oh, you pathetic, lost soul." His voice was honey, but his face was a glowing ember. "Grief has made you lose your senses. The shock has shattered your poor mind. No matter. We shall heal you, dear, as best we can. Guards!"

He snapped his fingers, and armed guards poured into the room. They were a special unit, provided as always by the Sisters of the Star. They wore bows and arrows slung across their backs and short, sharp swords sheathed at their belts. Their long braided hair looped around their waists, where it was cinched tight—a testament to their years of contemplation and combat training at the top of the Tower. Their faces were implacable as stones, and the Elders, despite their power and stature, edged away from them. The Sisters were a frightening force. Not to be trifled with.

"Remove the child from the lunatic's clutches and escort the poor dear to the Tower," Gherland ordered. He glared at the mother in the rafters, who had gone suddenly very pale. "The Sisters of the Star know what to do with broken minds, my dear. I'm sure it hardly hurts at all."

The Guard was efficient, calm, and utterly ruthless. The mother didn't stand a chance. Within moments, she was bound, hobbled, and carried away. Her howls echoed through the silent town, ending suddenly when the Tower's great wooden doors slammed shut, locking her inside.

The baby, on the other hand, once transferred into the arms of the Grand Elder, whimpered briefly and then turned her attention to the sagging face in front of her, all wobbles and creases and folds. She had a solemn look to her — calm, skeptical, and intense, making it difficult for Gherland to look away. She had black curls and black eyes. Luminous skin, like polished amber. In the center of her forehead, she had a birthmark in the shape of a crescent moon. The mother had a similar mark. Common lore insisted that such people were special. Gherland disliked lore, as a general rule, and he certainly disliked it when citizens of the Protectorate got it in their heads to think themselves better than they were. He deepened his frown and leaned in close, wrinkling his brow. The baby stuck out her tongue.

Horrible child, Gherland thought.

"Gentlemen," he said with all the ceremony he could muster, "it is time." The baby chose this particular moment to let loose a large, warm, wet stain across the front of Gherland's robes. He pretended not to notice, but inwardly he fumed.

She had done it on purpose. He was sure of it. What a revolting baby.

The procession was, as usual, somber, slow, and insufferably plodding. Gherland felt he might go mad with impatience. Once the Protectorate's gates closed behind them, though, and the citizens returned with their melancholy broods of children to their drab little homes, the Elders quickened their pace.

"But why are we running, Uncle?" Antain asked.

"Hush, boy!" Gherland hissed. "And keep up!"

No one liked being in the forest, away from the Road. Not even the Elders. Not even Gherland. The area just outside the Protectorate walls was safe enough. In theory. But everyone knew someone who had accidentally wandered too far. And fell into a sinkhole. Or stepped in a mud pot, boiling off most of their skin. Or wandered into a swale where the air was bad, and never returned. The forest was dangerous.

They followed a winding trail to the small hollow surrounded by five ancient trees, known as the Witch's Handmaidens. Or six. *Didn't it used to be five?* Gherland glared at the trees, counted them again, and shook his head. There were six. No matter. The forest was just getting to him. Those trees were almost as old as the world, after all.

The space inside of the ring of trees was mossy and soft, and the Elders laid the child upon it, doing their best not to look at her. They had turned their backs on the baby and started to hurry away when their youngest member cleared his throat.

"So. We just leave her here?" Antain asked. "That's how it's done?"

"Yes, Nephew," Gherland said. "That is how it's done." He felt a sudden wave of fatigue settling on his shoulders like an ox's yoke. He felt his spine start to sag.

Antain pinched his neck—a nervous habit that he couldn't break. "Shouldn't we wait for the Witch to arrive?"

The other Elders fell into an uncomfortable silence.

"Come again?" Elder Raspin, the most decrepit of the Elders, asked.

"Well, surely . . ." Antain's voice trailed off. "Surely we must wait for the Witch," he said quietly. "What would become of us if wild animals came first and carried her off?"

The other Elders stared at the Grand Elder, their lips tight.

"Fortunately, Nephew," he said quickly, leading the boy away, "that has never been a problem."

"But—" Antain said, pinching his neck again, so hard he left a mark.

"But nothing," Gherland said, a firm hand on the boy's back, striding quickly down the well-trodden path.

And, one by one, the Elders filed out, leaving the baby behind.

They left knowing—all but Antain—that it was not a matter of *if* the child were eaten by animals, but rather that she surely *would be*.

They left her knowing that there surely *wasn't* a witch. There never *had* been a witch. There were only a dangerous forest and a single road and a thin grip on a life that the Elders had enjoyed for generations. The Witch—that is, the belief in her—made for a frightened people, a subdued people, a compliant people, who lived their lives in a saddened haze, the clouds of their grief numbing their senses and dampening their minds. It was terribly convenient for the Elders' unencumbered rule. Unpleasant, too, of course, but that couldn't be helped.

They heard the child whimper as they tramped through the trees, but the whimpering soon gave way to the swamp sighs and birdsong and the woody creaking of trees throughout the forest. And each Elder felt as sure as sure could be that the child wouldn't live to see the morning, and that they would never hear her, never see her, never think of her again.

They thought she was gone forever.

They were wrong, of course.